Praise for

JESS KIDD

"Jess Kidd is so good it isn't fair."

—ERIKA SWYLER, bestselling author of
The Book of Speculation and *Light from Other Stars*

"A few pages in and I was determined to read every word Jess Kidd
has ever written."

—DIANE SETTERFIELD,
on *Things in Jars*

"Jess Kidd is an author who shows a poet's way with words and
rhythm."

—*Electric Literature*

Praise for

THE NIGHT SHIP

"Jess Kidd uses two alternating narratives . . . shrewdly illuminating the loneliness and violence that make two children kindred spirits, even though they live centuries apart."

—*The New York Times Book Review*

"Kidd shows a keen understanding of how thin the boundary between the magic and the mundane is for children and treats their understanding of the world with seriousness and compassion. Her prose has an arresting simplicity that evokes fairy tales, and the echoes between Mayken's and Gil's experiences are treats for the reader to discover. An ambitious, melancholy work of historical fiction that offers two wondrous young protagonists for the price of one."

—*Kirkus Reviews* (starred review)

"Kidd's latest weaves a spell around the reader, transporting them across centuries, between a doomed ship and a dying island. The result is a true work of magic, and one that will haunt me for years."

—V. E. SCHWAB,
internationally bestselling author of
The Invisible Life of Addie LaRue

THE
NIGHT
SHIP

THE
NIGHT SHIP

A Novel

JESS KIDD

ATRIA PAPERBACK
NEW YORK LONDON TORONTO SYDNEY NEW DELHI

ATRIA
PAPERBACK

An Imprint of Simon & Schuster, Inc.
1230 Avenue of the Americas
New York, NY 10020

First Atria Paperback edition August 2023

ATRIA PAPERBACK and colophon are trademarks of Simon & Schuster, Inc.

For information about special discounts for bulk purchases, please contact Simon & Schuster Special Sales at 1-866-506-1949 or business@simonandschuster.com.

The Simon & Schuster Speakers Bureau can bring authors to your live event. For more information, or to book an event, contact the Simon & Schuster Speakers Bureau at 1-866-248-3049 or visit our website at www.simonspeakers.com.

Interior design by Yvonne Taylor

Manufactured in the United States of America

1   3   5   7   9   10   8   6   4   2

Library of Congress Cataloging-in-Publication Data has been applied for.

ISBN 978-1-9821-8081-2
ISBN 978-1-9821-8082-9 (pbk)
ISBN 978-1-9821-8083-6 (ebook)

For
Gavin Clarke

THE
NIGHT
SHIP

CHAPTER ONE

1628

The child sails in a crowded boat to the end of the Zuyder Zee. Past the foreshores of shipyards and warehouses, past new stone houses and the occasional steeple, on this day of dull weather, persistent drizzle and sneaking cold. There are many layers to this child: undergarments, middle garments, and top garments. Mayken is made of pale skin and small white teeth and fine fair hair and linen and lace and wool and leather. There are treasures sewn into the seams of her clothing, small and valuable, like her.

Mayken has a father she's never met. Her father is a merchant who lives in a distant land where the midday sun is fierce enough to melt a Dutch child.

Her father has a marble mansion, so she's told. He has a legion of servants and stacks of gold dishes. He has chestnut stallions and dapple mares. Red and white roses grow around his doorway, they twine together, blood and snow mixed. By day the roses raise their faces to the sun. By night they empty their scent into the air. Cut them and they'll live only an hour. Their thorns are vicious and will take out an eye.

Mayken's father left just before she was born. Mayken's mother would boast about the absent man. So wholesomely dedicated to the making of wealth. So staunch in the face of native unrest and strange pestilences. But she had no intention of joining her husband, being too delicate for such a perilous journey. Mayken doubted this. Her mother had sturdy calves and a good appetite. She had a big laugh and glossy curls. Her mother was as durable as a well-built cabinet. Until a baby got stuck inside her.

Mayken must not say a word about the baby because it shouldn't have been up there in the first place. She has practiced with her nursemaid.

"Your mother, she's dead?"

"Yes, from the bloody flux."

"How did your mother die, Mayken?"

"My mother died from the bloody flux, Imke."

"Tell me, child, how is your mother?"

"She's dead, unfortunately, from the bloody flux."

Bloody flux, says Mayken to the rhythm of the oars and the slap of the water on the bow of the boat that rocks her toward the East Indiaman. *Bloody flux*, she answers to the cows swung on high. They bellow as they are lowered into the ship. *Bloody flux*, she says to the people that swarm over her decks. The sailors and fine merchants, the plume-hatted soldiers and the bewildered passengers. *Bloody flux*, she replies to the *pip, pip, pip, toot* of trumpeters relaying commands. The ship waits in the water. Around her a chaos of people and goods are loaded from a flotilla of vessels. Like flies circling a patient mare.

Bloody flux, that is a big ship.

She is beautiful. Her upper works are painted green and yellow and at her prow—oh, best of all—crouches a carved red lion! His golden mane curls, his claws sink into the beam. He snarls down at the water.

Mayken's boat rocks round the ship's bowed belly. High up, the ship is lovely with her bright gunwale and curved balustrades and stern decks reaching up, up, into the sky. Lower down, she's a fortress, an armored hull studded with close-set, square-headed nails, already rusting.

Mayken cries out. "The ship is bleeding!"

A passenger sitting on the plank seat opposite laughs.

"The iron nails keep the shipworms out. They love to eat fresh juicy wood." The passenger leans forward and demonstrates with his finger on Mayken's cheek. "They burrow and twist and gnaw tiny holes."

Fortunately, Mayken, too, has teeth.

The man recoils. "She bit me!"

"You poked her." The nursemaid turns to the child. "What are you? A stoat? A rat? A puppy? Put your teeth away."

The man, good-naturedly, raises one gloved hand. "No harm done."

He wears the black costume of a preacher, a *predikant*. There is a Mrs. Predikant in a gown cut from the same cloth. Between them a line of children, big to small, dressed in the same dark wool as their parents. All with clean white collars. A minister and his family dressed for a portrait, pressed together like barreled mackerel, bumping knees with the other passengers. The eldest daughter cradles a carefully wrapped package, Bible shaped. The youngest son, a ringleted cherub, picks his nose and wipes his finger on his sister's leg.

Mayken addresses his father politely. "Speak more about the shipworms, if you please."

"The holes they bore are tiny," says the predikant. "But enough tiny holes—"

He makes a glugging sound and a motion with his hand: a ship sinking. The cherub pouts and his sister rolls her eyes.

Rounding the ship's flank, they see gunports painted red. The predikant points them out to the cherub.

"For the big cannons, Roelant. Against marauders," he adds darkly.

Decorating the stern of the ship is a row of great wooden men. Great in that they are almost life-height and full-bearded. Great, too, in that they wear long robes.

"They're to keep pirates away."

Mayken frowns at the predikant. Of this she is doubtful. One of the carved men looks like a pork butcher from Haarlem market, only he holds a sword, not a pig's leg. The other three just look peevish.

She glances at her nursemaid. Imke is rapt. Imke believes all sorts of pap. Eels are made from wet horsehair. Blowing your nose vigorously can kill you. Statues and carvings can occasionally come alive. Because an object crafted with love can't help but live.

They tried it with a pie. Mayken made pastry snakes to go on top. She rolled them carefully, pricked eyes, and kissed them. When the pie was baked, the snakes were still pastry, only golden. There was no wriggling or seething. Mayken ate them in disgust. They didn't even taste like snakes. Imke said the snakes were merely sleepy, that they had been basking in the heat of the oven.

Another time, Imke took Mayken to the Church of Saint Bavo, the jewel of Haarlem. The old nursemaid told her to open her eyes and take notice. Mayken opened her eyes and took notice. Even so she missed the grin of a stone gargoyle and the wink of a wooden toad on the choir stall.

And now her heart hurts to think of Haarlem and all the things they are leaving behind, the tall clean house, the market boys, the kitchen cat, Mama and the secret stuck-inside baby. He was a brother, of that Mayken is sure. She only ever wanted a brother.

The great-bellied ship looms above. One, two, three masts—rising up through a web of rope. The pennant flags snap and stream against a sky of lowering clouds.

Imke pipes up. "When they loosen the sails, it will be like all the washdays have come at once."

Gulls are nervously testing the yardarm, clumsy-footed compared to the sailors who are all over the rigging: climbing, dangling, rolling, lashing, hollering, and cursing.

Mayken loves the sailors instantly. The daring of them, their speed along the ropes, the heights they climb to! The predikant is pointing out the Dutch East India Company cadets and officials gathering at the top of the stern castle. Look, there is the upper-merchant in his red coat and plumed hat. Flanked by the under-merchant, also well hatted, and the stout old skipper, hatless. Three men entrusted by the Company with a cargo richer than the treasuries of many kingdoms, the lives of hundreds of innocent souls and this wonderful ship, newly built—her maiden voyage! Imke nods as though she's interested. Mrs. Predikant stares ahead with her mouth turned down, trout-like, abiding.

Mayken's vessel holds back. There's another boat unloading alongside the ship. The passengers look sick and pinched-faced as they wait their turn to board. A fine lady is hauled up the ship's flank on a wooden seat, her expression one of horror as she grips the ropes. Above her, a chaos of shouting sailors. Below, dirty October waves.

Mayken's nursemaid looks on with satisfaction. Imke revels in the trials of others with a pure and shameless joy.

"What is the ship's name, Imke?"

Mayken knows it, of course; she just likes hearing the way Imke says it.

"*Batavia*."

"Is that a *charmed* word?"

Imke doesn't answer.

Imke says *Batavia* like a charmed word, carefully, with a peasant's respect for the hidden nature of things. A charmed word carelessly uttered curdles luck.

The ship is named for their destination. There must be a store of luck in that: a ship that looks ahead to a new life somewhere hot and strange.

"*Batavia*," Mayken the unruly sings. "*Batavia. Ba-tahhhh—veeee-ah*." She waits for a catastrophe.

A rope falls, a cask drops, a sailor stumbles on the rigging.

Imke looks alarmed; she is superstitious even for a peasant. "Close your mouth."

Mayken does. Imke is not to be messed with.

She is broad of beam and shoulder, short of leg and large of foot.

She is almost as wide as she's tall so will stand in any storm. She has eight teeth, of which she is proud. If she smiles pursed (which she does among strangers) you'd think she had a full set. Imke is not young. The hair under her cap is white and as fine as chicken down. This is on account of the worry Mayken causes her. Imke has pale blue eyes, as watery as pickled eggs. When Imke is angry her eyes bulge; when she's loving, her eyes look soft enough to eat.

The best thing about Imke is her missing finger tops. Mayken gets a thrill just looking at them. Second and third fingers, right hand, nubbed joints smoothed over where nails ought to be. Imke will not tell how she lost her finger tops. Mayken never tires of guessing.

Mayken is a fine lady so she gets the winched seat, which is a plank with ropes attached at the corners. An old sailor wearing an India shawl around his head helps her up.

Mayken's legs shake. Imke is watching so she makes her expression grave and enduring.

The sailor smiles at her. "Are you ready, little grandmother?"

Mayken nods.

"Be brave." He puts his big hands over her small hands. His old scarred knuckles gnarled like knotted wood.

"Hold fast," says the sailor.

Mayken doesn't bite at his touch because her teeth are chattering. The seat lurches skyward. The boat below gets smaller and Imke too. Mayken is hauled up over the wide flank of the ship, hands gripping, feet dangling. At the top the winch stutters and her heart leaps but then she is hoisted briskly on board and tipped onto her feet. A boy sailor takes her to where she must stand and wait for the other passengers to be loaded. Like the other sailors he wears loose trousers and no shoes with a neckerchief tied about his head.

"Don't move," he tells her. "Danger everywhere, see?"

He points: hands run up the rigging, men cart heavy goods across the deck, open hatches lie in wait, dark apertures down into the belly of the ship.

Mayken doesn't doubt it.

Lesser passengers must climb a rope ladder to board. Imke is landed over the side, breathless. She shows her palms to Mayken, rubbed raw from the rope. The predikant and his family struggle after. Mrs. Predikant floundering, skirts flapping, face red, counting her children, taking Roelant from the back of a sailor. The child clings on, his small fingers must be prized open. Soldiers are boarding now, one after another, tight-lipped and grim-eyed. Mayken looks at them with interest, their different hat shapes, various breeches, not all of them Dutch. They carry their few possessions in canvas sacks and move with hesitation. This is not their world. Some of them are very young but all look battle-worn. Mayken would pick a fight with none of them.

A formidable figure elbows down the deck. A giant of terrifying proportions with a full blond beard and shorn head dressed in a leather tunic with no undershirt. Bands of leather go about his bare thick arms.

Mayken turns to the boy sailor. "Who is he?"

"Stonecutter."

Mayken watches in fascination as Stonecutter swipes one of his soldiers around the head with the easy savagery of a bear. As he paces along the line several of the men flinch. No one meets his eyes.

"He was a mason," adds the boy sailor. "He can break rocks and crush skulls with just one hand."

Mayken would like to watch to see if Stonecutter crushes any of the soldiers' skulls but now the passengers must follow the boy sailor.

"You are aft-the-mast," he tells them, pointing to the vast main-mast. "You can never go forward of that."

Mayken frowns. "What happens if I do?"

"Stonecutter crushes your skull."

☙

The cabin is the size of a linen cabinet.

Mayken catches Imke's look of panic before the nursemaid re-arranges her face. There are two shelves on the wall, one above the other. This is where they will sleep, stacked like crockery. Mayken climbs up onto the top bunk and surveys their domain.

As tiny as it is, the cabin contains a lamp, a slatted window, and a narrow table and stool. Their chests are already waiting in the corner. Imke's chest contains three wheels of cheese, a spare skirt, and a needlework box. Mayken's contains mostly silverware.

"Your father has a house of marble," reassures Imke.

"Red and white roses and dapple mares."

Imke nods. "Gold plates and shaded courtyards."

Because Imke looks as if she might cry and Mayken loves her, she reaches out her hand and strokes the tops of the old woman's missing fingers.

"Leave off my bloody fingers."

"Tell me how you lost them," Mayken wheedles. "Just this once."

"Guess right and I will."

Mayken thinks a moment. "You were feeding pigs and they were very, very hungry—"

"Not even close."

It is very early. Mayken and Imke slumber yet. The nursemaid, a poor sailor, still cradles a bucket, her old head nodding. On the bunk above, her charge, lulled by the ship's motion, cleaves to the wall breathing new-sawn wood. They have spent their first night on board at anchor in the lee of the island of Texel. There's no improvement in the weather; the air is heavy with drizzle.

Batavia the beautiful is almost ready to depart. On the quarter-deck stands the upper-merchant, Francisco Pelsaert, a fine-boned man in a splendid red coat. The rat-faced under-merchant, Jeronimus Cornelisz, is at his side, laughing and pointing. Pelsaert inclines his head and smiles politely. The skipper, Ariaen Jacobsz, with shaved head and drab garb, stands behind the two merchants. His meaty legs planted, eyes everywhere. The sailors look only to him.

The anchors are raised in readiness now. The *Batavia* wears them close to her sides, inverted. Her gunports are closed. A break in the clouds, the sun catches the wet deck, the unfurling sails and the ship's stern lamp polished to a dazzle. This lamp will show light to the other ships in the *Batavia*'s convoy. Her sister ships are a day out ahead. The *Dordrecht*, the *Galiasse* (poor *Gravenhage*, storm damaged, is already turning back to port), the *Assendelft*, and the *Sardam*. The little messenger ship *Kleine David* and the sturdy warship *Buren*. The *Batavia* will not be alone in the vast seas.

The frustration of the wait builds to the excitement of the leaving, now that her final treasure has been loaded. Twelve coin chests of considerable weight and ridiculous worth have been rowed to the ship under guard, hoisted under guard, lugged by six men apiece into the Great Cabin in the stern, and set down with a guard to watch over them at all hours.

What else does the *Batavia* carry?

Goods, declared and otherwise. Plate, velvet, brocade, jewels, a Roman cameo the size of a soup bowl, silver bedposts, an ugly agate vase of vast worth. Crew, declared and otherwise. Passengers ditto.

What else does the *Batavia* carry?

Thirty cannons, iron and bronze, bow chasers and big firers, some new-cast, some survivors from past campaigns. Beloved by their gunners, each cannon is wheel blocked and lashed into place. Massive and fickle, there's no telling if they'll buck or leap or explode on firing. To deafen, blind, or crush the men who serve them.

What else does the *Batavia* carry?

Salted meat in tight barrels, buckwheat and peas, three thousand pounds of cheese, hardtack biscuits (worm castles, teeth dullers), and pickled herring by the ton. Lining the hold, a stone archway for Castle Batavia.

All secure now, the ship is under way.

The *Batavia* sails!

From a distance, a queenly glide; on board, the frantic effort of all hands. Roars and curses and trumpeted orders. The new ship must be learned and felt. A week at sea and ship and crew will be one.

The *Batavia* heads out to meet the stormy Noord Zee with her cargo of wealth and wharf rats and souls.

Mayken, woken by the change in the ship's movement, slips out of her bunk. She peers at her nursemaid. The old woman sleeps on, mouth open, breath evil, cap crooked.

The corridor outside the cabin is empty. Mayken opens the heavy door to the deck with difficulty and fights her way out. The quarter-deck is heaving with Company men and cadets and first-class passengers. The main deck below is worse: sailors and before-the-mast passengers crush between the pigpen and the goat pen and the two upturned boats lashed on the deck.

The *Batavia* is picking up speed with a sudden southwesterly breeze that sends canvas scudding and sailors shouting and the deck tilting. Mayken reaches out for a balustrade and, on it, a carved wooden head, bearded, eyes popping.

"There, there," she says to the head. "Hold fast now."

The predikant greets Mayken like a favored member of his congregation.

Mrs. Predikant adds sourly, "Where is your nursemaid, Mayken van den Heuvel?"

"In the cabin, madam."

Her fish mouth twitches. Her cold eye kindles. "Is she unwell?"

"Oh, heartily, she's filled a whole bucket with sick."

The grown daughter, listening, hides a smile.

"Your father will be overjoyed to see you in Batavia."

"I don't know about that."

"Your late mother—"

"Bloody flux," says Mayken, one eye on the skipper as he aims a long spit overboard.

Mayken would love to spit like that.

She feels a soft touch on her arm. The grown daughter is saying something earnest about mothers and angels.

Mayken's attention is elsewhere. Rapt by the salvo of exquisite swearing erupting from the skipper.

Later, a rap on the cabin door and a tall boy outside.

"I am the upper-merchant's own steward."

"Good for you," says Imke.

"You are sick. May I come in?"

He's already over the threshold.

Mayken sits up on her bunk and watches the steward with interest. He has a narrow face and a wide mouth and prominent dirty-green eyes. His head is shaved and he goes barefoot. The steward smiles up at her, quick and wolfish.

He is all action, everywhere at once. Taking out the bucket and bringing it back sluiced clean with seawater. He mops the floor and brings hot ginger tea for Imke and kneels by her side. Her hand's in his as she sips.

"You're a good boy," says the old woman. "What's your name?"

"Jan Pelgrom."

"And the upper-merchant sent you?"

"It was reported that a well-to-do passenger was roaming the decks without her nursemaid."

Mayken hangs over the side of the bunk to see Imke's reaction but the old woman is asleep. Pelgrom extracts his hand from Imke's and wipes it on the blanket. He glances up at Mayken. "What?"

"Have you been in the Great Cabin?"

"Of course."

"You've seen the treasure chests?"

"I've seen *inside* them." Pelgrom sniffs. "The upper-merchant opened them to make sure there were coins, not turnips, inside."

"You saw the silver?"

"I saw the glitter of a thousand fallen stars. There's other treasure, too, better treasure."

"What better treasure?"

"The upper-merchant's jewels. Sapphires and rubies the size of duck eggs and a golden crown. He puts it on, just so." Pelgrom mimes, his expression serious. "He sleeps in it every night."

Mayken smiles. "He doesn't!"

"He keeps the keys to the treasure chests in the crack of his arse. Pirates wouldn't dream of looking there."

Mayken roars laughing. In her bunk, Imke stirs.

Mayken whispers, "I don't want to think about pirates."

"Fair enough. When the pirates attack, it's worse for children."

"How?"

"Pirates love small toes and fingers. If they take the ship, they'll cut them off and eat them. Then they'll hang you from the yardarm. Then they'll skin you, jug you like a hare, and throw you overboard in pieces. Then they'll wear your face as a hat."

Mayken is thrilled and horrified. "I'm not so scared of pirates."

"Are you not? I am."

"Where else have you been in the ship, Jan Pelgrom?"

"Where haven't I been, Lady Mayken?"

"Down there," she points to the floor, "in the belly?"

Pelgrom looks at her slyly. "The Below World?"

"What happens there?"

"First of all there's the gun deck. Where sailors bicker and curse, eat and sleep and the ship's barber lops off legs. Where the cook's galley gets hotter than Hell and the rats the cats can't catch grow big enough to steal babies." He glances at her. "The orlop deck below that is for cows and soldiers. And below that, there's the hold."

They sit, listening to the wheeze and slump of Imke sleeping.

"I want to go," says Mayken quietly. "To the Below World."

"You can't. You belong here, in the Above World."

Mayken reddens. "I can go wherever I want. Just like you can."

"No, you can't. They'd bring you back and tie you to that bunk like a bad puppy."

"They'd have to catch me."

Pelgrom looks amused. "You believe you could pass unnoticed on this ship packed with people?"

"Yes!"

"And what of the thousand misadventures that could befall a fine lady—"

"I like misadventures." Mayken gathers a spit in her mouth, thinks twice, swallows it. "And I'm not a fine lady."

Pelgrom looks closely at Mayken with his mouth pursed and his eyes narrowed. The exact same way Imke would regard a salmon held up by a Haarlem fishmonger. Mayken tries to look bright-eyed and fresh.

"There is a way to go anywhere you want on this ship," he says. "Even to visit the Below World."

"Tell me!"

Pelgrom smiles.

CHAPTER TWO

1989

The child sails in the carrier boat to Beacon Island. The boat left Geraldton at first light. Now, late morning, they are nearing their destination and sea and sky are dazzling blue. Gil is made of pale skin and red hair and thrifted clothes. His shoes, worn down on the outsides, lend an awkward camber to his walk. Old ladies like him; they think he's old-fashioned. Truck drivers like him because he takes an interest in their rigs. Everyone else finds him weird.

Mum said relating to other people is a trick that takes practice. Look a person in the eyes when you are talking to them. Not *all* the time. Sometimes look away.

Gil can't see the skipper's eyes because they are shaded by a baseball cap. As for talking, the skipper shouts sometimes over the engine. He doesn't seem to want replies. Gil sits up with the skipper because this is the farthest point from the sacks of bait reeking at the stern. A crayfish's favorite food is the spines and hooves and heads of sheep. Gil would like to look at the bait, out of interest, but not to smell it close-up. Sights are one thing, smells are another. Smells go inside a person in a different way. The worst kind of smell you can taste.

The skipper tells Gil not to get too excited. Beacon's barely an island, just a lick of coral rubble. You can walk all round it in twenty minutes. Now, if it were the other islands he was heading to, Pigeon, for example, he'd have a basketball court, a club hall, a bit of bloody life. As it was, he'd have bugger all, not even a school.

"I knew your mum," bawls the skipper. The peak of his cap turns in Gil's direction.

Gil looks overboard. Waits.

No further questions.

Gil is braced. He went over this with his and Mum's former neighbor.

"Your mother, she's dead?"

"Yes, from a mishap."

"How did your mother die, Gil?"

"My mother died from a mishap, Mrs. Baxter."

"Tell me, lad, how's your mother?"

"She's dead, unfortunately, from a mishap."

Mrs. Baxter said that anyone who actually knew what had happened to Gil's mother wouldn't be asking. Besides, he owed no one an answer but it didn't do to be impolite.

Mishap. The word didn't cover it.

Gil takes a furtive peek at the skipper. The man raises his head. His mouth is going, he's working over a sentence, gathering it, as he would a spit. Hawk it out.

But the skipper keeps silent.

Up ahead, a blip in the glare. The blip gets bigger.

Even on this sparkling day of sun and sea-dazzle, the island looks bleak. A collection of rough-made huts, dunnies, and water tanks amid shingle banks and low scrub.

The skipper tells Gil they'll put in at the northeast point of the island. The scientists have a jetty built out into the deepwater passage so their workboats can be unloaded onto the island. The scientists have a good setup here now. A hut that sleeps six, workshop, storage shed, darkroom, water catchment tanks for the rainy season. Like the islanders, they rely on the carrier boat for supplies. There are four fishing families on the island: Walker, Villante, Nord, and Zanetti. The Zanetti family are the first and most established, running two boats, a father and son team.

"Then there's your grandfather. Joss Hurley."

He says the name as if he's really saying *knob pox*, or *road traffic accident*. As if Joss Hurley is something to be avoided.

The carrier boat draws up to the jetty, a smattering of people waiting. A clutch of old men and a young woman, her arms folded, wearing a man's singlet vest and a belligerent look.

Another group stands apart in swimmers and open shirts. Two young men and an older woman. The woman wears her dark hair loose. One of the men cracks a joke and they all laugh. The other man has a camera round his neck. He lifts it, takes a look at the scene in front of his eyes, then puts it down again.

"Scientists," says the skipper. "Come to dive the wreck."

He gestures at a wide-bed reef boat with a substantial winch, the only craft moored at the jetty. "They bring shit up from the seabed. Cannons." He glances at the boy. "You know, cannons?"

Gil makes no sign that he knows cannons.

The skipper cuts the engine. The mate stirs himself and drops the fenders. The skipper pulls down the peak of his cap. "Mind how you go," he says to Gil.

Gil disembarks. His bag follows. The islanders come down the jetty. They move without haste, but even so the goods are unloaded rapidly, the heaviest crates and boxes wheeled in barrows along weatherworn boards.

Gil's grandfather makes himself known by picking up the boy's bag.

Joss Hurley is short, not much taller than his grandson. He goes hatless, tanned creosote brown, his bald pate blotched with cancerous-looking sunspots. There's a dark-eyed glance under full eyebrows. A beard stiffly bristled, like the ruff of a tomcat, shot through with gray. He's dressed, like the others, in the island uniform of singlet, shorts, and thongs. There's a bow to his legs and a paunch to his gut. He grunts and throws Gil a sack of tins to carry.

Gil rushes after his grandfather. The old man is deft with a wheelbarrow stacked with supplies, Gil's bag rolling on the top.

A few of the old men nod at Gil in passing. The young woman in singlet and shorts smiles at him, quick and wolfish. She is carrying more than her share, more than the men, and hardly showing the effort.

As Gil's grandfather passes, the islanders draw back. There are no nods or smiles in Joss's direction, just hostile glances. Joss singles no one out for his attention but neither does he look away. Gil follows. Slipping over coral shingle. The sack heavy, feeling like a test.

"There's a wreck out here?" he asks his grandfather's back. "With cannons?"

The distance widens. Gil scrabbles to keep up, listening for a reply.

But the only sounds are the call of birds and the lull of the sea and the throb of the carrier boat's diesel engine as it pulls away.

Theirs is the farthest hut from the jetty. It stands at the south end of the island behind a bank of scrub, as if sloping away from company. As if it would rather launch itself into the sea than converse with its neighbors.

The hut is built from coral slabs and roofed with corrugated iron. The windows are small and have storm shutters. There are a few scorched plants in buckets that might have been tomatoes. A screen of ornamental brick shelters the doorway, and a veranda has been made by extending the roof's overhang. There are outbuildings: a dunny, a generator shed. The plot slopes to shingle at the water's edge, which is six meters away from the one door.

Gil follows his grandfather through this door into a small porch, then onward into a narrow kitchen that smells of mice. Despite its modest size, the kitchen holds a dresser, a table, four chairs, a fridge, and a kerosene stove, giving the room an overstuffed feel. A serving hatch gives out, inexplicably, into the hallway beyond.

Gil has a bedroom farther along the hallway. It's dark and poky with a view of the wall of the generator shed. There's a camp bed, a hook on the wall without a picture, and an upended wooden box with a torch on it.

The old man clears his throat and that serves for his grandson's name, it seems. "There's grub in the kitchen."

He drops Gil's bag in the corner and then Joss is off, back along the hallway, through the mouse-musty kitchen, the screen door slamming behind him.

With his grandfather gone, Gil takes a proper look around. The rooms in the hut are cramped but it's still bigger than the caravans and motels he and Mum would stay in. The asbestos panel walls have been painted bruised colors: sooty purple, dirty green, dull yellow. Gil begins at the beginning. The small porch, with its shelf for torches, its hooks for boat gear, and the smell of diesel and brine. The kitchen, where every surface is tacky with grease, and drowsy flies circle low. Gil peers into the chest freezer in the hall, a jumble of icy plastic with meat parts inside. He slams shut the lid. At the end of the corridor is the lounge room. A couch with antimacassars, a cabinet full of dusty dancing lady figurines.

Joss's bedroom is opposite Gil's. There is a double bed with a sag to it and nightstands on either side, an ashtray on each, one full, one empty; a kidney-shaped dressing table with a mirror you can move. A frilled stool is set before it. Gil finds, not without surprise, that he knows this dressing table.

He remembers a woman sitting there. Not her face but the motion of her hands. She was setting her hair, dipping a comb into a cup of water, working quickly, little bright splashes, the neat row of rollers growing, tight-wound wisps, white-pink scalp showing between.

This is his own memory, not one given to him by Mum. If it was Mum's memory it would have an element of drama: an eel curled in the cup of water or the Devil appearing in the mirror.

Now the memories are jostling to come in. Gil frowns. Let one memory get a foothold and they'll all be clamoring, elbowing their way forward.

He walks through the hut, wary now.

The plush chair in the lounge room he remembers and the window above it that looks out onto blue. These windowpanes rattle in the wind and the tin roof hums in the sun. In the kitchen Gil knows the door to the left opens onto the pantry, as he knows what the pantry will smell of: ant powder and spilt vinegar. Heading back outside, Gil recollects sunlit buckets in the porch and the contents of those buckets moving. Here on the veranda, on this swing seat, canvas canopy gone, frame rusted and buckled, he sat on Mum's lap. Her hands under his armpits, she held him up to a big-sky sunset that filled the whole world, his baby eyes wide open.

If Gil has any memories of this grandfather, he can't find them. But then Mum's father was an incidental character. She never called him "Dad," it was only ever Joss Hurley. Joss Hurley was a walk-on who marked the start and the end of something.

When Joss Hurley left the camp that morning, the kids set out . . .

. . . and then the kids had to stop because Joss Hurley returned.

Gil sits and waits on the veranda but the old man doesn't come home. When he's hungry he goes back inside. He's used to finding his own meals and the pantry is stocked for a siege. Gil opens a can of peaches and eats the fruit, spoon to tin. He drinks the syrup, sweet and tepid, spilling some because he is holding the jagged edge away from his mouth.

A sound at the screen door. Gil startles and turns, cutting his lip on the tin.

A young woman lets herself in, grabs a dishrag and holds it against his bleeding lip. Her other hand is on the back of his neck but very gently so it's okay.

"It looks worse than it is," she says. "Mouth cuts always give a good show but they're quick to heal, all right."

Gil remembers her from the jetty, with her man's singlet and fierce expression. Deep-tanned and flushed with the afternoon heat. Her eyes are brown and prominent. Her face is round and her nose snubby. She is not tall but her limbs are sturdy. Her feet in thongs are splay-toed.

She puts Gil's fingers over the dishrag, at the place he should press.

"Never bleed on the ground here." She quickly wipes the floor and then the counter. "Not even a drop. This island has drunk enough."

Gil presses hard with the rag. She takes off her cap. Her hair is stuck down with sweat, a bad bleach job, fried white at the ends, black at the roots. Her face is kind, even if her smile is filled with wickedness. She is about Mum's age, which was twenty-five.

"You're the grandson, yeah?"

Gil tries to respond.

"Don't talk. Catch the blood."

Gil watches her move about the kitchen. Her name is Silvia Zanetti and she's brought with her magazines left behind by Roper's kids on their last visit.

"Roper is my stepson. Keep pressing."

Gil presses on his cut.

"My husband's son is older than me. Can you imagine being mother to someone older than you?"

The magazines are lame, for younger kids. Gil flicks through them and Silvia keeps talking. She knocks about the island on her own all day every day but she's from a fishing family so she understands this life. Her husband, Frank, is the foremost fisherman. Frank is highly regarded.

His son, Roper, isn't highly regarded on account of him being an arsehole.

"He has a metal plate in his head. It ate into his brain."

Gil is interested, she sees that.

"He brushes his hair over the join." Silvia puts her cap back on. "Show you around?"

"Okay."

Silvia inspects his lip. "It's stopped." She folds the dishrag and has Gil pocket it. "But you really don't want to bleed on this island."

They walk and it's hot and there's nothing to see.

"There's always something to see," says Silvia.

The sky, the sea, the shingle ridges, the rubbled tracks, clouds, if there are clouds—everything changes moment to moment. Gil is not convinced. He listens because he likes her accent.

"Every walk, a different island."

"What's your accent?"

Silvia smiles. "Italy, Big Pigeon, and now here."

"Okay. Carry on." Then, because it might be expected of him, Gil returns her smile but it splits his lip.

"Wipe that blood! Don't smile with your mouth. Smile with your eyes." She wrinkles the corners of her eyes. "Get it?"

Gil doesn't but squints back at her all the same.

They walk and Silvia tells him that these are the Abrolhos Islands and Abrolhos comes from the Portuguese for *open your eyes*, or *watch out*, or maybe *put your frigging eyes back in*, or all of these things.

"Why?"

"There are reefs around here, great for sinking boats."

They stop and stand by the coral cairn, a stacked beacon, eight foot high.

"This is what the island is named for," Silvia says. "The old-time snapper fishermen wanted to be able to tell this island apart from the others. Frank says that from a light aircraft they all look like scabs."

Gil tries to imagine it: the clusters of ugly flat islands.

"The sea is dark today," observes Silvia, "which means she has bad designs. You can't tell what she's going to do next, she's unpredictable."

Gil glances out at the unpredictable sea.

"You know how Roper got his metal plate? The sea took the top off his head."

Gil looks out at the sea with renewed respect.

"He was fishing on the reef when a wave upended his boat. He fell in the water and the propeller minced him up pretty bad." She looks satisfied. "He swam back through the breakers with his head tapped open like an egg, the top of his skull lost. The doctors welded him a new one."

"Are you telling the truth?"

Silvia smiles her wolfish smile. They stand for a while looking at the sea that tapped Roper's head open like an egg.

"It wasn't the sea's fault," says Gil. "It was the propeller that did it."

"You want to split hairs? You'll need to respect the sea when you're out fishing."

"I don't want to go out fishing."

"That's what it's all about. Joss'll train you up as a deckhand."

"I don't want to be a deckhand."

"It's about time your granddaddy had a deckie. Forty pots in the water, a handful even for a younger man. But Joss likes to work alone."

Gil shrugs. Seems like a good idea.

"He doesn't have a choice." Silvia bites a fingernail and glances slyly at Gil. "No one will work with him."

A circuit of the island is punctuated by three hand-rolled cigarettes, smoked standing and in silence. Silvia delicately extracts the rollies from a battered Drum tobacco tin. She uses a windproof lighter with a wild flame and makes a big point of it. Silvia smokes facing away from the wind with her eyes narrowed and the rollie kept alight in her mouth by constant puffing.

Gil asks for a rollie. Silvia looks at him sternly. "How bloody old are you?"

"Nine." Gil hesitates, then says it. "Mum let me."

"That's as may be."

Gil stands next to her, breathing tobacco smoke and mineral air. She smokes the third rollie contemplating an area of scrub. One of the bushes is bigger, more gnarly and set apart. Its branches are hung with ribbons and beads. Around the base of the bush, children's toys are arranged. Some of the offerings look new: a yellow plastic yo-yo, a tiny red bus. Some look old and weathered: faceless dolls, faded bears.

"That's the Raggedy Tree. Now you've seen all the landmarks, apart from Bill Nord's new dunny."

Gil watches the ribbons flutter. "What's all this for?"

"The dead girl who haunts the island. She hangs out here mostly."

Gil, suddenly breathless, thinks of his mother. She was young here. "What dead girl?"

"Old-time ghost, from the shipwreck."

Gil feels himself calm. "There's no such thing as ghosts." He moves forward, touches the ribbons, straightens a fallen toy at the foot of the bush.

"You know about the shipwreck?" Silvia takes a few deep, reflective puffs. "Way, way back. They were Dutch. One lot went about murdering the other lot. Their boat was called the *Batavia*."

Gil notices how Silvia says *Batavia*. Quietly, carefully. He repeats the word inside his mind, feels the thrill—*Batavia. Batavia. Batavia.*

Nothing happens.

But the saying of it will have set something in motion, Gil knows this.

There were words Mum said quietly and carefully because they were dangerous. *Devil. Hangman. Tutankhamun. Cancer.*

"They were finished from the start because they set sail with a psycho on board. Then the ship sank and everyone washed up here. Imagine some psycho after you on this island, you'd be screwed."

"Yeah."

"Where would you hide?" Silvia waves her hand, taking in flat landscape and sparkling sea.

"You couldn't."

The ribbons on the bush flutter, the birds turn above and shriek. Gil is struck by the loneliness of the place.

"She could be a little friend for you." Silvia's tone is taunting. "The dead girl. Seeing that you're the only other kid on the island."

Gil throws her a look. Silvia hides her smile. She pinches the spark off her rollie and pockets it. "Come on, I'll show you the scientists."

The scientists are outside their hut by the jetty, scrubbing small things over buckets. They do this when the sea conditions won't let them dive. Silvia advises Gil to go no nearer.

One of the men looks up and waves.

"Don't wave back," says Silvia. "You don't talk to them."

The man glances at Silvia and returns his attention to the bucket.

She lights her rollie stub, puffs fiercely, glares at the sky. "Disturbing the dead."

Gil thinks of the cannons, the silver coins glinting on the seabed. "They're looking for treasure?"

"If you'd call bones and teeth and rusty nails treasure," Silvia murmurs through her rollie.

"Aren't there coins?"

"They were all found years ago."

The woman scientist is watching them. She stands up, as if she's about to come over. Silvia scowls. "Let's go."

"You're smoking," says Gil.

"I can smoke and walk if I have to."

They head back up the path.

"Disgusting, what they're doing." Silvia throws away her rollie and stamps on it. "Raising ruddy ghosts."

Gil snatches up the rollie and puts it in the pocket of his shorts.

They reach Silvia's camp. The Zanetti family's hut is bigger and better maintained than his grandfather's. It has a new-looking metal roof and blinds pulled down at every window.

"You can't come any further. Frank won't have you inside, on account of what you did and who your granddaddy is." Silvia flashes her wolfish smile. "I can only see you when the boats are out."

Feeling himself redden, Gil turns and kicks back up the path.

Silvia calls out to him. "It was Pop Marten that started it. Brought the scientists here. It was Pop Marten who found the first skull."

Gil keeps walking.

"Under his bloody washing line."

A bird dive-bombs. The scrub shivers in the breeze off the sea.

While Joss cooks, Gil sits at the table and traces on the oilcloth with his fork. Mazes and labyrinths. He knows the difference.

"You'll come fishing tomorrow," says the old man to the cooking pot.

"When can I go back?"

Joss balances his rollie on the edge of the counter, shakes salt into the mix on the stove.

"I could live with Mrs. Baxter, she said I could."

This seems to annoy Joss; he prods at the contents of the pot with a vengeance.

"What are we having?"

"Stew."

"You could teach me how to make it? I could get it ready," Gil tries.

"You throw everything in the pot and boil the shit out of it. What's there to learn?"

Gil looks down at his fork, digging hard into the oilcloth. Joss switches off the burner. He brings the pot to the table and two bowls. Two slices of bread are on one plate, one for each of them, buttered and folded over. Joss gestures at the bread. Gil takes a piece and just holds it.

The old man sits down with a noise, as if there's a big effort in sitting.

Gil keeps his eyes low. He takes in nips of nasty detail every time he looks around. The gunge around the neck of the sauce bottle, the full flypapers decorating the ceiling, the old man's open shirt showing a grizzled fuzz of chest hair.

Joss stirs the stew in the pot with a teacup, then ladles it out. Two portions. There is a greasy film over the stew. Like everything else in this kitchen.

Joss holds a bowl out, his hand ingrained with filth and oil. Gil notices his grandfather's missing fingers. Second and third, the nubbed joints smoothed over where nails ought to be. It gives Gil a jolt. He wonders how he lost them.

"Take it." Joss motions. "What's the matter with you?"

Gil takes his bowl. Joss eats quickly, resentfully, as though he wants to get it over with. Gil watches the stew cool and solidify, grow skin. He tries to think of something to say. About the island and the huts, about the birds and the sea, about the scientists and the bones, about the shipwreck. About Mum and how it had been. About why he'd done what he did.

"Pop Marten found a skull, didn't he?"

His grandfather glances up. "You've been talking to Silvia Zanetti?"

Gil nods.

"Don't. Silvia's full of shit." Joss pushes his chair back. "Be ready early."

CHAPTER THREE

1628

The *Batavia* is the whole world and the whole world is always moving. Mayken has learned to walk again by watching the skipper's soft-kneed swagger with the pitch and roll. A sailor doesn't fight to stand upright because there is no upright. They let the ship come to their foot. And, like a good skipper, Mayken keeps a ship's log.

Ate a ship's biscuit and it made my teeth loose. Imke says I must hold on to my full-grown teeth now that I'm nine as no more will grow in their place. I had to do sewing with the ladies on deck, Mrs. Predikant and her grown daughter Judick. I taught the little boy Roelant a clapping game. Judick smiled over us like a warm sun. Mrs. Predikant gloomed like a rain cloud. Then the skipper came on deck without a tunic on, so we had to go back inside. Today the waves are big and the ship jumps into them, the lion on the bowsprit dips his great paw right in! I practice spitting and swearing when Imke's asleep. I can spit quite far. I would make a great sailor. We have been eleven days at sea.

Mayken thinks about adding Jan Pelgrom's news to her ship's log. That the ship is clear of the English Channel and heading across the Bay of Biscay. That the skipper is angry at having to stay in the convoy because he could drive this boat like a bitch and arrive in Batavia two months sooner.

Pelgrom collects news as he pours wine and picks up fish bones in the Great Cabin. There's a big round table. Skipper Jacobsz and upper-merchant Pelsaert dine in the Great Cabin on alternate nights because they will not eat at the same table, however big and round it is. The two men have history. They have a boiling hatred for one another. Pelgrom likes the skipper's nights better because everyone gets drunk and there are high japes. He's run ragged with the jug but he can eat and drink his fill without anyone noticing. He falls asleep standing on the upper-merchant's evenings because everyone talks softly and makes the wine last.

Mayken reads back her log entry and decides there's quite enough news for the day. She puts her writing things away. Now she will do a patrol. Her permitted area, strictly aft-the-mast, includes her own cabin, the poop deck, and the quarterdeck.

If she chooses to roam outside these areas, she'll bring a horrific accident upon herself. There are ropes that lash, pulleys that twist, sails that swing, and a sea to be swept into and the ship turns back for no one.

Imke accompanies Mayken on deck on calmer days. The old nursemaid settles in a sheltered corner while Mayken winks back at the sailors. Then Imke gives readings of maritime portents (clouds, wave formations, seabirds passing at funny angles). Well-to-do passengers and cadets seek out her wisdom in person. Messages are sent up from below decks. And so Imke's reputation grows.

This is nothing new. Imke was renowned in Haarlem for her ability to accurately forecast love matches and business affairs using no more than turkey giblets and a bag of dried peas.

When Imke tires of her audience she beckons to Mayken. On the way back to their cabin, Imke is sure to stroke the beard of a wooden sailor's head for good luck.

Pelgrom says they are going to need it.

He tells Mayken what's in store. Extremes of hot and cold will send the *Batavia's* timbers shrinking and swelling. The caulkers and carpenters will work all hours to stem the leaks. Barnacles will attach to the ship's underbelly. A skirt of seaweed will grow, slowing her in the water. Ropes will weaken. Sails will stiffen. The painted works will fade and the decks dull. Salt, wind, sea spray, feet in their hundreds are wearing out this wooden sea castle. The ship will spoil as the food will spoil. The fresh water is already tainted. By the time they reach the equator the barrels in the hold will contain more worm than water. The people will spoil too. They'll grow sick.

Mayken learns from Pelgrom about the six-month scurvy. The terrible weakening of the muscles and the swelling of gums and the blotching of legs and the gushing of blood from every orifice. Then it's into a canvas sack and a stitch through your nose and heave-ho over the side. Mayken checks Imke nightly for signs of scurvy. She pulls out the old woman's bottom lip and pokes the gums with her finger. Then she rolls up Imke's shift and scrutinizes her big, blue-veined legs.

Mayken wonders if she'll die of boredom before she dies of scurvy. She wishes for a storm. Not the epic kind, like the storm that ran them aground a day out of harbor, just some interesting weather.

A storm comes.

They smash and tumble through biblical waves with the crying of the passengers and the shouting of the crew and the deck sea-whipped and the sails furled tight against the screaming wind. The waves reach the hens in their poop deck aerie. If the ship sinks, it will be her fault.

Mayken makes a deal with God: in return for the ship not sinking she will think only good thoughts, refrain from swearing, and mind Imke.

The weather is fine.

Imke refuses to teach her how to read the portents. It's not fitting for a lady.

Mayken pipes up during Imke's next session and rattles off a reading to a rapt sailor. Why, his past, present, and future are laid out in the sky! Right there in the flap of the canvas! In the color of the sea! The sailor is astonished—the child sees clearly. Mayken grins at Imke. Imke looks back, tight-lipped.

Imke's second sight has likely rubbed off on Mayken. The old woman vows to be more circumspect with her visions.

Their cabin is getting smaller. Mayken has measured it. Five strides from one end to the other. On the first day it was nine. She has not grown any bigger and Imke has shrunk with the seasickness, so, if anything, they ought to have more room. The contents of the cabin are unchanged: two chests, two sleeping mats, blankets, a bucket, a table, and a stool.

The stool that Mayken is at this moment balancing on.

"What's happening?" whispers Imke.

Mayken applies her ear to the hole in a corner of the ceiling. This hole is for eavesdropping on conversation from the neighboring cabin. Mayken listens hard. Nothing is happening.

"Well?" Imke, propped up on one elbow, looks hopeful.

"The lady is telling the maid off," reports Mayken.

"Use their proper names!"

Mayken rolls her eyes. "*Lucretia Jansdochter* is giving out to *Zwaantie Hendricx* on account of the maidservant giving encouragement to sailors old and young."

Imke nods sagely. "Has Zwaantie answered back this time?"

Mayken shakes her head. "No, but I can hear furious anger in her silence."

"You would do."

"Zwaantie is to rein in her bosoms."

"Wise advice."

Mayken makes to climb down.

"Keep listening, child!"

"They've gone."

"Where?"

"To drink wine in the Great Cabin with the upper-merchant."

"He has a notion for Lady Lucretia." Imke frowns. "Zwaantie is going too? A maidservant is allowed in the Great Cabin?"

Mayken thinks quickly. "No, she has to wait outside in case her mistress needs anything, like a comb, or some pearls. She can sit with the guard as long as she keeps her bosoms to herself."

Imke lies back satisfied. "Come down now."

Mayken is relieved. She has better things to do than make up overheard conversations all day. Besides, it's hard to stay balanced on a three-legged stool on a rocking ship. She cannot understand this fascination for Lucretia Jansdochter, or Creesje, as she is known to her friends. Even Imke, who usually sets no store with wealth, breeding, or beauty, is caught up in the mysteries surrounding their neighbor. The biggest mystery being: why would a woman of wealth, breeding, and beauty risk a long and perilous sea journey? To join her husband, a senior Company man, is the story.

Mayken hasn't forgotten the expression of terror Creesje was wearing when she first saw her—the fine lady being hoisted up the side of the ship like a bag of flour! Now terror has been replaced by a customary expression of dismay. As Imke puts it, she's probably not had to wash in her own piss before.

There is an elaborate knock on the door and it's Jan Pelgrom.

"How are your neighbors?"

Imke sniffs. "The lady is going to drink wine in the Great Cabin with the upper-merchant. The maid is to rein in her wayward bosom."

Pelgrom is to thank for the distraction of the listening hole. Him and his borrowed carpenter's tool. Pelgrom the shipworm.

Mayken takes advantage of Imke's improved spirits. "May I go out? There's sewing."

Imke hesitates. She's been a mare since Mayken's adventure in fortune-telling.

"Mrs. Predikant is teaching embroidery to the young ladies on the deck," supplies Pelgrom. Imke nods. He produces a nugget of ginger from his pocket. "To settle your stomach, Lady Imke."

"Obliged."

"And this, to stir your mind." He kneels down to whisper in her ear.

Mayken watches the glee spark and spread across her nurse-maid's face as Pelgrom speaks hushed and fast. He makes a quick unfathomable gesture with his thin hands. Then he squats back on his haunches and waits.

Imke erupts with a rich fat giggle that runs to a generous laugh that Pelgrom heartily joins in with. Finally, Imke's laughter subsides into the dabbing of tears and a look of gratitude.

Pelgrom, it seems, has a particular gift: the gift of knowing exactly what you need and then giving it to you.

For Imke, it is ginger tea and crying in a good way.

For Mayken, it's the key to the Below World.

Pelgrom rummages in the corner of the dim cabin. The cabin is shared by five clerks and it's half the size of Mayken's. The clerks are presently busy in the Great Cabin, writing lists for the under-merchant.

"Your key to the Below World," says Pelgrom grandly. He brings forward a sour-smelling bundle. "A disguise. You can't trot around down there in your fine gown and lace collar. They'll see at once that you don't belong."

"Does the disguise have to stink?"

"It's from a Below World boy."

"He reeks."

"So do you."

"I reek less than he does."

"Quickly, I'll help you." Pelgrom's hands are not gentle. He tugs at her bonnet bow.

"I can do that."

She steps into canvas breeches, stiff-legged with filth. Pelgrom adds an itchy tunic and a thick leather belt. Mayken suddenly feels scared. Small and lost in someone else's clothes.

"I want to go back to my cabin."

"And miss the chance of an adventure?"

Mayken hesitates.

"Go on, go back to your cabin! Sit with that old girl hauling up her guts."

"Imke can't help being sick." Mayken takes a deep breath, feeling her fear and curiosity battle it out. "I'll go."

"'Course you will." Pelgrom pulls a cap onto her head and surveys her with satisfaction. "My, you are exactly a cabin boy! You must have a name."

Mayken thinks. "Obbe. Like our cat in Haarlem."

"Pleased to meet you, Obbe."

Mayken takes a few short strides. Scratches her arse. Tries spitting.

Pelgrom laughs. "When Imke dies, you can stay that way. We'll shave your head and get you a beer ration."

Mayken feels a sudden flare of anger. "Don't say that about Imke. She's not dying."

Pelgrom shrugs. Mayken tries to scratch under her cap, only her sleeves are too long. Pelgrom rolls them up. His smile is charming.

"What do you want?" asks Mayken.

"Can I sell your old clothes, Obbe? Your fine wool dress with the hidden gems?"

"No. I'll still need to be Mayken. And there are no hidden gems."

Pelgrom feels along the hem of her dress, then stops, raises an eyebrow, and bites at the stitching. Mayken grabs at the dress but Pelgrom holds it up and away from her.

"I'll push this behind the pigpen. You can crawl through the loose board and change back into yourself there."

"I'll be seen!"

"You won't, and if you are, what's better: to be caught as Mayken on the main deck or hung from the yardarm as Obbe for entering a lady's cabin?"

"I'll stink."

"You will."

Mayken scowls but nods.

"Watch yourself," warns Pelgrom. "Aft-the-mast you're protected. The rest of the ship has different rules. Don't expect people to treat you nicely. You're not fine anymore."

Mayken spits, one hawked from the deep.

Pelgrom is grave. "Avoid the corporals, especially the man known as Stonecutter."

"The giant who crushes skulls?"

"The same. He makes it his business to know every last soul on board. Stonecutter counts the bloody rats. He'd know straightaway that you are an impostor. And if you get caught—"

"It has nothing to do with you."

"Remember that."

Mayken moves as fast as she can through the bustle of the main deck. She keeps her eye on Pelgrom, who slows near the waist of the ship. He glances back at her, then ducks behind the pigpen. Mayken follows. He gestures to a loose board and pushes the bundle of her fine clothes behind it.

Pelgrom straightens up, on the alert. Mayken watches. She must wait for his signal to make the final dangerous dash to gain the steps down to the gun deck. He is turning his face everywhere. Who might see them slip through? Who is paying attention? Who is likely to care?

From high above a sudden volley of notes from the fat trumpeter on the poop deck. The bosun's orders translated. The bosun is a big scarred brawler with a flat nose, and right now his eyes are lifted to the sails and the sky. Sailors scramble, ropes tauten, and canvas swells. The *Batavia* ducks and noses and the ship's bell rings another half hour.

Pelgrom raises his hand. *Get ready* . . .

Mayken waits. Her old life behind, her new life before, watching only for the signal. One breath, two breaths—

He drops his hand. *Go!*

CHAPTER FOUR

1989

He can tell by the smell it's how Mum made it. Some trick involving instant coffee and canned milk, with whipped froth on top. Magic. Gil keeps his eyes closed. He and Mum are in a caravan, a motel, a rented room, a borrowed house. Mum is smoking out of the window, or twisting up her hair, or emptying her handbag onto the bed.

Gil decides they are in a house, the last place they lived.

What about the flies, beating themselves senseless to get out of the windows?

Gil takes a breath. Start again: their house.

The house wasn't really theirs. It belonged to the owner of the service station where Mum worked. It was easily the best place they'd lived, although nothing worked and it was full of cockroaches. When you stay in one place, you have to sort things out and clean regularly. You can't just move to get a fresh outlook, like with the motels and caravan parks. Sometimes Mum got pissed off about that.

The house was on the edge of town, up a long drive, meaning visitors were not accidental. It had belonged to the aunt of the service station's owner. She'd expired there. Mum would take a guess as to the whereabouts of Auntie's death. She'd decide on the old chair in the back room. Then she'd laugh.

Gil hated it when Mum talked like that.

Mum said he had sensitivities to other realms, special gifts. If he told Mum not to drive down a road, she wouldn't. Neither of them really knew why. Gil didn't like to sit on the old chair in the back room. It looked haunted. Dips in the cushions from ghostly buttocks. The springs groaned when Mum tried it. Maybe she too felt uneasy sitting on the dead woman's chair, because she usually went for the couch.

The place where he found her.

Gil takes a breath.

Start again: their house.

The first few weeks Gil and Mum worked hard to set the place right. They threw out the commode and unscrewed the bath seat. They scrubbed the floors and windows and painted furniture. Gil arranged candles in jars and Mum sewed cushion covers. They had a bedroom each and for the first time slept apart.

Their house came with rodents, a cat to kill the rodents, a patio with a swing seat, a moldering library of romance novels, a temperamental boiler, and a man named Carlo.

Carlo would call by the servo when Mum was working. Carlo knew how to fix boilers but not well enough so that Mum didn't have to call him out every Friday night. Carlo would come over with his tools and the ingredients for a meal: steak, potatoes, veggies. Then Carlo would cook while Mum watched. Smiling at the big novelty of a man being useful in the kitchen. Gil would take his meal outside and throw it in the bushes. Then Carlo and Mum would drink stubbies and put music on.

Things started to change. Carlo's car was outside. Carlo's bag was in the hallway. Carlo was everywhere. In every part of the house. His aftershave would fill the hall as he strode out of the bathroom. His fried-butter smells would linger in the curtains as he whipped up pancakes in a bathrobe with his nuts showing. Soon Carlo made the coffee, not Mum. Carlo and his shit coffee were the beginning of the end. Her end.

Gil opens his eyes and looks at the mug on the crate next to his bed.

Joss doesn't look up from the mess of papers spread out.

Gil brings his mug to the table. "Mum made it like this."

The old man reads. Gil, with an eye on his grandfather, puts a sugar in and then another and another. He stirs the sugar with a grating sound and then a clanking sound. Then he taps the spoon on the rim of the mug. Quietly, then louder.

Joss, reading, necks his coffee. With the handle of the spoon Gil begins a labyrinth dug into the oilcloth. Joss collects the papers, puts his mug in the sink, and goes to the back door. "Get ready, we'll head out."

Gil moves the sugar bowl, and his labyrinth unwinds.

The boat is moored at the end of a spindly jetty a short walk from the hut. The jetty appears to be lashed together by rope and there are planks missing so that Gil has to hop across. Joss just widens his swagger. *Ramona* is smaller than Gil imagined, not much more than nine meters long. A little cabin out front, white belly and pale blue trim, stacked with craypots and bait buckets. Joss steps in, setting the boat rocking.

"Get in," says Joss.

"I'd rather stay at the camp."

The old man throws him a dark look. Gil climbs in. The boat shifts under his feet. He clings to the side.

"Watch what I do, boy. You might learn something."

Gil has learned enough. He can read a road map, do a decent French manicure, put a grown woman in the recovery position, and shoplift a square meal. Mum called these life skills. Life skills are better than school skills. Mum would tell well-meaning stickybeaks that Gil was home-schooled. Gil understood this to involve learning song lyrics, completing sticker books and doing quick-fire mental arithmetic. When Mum was a waitress, he'd calculate the bills. When she was an usherette, he'd give reports on the films. Gil knew loads of stuff other kids didn't and none of the stuff they knew. Fraught attempts to communicate with another species. For this reason, Gil preferred the company of adults.

If they stayed in a place more than a few weeks, Gil knew there was a danger that Mum would cave in to convention and send him to the local school. This riled them both. Presentation this day, project that day, try not to stand out, forever the new kid. Hide the bruises, hide the notes home, or else Mum might appear at the school stumbling and swearing. The other kids looking on, excited to see an adult unravel.

It was then that Gil hated Mum the most. He'd think: *Suppose she dies.* There's a robbery at her work. Driving home she wraps her car round a tree.

He would visit the scene. Bloodstain on linoleum. Tire marks and broken branches. He could go and live in the kids' home. Have regular bedtimes and maybe make friends. Without Mum, Gil reckoned, he could be average. With Mum, he was always going to be weird. She put the weirdness in him, or else she brought it out.

Don't let her be dead. Don't let her be dead. Don't let her be dead.

Three sets of three. Always in threes. Unless the three sets of three become nine. Nine sets of nine.

Ramona moves out through a reef maze, her engine noise low and throaty, a small dog with a deep growl. Joss shouts over the engine and the wind. He names the other islands in the archipelago, a long one, two higher ones. Gil, standing next to his grandfather, is not tall enough to see through the windscreen. Joss ties the controls with a bungee and finds a box for Gil to stand on. Now all Gil can see is dazzling water. And all he can feel is blind panic as they lurch and dip. He concentrates on holding on, holding fast.

The sea changes color as they motor out. This is lost on Gil. He is rigid with dread at every dip of the bow as *Ramona* snouts down the big waves. Every time he is certain he'll be washed off the deck or the boat will capsize. Gil glances at his grandfather's face. Joss looks out at the sea with a squint, the kind that measures, calculates. For all this the old man looks comfortable, feet planted on the deck, arm draped over the wheel.

Joss brings the boat to buck and roll over a spot that feels hours away from the island, where there are not even spits of coral, only perhaps the stony teeth of reef. Gil wouldn't know, other than the water looks dark and oddly stippled. Joss moves with deliberation, the way that those used to perilous work move. And this does feel perilous to Gil, who stays where he is, holding fast to the side of the boat. With the waves skittering across the deck and the old man wet with sea spray bending to haul the first pot. Joss hooks the float, grapples the line, and pulls in by hand, his stance wide-legged, his deck boots gripping. He rocks the boat and heaves with the rhythm, letting the roll of the boat lift the pot, then pulling up the slack line after.

Gil tries to pray. He fixes on *Jesus Christ, please save me.*

With a last effort on Joss's part that sends the boat careening, the first pot is up. Inside it crawl submarine monsters. Sedately furious, testing the boundaries of their prison, their tails pulsing. Limbs and antennae poke through the gaps. Joss clears the ropes and upends the pot into a tub lashed to the deck, deftly extracting the stragglers. They twitch a moment in the air like awful newborns. Sometimes he pauses to measure them against a metal rule and throws the too-small cray back into the sea. He re-baits the pot with stinking mix from a lidded bucket. The smell is overwhelming, even amid the fresh mineral brine of a whole ocean. Joss starts the engine, which splutters and farts and dies. Joss frowns. The third time he tries, the engine jumps to life and Gil breathes again.

By the fifth pot the weather is changing. Big breakers are coming in. The sea darkens. Joss hooks the float, grapples the line, and begins to heave in, and the engine cuts from idle to silence.

He pushes past Gil, who's an obstacle now, as inanimate as a bucket. Joss works quickly, opening covers, checking dials, as the boat bucks and slams in the water. Without the sound of the engine the world seems to close in around Gil. The sea and the sky. The waves and the wind.

With a bang and the sudden stench of diesel and hot rubber, the engine turns over. But Joss stays on his knees, bent in on himself, his right arm clamped against his body, blood running down along his fingers. He stems the flow with engine rags. Gil, rooted by fear, cannot help.

Joss steers into the worsening weather, sea spray plastering his remaining hair to his head, his cap taken by the wind. Gil listens for the engine sound above the keen of the wind, predicting every falter. The old man has added a plastic bag to his wound dressing, binding it with cord, using his teeth. Blood pools against the plastic.

Gil does not see the island until they are almost upon it. He feels relief and, alongside this, a sudden exhaustion. His grandfather motions him to get out and tie up, which Gil does badly. Joss revises one of the knots but stooping to the second knot he totters, straightens and wipes his face with his good hand. His lips are pursed and his eyes dull as he gestures to Gil to carry the wire-handled bucket.

Gil slips behind Joss over coral shingle, the few crays he carries slipping with him.

The storm worsens so that the waves grind the shingle banks and the tin roof of the hut whistles. When the generator cuts out, Joss finds lanterns. He brings one into the lounge room where Gil is pretending to play patience.

Joss has changed the dressing on his hand; it is bandaged now, bulky but clean.

Gil draws cards and quietly places them.

Joss has a glass of brandy in his good hand. He sits down heavily, downs his drink, and closes his eyes.

With Joss asleep in the chair, there's no cooked dinner. Gil goes into the kitchen. A lantern has been left lit on the table, flaring patterns on dark walls.

The brandy bottle is on the dresser. Gil pours some into a mug and sticks his tongue in. It tastes sweet and nasty and burns. He takes sips until he feels hot and poisoned. He opens tinned ham, turning the key so the metal strip winds off. He pokes the ham out onto the counter with a knife and cuts the flabby bits off. When the slices break, he eats them straightaway. The perfect slices he slides onto crackers and dots tomato sauce on top. He arranges the crackers nicely on the table, because you eat with your eyes. He has his snack while the weather pounds on the windows and shakes the door. Outside the sky is dark, the ocean darker. Somewhere inside him Gil still feels the tip and reel of the boat.

Joss hasn't moved. Gil wonders if he should find a mirror. If the mirror fogs, a person is alive. If the mirror stays clear, they are holding their breath or have no breath.

The old man's eyes are closed and his mouth is open and his chest is still. He doesn't look dead.

Mum looked dead.

Stop. Breathe. Think of what to do.

Don't let him be dead. Don't let him be dead. Don't let him be dead.

Gil gets right up close to his grandfather, smelling the booze and tobacco off him, smelling dried blood and diesel. He listens hard.

Nothing.

Outside the squall has blown over. The waves on the shingle banks have calmed to a rasp. Gil waits. Joss suddenly takes an in-breath, like he's being born or something. It starts up a ratchety but regular snore.

Gil goes to bed.

CHAPTER FIVE

1628

Mayken goes across the deck, down the ladder, following Pelgrom into the belly of the ship. As she descends, the heat and the smell rise. It's dark, with a crush of people going in all directions. Pelgrom disappears. Mayken panics to lose sight of him. She tracks back and there he is waving at her through a gap between the ship's hull and a cabin. She squeezes in.

"My offices in the Below World," says Pelgrom.

A stool has been dragged into the cavity. The steward folds himself into the small space, his knees at his ears. Mayken wonders at him. Making holes, moving boards, burrowing into tiny places. This ship needs neither worm nor rat with Jan Pelgrom on board.

A clanging bell. Crowds of people press through the main thoroughfare. Mayken can see legs, bare filthy feet.

"We'll wait a while."

Mayken puffs. "Why is it so hot?"

Pelgrom taps the wall. "Tin-lined brick. Behind here the cook roasts himself daily." He pulls a sour face and makes his voice old and grumbly. "Three hundred and forty fucking souls to feed."

She wipes her face on her sleeve. "I couldn't stand this."

"You weren't reared on eel spines and pebbles in a hovel in Bommel like I was. Jan Pelgrom will never be warm. My crib was cut in the mudflats."

Mayken suspects a story.

"Meet me here at the next change-of-watch bell. You know how that sounds?"

"'Course."

"On no account leave this deck. Don't go up. Don't go down."

"What's beneath here?"

"Nothing. I told you: soldiers and cows." Pelgrom's face is grave. "Talk to no one. And if you're caught—"

"It has nothing to do with you."

Pelgrom nods. Then smiles. "Go, Obbe! You're a cabin boy now and the Above World is lost to you. The Below World is yours to explore."

The Below World is a dim realm. The only light comes from the hatches above and the gunports, open in today's fine weather. The gun deck runs the length and breadth of the ship, sectioned by the cannons that hulk at intervals along the side. There are cabins housing the offices of the provost and the ship's barber-surgeons. Families live on the gun deck; canvas sheets have been rigged up for privacy. Some don't bother. Sailors bed down between the cannons, some with their women, trying to sleep despite the constant traffic. Mayken does a full circuit, looking at everything, her eyes used to the gloom now. Her route takes her back toward Pelgrom's hiding place, past the galley. The door to the galley is open this time round. The fire is out. A lull between meals.

The kitchen boy, bare limbs, shaved head, wearing a flour sack, looks out. He stares at Mayken and recognition dawns. "My breeches. You fucker! Those are my breeches!"

Mayken runs, dodging people, tripping over feet. Ahead, there's a gaggle of sailors. She presses herself in among them and the kitchen boy runs past.

The sailors are crowding round a man, another sailor, on his neck a suppurating boil the size of an apple. His shipmates are taking turns touching it for good luck. The boil is a wondrous red. The sailors debate it.

"There's something inside wanting out."

"A face, look."

"A baby's head."

"No kind of fucking baby I'd want to meet."

The sailor is patient; Mayken can tell he's unwell, pale in the half-light and sweating. He smells dreadful, a fishy sweetness over the usual sailor stench of piss and foul breath.

The sailor is called into the cabin. Mayken crowds round the door with the other onlookers.

The barber-surgeon's cabin is cramped, the floor strewn with sawdust. Two buckets, one full and one empty, are roped to the wall, which, to Mayken's fascinated horror, is splashed with blood. Lipped shelves are fitted floor to ceiling, holding rows of bottles and jars. There is a long narrow bench with tools laid out. The cabin is well lit. Three lanterns swing high, burning bright, on chains that can be lowered. They cast strong shadows in the cabin and on the barber-surgeon himself, a young man wearing a long apron so stiffened with blood and pus that it would stand upright without him. His sleeves are rolled up and he wears a skullcap. His expression is one of regal disdain, a smear of gore on his cheek. He is half prince, half butcher. Mayken stares at him in wonder.

The sailor with the boil strips off to the waist and is positioned on a low stool. The onlookers, including Mayken, press forward. The butcher-prince pulls down the chained lanterns. The sailor and his boil look even worse in the light. The sailor, waxen. The boil, livid.

Mayken notices the chair in the corner. It is bolted to the floor and has leather restraints for the arms, ankles, and chest. In a box on the wall next to it is a saw, a chisel, and a hammer.

Mayken is overcome with excitement. "Is that where you take off the legs?"

The butcher-prince glances over with a frown. Mayken remembers to speak like a cabin boy. "Is that where you take off the *fucking* legs?"

"And you are?"

Mayken catches herself. "Obbe."

"Obbe, *sir*."

"Obbe, *sir*. And you are?"

Some of the waiting sailors laugh.

"Under-barber Aris Jansz." He swabs the boil with a rag and something tarry from a jar. "Do you always use oaths, Obbe?"

Mayken nods with enthusiasm. "Yes, I fucking do."

"You don't fear a thrashing like the other cabin boys?"

Mayken startles. There is a hint of a smile on the under-barber's face.

"Then you are stout of heart, Obbe."

"Depends."

Aris taps the sailor lightly on his boil. The sailor flinches. "This has grown big enough for its own beer ration."

Everyone laughs. Aris glances at Mayken.

"Come stand beside me, boy. I need an assistant."

The crowd makes way and Mayken steps into the cabin.

"Prodigious quantities of pus," Aris notes. "What do you make of it, Obbe?"

Mayken looks up at the under-barber. He's older than she first thought, or maybe just more tired. His eyes are a clear blue gray. His nose sharp. Beard fine.

"Yes, prodigious," she concurs. "Pus."

Aris hands her a sponge and a bowl and leans down to her ear. "Sailors show no pain but what I'm about to do will hurt. A little performance to distract this man's audience can only help. Do you understand?"

Mayken nods and grips the sponge.

"Get through this and you can watch me take a leg off." Aris straightens up. "Right, I'll lance. Obbe, are you ready to catch whatever the hell comes out of this?"

Mayken holds up the sponge and the bowl, dancing on the spot. The audience laughs.

"Ready?" Aris raises a knife. "There's no way of knowing which way she'll blow."

The audience draws back.

The sailor, his neck bandaged, makes his way through the crowd, far paler now. Aris throws the sodden rag in a bucket and wipes his forehead with the back of his arm.

"I've another job for you, Obbe. Are you strong of mind?"

"Depends."

"'Course it does."

From a low cupboard Aris takes out an ornate box. He places the box carefully on the workbench and unlocks it. Inside there are rows of tiny stoppered bottles. He selects one, wraps it in a clean rag, and hands it to Mayken.

"Go to the deck below, where the soldiers are. Find the Englishman called John Pinten."

"John Pinten." The shape of the name is unfamiliar to her mouth.

"Give him this. Hide it. Don't let anyone see. Understand?"

"Yes."

"Bring his payment straight back to me."

Mayken nods.

"Good. Then I will give you a coin of your own."

"I'd rather see you take a leg off."

"You would?" Aris looks at the cabin boy closely. "Well, get on with the delivery, then."

Mayken keeps the bottle hidden in her breeches. Intent on finding a way down to the lower deck, she doesn't see the kitchen boy stalking her.

He flies at Mayken. She turns and delivers a smart punch to his nose. His face erupts with blood and tears.

They sit behind a cannon away from the main thoroughfare. The red stream from the kitchen boy's nose is abating but the tears still fall.

"Less of that," says Mayken kindly. "Or I'll kick you."

The kitchen boy stops weeping.

His name is Smoert. He is small and thin with a blasted, reddened look to him. Pink-rimmed eyes like a rabbit, brows and lashes melted away in the heat of the galley. His shaved head, hands, and arms are stippled with scabs and healed burns from meat-fat splatters. He's a little gargoyle; his face naturally finds a grimace.

Smoert tenders his complaint: Mayken is wearing every stitch he previously owned. The breeches he sewed himself, the belt a gift from his old master, the tunic issued to him when he boarded the ship. Smoert had taken everything off two days ago to get deloused. After a bucket of seawater had been emptied upon his head, he'd looked around to find his things gone.

"I didn't take them," says Mayken.

Smoert looks unconvinced.

"Do you know where the soldiers sleep?"

Smoert nods.

"I will give your things back," she says. "But first you must help me find the soldier John Pinten."

Smoert picks at the blood coagulating in his nostrils.

"I will also give you a coin," promises Mayken.

Smoert narrows his rabbity eyes. "Show me."

"When I'm paid. You have to trust me."

Smoert considers. He nods shyly.

❧

"Wait," whispers Mayken into the dark hatch. "What's even down there?"

Smoert, his feet on the staggered steps, stops and looks up, his blasted face pale in the dim. "Soldiers and cows."

"Is that all?"

"What else would there be?"

"It smells like Hell."

"How do you know what Hell smells like?"

"Imke told me: dead souls and roasted devil shit."

"Who is Imke?"

"My nursemaid."

"Nursemaid?"

Mayken bites her lip. "Never mind. Go down. Hurry."

By the bottom of the ladder the heat and the stink overwhelm Mayken; cow dung and something acrid and tarry. A hot stench that suffocates like a grip over the nose and mouth. Mayken breathes as best she can, ignoring the panic rising inside her. It is even darker here than on the gun deck. With no gunports the only light comes from the lanterns that punctuate the darkness, hung at wide intervals from crossbeams, flames turned low. This stifling, perpetual night is made worse by the low ceiling, which seems to press down in the gloom. The orlop or cow deck is the height of the beasts penned near the hatch. No grown person can walk upright; they must bend and scuttle, taking care not to crack their skulls on the beams.

Mayken is small enough to stand upright. If she reaches up, she can touch the glistening ceiling, which drips wet from the cows' breath and soldiers' breath. A quick movement in the shadows tells her this deck is alive with vermin. They thread between the bars of the pen and run among the cows, who stand hock-deep in filth.

The cows are chewing, their eyes large in the dim. As they dodder against the motion of the ship, their nostrils flare and ears twitch. Mayken feels sad for them, these creatures of soil and fresh grass who never in their cow dreams could have imagined such a life! In the next pen, steers huff out the remainder of their lives before they are butchered for the Great Cabin's table.

"The soldiers sleep down there." Smoert points into the dark.

He hangs back as Mayken sets off along the boarded walkway at the center of the deck.

"Wait there if you want," she whispers. He looks relieved.

Mayken proceeds. By the pockets of light thrown down by the lanterns, she sees soldiers lying packed in rows. They stare dead-eyed at the ceiling, as ghastly as corpses.

Mayken calls low. "John Pinten."

No answer.

She tries again, louder. "John Pinten."

"Farther," says a rasp from the murk. "All the way."

Behind her: the dwindling comfort of lanterns. Before her: blackness.

But she promised to deliver the bottle.

Coming to the end of the walkway, she tests the edge with her foot, a drop into what? She fights to breathe, overcome by the heat and the airless dark.

"John Pinten," she gasps. "Show yourself!"

There's a noise. A spark is struck, a lantern flares—a face!

Mayken cannot bring herself to run.

CHAPTER SIX

1989

Joss Hurley was seen leaving for the mainland on the carrier boat this morning. He was in a bad way. Bill Nord made him go. Bill, who was a medic in the forces and knows his shit, said that the quacks would need to lop off the hand. But if the infection has spread, as it likely has, they'd take the arm. If that didn't fix it then the old man will be royally fucked.

So goes the news Silvia Zanetti brings to the door.

Gil already knows the news. His grandfather has gone to the mainland to buy parts to fix *Ramona*'s engine. Joss didn't mention having his hand lopped off, only that he'd stay overnight in Geraldton.

He wasn't well. His face was greenish, eyes rheumy. Gil had waited out front, his bag packed for the trip.

Joss had barely looked at him. "You'll be all right here. Silvia can look in."

Silvia sets about making breakfast, her bad-bleach-job hair pinned up, her uniform of singlet and shorts fresh on. Gil is wearing his school shorts and the T-shirt that Mrs. Baxter bought for him, a violent yellow that clashes with his red hair. Mrs. Baxter said it is cheerful, which is the main thing.

"I've nothing personal against your granddaddy, you understand." Silvia puts mugs on the table. "But Frank would roast me if he knew I was here."

Gil adds three sugars, four, then stirs quietly.

"Still. If you can't do a good turn." She puts her feet up on a chair and flicks open a magazine.

Gil and Silvia play cards for matches. He catches her looking at him, her expression curiosity and pity mixed.

Gil looks down at his cards, waits for it.

"Is it true that you kept her in the house?"

Gil keeps his eyes on his cards.

"All that time?"

Gil keeps his eyes on his cards.

"You knew she was . . ."

Gil's cards go blurry.

When they get hungry, Gil goes to the pantry and takes out meal ingredients: tinned ham and crackers.

"Is that all you have?"

"There's stew left."

Silvia looks in the pot and pulls a face. Then she sticks her head into the pantry. "Your granddaddy eats like the end of the world has happened. Nothing fresh. The fishermen all do."

"I don't mind."

Silvia puts her baseball cap on. "We'll go to mine and have a proper meal."

"Won't Frank be there, and Roper?"

"I wouldn't take you if they were."

❧

The sea and sky are searing blue, the breeze giving a freshness that masks the heat. Lizards bask in sheltered dips in the coral rubble. Gil's arms and legs redden. His skin feels the sun's burn even with the wind.

They walk past Bill Nord's, the place where the skull was found.

"The scientists want to dig trenches under our camp," says Silvia. "Frank won't let them. He says there's nothing buried around our place."

"How does he know?"

"He doesn't." She glances at Gil, lowers her voice. "Sometimes I go out with a trowel. I've found things."

Gil finds himself straying nearer. "What things?"

"Never you mind."

Gil knows this means Silvia has found nothing.

"I'm looking for the remains of someone."

"Who?"

"The dead girl, from the Raggedy Tree. The fishermen call her Little May."

They walk on.

Silvia looks thoughtful. "If I can find her and give her a decent burial, she'll stop walking the island. All the dead really want is to rest in peace."

"There's no such thing as ghosts," Gil spits, surprised by his own anger. "The dead don't bloody come back."

Silvia glances at him coolly. "Not if their bones are treated with respect. You ought to know that."

Gil, stung, drops back. He looks at Silvia's ugly shorts, her dumpy legs, her nasty hair scooped into her hat and he hates her.

She glances over her shoulder. "Do you want ice cream, or what?"

The Zanetti camp doesn't have a serving hatch to nowhere, or a kidney-shaped dressing table, or low buzzing flies and sticky surfaces. Everything inside is functional and wipe-clean in a shade of beige or cream or orange. The dunny, adjacent to the main hut, is a wonder, gleaming white porcelain. The main hut has three bedrooms and a wide veranda under the new galvanized roof. There's a good-sized kitchen and a walk-in pantry that doesn't smell of mice. The deckie's hut next door is well fitted-out but messy: a surfboard propped against the wall and a tangle of gear heaped in the corner. There are two bunks but only one mattress rolled out.

"We used to have two deckies. One left on account of Roper being an arsehole."

There's a lean-to out the back of the main hut with a pool table and bar built from pallets. Framed photographs of boats hang above the bar. Frank's boat *Sherri Blue* and Roper's boat *Waygood*.

Another photograph is propped behind a keg. "I gave this to Frank on his birthday."

They look at the photograph: four men on a jetty.

"That's my Frank, in the middle."

Frank is dour-looking, fifties, dark hair graying.

"He's old."

Silvia laughs. "The old ones are more grateful." She points at the man standing next to Frank. "That's Roper."

Late twenties, short legs, good-sized gut, pumped-up arms. Roper holds his cap in his hand, red-faced and sweaty-mouthed with receding fair hair.

"The ugly duckling." She points to the men flanking father and son. "The deckies."

On one side a young bloke, well-built and sunburnt. "Cherry, he's still here." The other deckie is stringy and older. "Dutch, he left."

Gil notices that in the picture Frank has his arm around Dutch, not Roper.

"Brilliant worker, Dutch. With the family for years. Until Roper kicked the shit out of him." Silvia glances at Gil slyly. "Your mum ever speak of Dutch?"

"No."

"You know they were sweethearts?"

Gil can't see it, Mum and a stringy old deckie. He says nothing.

Silvia smiles. "Do you like eggplant?"

"I don't know."

Silvia bustles about the kitchen. Her bare feet flop on the lino as she sings along in Italian with the radio. She holds up a vegetable. "Eggplant."

"No."

"You're nine." She says it like an accusation. "I'll put it on a pizza."

The pizza is good. Gil picks off the eggplant. Then Silvia brings out a cardboard pack of ice cream. She cuts a thick slice, slips it into a glass, and pushes the glass to Gil.

She licks her finger. "After this, I'll show you the grotto."

"What's a grotto?"

"A decorative cave, very spiritual." Silvia takes up a spoon and eats straight from the cardboard box. "Frank built it."

Gil stirs his ice cream to sludgy melt.

"It's my haven," she continues. "You know what a haven is?"

Gil slurps his dessert.

Silvia's grotto looks out to sea. Perhaps it was a dunny once; now it's something else entirely. An ugly structure made from molded concrete set with shells and rocks in wavy patterns.

The doorway is low and arched. Silvia, short as she is, has to bend her head. There's a curtain she sweeps aside with the air of a fortune-teller. "Enter."

Gil's eyes adjust to the dim. The walls and ceiling are set with fragments of glass and pottery. There are alcoves with candles in jam jars.

A short bench holds them both, closer than Gil would like. Silvia smells of smoke and sweat and laundry detergent. Gil has no idea what he smells like, probably damp underpants, mice, and engine oil, like Joss's hut.

They look out through the low arch at the sea, framed like a bright picture.

"You should find a place," Silvia murmurs. "Somewhere you can be truly alone on this island."

"I'm alone when he's out fishing."

"I wouldn't bet on it."

Gil can tell from the tone of her voice there's some weird shit coming.

"One of the fishermen followed her once."

Gil concentrates on the blue sea.

"It was just after dawn and not a soul in sight when he saw Little May rise out of the Raggedy Tree and set off across the scrub."

A seabird flies through the framed picture.

"It scared the crap out of him but the fisherman still followed her." There's a wicked smile in Silvia's voice. "But you don't believe in ghosts and ghouls, which is just as well."

"Why?"

"You know where she went?"

Gil keeps his eyes on the sea but can feel Silvia looking straight at him.

"She took the path right up to your granddaddy's."

CHAPTER SEVEN

1628

The glim is a lantern; the lantern illuminates eyes, bloodshot, pupils huge. The face is pale and the beard is matted.

"You called my name. I am John Pinten."

He speaks Dutch with an accent of elsewhere. He's broad of forehead, heavy of brow, with a nose that hasn't gone unbroken. He's seen fighting. The scar on his face attests to this. It runs down his cheek, carving a channel through his beard to flick across his filthy neck.

The sight of him thrills and terrifies Mayken in equal measure.

"Come forward. Quickly, boy."

Mayken takes the bottle from her breeches and, moving as near as she dares, places it on the floor beside the soldier and retreats. She smells the sourness of the man's body and the rank hay smell of the bales surrounding him. No others lie nearby.

"My English castle." He points past the bales. "The French are over there. The Dutch are nearest the hatch."

With effort the man sits up and takes up the bottle, cursing in words Mayken doesn't understand, although she knows them to be curses by the way the soldier spits them out.

"The barber sent this?"

Mayken nods.

"He no longer attends his patients in person. Your name, boy?"

"Obbe."

"Sit, Obbe."

Mayken hesitates.

"You must wait for payment. Yes?"

Mayken sits in the hot airless dark and feels like a landed, drowning fish.

"Breathe through your mouth," says the soldier. "Slowly. Don't gulp. That's it."

"Why do they keep you down here?" asked Mayken.

"Soldiers and sailors are enemies."

"You are their prisoners?"

"Not at all. At sea the sailors must have the run of the ship. This is their world. They celebrate by pissing down on us. Near the hatch there is air but also water."

He bites off the lid and raises the bottle to his lips. He drinks with an eye on Mayken.

"Now talk to me until the barber's potion works."

"What does the potion do?"

From the hay bales, a squeal and tumble.

"It grants me the sleep of a stone," replies the soldier. "Then the rats can play in my beard."

"Rats are a problem for everyone," says Mayken sagely.

"They start low and work up. By the time we reach Batavia they'll be sitting in the Great Cabin eating from the silver plates."

Mayken laughs.

The soldier smiles bitterly. "But they like it best here, under the waterline."

"We are below the waterline?"

"Come." John Pinten turns and puts his palm against the hull. "Do as I do."

Mayken crawls forward and puts her palm next to his, flat against the planks. She sees how much smaller and cleaner her hand is. Too clean for a cabin boy. But John Pinten doesn't seem to notice.

"She's all that lies between us and the deep dark fathoms of the sea." John Pinten's voice grows quiet, grave. "Can you feel the ocean pulling at the nail heads, pressing against the planks, prizing the caulking? The water wants in."

Despite the heat Mayken suddenly feels cold. She pulls her hand away.

"Out beyond those planks there could be a big blue nothing. Or shoals of glittering fish. Or a whale bigger than your Dutch village. Or a line of jagged rocks waiting to smash us to pieces."

Mayken shudders. "Don't!"

The soldier smiles at her. "You're easily frightened, boy."

"I'm not frightened."

John Pinten lies back, stretches his arms out behind his head, closes his eyes. "There are worse ways to die."

Mayken watches as his breathing slows. He's turning to stone.

"John Pinten, I must take back payment."

He opens his eyes, gestures toward the bale. "Pouch under there."

"The rats—"

"You're scared of rats as well?"

"I'm scared of nothing." Mayken feels around under the bale. "Fuck off, rats."

John Pinten laughs as she finds the pouch and passes it to him. With effort he counts out several coins, pressing them into her palm. Mayken makes to go.

"Wait. Stay. Until I fall asleep."

Mayken sits back down. He turns his head to her, his pupils wide and black in the lantern light. He whispers urgently. "Between asleep and awake I hear it; down in the hold, stirring."

"What stirs?"

"Your Dutch bloody monster."

"What monster?"

But the soldier is stone now.

❧

Smoert is waiting for Mayken at the top of the ladder. She sees him squinting down into the dark as she climbs up, the air on the gun deck sweet and fresh in comparison.

"You could have come to see the soldier."

"I took you to the orlop deck, didn't I? An' you found him, didn't you?"

"And you'll have your coin."

Smoert wipes his nose. "Obliged."

Mayken pushes through the queue outside the barber-surgeon's cabin. Smoert holds back. The kitchen boy holds no store with them. Their ointment hurts worse than any burn.

The under-barber is wrenching something from the mouth of a sailor. He glances at Mayken, then holds his hand out. She drops the coins in, Aris slides them in a pouch at his waist and pulls out another, smaller coin. It's blood-smeared. She takes it anyway.

"Come again." He lowers his voice. "And tell no one what you did."

Mayken is true to her word. She gives the kitchen boy the coin.

"My clothes," he says. "Please."

They go round behind a cannon. Smoert changes, head down, face burning, all knees and elbows. He looks better in breeches even if he has to wind the belt three times around himself.

Mayken adjusts the flour sack as best she can. It's down to her ankles and far itchier than it ought to be. "Have you got lice?"

"Are you a girl?"

They look at each other in the half-light.

Smoert rubs his nose on his sleeve. "I don't care if you are a girl."

"I don't care if you have lice."

And then the clamor of the watch bell.

Pelgrom is waiting for Mayken in his hiding hole behind the galley.

"Where are your clothes?"

"I gave them back."

Pelgrom gives her a sour look. "You kept me waiting. I'm wanted in the Great Cabin."

"Sorry."

"You went to the orlop deck."

"I didn't."

"I can smell the cow shit off you."

Mayken follows Pelgrom back through the gun deck. She keeps up, although he doesn't make it easy.

"You know every part of this ship, don't you, Jan Pelgrom?" She's wheedling. "Better than anyone."

He catches her tone and slows. "So?"

"What's in the hold?"

"Beer, grain, bricks—"

"Is that it? Nothing *stirs* there?"

Pelgrom shoots a look at her. "Like what, rats?"

Mayken hesitates. "Not rats . . . something else."

Pelgrom reddens. "You were to talk to no one! You were told to stay on this deck! I won't bring you here again."

"Please!"

"I should risk the noose so you can play cabin boy and gab non-sense with Lord knows who? Say goodbye to the Below World, Lady Mayken."

CHAPTER EIGHT

1989

Walking back to his grandfather's camp, Gil imagines he hears the voice of the dead Dutch girl on the wind. The crunch of her steps behind him. Although, ghosts probably don't have footsteps; they likely float. And it's no use her calling out, because he can't speak Dutch. Once or twice, sensing someone following, he looks round, quickly, so she hasn't time to disappear. But there's nothing but the breeze through the scrub or the waves on the shingle.

Gil resolves to tighten the screws and not listen to another bloody word Silvia Zanetti says. She's promised to look in on him later with a dinner. Well, he can plug his ears while he eats. Mrs. Baxter had the same love of feeding him. Maybe it's because he's an orphan.

Gil doesn't know he's an orphan for sure. Technically his dad would also need to be dead. But Mum never divulged and Gil never prodded. His dad was likely some loser. If he'd been a big shot, Mum would have been on to him for money. Mrs. Baxter said that whatever else Mum was, she wasn't backward in coming forward.

On reaching the camp Gil finds the screen door open, banging in the wind. It spooks him, so he goes through all the rooms. Not a living soul.

Gil knows the signs of haunting. A kid ghost will give you cold knees. A woman ghost turns silver jewelry black. If furniture's thrown around, your ghost is a man.

Gil's knees are fine, thank you.

He mixes up a frozen juice for himself. He makes it strong how he likes it and carries it into the back room. He looks at the dancing lady figurines in the cabinet while he crunches his icy drink. He lifts one out to look at her dress, her face, her tiny slippered feet. He sets her back carefully on the clean patch in the thick layer of dust. As he shuts the cabinet doors the catch sticks. A shadow falls across the floor, like someone's outside watching at the window. A cloud passing on a cloudless day.

He tries the door again, slamming it a little. A sliding noise; something slips out behind the cabinet. Gil discovers an old picture book.

On the cover is a tall, monster-shaped shadow and a girl looking up at it with her eyes big. A dark and creepy-looking water hole lies between them. The title, *What's My Name?*, bubbles up in twisty letters on the surface of the water.

Gil opens the book. The story goes that the girl, on her way home, wanders off the path and amuses herself by throwing pebbles into a water hole.

A voice rises out of the water, startling her. But it's a sweet-talking voice. The girl listens and is lulled. A monster-shaped shadow, massive and eel-like with a jutting spine and fishy eyes, rears up before her. The girl remembers what her mother told her about talking to big, shadowy, monster-shaped strangers.

"I'm no stranger!" exclaims the shadow-monster. "Don't tell me you've forgotten my name!"

Sensing a trick, the girl walks on.
But the shadow-monster follows her.

Gil turns the page and it's there in the entrance of a cave, or skulking in the bushes, or flattened behind a rock, its fishy eyes peering over.

The girl stops. "What is it you want?"
"I followed you and now I'm lost!" wails the shadow-monster.
"Take me home to my water hole!"
"I'll be late for tea!" says the girl.
"That's never worried you before," replies the shadow-monster.
The girl tracks back to the water hole and the shadow-monster follows. There it is behind the rock, in the bushes, in the cave.
When they get to the water hole the shadow-monster has another request.
"Make me real. All you have to do is say my name. Only the things you humans name become real."
"What happens if you become real?"
"I'll wait nicely by the water hole and you can come and visit. I could eat your enemies, if you like."
The girl's face brightens. "You'd eat my enemies?"
"Yes. What's my name?" asks the shadow-monster. "Go on, say it!"
"I really don't know."
The shadow-monster whispers in her ear.
"Bunyip," repeats the girl.
"Louder!" says the shadow-monster.
"Bunyip."
"LOUDER!"
"BUNYIP!"
The shadow-monster darkens and becomes solid. It is terrible. Slime slicks and drips over ancient barnacled scales. Eyes, luminous and bulging. Gills rattling venomously.

A great, festering eel-king.

The girl—too late—realizes her mistake.

Bunyip lashes its tail around her and squeezes tight—"You're mine, sucker!"—and drags the girl straight down into the water hole.

The final picture shows the water hole. On the surface of the water floats Bunyip's grin, stretched thin and wide, and its gleeful gleaming eyes.

Gil frowns. It's disturbing. Closing the book, he catches sight of a name written inside the cover in little kid's handwriting.

DAWN HURLEY

He touches the name. Once, when she was smaller than him, even, Mum's hand had crossed this page, spelling out these letters carefully. Maybe she was sitting in this room. Sea light playing across the ceiling. The sound of waves and seabirds.

Then Gil sees another name, written just under the picture of the girl as she runs happily toward the water hole, her pigtails flying.

LITTLE MAY

Gil pushes the book back behind the cabinet. There's something in Bunyip's grin he wishes he could unsee. Maybe that's why Mum left it there. Despite the afternoon heat of the room, he feels a sudden chill. And an urge to be elsewhere.

He takes the scrubby path down the center of the island. The sky is white blue and the light beats up off the coral shards. Gil doesn't want company but wouldn't mind knowing that living, breathing people are nearby. He'll go and watch the scientists.

They are digging up at Bill Nord's. There's a cordoned-off area with lines of tape held up by rods. Not police crime scene tape, just plain white tape that bounces in the breeze off the sea.

The scientists are down on their hunkers. They wear shirts and khakis, boots and hats. The woman's dark hair is plaited in a long tail down her back. One man, thin with a sparse beard, smiles at Gil. The other man is muscled and brooding and scraping around with a trowel as if his life depended on it.

The woman gets up, brushes off her knees, and heads toward Gil. "I've seen you with Silvia Zanetti. Didn't she warn you off us?"

Gil feels awkward. "No."

She smiles. Her smile says she doesn't believe him.

Her name is Birgit; the thin, bearded man is Sam; and the broad, surly man is Mick.

On hearing his name, Birgit nods as if she already knows it. "Come and see, Gil."

He follows her over to a pit sectioned out with markers. On a trestle table set behind windbreaks there are tools, tubs, and plastic bags.

"This trench has given up what looks like butchered animal bone, fragments of an iron ring, pottery shards."

"All in that dirt?"

"All in that humus, compact sand, and coral rubble."

Gil likes the way Birgit talks to him, just normal, not overenthusiastic like some adults are with kids.

"This is a difficult site to excavate," she explains. "Everything gets churned up with the birds burrowing."

"They have to live somewhere. There are no trees."

"You're right." Birgit picks up a plastic pot from a nearby crate, holds it out to Gil. "What do you reckon this is?"

Gil frowns into the pot. A tiny misshaped ball on a bed of cotton wool. "A gallstone?"

"Shit." Birgit laughs. "Is that what gallstones look like?"

Gil is pleased. "Mrs. Baxter's did. She minded me when Mum was crook," he adds, not knowing why and then wanting to kick himself for giving a way in.

But Birgit's attention is on the plastic pot. She nudges the cotton wool with her fingertip. "It's a musket ball. A musket is an old muzzle-loaded gun."

"Did that kill someone?"

"Likely not." She glances up at him. "Visit our hut sometime. I'll show you what else we've found."

"I don't want to just see skulls, you know."

"You've an interest in gallstones, too."

"Silvia is looking for bones." Gil forces a laugh. "So some dead girl stops haunting."

Birgit nods, her expression surprisingly serious. "Little May, is it?"

"There's no such thing as ghosts."

Birgit's eyes kindle. "But wouldn't this be just the place for them? This lonely island."

She lifts out a flask from the shade under the table and pours two beakers of squash for them. They drink looking down into the pit.

"You know something, Gil? I sleep uneasy here. I feel watched."

Gil doesn't miss a beat. "That's probably Silvia Zanetti."

Birgit smiles and it's a real one, because her eyes crinkle at the edges.

It's not as if Gil isn't used to being alone. Mum sometimes worked nights and the nights sometimes turned into days before she came home. Sometimes she came home with a bag of groceries and cleaned the house. More often she came home and drew the curtains and told Gil to be quiet and leave her the fuck alone.

Gil sits out on Joss Hurley's veranda. The sea and sky are still searing blue. When he closes his eyes, the sea gets louder. The sea-birds are loud either way. Sometimes you forget they are there, the sea and the birds. Then suddenly you can hear only them. The sea and the birds are like your breath and heartbeat. They are constant, whether you notice them or not.

Gil picks at the sun blisters on his shoulders for a while. Then he gets up and goes inside to look at the clock. Hardly any time has passed. He lights the kero burner to hear the pop of the flame and puts the kettle on to boil. He takes out Silvia's squashed rollie, the one he picked up. He lights it, inhales, and heaves over the sink. A taste on his tongue like cat crap. He opens his mouth under the tap. The burble of the water is fast and loud down the drain.

A wide, stretched grin. What's my name?

Fuck off, Bunyip.

He wipes his mouth and watches the kettle. Then he remembers that it won't boil if it's watched, so he closes his eyes until the whistle starts. The coffee he makes is nothing like Mum's. Gil pours it away and mixes another. It's still not right but he will drink it anyway. He takes the coffee into Joss's room, setting it down on the nightstand.

Granddaddy's boudoir.

Boudoir was Mum's favorite word, along with *magnificent* and *sparkle. Gusset* was her least favorite word, along with *adenoids.* Gil likes *moon* and dislikes *nits,* other than that he's easy.

The humped sag of Joss's bed. The kidney-shaped dressing table. Gil approaches it with care, a more skittish-looking piece of furniture you couldn't imagine. It wears a mauve frill around the base. He imagines it hoisting its skirts and galloping away. He opens the drawer and smells stale talc and dust. A perfume as faint as Granny Iris, that faded memory. In the drawer there's a ceramic dish with hairpins. A comb with a wispy gray hair tangled in the teeth. Gil holds it up: all that's left of Granny Iris.

At the back of the drawer are the fossilized remains of makeup. Clotted eyeliner and ancient rouge. Gil winds up a lipstick with satisfaction. Red against the shiny gold casing. He turns it over to look at the base but there's only a number. Mum liked naming colors. He considers.

Jamboree Lips
Scarlet Floozy
Crimson Hussy

Gil rubs the lipstick carefully against the side of his finger, removing the surface that touched Granny's old lips once upon a time. Looking in the dusty mirror, Gil draws himself a movie star mouth. Bigger, better, redder than his own.

The wind is picking up when Silvia arrives with cannelloni.

"Are you wearing lipstick, Gil?"

"No."

"Suits you. What did you get up to this afternoon?"

"Nothing."

Silvia looks narrowly at him. Gil looks away.

"Birgit showed me a musket ball," he admits.

"You spoke to the scientists?"

Gil hesitates. "Not much. Hardly at all."

"That bitch thinks she owns the place." Silvia disappears into the pantry. "But guess what, the island doesn't want them here."

Rummaging, clink of glass.

"Bingo." Silvia brings out the sherry bottle.

She finds two dusty tumblers in the lounge-room cabinet and pours a large sherry for herself and a speck for Gil. He tips his tumbler back to get it. He notices the red crescent smears around the top of his glass and likes them. Slutty business.

"They'll sew his stump up nicely. Bill Nord can keep an eye on it."

Gil shudders. He hears again the grunt the old man made when he was injured. Sees his blood dripping on the deck, pattering inside the plastic bag.

"Your granddaddy will need a deckie now. He can't haul pots with one hand." She gives Gil a sly glance. "You'll have to step up."

Gil lets this go.

"You'll be joining him one day."

"No. I won't. I don't want to be a fisherman."

"What will you do, then?"

"I dunno, but not that."

"What did your mum do?" Silvia is pretending to read a newspaper.

"Hairdressing," Gil lies.

She turns over a page and squints at headlines. "She sounded like a lovely person."

Gil thinks about this. "She liked sunsets."

Silvia smiles. "'Course she did."

"And singing and dancing. And dressing up."

"Fabulous! I'll bet you did that together, mother and son?" Silvia says sweetly.

Gil glances at her, waiting for the twist of some knife. But she's reading properly now, her eyes moving across the page. Gil breathes out.

"It's a tragedy when someone so full of life does themselves in," she adds.

Gil sits in the dunny. He listens to the sea bashing the shingle and the seabirds killing one another. After a while he wipes his eyes.

Silvia heats the dish through and Gil likes the rich sauce and has loads of triangles of white bread and enjoys it. Silvia lights a cigarette and watches him as she plays with the frazzled ends of her hair.

It's dark, they've sat at the table that long. Like they do in Italy, says Silvia. Eating, talking, except she's the only one doing the talking. Gil picks at the burnt cheese on the cannelloni dish. Silvia knocks back the sherry. She sways when she gets up to butter more bread.

"I'll stay here tonight to annoy Frank." She lights her rollie with a flourish. "Your granddaddy is his enemy because of the feud."

"What feud?"

"I can't talk about it. Island business."

Gil picks up a fork and starts tracing a maze on the table. A complicated one.

"You know what a feud is?"

Gil carves.

Silvia pours another sherry; she's revving up to tell.

A bang at the kitchen window. The pair of them jump.

A shadowy bulk outside.

What's my name?

The shadow swears and shuffles. It's a man who has taken drink.

"Quick, switch off the lights," says Silvia. "It's Roper."

Gil hits the light switches for the porch and the kitchen. The place is in darkness. Outside is lighter. Roper framed at the window.

He bangs on the glass again. "Dad says come back."

"Fuck off," breathes Silvia.

"You hear me? Get out here." Roper bangs harder and the window frame judders.

Silvia calls out: "I'll come back later."

"You'll come now." Roper tracks back to the screen door. He kicks it with each word he shouts. "Or I'll fucking drag you out."

"No." Silvia gets up and goes to the door. "You fucking won't."

In the dark kitchen, Gil opens the window a crack to hear.

Silvia is on the doorstep talking fast and low. She has the door held ready to slam in Roper's face. They've the porch light back on to keep him in view. He stands before the door, swaying, fists clenched. Roper's of average height but there's a muscle and mass to his shoulders. There's a sizable paunch to him. His shorts are overlong and his hands are overbig and when he takes off his cap, fluff clings to his balding head. A long comma of a scar and a dent on the left side of his head. Silvia wasn't lying about his scalp.

"Dad's going to beat the shit out of you. Shagging that old man, Dirty Hurley."

"Joss is not here. I'm not shagging him."

"What is it with you and old blokes?" His hand rummages at his shorts. "You should try a young one."

Silvia says something Gil doesn't catch. Roper goes wild, lunging forward, hand out, grabbing her hair.

Gil feels the blood in him slow.

Silvia twists away, slams the door closed, draws the bolt. Then her voice, nervy, over-high. "Go home, Roper, just fucking leave it."

Roper raises an emphatic finger. Stumbles back. Lurches onto the veranda. Shoulders along the wall. Gil ducks. Roper leans in, his fingers finding the open kitchen window. He tugs it, slipping the catch. Gil shrinks back.

Roper stares inside, mimes a gun with his pointing finger, and pulls the trigger.

CHAPTER NINE

1628

Mayken and Imke lie on their bunks. Mayken above, Imke below. The ship rocks. The gimballed lantern above them is rocking too. The lamp is left lit for Imke, who will not sleep in the dark.

Mayken peers over the edge of her bunk. "You're sad, Imke."

"Yes, Mayken, so are you."

"Only a bit. Why are you sad?"

"Because I'm a sick old lady. Why are you sad?"

Mayken thinks about this. Because she would like to return to the Below World and see Smoert the kitchen boy and Aris the butcher-prince. She would like to visit John Pinten again and ask him what stirs in the hold. Although she half doesn't want to know.

"Because I miss Haarlem."

"Who wouldn't?"

"Let's play How You Lost Your Fingers," says Mayken.

"Do we have to?"

"You were playing in a forest and came across a hungry wood-cutter with a sharp axe."

Imke laughs. "Not even close—and not much of a meal!"

Mayken smiles in delight. "He'd take a leg!"

Imke holds out her leg, gives it a wobble. "Better eating on that."

"Let's play another game called What Will Be the Best Thing About Living in Batavia?"

"I can get off this bloody boat."

"Think, Imke. Batavia."

Imke thinks. "I can sit on my arse and eat figs in the sun."

"The sun that melts little Dutch children."

"You are a horror. Now let me sleep!"

Mayken lies back down. In her mind she drafts her next ship's log entry.

Twenty days at sea. I don't know where we are. I am sewing breeches for the poor cabin boys with Mrs. Predikant and Judick. The ladies are dismayed to find young crew members dressed in rags. But the breeches are for me. I have made a tunic too. If I ever get back to the Below World then I won't be wearing a flour sack.

Mayken listens to the nighttime noises of the ship. Nearest to her: Imke's snores. Farther away: feasting in the Great Cabin, muffled roars and shouts. It's the skipper's night. And the constant rhythmic creak of the ship. A plain, easy-sailing night. The night ship rocks everyone in her round wooden belly.

A soft knock at the cabin door.

Mayken slips from her bunk. Imke sleeps on.

From the corridor comes Pelgrom's voice with a stifled giggle in it. "Take the air with me, Lady Mayken?"

They sit in a dark corner of the quarterdeck under the canvas rigged to protect the well-to-do passengers from the sun in the daytime. Mayken wishes they were under open sky, the better to see the stars. The great stern lantern is lit. It shines a glittering path on the newly washed deck.

Pelgrom nudges her and offers a jug. She cannot see his face in the dim but she can tell from his breath that he's drunk.

He whispers, "Wine, from the skipper's table."

She lifts the heavy jug to her lips. It tastes nasty.

Pelgrom takes the jug back. "Do you want to know what they ate in the Great Cabin tonight?"

Mayken always does.

"Three baby pigs. Fancy carrots. Fishes slit and stuffed. Hens' eggs, marbled."

"How many fell down drunk?"

"One junior cadet, with his face in the soup, but the night is young."

Pelgrom lifts the jug, Mayken sees the motion in the dark.

"Where are we now in the sea?"

"You mean you don't know?"

Mayken hears the smile in his voice.

"We are seven months from Batavia, Lady Mayken. Much can happen in seven months. People may be born. People may die. We'll all go mad and our teeth will fall out."

Mayken pulls her lips over her teeth, gumming in the dark.

Pelgrom raises the jug again. "You had a question about the hold. Remember?"

Mayken thinks of John Pinten's words. They still raise prickles on her nape and make her tummy lurch. "What stirs in the hold?"

"I'm here to give you the answer . . ."

Mayken waits.

"Biscuit weevils, water-barrel worms, and rats by the thousands. They wake in the hold!"

"If you're not going to tell—"

"All right!" Pelgrom lowers his voice. "I have it on good authority that we have a stowaway on board. An *unnatural* stowaway."

Mayken's eyes widen in the dark. "Go on."

"Something monstrous stretched out along the keel, licking the moisture there, breathing the close black air."

"Have you seen it?" Her voice is a whisper.

"The hold is deep and I wouldn't poke around down there if you paid me."

Mayken thinks a moment. "Who told you about the stowaway?"

Pelgrom drinks again from the jug, a soft slurp. "A sailor, honest and true."

"What's his name?"

"You'd only go bothering him. I'll tell you what he told me. Only I warn you," says Pelgrom, "it's not a story for children."

"I still want the story."

"You would."

There was once this village, just like any Dutch village, only unluckier. Vegetables grew spindly, the animals were sickly, and the people were ugly. On top of this came a terrible summer and worse autumn, wet and stormy, bringing every chance of floods and ruined harvests. The villagers had tried to drain the land but they were very poor. They had no money to build windmills or buy timber to shore up the banks. Neither had they sheep to graze and stamp down the soil with their golden feet and deposit muck to make the grass grow long and bind the land together to keep the whole place from slumping to mud.

It continued to rain and the water continued to rise and the villagers continued to fear.

Then came a stranger to the village.

"What did the stranger look like?"

"A very old man with a bundle on his back. Bent over he was, like a tree in high wind."

"What was in his bundle?"

"Have patience, will you?"

The villagers gathered around the stranger, for they rarely got visitors.

"We have no food to offer you, old father," they cried. "The land is drowning and our crops have failed. Our babies are hungry and our animals marked for slaughter, even the cats and dogs—"

"Just like in Haarlem during a siege long ago! The sign in the church says 'dogs and cats were considered roast game'—"

"Do you want this story at all?"

"You are in the shit," said the old man. "Luckily I can make the rain fall upward."

"Then help us, kind stranger!"

"I can save your crops and your land, for a price."

The villagers hardly had a choice. "Name it."

"The next baby born of the village is mine. I'm too old and bent to go walking about forever, I want to train up an apprentice."

The villagers readily accepted his terms. "Lijsbet will have her baby any day now. You can have it."

Lijsbet knew none of this. She was at home with her feet up.

The old man untied his bundle. "Three nights it will take to dry out your land. At dusk on those three nights, you must all go home and lock your doors and shutter your windows. You must not look out, not a peep, through crack or keyhole, until morning."

The villagers agreed.

As dusk fell on the first night, they all went home and locked their doors and shuttered their windows and didn't look out, not a peep, through crack or keyhole, until the morning.

Then they discovered two things: the land was drier and Lijsbet's baby had been born.

Dusk fell on the second night and the villagers again did what they were told. The following day the land was drier still. Everyone was delighted apart from Lijsbet, when she was told her baby would be payment for the old man's help.

Dusk fell again on the third night. The villagers went home and locked their doors and shuttered their windows. All except Lijsbet, who was determined to see what variety of old man would take an infant from its mother.

She hid herself in an apple barrel with a good view all around. Presently the old man appeared with a jar, a lantern, and a sturdy stick. He lit the lantern and put it on the ground next to the stoppered jar. Then he unstopped the jar and tapped it with the stick.

Out of the jar flipped a horrible creature. Notched was its spine, gleaming were its eyes. It writhed on the ground and it hissed. Like an eel it was, only seven times longer and five times fatter. The old man hit the creature with the stick and the creature shivered. The old man hit it again and the creature went headfirst into the soil. The next time the old man hit it, the creature began to make slurping noises.

The creature grew bigger and bigger and bigger as it sucked up all the water in the flooded land. When the creature was the size of a hill, the old man waved his stick in the air and shouted, "Spit!"

The massive bloated creature raised itself up and hissed.

The old man threw his stick in temper. "SPIT, I SAID!"

The creature opened its mouth and all the water it had sucked from the land streamed high into the sky, higher than the clouds, higher than the moon. All at once the creature was small again, like an eel, only seven times longer and five times fatter.

Lijsbet jumped out of the apple barrel. She took up the old man's stick lying on the ground and hit him with it for his dark magic and mistreatment of innocent eel creatures.

"Leave me be!" he shouted at her. "Don't let that bastard get away!"

But it was too late. The creature was gone.

"You fool!" said the old man to Lijsbet. "You have set a terrible monster loose on the world."

Lijsbet shook the stick at the old man. "You get out of town or I'll ram this stick up your hole."

The old man hopped. "Gladly. That monster is a baby yet. I wouldn't want to be around here when it comes slithering back fully grown."

Mayken frowns into the darkness. "Lijsbet should have got after that eel creature with the stick."

"Well, she didn't."

"Never mind. Keep going."

The villagers rose in the morning to find their land perfectly dry. The old man had gone and Lijsbet still had her baby. She told no one about what she saw or the old man's warning words. In the days that followed, a shadow grew wherever water was to be found—

"In a jug, in a puddle, in a tear," says Mayken, because she can't help herself.

"Do you want me to continue?"

One by one the youngest villagers met their ends. First, the babies. They were found lifeless in their cribs, just tiny wizened skins of themselves, as if all the moisture had been sucked out.

Then the children, who tragically drowned in various ways—

"I want the various ways!"

"All right!"

One little girl was found upended in a bucket with her belly full of water and her eyes sucked out. A little boy was discovered drowned in a puddle, covered in fish slime with his face gnawed off. Several more were found strangled near a horse trough with their mouths full of sea lice. In all cases an eel-like creature had been seen slithering away.

Lijsbet told the village elders what she knew.

They said they would communicate with knowledgeable elders elsewhere.

The answer came back from the knowledgeable elders elsewhere.

The eel creature was an ancient monster and foe of all humankind. Its name was Bullebak.

"Big bully? The creature was called *big bully?*"

"Just so."

"Fair enough," says Mayken. "Carry on."

Bullebak was a canny creature. Although eel-shaped, it could change its appearance, like the water it lived in. While Bullebak enjoyed drowning children and eating them, it liked to give grown people fatal bites or just play tricks on them, like taking over their minds. Bullebak would worm in through the nostrils or the ears and turn and turn about inside the skull until the brain was plash. By then the person would be dangerously insane, of course. Behind their eyes lay the gleam of the creature inside. But before Bullebak could be caught it would slip away again and lie low. Waiting for its next victim.

Lijsbet pledged to spend her life hunting Bullebak. As her child grew, he would help her. Mother and son followed Bullebak tirelessly, through canals, rivers—

"But they didn't catch it?"

"No. One day Lijsbet was found dead in a chair by the fire, her brain plash running out of her ears."

"Bullebak got her in the end!"

"Her son vowed to avenge the death of his mother and follow the creature across all the seas and every country."

"Did Bullebak get him too?"

"No, he's still looking."

"Good for him."

"So, to this day," says Pelgrom, "Bullebak lies in wait for the unwary."

He pinches Mayken's leg. She screams. Laughing, he holds his hand over her mouth. She bites his fingers. Pelgrom lets her go.

Mayken has a question brewing inside her like a storm cloud. "So you're saying it is Bullebak that wakens in the hold?"

"More or less."

"I don't believe you. You made that story up, a sailor didn't tell you. There was no old stranger, there was no Lijsbet."

Pelgrom's voice is grave. "Believe what you want, Lady Mayken. I swear on God's robe that is the truth as I heard it."

Mayken whispers, "Why did Bullebak stow away on this ship?"

"It's the best ship ever made! With the juiciest cargo, plenty of people to feed on, and a fast passage to a new land."

"How did it even get on board?"

"In a jug, in a puddle, in a tear."

CHAPTER TEN

1989

They sit at the kitchen table, Silvia holding a rollie in her shaking hand, her eyes flitting between the locked door and the shut window. Roper, it appears, has gone.

"When I first came here," she says, "after Frank and me married, I made a plan: when we got back to the mainland, I'd steal the season's earnings and run."

"Did you?"

"'Course not. I lost my nerve."

Gil thinks about this. "If you do run away, will you take me?"

"It's a deal." Silvia smokes hard and starts to look calmer.

"Will you still stay over?" says Gil.

Silvia squeezes Gil's arm. "If that's okay?"

Gil nods.

Silvia stubs out her rollie. "What would you say to a jigsaw?"

Canals, canyon, Easter rabbits, space station. Every box contains a mismatch of moldering, chewed-looking pieces.

"We could dress up," Gil suggests, as if he doesn't care.

"As what?"

"Fashion models."

Silvia gestures at her own outfit. Frank's old singlet by the looks of it.

"There's loads of stuff in the wardrobe, from Granny Iris."

"Jesus, Gil!" Silvia cackles. "You want to dress me up as your granny?"

Gil smiles.

The left side of the wardrobe holds Joss Hurley's few clothes. A couple of shirts, shorts. The right side of the wardrobe holds his dead wife's clothes.

"You think your granny would mind?" Silvia's voice is respectfully low.

Gil has no idea.

Iris Hurley had rigid curls and blue eyes. She had a white patent-leather purse that matched her white patent-leather sandals. She had frosted peach lips that matched her frosted peach nails. Meeting her would involve a whole day's drive to some café. A midway point, only Mum would grumble that she had to drive farther, so it wasn't midway at all. Gil would get a sundae so big he'd have to stand up on his chair for the last knockings.

Granny Iris said let the child have whatever he wants.

Mum and Granny Iris would hiss at one another over coffee cups. Then Granny Iris would press her lips closed and open her handbag. She would pull out a fat envelope and push it across the table. Mum would slide the envelope into her bag without looking at her mother.

On the drive home Mum would cry and Gil would puke.

Silvia is rapt. "Did your granny actually wear this stuff around the island?"

First, they arrange the dead woman's clothing according to color: white, yellow, pink, peach, apricot, orange, red, brown, beige, taupe, sand, green, aqua, blue, and black. Gil already has his favorites: a jacket in lovely stiff emerald brocade and a raspberry silk blouse, cool and slippery. At the bottom of the wardrobe a chorus of shoes, imprinted with the ghosts of Granny Iris's toes.

"I wonder why he keeps it all?" Silvia looks sad. "He must miss her."

"Do you want a day or a night look?"

"You choose."

Silvia sits before the triptych of mirrors at Granny Iris's dressing table. Gil has set up two lamps to offset the harsh overhead strip. It's not exactly a Hollywood mirror but it will do. He has brushed out Silvia's hair and pinned it up so it's soft and flattering for her round face. There's nothing he can do about her bad dye job. A fierce streak of rouge creates cheekbones and a smudge of eyeliner for drama. Silvia wears a blush satin strappy dress with a pair of crocodile slingbacks, her callused heels hanging off the back.

She smiles wolfishly and is entirely gorgeous.

"Now it's your turn," she says.

Gil wears the emerald jacket. Silvia has belted it and rolled up the sleeves. They agree it looks better like that, more modern.

"The David Bowie look," she says.

Silvia adds a brooch, then rummages in Granny Iris's jewelry box and fishes out some clip-on pearl earrings.

Gil nods and holds still.

The both look in the mirror.

The green brocade makes Gil's face look paler and his hair look redder and the cut on his lip, healing now, more obvious.

"Your eyes, Gil!"

Peering into the mirror, he sees what Silvia means. His golden-brown eyes glow amber: some trick of the light and of the brocade. He looks like a dream; he looks like a painting; he looks like a prince.

Gil likes it.

They each choose a handbag and walk out into the kitchen. Gil has no problem managing a too-big pair of courts. He gives an accomplished stride down the hall runway. He turns at the end, snapping his head round, leg out to the side, giving it attitude. Silvia goes wild clapping. Gil gets better with every turn but then goes over on his ankle. Silvia is rubbish, she can't walk for laughing, which makes Gil laugh too. She crosses her arms and hunches her back and does a funny sashay. They call it a day as supermodels.

"We'll have some music." Silvia wipes the dust off the cassette player above the kitchen sink and switches it on and it works. "It's some kind of Ella Fitzgerald."

Silvia dances and sings along with her own words about what fuckers Frank and Roper are and how she'll be stealing all their money soon. Gil claps along and does the backing vocals.

Then there's a power cut and all the lights go out. Silvia's laughter winds down in the dark because maybe the power cut isn't a power cut. Maybe it's the ghost of Granny Iris angry at their wardrobe raid. Gil says he doesn't think Granny Iris would haunt them over a few outfits. She would probably be glad her things were getting an airing.

Silvia won't meddle with the generator. It will blow up, maiming her, or she'll break it and Joss will go nuts and she'll find herself buried with the Dutch people under this camp. They light lanterns and take them into the lounge room. And the room looks cozy in the soft flickering light.

Gil finds a box of dominoes but Silvia can't put her mind to it, lying the length of the couch, slap, slap, slapping Grandma Iris's shoe against her grubby sole, slinky in silk.

Gil studies the tan lines on Silvia's shoulders. He thinks about how things, now gone, might leave a mark: singlets, mums—

"We'll go to Perth city," Silvia says. "Buy a van, get a dog. Dye our hair, you know, for a disguise."

"Can I get a pearl-blond pixie cut?"

Silvia laughs, then falls asleep with her head under a cushion.

Gil isn't sleepy. He returns to his grandfather's room to hang up Granny Iris's blouses and dresses and tidy away the ancient makeup. He crouches on the floor to neaten the shoes in the bottom of the wardrobe, walking them back into line.

Tucked away in the far corner of the wardrobe, he sees a small box, like you'd keep money in. There's no money inside, just a shuffle of papers and two tobacco tins. Gil ignores the papers and opens one of the tins to find a yellowish shard and a slip of paper. Gil reads the words:

> **BATAVIA FIND**
> **IVORY BOBBIN**

Whatever a bobbin is. He opens the second tobacco tin: a dry strip of gristle. On the slip of paper:

> **BATAVIA FIND**
> **CHILD'S FINGER**

He drops it on the bed in disgust. Then looks at it in fascination. He compares it to his own, then puts it carefully back in its box, wiping his hand on the bedsheet. Granny Iris must have collected these, in her patent sandals and patent bag, digging about in the humus, compact sand, and coral rubble. He pockets the bobbin tin and puts the money box back in the wardrobe.

Gil checks the door three times. Locked. Locked. Locked. Then he checks the windows, three times per window, although Roper surely wouldn't go to the trouble of climbing in the windows with his fat arse. He'd just kick the door in. Then he'd kill them with an axe, something bloody and violent. He'd scream with every blow he struck. He'd scream louder than them, even. Gil gets into bed with his shorts on; he's ready to run out.

Sometimes he and Mum went to bed in their clothes so they could do a bunk because they owed rent. When Gil was small, Mum would wrap him in a blanket and carry him out to the car. He would sleep a while and when he woke they would be far away and the sun would be coming up and Mum would glance at him in the driver's mirror. *Good morning, starshine.*

Gil thinks about the lights cutting out. He imagines a ghostly

Granny Iris tutting up and down the hall. Ghostly fat envelopes in her ghostly handbag. Or maybe it was the olden-days Dutch people that doused the lights? Disturbed by the laughter and the Ella Fitzgerald music. All the murdered people jostling about in the hallway, shaking their heads, frowning through the serving hatch.

Maybe Little May was there with them? In an olden-days dress and bonnet and a sad face. Maybe it's her finger in the wardrobe? Maybe she wants it back?

Gil has a watched sort of feeling. He reassures himself that his room is too small for any quantity of ghosts, unless they can overlap. But then the dead can't harm you, it's the living you should fear. The ghosts ought to make themselves useful and go out and haunt the veranda in case Roper returns.

Gil dozes despite himself. Bad dreams come like beetles, crowding and clicking, overturning one another, scrabbling.

A house on a road that led nowhere.

Mother and son sing on the swing seat in the yard. A gray cat turns up during a thunderstorm and has kittens. She carries her babies out mewling, one by one into the rain. In the morning, a huddle of tiny wet pelts.

Mother comes home and draws the curtains. Son plays quietly.

Flies at the window, knocking themselves to pieces, trying to get out of there—

Gil startles awake in his bed. He listens. Nothing. The camp is quiet. He lies back down. All the island slumbers, think on that. Silvia sleeps stretched out on the lounge-room couch. Fishermen snore under corrugated roofs. Scientists nod surrounded by skull scraps and musket balls. The ghost crabs dream, curled up under the dunny. Even the sea eagle dozes in her nest of fishing twine and rag. Only Little May is awake; ghosts don't sleep. She'll be drifting down quiet paths or inspecting her gifts at the Raggedy Tree.

Gil will keep his mind here, on this lonely island, and not let it go back across the water, back across the land, to where the real ghosts live.

CHAPTER ELEVEN

1628

Six weeks at sea. Pelgrom says we are sailing south along the coast of Spain. Spitting practice is going well. I am aiming for halfway across the quarterdeck, like the skipper. This is harder on windy days. I have finished sewing my cabin-boy breeches but I fear I will never wear them again, that I am stuck forever in the Above World. Mrs. Predikant has a boil. I wonder will she let the other passengers rub it for good luck?

Mayken thinks for a while. She could write about Smoert the kitchen boy and Aris the butcher-prince and the stone soldier John Pinten. But her journey to the Below World feels like a dream now. Her life is in the Above World, with Imke.

Mayken loves the old woman fiercely. Who wouldn't? Imke's eyes water when she laughs. Imke's songs are hilarious and rude. Imke's embraces are surprise attacks that make Mayken hiccup with delight.

Or, at least, that's how things used to be. Now there's a growing sadness in Imke's eyes, all her songs are about withered roses and night falling. Before, back in Haarlem, Mayken enjoyed hiding from her nursemaid. Now she dogs Imke's every step.

"Go and sew with the ladies. Go and take the air with Lady Creesje. Go and practice your spitting, yes, you've been seen."

Mayken pulls a face. "I want to stay with you. I have a new game you might be interested in playing."

Imke looks weary. "Go on."

"It's called The Skipper is a Wolf. You have to say the animal the person is most like."

"And be thrown overboard for mutiny!"

"It's not a mutiny: wolves are nice. What about the upper-merchant?"

"I'm not playing."

"Come on, Imke!"

The old woman thinks. "Pelsaert is a magpie: smart feathers, sharp-eyed, likes a bright coin."

They both smile; it's very good.

"Lady Creesje?"

Imke ponders. "A swan."

Mayken rolls her eyes. "My turn. Make it a tricky one."

"Jeronimus Cornelisz."

Mayken considers. She pictures the under-merchant in her mind. He is third in command. It goes: upper-merchant, skipper, and then under-merchant. Mayken knows from her races around Haarlem with the market boys that third place is no place. Jeronimus Cornelisz knows it too; this explains the bitterness about his mouth and the shiftiness to his gaze. He's always muttering into people's ears, huddling close while looking past them. On to the next trick. The next plot. He's a failed apothecary from their own town. Imke says there was a scandal but she can't remember the details, meaning it is too rich a sauce for Mayken.

"He's a weasel," says Mayken. "In a plumed hat."

Imke hoots. "Exactly right! The steward?"

"Jan Pelgrom is a snake," says Mayken, without thinking.

Imke frowns, looks at her closely. "What's happened between the two of you?"

Mayken studies her knees. "He just is, that's all."

Imke wants to sleep, or use the pan, or have a peaceful think. She can do none of these things with Mayken watching her.

"Isn't it time for your patrol, Mayken?"

"But are you quite well, Imke dear?"

"Never better."

"What if you should need me?"

"Then I'll send for you."

"What if you should fall, or become sick, or—"

"Get out from under my feet, child!"

"Your nursemaid is failing," Mrs. Predikant observes coldly. Her needle stabs, her mouth is pursed, the fabric taut in her hands. "She's half the size she was when she boarded."

Mayken is so angry she could spit. From this distance she could easily hit Mrs. Predikant.

"Mother, we are all diminished versions of ourselves after weeks of imbibing weevils and carrot tops." Judick glances kindly at Mayken.

But Mayken knows that Mrs. Predikant is right. Although Imke has recovered from her seasickness, there's a sunken look about her. A slackness and a slowness that wasn't there before. Now Imke falls asleep midstory and her plump chest is just skin flaps. Now there are bones that jut. In her nightgown she looks like an old milk cow, all hip and rib.

Mayken puts down her sewing and takes a ramble along the deck. Pelgrom passes, running with jug and bowl. Mayken hails him.

"I need something."

"Go on—quickly."

Mayken lowers her voice. "A tonic for Imke."

"Because she's failing?"

"She is not!" Mayken frowns. "She just looks a bit thin, that's all."

"Maybe your old friend Bullebak is poisoning her? Check for eel bites." Pelgrom throws her a wry glance and continues on his way.

"Don't be stupid." Mayken hesitates, then calls out after him. "What do eel bites look like?"

Mayken must wait for Imke to be truly asleep before she starts. The examination will take place during Imke's afternoon nap. Today Mayken will be searching her nursemaid for Bullebak bites as well as scurvy. First, she lifts Imke's lip and scrutinizes her gums. Then she peers into Imke's ears and up each nostril. Next, she listens to her nursemaid's breath; then bravely smells it. Then she squeezes Imke's fingers one after the other, even the stubbed ones.

Mayken saw the physician do this when he attended her mother. The physician came often to Mama. Some days she waited nicely for him by the window, her round belly swathed in a fine gown, her face clean and her hands fresh. Other days Mama was crawling over the bed like a spider, big bodied and twiggy limbed. The physician left drops. Mayken liked the look of them swirled in water, inky. Mama always took them in the same glass, only the preparation changed and grew darker.

Next Mayken must inspect Imke's belly. Mayken rubs her hands together like the physician did, then lays them on Imke's belly, raising her eyes to the ceiling, nodding. *Yes, precisely as I expected.* Now she'll press more firmly at Imke's wide middle. This sometimes makes Imke fart. When this happens Mayken scrutinizes the nursemaid's face for the twitch of a smile that appears.

Today all is as it should be. Imke's gums are fine, her breath isn't too sour, her nostrils are clear, her knees are both there—

"Imke!"

Imke wakes.

"Your toe!" Mayken is aghast.

The familiar old feet have their horny nails, cracked skin, and slight smell of washed cheese. But the big toe on the left foot is double the size of its right-foot counterpart. An angry red. Hideously swollen. At the base of the toe there are teeth marks. The yellowed toenail is peeling off, like a curl of butter.

Imke sits up on her bunk and squints down at herself. "A rat was worrying at me last night. I thought it was just my stocking he ate."

Pelgrom comes to look at Imke's toe. He raises his eyebrows and glances at Mayken with a *What did I tell you?* expression.

"Madam Imke, you've been bitten it seems. Allow me to fetch the barber-surgeon."

"I don't want him."

"He might be able to alleviate your suffering."

"He'll lop off my leg!"

Pelgrom draws Mayken to one side. "A creature inflicted this bite—"

"She said it was a rat."

Pelgrom turns back to Imke, whose face is a picture of fear. He takes from his pocket a small bottle, like the one Aris sent to the soldier.

"Take this before bedtime." He hands the bottle to Imke. "Give a nip to the child too. A nice deep sleep will do you both good."

Pelgrom also gives Mayken a pot of ointment for the toe. It smells suspiciously similar to rancid goose fat. Then he excuses himself to serve dinner in the Great Cabin.

Mayken paints the goose fat on Imke's toe.

"Will you have some wine, Imke dear?"

"No, Mayken."

"A small morsel?"

"No, I'll take my nap now."

"Good for you, Imke dear."

Imke closes her eyes. "I'd rather you didn't watch me nap."

"I'm not," says Mayken, her gaze riveted to her nursemaid.

Night falls. In the fug of their cabin Imke sleeps. Mayken dozes with her head on the edge of her bunk so that if she opens her eyes, she can see the nursemaid's old hand thrown out, palm upward, fingers furled.

They have taken Pelgrom's preparation. Imke insisted.

The gimballed lantern swings overhead, casting patterns on the wall. The flame is dimmed tonight, for Imke confessed to a headache.

Mayken falls asleep.

And dreams of eels.

Opening her eyes, she sees them flopping in through the gap under the door. Writhing, glistening. There is a dank, canal smell in the cabin. The eels multiply, the floor seethes with them. The lantern sputters, the flame burns blue.

Mayken peers over her bunk at Imke. She snores with her mouth open. Eels slip across the sleeping woman's body, nuzzling at her ears, winding about her neck. Mayken looks on with frozen horror as the door opens and into the cabin a shadow comes.

The shadow begins to rise, stacking upright, sharpening, deepening into a hunched figure that reaches halfway across the ceiling.

A smell grows stronger: bilge stink and sea spray.

The shadow moves across the room, the writhing eels part, it hovers near Imke's foot, sniffing at her swollen toe. It pulls back—it's getting ready to bite!

Mayken tries to call out, to jump down—but finds herself unable to speak or move. Imke stirs, gulping breath. The shadow darts head-first into her open mouth, disappearing with a flick of a shadowy tail.

Mayken wakes sobbing.

The floor is dry. The lantern burns with a yellow flame.

Mayken slips from her bunk.

Imke sleeps. She looks inside the old woman's open mouth. It is empty. She pulls back the blanket to see the redness and swelling have spread from Imke's toe to her entire foot. The toe is the color of liver and the nail has gone. A sudden movement under Imke's nightgown catches Mayken's eye. Mayken pulls up the gown and screams. Nestled at Imke's hip, curled like a worm cast, a tiny eel.

It is not easy to kill an eel. They never die, not quite. Gut them, cook them—turn to grab a wedge of bread—and your dinner will be gone from your plate. Mayken expects a fight, even with a small eel. She traps it down behind the table and flattens its head with her clog. It moves halfway across the floor, leaving a trail of eel brains. Finally, it grinds to a halt and is still.

Imke sleeps through the great slaughter.

Mayken holds up the eel, feeling triumph rise in her alongside the queasiness.

But this poor mashed creature is not Bullebak. It's one of its subjects, and proof if proof were needed of the monster's visit.

Mayken ventures out on deck. The breeze is fresh and the dawn is rosy and the ship moves well in the water. The painted Lion of Holland on the prow is aglow, pinkish in the new light. The hands aloft in the canvas are taking a breather, balanced, sure-footed, looking down at soft-peaked waves, waiting for next orders. The watch is alert yet. The ropes sing, the ship noses, the passengers sleep.

All is as it should be.

Knowing Pelgrom's duties start and end in the Great Cabin, Mayken makes her way there, with an expression of flinty purpose and a dead eel clasped in her fist.

❧

Two soldiers guard the door to the Great Cabin. They sit on the bench built into the wall, with a view of a narrow corridor and nothing else. They are men drawn from the orlop deck. The younger soldier, who wears a sword, is resting his eyes. The older soldier, who wears a cape, looks to be praying, at least his lips are moving. Neither are John Pinten, but they have the same look about them: weathered, accepting, but not to be roused.

Mayken nods to the soldier in the cape and uses her haughtiest voice. "I wish to talk to the cabin steward Jan Pelgrom."

The soldier in the cape nudges the soldier with the sword awake.

"What makes you think the cabin steward is within?" asks Corporal Cape.

"He starts work in the Great Cabin at first light."

Corporal Cape ponders. "Are you here to steal the silver?"

"No."

"What's that in your hand?" asks Corporal Sword.

Corporal Cape is indulgent. "Her pet!" He looks closer and frowns. "A leech, sweetheart?"

Mayken is indignant. "It's a dead eel."

Corporal Sword laughs. "State your name."

"Mayken van den Heuvel. State yours."

"Corporal Hayes." He points to Corporal Cape. "He is Corporal Hardens."

Mayken nods with stern formality to the pair of them.

"Will you give me your word," asks Hayes, "that once inside you will refrain from thieving the silver?"

"Yes, I give you my word: no thieving."

"Good," says Hayes. "What's with the eel?"

"I'd rather not say."

"Fair enough." Hayes has a wide, friendly face and a sandy beard. "But don't be too sure it's dead. You know what they say about eels."

Hardens smiles at Mayken. "I've a little girl about your age. She plagues me for ribbons."

"Does she live in the dark with the cows and John Pinten?" Mayken instantly wishes she could bite the words back.

Hayes regards her closely. "You know John Pinten?"

Mayken inspects her eel.

"We live on the gun deck, not with the cows," adds Hardens stiffly.

Hayes nudges him. "Let the child in."

"Watch that Pelgrom," murmurs the soldier, opening the door. "He's more slippery than your eel there."

The Great Cabin is empty of its denizens: there is no skipper, upper-merchant, under-merchant, no clerks, cadets, or well-to-do passengers. Dawn light shines through the ship's one glazed window, currently open, to let out the smell of onions and farts. The table is big and round and polished. The steward is asleep under it.

Mayken nudges him and holds up the eel. "I know what bit Imke."

Pelgrom opens his eyes, glances at the eel, and looks not a bit surprised.

They sit at the Great Table. Mayken tells Pelgrom of her dream. The memory of it fills her with terror but she tells it, plain and exact. After listening, Pelgrom fishes a carrot from his pocket and begins crunching it. The carrot has two tails of the kind discarded by the gardener because the Devil's vegetables have no place on the skipper's table.

"It wasn't a dream," says Pelgrom bluntly, mouth full. "How else could the eel have got into the old woman's bed?"

"Then the shadow creature climbed inside her!"

"Oh, certainly, Bullebak is well able to do that. Whether it stays inside her is another matter. Imke isn't a very exciting host. She doesn't really get around."

"And her toe? The bite marks?"

"No point in lopping it off now," says the steward brightly. "No one can survive Bullebak's bite. This will claim her."

Mayken looks at the eel on the table. It's unmistakably dead, the ooze from its battered head drying. Her tears come heavy and quiet; she wipes them away with the hem of her skirt.

Pelgrom, chewing, watches her. He looks as if he's deciding something, making a difficult calculation.

"There might be a way to save your nursemaid," he says. "But it's a long shot."

"Tell me, I'll do it!"

"You must catch Bullebak and order it to suck the poison out and spit back the goodness it has taken from her." The steward finishes his carrot, stalk and all. "Your nursemaid has shrunk, there is less of her now, yes?"

"Yes."

"Then Bullebak has been feeding on her regularly."

Mayken shudders. "How do we catch Bullebak?"

Pelgrom takes up a rag and starts listlessly buffing the table. "There's no *we* in this. I'm too busy fetching and cleaning, serving and stewarding—"

"But Imke is sick!"

"I could give you the wherewithal to catch this creature and escort you to the hold. The deep dark place where the creature sleeps." Pelgrom stops polishing. He looks at Mayken with a sly smile. "But I must inform you that trying to trap Bullebak will not be without danger. You will likely become its next victim."

"I don't care!"

"Your death would be horrible. Do you want to hear the various ways?"

"No."

Pelgrom appears to bite back a laugh. "Well, you ought. Bullebak might slip inside you, then grow quickly so that you explode into gobbets of blood. Or bite you a thousand times so that your whole body turns red and fills with pus. Or—"

"That's enough. Just tell me how to save Imke."

"All right." Pelgrom goes back to polishing the table. "But it will cost you. If I'm caught helping you flit about the ship, Lady Mayken, I'll be hung from the yardarm."

"You won't get caught. And I'll pay."

Two lace collars and a silver comb buy Mayken another trip to the Below World, only she must wait on Pelgrom's word. In the meantime, she rarely leaves Imke's side. The nights are terrible. She watches until she falls asleep, then wakes herself up again. Mrs. Predikant comments on the dark circles beneath her eyes.

Bullebak does not return.

The dead eel, which Mayken stowed under her sleeping mat—evidence that her dream was real—promptly vanishes.

The steward is unapologetic about the delay. Imke may be failing but he must time things right. The stars must align, so to speak. The skipper must be looking out over the stern scratching his arse. The upper-merchant must be gazing into Creesje's eyes on the quarterdeck. All the hands must be busy with hauling or tacking or trimming. Stonecutter and a whole raft of no-shit-and-nonsense watchmen must have their attention elsewhere.

Mayken pulls a face but knows better than to argue. She has no wish to be caught by the terrifying Stonecutter. He would burst her skull like a bad nut.

There is nothing for it: she must trust Pelgrom.

The day comes. A soft tap on her cabin door.

"Now's the time."

Mayken leaves quietly with a last glance at sleeping Imke. The old lady's face has a green tinge to it and her breathing is ragged.

In the corridor the steward gives her leather gauntlets, way too big, a fishing net, and a bag of table scraps.

"What are these for?"

"Catching Bullebak."

Mayken suddenly feels overwhelmed by the enormity of the task. *"How?"*

Pelgrom rolls his eyes. "Scatter the scraps. When it comes to eat, throw the net over. If it bites, you've the gloves there."

"What if it changes shape?"

"That net's good for all sizes, sprats to sharks."

"What if I don't catch Bullebak this time?"

"There will be no other times."

"But Imke—"

Pelgrom shrugs. "You've bought only one more trip."

"I have jewels—"

"Worth me being hung from the yardarm?"

"I have coins—"

"No use for a dead man. Enough. Follow me."

Mayken's dash across the deck goes unnoticed, with a quick change behind the pigpen. She climbs down to the gun deck just behind Pelgrom. He moves fast and she fears she will lose him. She can hardly take note of the route, just the usual press of people, the smell, and the dim. Then they are climbing down the steps to the orlop deck. At the bottom Pelgrom unhooks a lantern and, crouching against the low ceiling, creeps to a locked hatch. He produces a key and makes a big point of unlocking the hatch. He takes the lantern and descends, throwing Mayken a tense glance. She follows.

The reek and the heat are overwhelming.

At the bottom of the steps Pelgrom holds up the lantern. Mayken can see that they are hemmed in on all sides by crates. They squeeze through a walkway so narrow that Pelgrom, thin as he is, must turn sideways and breathe in. There are crates packed to the ceiling, stacked barrels of vinegar and wine, cannonballs racked neatly. Bundles of wood for the cook's stove are pushed into every crevice. There is no space for air.

The walkway joins the main thoroughfare, the width of Pelgrom if he rounds his shoulders. Beneath their feet is ballast, bricks destined for Batavia.

Pelgrom stops. "Kneel here, put on your gauntlets, and ready your net."

Mayken does what she is bid. On either side of her are walls of cargo. Before and behind her runs the dark ribbon of the narrow walkway.

Pelgrom dims the lantern.

"Don't leave me!" whispers Mayken, horrified.

Pelgrom's eyes glitter in the half dark, his expression amused. "I've no intention of facing the creature you seek. Scatter the scraps and ready your net. I'll wait for you above."

Mayken watches as the steward walks away and is swallowed by the dark. She glances at the lantern, the flame so low—if it should gutter, she'd die of fear! She throws scraps into the gaps between the crates.

A distant scrabbling.

Mayken kneels down and waits.

Noses appear, just the tips. Then, by degrees, heads and bodies and wormy tails. The ship rats are long and thin and sharp featured. In a matter of moments, they grow bolder. Soon they grow bold enough to brush past her. Soon they run over her toes.

Still kneeling, Mayken holds tight to the net.

The rats swarm.

They are multiplying. She feels the first skim of teeth and then a nip on her ankle. She struggles to her feet and the rats follow, a rising tide of leaping bodies. There are no scraps left. Perhaps realizing this, the rats become frantic in their hunger. Ever more rats are running out from between the crates.

A rat hangs by its teeth from her breeches and another from her sleeve.

And now Mayken understands that the rats will almost certainly kill her. They will rip the clothes from her back and gnaw open her stomach and crawl into the cavity. They will squabble over her entrails and tug out her hair for their nests. Their fur will be spiked wet with her blood and scraps of her will be dragged off to all corners of the ship.

Pelgrom brought her here to die!

She screams and more rats come, swarming up her legs. All of a sudden, a noise—a low boom that displaces the air. The rats drop and scamper and are gone. Mayken stands in the empty walkway, her heart stopped in her chest. Then she hears it—something is coming toward her.

Plash. Plash. Plash.

A sucking quality to the sound, as if someone is walking in boots full of mud.

Plash. Plash. Plash.

Mayken stands in the lantern's ring of light, net lifted.

Her blood pounds in her ears.

Imke says you must never run from what scares you. It will only follow. You must stand and face it.

The flame gutters.

Mayken drops the net and runs.

CHAPTER TWELVE

1989

Gil is woken late morning by the sound of whistling. Mum said there are two kinds of whistler. The first kind can whistle an identifiable song and are plumbers. The second kind of whistler has no tune, because they are whistling their anger and anger is always tuneless. This kind of whistler is a murderer.

The stranger in his underpants frying tinned ham on the stove can hold a tune.

When he sees Gil, the stranger puts down the pan and offers a hand. "Dutch."

Gil looks at the hand and then skirts round to the table, one eye on Dutch.

"And you're Gil." Dutch turns back to the pan.

Gil takes a seat next to his grandfather at the kitchen table. The old man is ignoring the breakfast before him. His right hand has been freshly bandaged, then wrapped around with duct tape. He smokes a rollie with his left. It gives him a hesitant air.

"You've still got your hand?" says Gil.

Joss takes a deep inhale.

"Now." Dutch brings over the food he's cooked, rearranging sauce bottles on the table, the tea towel slung over his shoulder. He turns to Joss. "The food is not to your liking?"

"The food is fine." Joss gets up with a scrape to his chair and goes out, slamming the screen door.

"He no longer has the use of that hand," says Dutch. "They wanted to operate but he wouldn't have it during the season."

The deckie sets down a breakfast for them, putting Joss's under a plate. He takes a seat and smiles at Gil. Gil looks away.

Dutch digs in. Gil glances at him. It's the deckie from Silvia's photo, only older, craggier. Wiry and spare with the look of someone who can't live soft. Dutch is deeply tanned, blue-eyed with a stubbled jaw, close-cropped hair, reddish brown, patchy gray in places.

Gil looks at his plate. The fried things are nicely arranged, like in a café. "Where's Silvia?"

"She's gone back to Papa Zanetti."

"Where you used to be?"

"Yep." Dutch smiles. "But I'm here now."

Gil eats his breakfast, taking sly peeks at the deckie. He notices the raised red-stippled skin on Dutch's throat.

Dutch catches him looking. "They say a birthmark is your death blow from a past life." He mimes frantic stabbing to his neck. Gil turns back to his plate.

"So you're the great Gilgamesh?"

"I'm Gil."

"Did your mother not name you for the great warrior?"

Gil moves a tomato to the edge of his plate. "Are you Irish?"

"Yeah."

"Then why are you called Dutch?"

Dutch, finished with his meal, pushes back his plate and deftly rolls a smoke. He lays down a long pinch of tobacco in a cigarette paper, licks the edge, pinches the end, and sets it in his mouth. Lights it.

"I got my name because I was among the first divers out to the Dutch wreck. You know about the *Batavia*?"

Gil nods. "Did you find treasure?"

"I did. Silver coins. I'll show you sometime."

"Any bones?"

"Jesus, no." Dutch laughs. "They're all under Silvia's bloody grotto."

Gil laughs too.

"How's island life treating you, Gil?"

"All right."

Dutch nods at the cardboard box on the counter. "You might want to have a look in there. Your granda won it for you last night."

Gil notices the air holes punched in the sides of the box. "What is it?"

"A pal for you to muck around with."

Gil lifts the flaps open and peers in. "It's an actual bloody tortoise!"

Dutch laughs. "It's an actual bloody tortoise."

Gil touches the shell of the tortoise, lightly, carefully. The creature edges away from him. A head that waggles and looks obscene. A shell like something carved. Two tiny malevolent eyes.

Gil loves it.

"Lift him out. Hold him by the middle. Mind those soft spots at his armpits. Take him gently, Gil."

The tortoise is the size of a dinner plate and surprisingly heavy. Dutch clears a space and Gil carries him to the table.

Gil strokes the tortoise's blunt nose. Two tiny air holes. He covers them with his finger, just for a second. The tortoise pushes with his feet against the oilskin.

"His name is Frisbee."

The tortoise seems to be doing a slow revolve.

"Who said?"

"The raffle fella. He pretended to throw him."

Gil frowns.

"He was a gobshite, Gil. You don't have to call the tortoise Frisbee."

The tortoise stops moving and has a little rest.

"What shall I call him?"

Dutch considers. "Enkidu. Gilgamesh's best mate."

Enkidu. Gil repeats in his mind. *Enkidu, Enkidu.*

Gil knows it's a magic word. What's more, it's exactly the tortoise's name.

"I'll think about it," he says.

The old man's breakfast is wrapped in greaseproof paper. They'll take it down to him. Dutch finds an old sports bag Enkidu can ride in.

Joss will be on the main jetty, says Dutch, where there's a hookup for electrics. He's frantic to get *Ramona* fixed. It's the height of the season and every day that passes loses him money. And his pots are out there. Gil wonders if that's where his grandfather's thoughts are too, tangled in the reef.

On the walk down, Dutch stops to look at a sea eagle nest, pulling out binoculars, small, foldable, good ones. The sea eagle, by chance, comes in to land. Dutch quickly hands the binoculars to Gil, helps him adjust them. The sea eagle puffs out its chest. It's amazing, Gil can pick out every feather.

"They're great ones for the nest building."

"That nest has tinsel, even," says Gil. "It glitters in the sun."

The deckie laughs, as if Gil has given him Christmas.

They walk past Bill Nord's camp, the dig site, but no scientists. The posts are still there and the tape. The trenches have been covered with canvas.

"Birgit will have them out diving the wreck. The conditions will be spot-on today," says Dutch, a winsome look about him.

"You know her?"

"I do. Sam and Mick too."

Gil remembers how Dutch got his name. "What's it like, diving the wreck?"

"The first time I saw the cannons on the seabed I cried, I literally did, into my bloody mask, it was magical. And the silver coins, shoals of them, twinkling. Like they'd just been scattered by some hand and sunk to the seabed. They were years looking for the *Batavia*; they couldn't fathom from the ancient records where she was."

"I suppose there's a lot of sea around here."

"There is, Gil, and desolate islands and killer reefs."

Gil goes to hand the binoculars back.

"You can borrow them, if you like. Keep an eye on that sea eagle."

Gil nods a thank-you.

"The fishermen found the *Batavia* long before the scientists, only they kept it to themselves. One fella had a hunch and went out on a calm day. He took a glass and looked down into the water and there was a cannon, crystal clear."

"Is the ship still down there?"

"They've been bringing up planks of her, sides and belly, what's left. What the sea hasn't scattered down the years."

They walk in silence, other than sea sounds and bird sounds and the trudge of their feet through coral shingle. Gil likes the way Dutch doesn't fill every moment with talk. And when Dutch does talk, his voice is soft, easy, kind to the ears.

"You're the spit of your mum."

Gil glances at him. Dutch has a smile on his face.

Gil looks away. But finds he has to ask. "You went out with her?"

"Let me guess: Silvia told you that?"

"Yeah."

"Silvia's a gobshite. Your mum and I were very young."

"Did you know my dad?"

"No. Do you?"

"No."

Dutch hesitates. "You have a name for him, Gil?"

"Mum never said."

Gil hands Joss his breakfast from the bag. His grandfather points to the tortoise sitting at the bottom.

"Get that out for a stretch of its legs."

"His name is Enkidu," says Gil.

Joss glances at Dutch.

Dutch grins. "The two great warriors."

Gil sits on the jetty with Enkidu while the men work on the boat. In their exchanges Joss and Dutch use few words. The engine cover is off, the smell of oil and diesel on the salt air. Enkidu doesn't seem impressed with the proceedings. The sides of his mouth are turned down.

Gil takes the tortoise for a paddle in the water. Enkidu looks sour.

Gil takes Enkidu for a slow crawl over the shingle. Enkidu looks sour.

Gil tries to feed Enkidu some shrubs. Enkidu gives him a sour look.

So back they go to sit on the jetty again. Gil has a juice from the esky cooler, the two men have a beer. Dutch pours a container of water for the tortoise to ignore.

The other fishermen return, heralded by engine throb, then the sight of the boats nosing in. The deckies jump out to tie up. Men, sunburnt and sweating, carry gear and crates of crays along the jetty. They greet Dutch loudly. He climbs out of the boat to shake hands with a few of them. They clap him on his back. A few, in passing, nod to Gil. They point to Enkidu, give a thumbs-up or a smile.

Joss Hurley might as well not exist. He keeps his head down, ignoring the proceedings, fumbling with his wrong hand under the engine cover.

The light is fading.

"Take the boy back," says Joss. "I'll keep at it for a while."

Gil and Dutch head up toward the camp. A nice walk, for it's warm yet.

"We'll call in at Papa Zanetti's, see what Silvia's cooking."

"I'm not allowed in her camp."

"She said that?"

"Because of Frank and Roper."

Dutch studies Gil a moment. "Balls to that. You can go anywhere."

"I don't like Roper."

"Sure, no one does, he's an arsehole. Don't worry about him."

Gil frowns. "Didn't he kick the shit out of you?"

"Who said Roper kicked the shit out of me?"

"Silvia."

"Well, truth be told, we kicked the shit out of each other. I kicked more shit out of Roper, of course; there's more in him."

Gil smiles.

"Gilgamesh, sometimes violence is a necessary evil." Dutch grins. "And it was a long time coming."

Silvia looks bemused when she opens the screen door. "You've got a nerve, Dutch."

"Miss me, Silvana?"

"Always."

"Is the big man in?"

"The lounge room. The other fucker is out."

Dutch glances at Gil with the hint of a smile. "You'll never guess what this fella has in his sports bag."

"Can I cook it?"

Dutch turns to Gil. "See what Silvia can rustle up for us while I make my peace with Papa Frank."

Silvia takes two stubbies from the fridge and hands them to Dutch. "You'll need these."

Dutch nods. "Grand, so. Call me when the tortoise risotto is ready."

Gil opens the sports bag slowly.

Silvia peers in, making a horrified face. "How do I open it? Like a can?" She winks at Gil.

Gil shows her the tortoise's main features, being that Enkidu is permanently angry-looking, can walk in a circle, and has really sharp gums. They crawl about on the floor with him. Silvia sings a gross song about tortoise risotto that makes Gil feel sick and laugh at the same time.

Then she is on her feet, pulling out pans, wandering into the pantry, finding lettuce for Enkidu, pouring lemonade for Gil.

"Finish my crossword, Gil. Make up the words if you want. I'm tormented by it."

Gil sits down at the table and takes a look. He did a lot of crosswords with Mrs. Baxter, so he's not bad at them. His writing's not great but it's better than Silvia's.

A holler from next door. Silvia disappears.

She returns directly, concern on her face. "Frank wants to see you."

Under the glare of the lounge-room strip light sits Frank Zanetti. His throne is an easy chair, part of a three-piece coffee-colored plush suite. Dutch sits opposite on a sofa. Between the two men is a smoked-glass coffee table. Dominating the room, almost the size of the whole wall, is an ugly painting of a lion. Midsnarl, mane curling. Gil saw the room before when Silvia showed him around. Now, altered by Frank Zanetti's presence, it has glamour and menace, as if it has turned into a casino.

Silvia brings drinks on a tray and swaps them for the empties on the table. Frank glances at her, then shakes his wrist and big gold watch there.

Silvia starts. "Thirty minutes."

"Make it twenty." He turns to Dutch. "You'll eat with us?"

"If you'll have me."

"I've no argument with you. I don't like the company you keep." Frank turns to Gil. "You're Hurley's grandson."

Gil nods.

Frank looks at him narrowly. Gil feels like a crayfish being weighed, evaluated, found lesser, and thrown overboard. Frank has a flinty aspect to him. A stillness. Like a stone in water that sets everything eddying around it while it stays firm itself.

"You can't help who you're related to. Dawn's boy?"

"Yes."

"She was a handful. Are you a handful?"

Gil doesn't know if he's a handful.

"You look like you're a handful," says Frank. "I was sorry to hear about your mother. Fucking stupid thing for her to do."

Gil looks away. He studies the ugly painting.

"The lion's eyes are glass," explains Frank. "That's why they glint."

"It's awful," says Gil.

"Yeah," says Frank. "It is."

Dutch smiles. Frank doesn't. Both men lift their beers and drink.

Gil listens at the table. Dutch does the most talking, then Frank. Silvia pitches in now and again in a sensible voice, saying nothing fruity about dead Dutch girls or bones. She tops up Gil's glass and kisses him on the head as she does it. He flinches because he doesn't see it coming. Enkidu mounts the broom by the back door and elicits Frank's first laugh of the evening. Frank's laugh is deep and rolling and contagious and everyone joins in.

Then Roper arrives. Roper, lightly drunk and heavily sweating, fills the doorway. Silvia gets up and starts to clear the table, like a bartender in a Western who senses trouble ahead.

Dutch stands and offers his hand to Roper. Roper looks around the room, dead-eyed, venomous. His glare momentarily fixes on Gil before sweeping back to Dutch.

Gil feels a rising sickness, a growing panic.

"Roper," says Frank, a growled warning in the word. "Shake the man's hand."

Roper slams back out, nearly taking the front door with him.

ை

Frank and Dutch are having a smoke in the lounge room. In the kitchen, Silvia is on the sherry and Gil has lemonade. Silvia has a plate wrapped for Gil to take back to his granddaddy. Silvia sinks the plate in Enkidu's sports bag with a smile. It's one thing to allow your enemy's grandson to sit at your table and another to be sending food home to your enemy himself.

"Our secret," she mock-whispers, weaving to the pantry. "Now ice cream! For you and me and Enkidu!"

Enkidu is resting in the sink with a wet tea towel over him, overcome by his exertions with the broom.

"No. He'll have a leaf." Gil is clear and brief. He knows from experience that this is the best way to manage drunk adults.

Silvia sets about slicing the ice cream, sandwiching the blocks with wafers this time. From the other room: Dutch's voice raised in a punch line and Frank Zanetti's deep laugh again.

"I've missed Dutch. He makes everything much better." Silvia wipes her fingers on the tablecloth. "Frank only ever laughs when he's around."

The wind is picking up as Gil and Dutch walk back along the coast path to Joss Hurley's camp. The moon seems smudged and the clouds overhead like rolling dishrags. The night birds returning to their nests have a mournful call. Dutch shines his torch to illuminate their burrows. He talks about the stars and points out constellations. Gil pays no attention. He would rather the stars stayed wild and not become something else he has to know about.

He keeps to his own thoughts. He has a mind to ask Dutch why everyone hates his grandfather and what kind of a feud the old man has going on with the Zanetti family. Instead, he surprises himself.

"Do you believe in ghosts?"

"Where did that come from, Gil?"

"Silvia says a dead girl from the shipwreck haunts the island."

"Silvia's full of shite, God love her."

Gil huffs; this is no kind of an answer.

"Little May, is it?" says the deckie, conciliatory. "Some of the auld island fellas swear they've seen her."

"Do you believe them?"

"The eyes and the ears can play tricks out here, with the weather and the seabirds and the loneliness. It's a tough life and fishermen can be superstitious."

"Loads of people were killed—"

"A long, long time ago."

"If there is such a thing as ghosts, they would live in a place like this."

Dutch changes the subject back to the stars.

They reach Joss Hurley's camp. The veranda light is on and the insects are killing themselves to be near it. The old man is asleep on a lounger with his mouth open. Moth shadows flit over his face.

"If you ever want to talk," Dutch says softly. "About your mum."

"It's okay," Gil says softly. "I won't."

CHAPTER THIRTEEN

1628

Running through the dark hold, Mayken sees light above—the open hatch to the orlop deck. Pelgrom will be at the top, waiting for her!

She races up the ladder.

Pelgrom isn't there.

Mayken tries to slam the hatch behind her—against the creature that surely follows—but it's too heavy to move. She abandons it and keeps going, heading for the ladder to the gun deck.

The hatch is closed. She stands below, shouting Pelgrom's name.

A gruff voice calls out. "Some of us are fucking sleeping here."

Mayken tries to calm her breathing. To think. She turns and picks her way past the shuffling cattle, the sardined soldiers, to the end where the lantern light doesn't reach.

She whispers into the dark, "John Pinten, help me."

A sudden fear—he may be sleeping like a stone.

Louder, "John Pinten, please wake up."

There is a striking of flint and the glim of a lamp. There is the English soldier, propped up on one arm, blinking, in his castle made of stacked bales.

Mayken crawls forward, sobbing with relief.

"Calm yourself, boy, you're shaking." John Pinten holds out a jug. "Take a drop."

Mayken gulps and retches; there is fire in the liquid.

"Drink it slowly, you'll feel better."

She sips. Warmth spreads through her and she is able to breathe. But in her mind she is still down in the hold, rooted to the spot—

"Now, tell me what happened."

"I went to the hold to catch the creature that bit my nurse-maid."

"You have a nursemaid?"

"I live aft-the-mast really," she whispers. "I'm Obbe here."

"Carry on, Obbe," says the soldier kindly.

"I scattered the scraps and got the net ready like he told me."

"Someone told you to go into the hold and do this?"

Mayken hesitates. John Pinten gestures for her to continue.

"All the rats came out and I feared they would eat me. Then there was this strange noise and the rats startled and vanished." She frowns. It sounds so unlikely now.

The soldier wears a grave face but Mayken is certain there's a hint of a smile under the wild beard.

"Something terrible was down there! The rats knew it."

John Pinten considers. "Perhaps this person was playing a trick on you? Sending you there?"

Mayken shakes her head. "You told me yourself—*something stirs in the hold.*"

"I told you that?"

"When you were falling asleep."

"I'd taken the barber's potion?"

Mayken nods.

"And you took my ramblings as real?"

"The creature is real. I dreamt it!"

John Pinten smiles into his jug. "A dream as real as the worms in the water barrels or the rats in my bed?"

"Listen to me! It bit Imke and now she's sick."

"Imke being your nursemaid?"

"If I can catch this creature, she'll get better." Mayken is furious to find herself crying again. "I know she will."

John Pinten looks thoughtful. "Then dry your eyes and let's work out how. Tell me everything you know about it."

Mayken nods, wiping her eyes with her tunic sleeve. The soldier listens as she tells him about the flooded village and the bent old man, about Lijsbet and her baby and the bite marks on Imke's toe. Then Mayken whispers the name of her enemy.

"Bullebak?" he repeats. "Meaning big bully?"

She nods.

"But this is a *story*, child."

"It's come true."

The soldier downs the last from his jug and holds it out to her. "To catch Bullebak you'll need this."

"What for?"

"Didn't the old man in the story keep it in a jug?"

"He did."

"Well, this is a Beardman, the very best jug for trapping monsters."

Mayken takes the jug in both hands. She's seen its kind before: fat-bellied with a loop for the fingers. On the neck of the jug a molded face, eyes staring, a straggling beard. The soldier finds the wooden stop and pushes it into place.

"Keep an eye on the jug's face. It changes. That's how you know if it holds water, wine, or quicksilver."

Mayken looks at the jug doubtfully.

"You'll also need some bacon rinds, for the catching of your creature."

"Bacon rinds?"

John Pinten nods. "In Ireland, a country not so far from my own, there's such a thing as a man-creeper. Take your time yawning and this newt will leap down your gullet. Holding the afflicted by the ankles over a bowl of bacon rinds is said to draw it out."

"I don't understand."

"Man-creeper, eel, Bullebak, similar kinds of thing, no?"

"Maybe."

"Leave the jug under your nursemaid's bed with a few bacon rinds inside. Once your creature is curled up inside, stopper it and throw it overboard."

A scraping sound comes through the dim, then a hollow clank.

"That's the hatch opening for the change of watch. Now's your chance."

Mayken is up on her feet.

"And see your way to some better friends, Obbe," calls the soldier.

That Pelgrom has abandoned her, Mayken has no doubt. She must make her way back to the Above World alone. Another bell sounds, far nearer than the watch bell. And with it, the stomping of feet and the wild calling of voices. Mayken climbs up onto the gun deck to be carried along by the crowd surging toward the galley. It's mealtime, she supposes from the brothy smell and commotion. The galley door is open and a bench has been set up outside. Smoert is behind it. Mayken fights her way out of the crowd and climbs on the brake block of a cannon to see him better.

Smoert, holding a bucketful of ship's biscuits, stands next to a rotund, red-faced cook. The cook ladles stew into the held-out bowls of jostling messmates and Smoert blesses the stew with a biscuit. Now and again the cook beats him viciously about the head for no reason that Mayken can see. After several bouts of this Smoert has a bloody nose and a glazed expression. Mayken flinches every time. The queue seems endless but finally the crowds thin out and Mayken catches the kitchen boy's eye.

"I never knew this was here," Smoert says in wonder, as if Mayken has shown him a gilded great hall.

They sit in Pelgrom's hiding place around the back of the galley, sharing a stool, half and half. The kitchen boy smells overpoweringly of smoke and rancid fat. He has many burns and blisters on his poor face, aside from the injuries inflicted by the cook.

"Your master beats you often?"

Smoert shrugs. He glances shyly at Mayken. "What work do you do?"

"Sewing," says Mayken. "But now I've a more important task. Do you want to know what it is?"

"If you like," says Smoert mildly.

"Hunting a dangerous creature who lives in the hold." She nudges him. "You could help me?"

Smoert considers. "All right."

Mayken goes fishing behind the stool and pulls up a canvas bag. "It's Jan Pelgrom's. This is where he comes."

"Put it back!"

Mayken opens the bag and shows Smoert. Inside is a stabbing knife, a silver soup ladle, and a tatty necklace of seed pearls. "He's likely stolen these."

"Don't mess with him," whispers Smoert. "He can cause trouble for you. He's into everything."

"Like a weevil," Mayken scoffs. "I'm not scared of Pelgrom."

A roaring voice, loud enough to hear through the wall.

"Don't you ever feel like pushing the cook in the cauldron pot?"

Smoert rises. "Too much gristle, ruin the stew."

"Would you have bacon rinds?"

"I can get some."

"They're for the creature we're hunting."

"If you say so." Smoert turns to go.

"And I'm making you some breeches like mine."

Smoert grins over his shoulder. "If it's all the same, I'd rather wear that bloody flour sack."

❧

There is nothing for it. Pelgrom is not here to judge when to cross back to the Above World, so she will have to make the decision on her own.

Mayken climbs up to the main deck. The fresh air hits her face. She hesitates at the top. The deck looks unusually clear: a few carpenters, rope menders, some sailors in the rigging, and the skipper prowling about the stern castle with a handful of men. There's a shout below; others are behind, wanting to come up.

She heads out across the deck, jumping coiled ropes, speeding toward the pigpen, she's almost there when—

She's lifted.

The world spins, canvas, sky, sea—rushing swelling waves cresting to meet her—she is thrown overboard! Deck again. She's dropped and lands awkwardly on her tailbone. Pain smashes through her body.

A giant's face, shaved head, and blond beard.

The giant shoots out an arm and grabs her, shakes her, and sets her on her feet. He cups the base of her skull, his fingers tighten. Mayken screams, an impressively loud, high-pitched scream. The giant releases her skull and clamps his hand over her mouth. Mayken bites his hand, hard. He throws her. She skids along the deck, her head knocking against something wooden. Now she will definitely die. Bloody flux.

"Who the fuck are you? And where the fuck do you think you are going?"

Mayken can't answer. She's watching the sky and the complexities of the rigging. Clouds and rope.

A new face swims into view. Aris Jansz, the butcher-prince! Too late to save her.

"Get up," he hisses. "Stand. Quickly."

Mayken gets onto her knees and sits back on her haunches. She puts a tentative hand to her head. It is attached, though it hurts very badly. Her cap has stayed on too. She is still Obbe. Miraculously, the jug in her hand is unbroken, the clay face pop-eyed with shock.

Aris is talking to the giant.

Mayken sways on her feet.

Aris turns and hands her a box. "Carry this," he says under his breath. "You're my assistant."

The giant lowers down at her. "What do you fucking know about barber work?"

Mayken wipes a trickle at her ear. When she moves her head, her thoughts jangle. "I know boils, sir."

This seems to amuse Stonecutter. He takes the box from her hands and opens the lid and looks at the vials inside. Then he closes the box. He shakes the box hard and hands it back to Mayken.

"On your way, and don't bleed on my fucking deck."

Imke is pale and frantic and bathed in sweat. She tries to sit up as Aris helps Mayken into the cabin.

Aris addresses her sternly. "Madam, stop this clamor and save your strength."

He unpins Mayken's cap and wipes the worst of the blood from her face and neck. He takes bandages and wadding from his case and wraps them tightly around her head, giving her one end of the cloth strip to hold taut.

"Stonecutter has half pulled off your ear. If we bind it flat, it might knit." He gestures at Imke, lowering his voice. "What ails this woman?"

"She was bitten by Bullebak," says Mayken.

Aris looks baffled.

"The ancient monster and foe of all humankind." Mayken uncovers Imke's foot. "I tried to catch it to make it suck the poison back out."

Aris takes a closer look.

"No knives," breathes Imke.

"Are you responsible for this child?"

Imke nods, her eyes are dull with pain. Aris leans down and talks low in her ear. He straightens up and waits. Imke nods. Aris pats her on the shoulder.

Aris takes out the tools of his trade and lays them on the cloth he has set on the table. Mayken sits at the old woman's side. Imke holds her hand out to Mayken, who takes it.

"I lied to you, child," whispers Imke. "You guessed right one time, about how I lost my fingers."

"It doesn't matter. At least I'll know how you lost your toe."

"I'll tell you now."

This is Imke's death confession.

"No!" Mayken is adamant. "I want to keep guessing about the fingers."

Aris will not allow Mayken to watch the operation or to handle the severed article on removal. Instead, hastily dressed in a gown and bonnet, with ribbons loosened to allow for her ear bandages, she stands outside the cabin door, listening. She hears a metallic click, a low moan, a dry snap, and a hoarse scream, quickly suppressed. After what seems like an age Aris opens the door and beckons her in.

Imke is swaddled and sleeping, her bad foot dressed nicely. There is a strong tarry smell.

Mayken sees the covered bowl on the table. "Will you throw her toe overboard?"

Aris frowns. "What else would I do with it?"

Mayken imagines Imke's toe spiraling down to the seabed. What if a fish snaps it up? And the sailors catch that fish? And they serve it in the Great Cabin? And the upper-merchant cuts open the fish to reveal a nursemaid's old toe?

"We could pickle it and then bury it in Batavia," Mayken suggests.

Aris gives her a look. "Send for me if she worsens. And stay aft-the-mast. You were lucky to get away with your skull intact this time."

Mayken has a thought. "You could do with an assistant."

"Haven't I just told you to keep away?"

"Not me. I know a boy—as long as you wouldn't beat him."

Aris smiles; it lights his tired face. "We'll see. Take care of your nursemaid. No more chasing around after your Bullebak."

Mayken closes the door behind him and sits down to watch over Imke. "It's hardly *my* Bullebak."

CHAPTER FOURTEEN

1989

The fishermen went out an hour ago. Barely awake, they trudge down to the jetty, load their boats, fire their engines, and motor out into the beautiful brightening dawn. Once they've gone, the only sounds on the island are the sea and the birds and the shingle underfoot.

Joss Hurley and Dutch leave before the others. This is Joss's way. First out, last back, no talk, need nothing, depend on no one. Gil walks down with them, carrying the esky full of the provisions Dutch has fixed for the day. Dutch leaves food for Gil back at the camp too, under plates in the fridge. Dutch also has the kitchen swept, mugs washed, and laundry pegged out: Joss's singlets, Dutch's own worn shirts, Gil's shorts. Their clothes dance all day on the washing line together, the best of friends.

Gil walks slowly back to the camp. Today the sea looks calm but then there are the rough waters beyond the reef. He can't think about his grandfather's boat out there without the memory of the heart-stopping silence of the cutout engine, of blood pooling in the plastic bag around the old man's hand, of weather and wave wild against the struggling boat.

Gil turns his mind to the long stretch of the day. Enkidu helps. There's the tortoise's breakfast, the tortoise's morning exercise, then circus training. This takes time because Enkidu is in no way tractable and won't be bribed like a dog. They usually have their Special Project of the Day. Yesterday it was building Death Castle down on the beach, a bleak place of dismembered crab limbs and a moat set with jagged coral shrapnel. Enkidu joined in, storming the battlements and taking no prisoners.

Today's Special Project will be having a nose through Dutch's things, for no particular reason, at least no reason Gil will admit to himself.

Dutch sleeps in the tumbledown hut downwind of the generator shed. On the island a deckie's lair fit for one is called the Love Shack. Dutch's new digs are nowhere near as good as those he had at Frank Zanetti's. The Love Shack has a sloped corrugated roof and two windows at awkward heights, one too low and one too high to see out of. Dutch has patched up the major holes and fixed the old metal bed frame. Gil helped him hang curtains with a staple gun. Joss visited, nodded at the repairs, and eyed the curtains suspiciously.

The one room is partitioned, making a narrow area inside the door. Dutch calls this his galley. It holds a picnic table, a portable stove, and a few pieces of plastic crockery. There's a yellowing cooler on the floor and a row of tinned potatoes on the shelf above. In the sleeping part, there's a chair with Dutch's few clothes folded neatly on it; propped against the wall, a surfboard and guitar.

Gil crouches and looks under the bed—jackpot! He drags out a battered briefcase lashed about with rope.

It likely contains drugs in little plastic bags, or body parts, or money in crisp piles with bands around them, or a gun. Or all of these things. Gil knows this from the late-night films he watched with Mum.

The lock is busted on the briefcase. As is the catch. Gil undoes the rope, the knots slipping easily with one pull of the loose end. Too late he realizes they were probably seafaring knots. Now Dutch will know someone was snooping in his stuff. Now Dutch will know *he* was looking. Who else? The old man?

Gil wavers, then opens the briefcase anyway.

Loose papers, a broken pocketknife, and a battered Irish passport for Patrick John Roche. The faded photograph shows Dutch, expressionless and with a beard. Tucked into the pocket compartment there's a book. The pages are yellowed and the spine buckled. A picture of an olden-days stone horse on the cover. *The Epic of Gilgamesh.*

Gil finds he wants to read about his namesake and Enkidu too.

He opens the book and his heart twists: here is Mum's handwriting. Her big, happy, loopy writing.

To the epic Dutch.

Love forever,

Dawn

The sea light plays on the ceiling and the breeze skips in through the open windows and he begins to read.

He can make no sense of the story. He skips pages. Advice from some goddess who might be a cow. Walking leagues. A tree hermit. The loss of Enkidu is hard to bear.

He carefully puts the book back where he found it, else Dutch will be onto him. He'll be asking in a soft voice if Gil wants to talk about his mum.

Not after seeing that bloody book, Gil bloody doesn't.

Love forever.

Without kisses. Which means it was a serious love. Mum probably did it with Dutch. Stringy old Dutch.

Gil feels weird. He won't look through Dutch's stuff again. So he has one last good search of the briefcase.

A brown envelope is tucked in another compartment. Gil gloats.

He's found the drugs and the money. He shakes out the contents: a pair of blue baby bootees. Gil puts his fingers into the bootees—knitted for the tiniest of feet—and walks them leagues across the bed then right back into the envelope.

The breeze picks up through the open windows and the seabirds pitch and argue. Gil lies on Dutch's bed and the briefcase lies on the floor beneath, tied about with rope, fastened with some kind of giveaway knot. On an upended crate, within arm's reach, there is a pouch of tobacco and a stone. Gil picks up the stone. Perfect, round, with a hole right through the middle. Smooth and cool and nice in his palm. A special stone—magical, even. Gil puts it to his eye and squints up at the ceiling but sees only dancing light reflected off the sea.

CHAPTER FIFTEEN

1628

Pelgrom visits their cabin with a bowl of pickled plums and a snake's smile. Even Imke is reserved. Mayken has not told her nursemaid that it was Pelgrom who costumed her as a cabin boy and allowed her to get half killed, but perhaps Imke has drawn her own conclusions. Mayken has recorded her fury with Pelgrom in her ship's log.

> *Nine weeks at sea. Please God, grant Jan Pelgrom scurvy. May his eyes fall out and his teeth fall out and his hair fall out and his limbs burn with a fiery pain. May he shit his own guts and die roaring and be tossed overboard in a sack with a stitch through his nose. And may there be rats in the sack. If not scurvy, Pelgrom could get his skull crushed by Stonecutter, please God. It would shatter like a bad walnut. Would I wish him bit by the Bullebak? He's probably one of the creature's own.*

That Imke hasn't mentioned her disguise and obvious wanderings is a surprise to Mayken. She can only conclude that the nursemaid *wants* her to find Bullebak. Imke is canny—she likely knows exactly what bit her! Mayken must take it upon herself to save this fierce old lady. Hasn't Imke cared for her all her life?

While Imke sleeps Mayken takes out the cabin-boy breeches and the jug. The old woman is no better; her foot stinks and she burns with fever. Mayken must find a way to trap Bullebak—and soon.

She sees with a jolt that Imke has woken and is watching her.

"Go and breathe the air on deck, Mayken."

"Go and do bloody sewing, you mean?"

Imke smiles, with effort. "Sit with the ladies, get to know them, for later."

"What *later*?"

Imke won't answer.

Mayken frowns. "I'd rather stay with you."

"All day in a sickroom? I'll be here when you get back."

"Promise."

"Promise."

It's blustery on the upper deck. Judick pats a place next to her on the straw-filled bolster under a canopy. A young cadet rigged it up for the passengers. The same young cadet who moons about after Judick and whom Judick ignores. Agnete, haughty, shuffles along, making room next to her older sister. Mayken pulls a face at Agnete, who responds with a disapproving stare. Agnete, young as she is, already looks weary. Probably from always having to sew and listen to the Bible read aloud.

The passengers are talking about rats. Every time the word is mentioned Mrs. Predikant purses her mouth as if she's actually tasting one and it's sour.

Mayken tries a line: "I heard a sailor say that there are many rats on this crossing. Rats, rats, and more rats. The rats are also very big. The rats are big enough to carry a child away."

She glances meaningfully at Mrs. Predikant's youngest child, a plump, happy tumble of a boy. It would take a fair few rats to carry Roelant away.

Judick touches her arm. "Let's talk about happier subjects." A sharp inhale. "Your face, Mayken, what happened?"

Evidence of her exchange with Stonecutter has flourished on Mayken's face. A vivid bruise to her cheek, her mangled ear only half hidden by her cap.

"She's been brawling," says Agnete tartly.

"I have, with Stonecutter."

Wybrecht, the family's maid, a country girl with a ribald sense of humor, laughs out loud. Mrs. Predikant silences her with a cold glare. Wybrecht continues with her sewing, glancing up to grin at Mayken, her brown eyes lit.

"Another thing about rats . . ." begins Mayken.

But the attention of the circle is suddenly elsewhere: Lady Lucretia, accompanied by her maid, has arrived on deck. Mayken can sense an excited flutter, the craning of heads, apart from Wybrecht, who calmly carries on sewing. Creesje traverses the deck with Zwaantie following and everyone pretends not to observe. Even Mrs. Predikant seems distracted by this illustrious passenger.

Mayken still can't see the fascination. She studies Creesje carefully. She's tall and thin but not in a spiky way. She has a long neck and a pale oval face. Her gown hangs very well and is not stained about the armpits. There's a glide to Creesje, some trick of the feet under the skirts.

Creesje draws nearer. She nods to Mrs. Predikant and bends to ruffle Roelant's curls. "May I join you?"

Everyone moves in all different directions at once, bumping into one another in a bid to make space. Creesje sits next to Mayken. She smiles down at her.

Zwaantie settles away from the shelter of the canopy, turning her face up to the sun. Although the two have come out on the deck together, it is clear they'd rather be miles apart. Creesje asks Zwaantie for her fan. Zwaantie delays, then passes the fan with a look of profound begrudgement. Noticing skipper Jacobsz watching from the lower deck, Zwaantie smiles right at him. Her face is transformed, all bright and dimpled. Skipper Jacobsz grins back, slowly, leeringly.

He is a wolf, thinks Mayken, a hairy old long-toothed wolf. Zwaantie isn't a lamb, though. Mayken can see that. She's rather a strong, young she-wolf.

Skipper Jacobsz returns to giving out orders with increased strut and swagger. Zwaantie watches him now.

Just above Zwaantie a sailor is doing something complicated with rope. Soon he is joined by another sailor, then another. Mayken knows this has something to do with the lure of Zwaantie's magical bosoms, which have risen half out of her dress, all glowing and doughy. Creesje leans forward and speaks to Zwaantie in a low, firm voice. The maid looks at her blankly, then gets up, moving in under the shelter of the canopy.

Mrs. Predikant watches with an approving pucker to her lips.

Creesje turns to Mayken. "I hear your nursemaid is very sick."

"She's much better. Aris cut off her toe."

Creesje doesn't recoil. "He's a talented healer. I trust she will be well soon. Who cares for you now?"

"Being quite grown, I take care of myself."

Creesje smiles. Her face is kindly but sad. Mayken sees that Creesje is as beautiful as they say and not just because of the curve of her eyebrows, her blue-gray eyes, and her lovely russet lashes.

Creesje hugs Roelant onto her lap, never minding her fine gown, and the women glance at one another with pity in their expressions. Mayken remembers that Creesje was an orphan and then her own little children died. Alone in the world, she decided to sail to Batavia to join her husband, her only remaining family. It's a lot to bear, all of that and Zwaantie with her bosoms.

"Be my guest at dinner tonight in the Great Cabin," says Creesje.

Mayken hesitates.

"Your nursemaid needs her rest and you need a feed." Creesje pinches her and Mayken laughs. "And I confess, I would like the company. It's skipper Jacobsz's night and he is disgusting to the eye.

If you sit next to me and distract me I might be able to swallow my food."

"I don't know, Creesje Jansdochter."

Judick is watching them with a mawkish look on her face: childless Creesje and motherless Mayken.

"Please say you will!" insists Creesje.

Mayken nods. "Only I won't eat fish."

"You don't have to eat fish."

"You shouldn't either."

"What's wrong with the fish?"

"Imke's toe. Aris threw it overboard."

"No fish for either of us," replies Creesje gravely. "I will send my maid to help you dress."

They both glance at Zwaantie. Zwaantie looks back at them with an expression of such venom that Mayken knows the hair brushing and face scrubbing will be spitefully done.

Tonight, the Great Cabin is lit by many candles. This is the only place on the ship where candles are allowed. There are buckets of water just in case but these are tucked away so that everything seems natural and pleasant. If not for the motion of the ship, and the strange angles the floor makes, they could be in a room in any fine house. Light from the stern lamp floods the glazed window. Creesje and Mayken look out at the bright glimmer trail on the dark sea.

The treasure chests are covered with cloths at mealtimes, so as not to distract the guests with dreams of silver. The table is set with fancy plate and crystal. There is a lovely scent of beeswax and rich sauces and the faces around the table are soft in the light and expectant.

Mayken takes a seat next to Lady Creesje, who, in her black dress and jewels, looks mysterious and splendid. Like an illuminated saint, the sort Mayken saw in Imke's chapel. Mayken's scalp still stings from Zwaantie's attack with the comb. Her gown is tight under the arms and too short; she has evidently grown since leaving Haarlem.

She imagines she hears Imke's voice telling her not to scratch under her bodice and pick at her nails but rather sit nicely so as not to draw attention. She is the only child in the room, after all.

Unexpectedly, it's upper-merchant Pelsaert's night to dine because the skipper is indisposed. Creesje is delighted. She says the young noblemen of the guard will be disappointed, because they love the skipper's ribald stories. With Pelsaert, the conversation must sparkle and be civilized. For some, this feels like a wasted evening or even a test. But at least the upper-merchant doesn't flick fish bones, wipe his face on the guest sitting next to him, and fall backward on his chair in a stupor. With Pelsaert, there will be more courses and less wine, clever anecdotes, not drinking games.

"Do they ever eat at the same table?" whispers Mayken.

"Never," says Creesje. "They take alternate nights. Francisco absenting himself one night to rest. Jacobsz away the next. If they do meet, the air bristles between them."

"Why?"

"An argument, long ago. This is the first time they've shared a ship."

Pelsaert takes his place, looking pallid and sweaty in his scarlet coat.

"He is unwell, an old fever returns to plague him." Creesje looks sad about this. "Next to him is Jeronimus Cornelisz."

The man seems to have heard his name, though it was spoken quietly. He raises his goblet to Creesje with a smile.

Creesje lowers her voice further. "He's a little slippery for my liking."

Cornelisz, a middling sort of man, wears his clothes with a flamboyant air. Tying his neckerchief just so, tilting his hat just so. He has longish hair and a complicated beard; the effect is one of an everyday man, a baker or a carpenter, disguised as an aging fop. He has a habit of leaning in closely when he speaks to people, as if he'd climb into their ears given half a chance. Mayken thinks of Bullebak's trick of worming into people's skulls to look out through their eyes. She wonders where the creature is now. Down in the hold perhaps? Or close by, listening to the people around this table talking? If it can change size and shape it could be floating in a goblet. Or lurking in a sauce. Or inside the droplet hanging from the under-steersman's nose.

As long as Bullebak is nowhere near Imke, she doesn't care where it is.

Creesje is naming the other guests, the ambitious cadets, the steersmen. Mayken knows most of them already. Then there's Mrs. Predikant, the predikant, and Judick, who is stalwartly ignoring the young cadet who gazes at her from the opposite side of the table.

Pelgrom and another steward circle the room, bringing the first course, filling goblets, bending to listen to the guests' requests. Pelgrom moves smoothly and quickly, more stooped than usual, a smile embedded on his face. He deftly deals out butter curls and ladles soup, pours wine and forks meat onto plates with precision. His ear always bent to the conversation. Pelgrom's eyes meet Mayken's and his smile falters for a moment.

In the Great Cabin there are many courses, on every plate an elegant construction. The soft candlelight makes it hard for Mayken to tell exactly what she's eating. Besides, there are flavors and textures she has never tried before. Mayken wonders how many more burns and blows poor Smoert had to suffer in the making of this meal. With this thought it becomes impossible to eat. The room becomes hotter, everyone talks at once, the under-merchant laughs through his nose, Mrs. Predikant looks sour, and Judick shows a frosty indifference to the handsome cadet who is imploring her to taste a radish.

Mayken is perched on bolsters so that her nose might clear the edge of the table. She tries to understand the snippets of conversation she hears. Worth of this, worth of that. Buy this here, sell that there. One compliments another on the quality of their expensive clothes. One compliments another on their promotion. Talk is of Amsterdam, who to know, who to avoid. And of trade, always of trade. She stabs at the coiled arrangement on her plate, something trapped in jelly and decorated with crystallized flowers. It tastes of juniper and tears. She's not entirely sure it isn't alive.

There is a hush. Mayken realizes that the upper-merchant is talking to her.

"I know your father," Pelsaert is saying, a wine-bright look in his eye. "A great Company man. Isn't he very strict?"

"I don't know, sir," answers Mayken. "I've never met him."

Pelsaert seems charmed by this. "So you know nothing of your dear papa?"

"I know he has red and white roses and stallions."

The guests join in with the laughing. The upper-merchant dabs at his forehead with a handkerchief.

"All that is true, of course," he says. "But what would you say if I told you that he tortures his roses on difficult archways and flogs his stallions for not prancing?"

"Are you his enemy?"

"Not at all!" Pelsaert laughs. "He is an excellent man in all respects!"

Mayken feels out of sorts. Her dress is tight, she doesn't know what her food is, and she has drunk all the wine in her goblet. Pelgrom coasts by and deftly tops up her goblet with the jug in his hand. He looks at her, his smile sly. It was a mistake to drink the wine, Mayken realizes. At first it made her burp pleasantly, but now, with the eyes of the Great Cabin on her, she feels hot and dizzy.

"Your mother—"

"Bloody flux."

Around the table, glances are exchanged.

"About that: I'm sorry." Pelsaert really does look sorry.

Mayken feels Creesje's hand on her arm, gentle and encouraging.

The under-merchant pipes up. "I gather you are quite the urchin aboard." He looks pointedly after Pelgrom, who continues around the table with a jug.

Pelgrom has revealed her secrets! Mayken feels her face redden, unsure how to answer.

Creesje intervenes. "Please consider who you are addressing, sir."

Cornelisz holds up his hands. "I meant no slight. We all of us live roughly at sea." He turns to Mayken. "Your father will soon polish up your manners, child."

Creesje sends him an icy glare.

Mayken looks miserably at her plate and whatever is coiled there. It swims before her eyes. "If Papa flogs his horses and tortures flowers then I don't want to go to him."

"Don't say that!" whispers Creesje.

"I hope we never get to Batavia," says Mayken.

There is silence. Something in the room shifts. Mayken looks around. The upper-merchant appears dismayed, the cadets aghast, there's fear in Mrs. Predikant's cold blue eyes, and the predikant seems to be praying. The under-merchant holds up his goblet and swishes the wine in there. The candle flames, hitherto steady, waver and splutter.

Mayken has cursed the voyage.

Then the moment passes and the candle flames burn upright again and the upper-merchant frowns and turns away to remark something to the person next to him and Mrs. Predikant lowers her eyes and the corners of her mouth and the predikant is all chatter and the under-merchant savors his wine. Mayken's face burns scarlet. She glances up at Creesje, who gives her a pitying look.

The ship sails on and Pelgrom pours the wine and the candles burn down and talk turns to trade and soon enough everyone has forgotten Mayken. She slips from her chair and out of the cabin, past the dozing guards.

As she passes through the dark corridor, Mayken notices it is crisscrossed by tiny beams of light. She stops and puzzles and sees rows of curious holes. They are not wood knots, being uniformly and deliberately drilled. She peers through one—she's at table level in the Great Cabin! She presses her ear to the hole and can hear the babble of conversation.

Looking holes and listening holes! Not unlike the one Pelgrom made for Imke's amusement. Pelgrom the shipworm. Pelgrom the spy. Mayken rips off part of her dress's lace hem. She rolls the threads carefully, filling the holes. The beams of light go out, one by one. Mayken steps out onto the deck, satisfied that Pelgrom will know someone has noticed.

There's a bluster tonight, the wind wonderful after the close heat of the Great Cabin. Mayken thrills to the ship's sway as she lets go of the doorway and steps out into the dark. She tries her skipper's swagger across the nighttime deck, spits a bit, and even growls.

A shadow above in the shrouds. Just a sailor! By night the hands have the moon to see by, or if there's no moon they have the feel of the ropes and the stitched canvas hems to guide them.

The shadow flits overhead, moving too fast for a sailor.

Mayken feels like a mouse that's strayed under an owl's gaze. She turns and patters back across the deck. Heart pounding. Above, the shadow follows.

In sight—the door to the cabins.

She almost makes it.

CHAPTER SIXTEEN

1989

Mum taught Gil early about the importance of neighbors. Whether you are living in a motel, car, or a rented house, if there are people nearby, they are your neighbors. Chances are they will have something that you need. Only choose carefully who you are neighborly with. Avoid people who eat out of tins, people who have out-loud conversations with God, and those poor souls with loads of cats. Mums with young kids will be too busy. Single men will be weirded out. Old people are ideal, an old couple the best of all. You need an entry. Borrowing something is a good way to test the water. Make it simple: a cup of sugar, a hammer. Soon enough your neighbors will be laying an extra place at the table for you. Take Mrs. Baxter. She went from buying the right kind of sausages for Gil's breakfast to offering him a home.

On an island this small, Gil has decided, everyone is your neighbor.

And Gil has a very specific request in mind.

He checks in his pocket for the tobacco tin with the ivory bobbin. If Birgit balks at handing over what he needs, maybe she'll consider a neighborly exchange? He trains Dutch's binoculars on the scientists' hut and waits.

Birgit steps out into the morning wearing a man's shirt and with her hair loose. She's a film star. Gil focuses the binoculars on the cigarette in her hand. She smokes fancy filter-tipped continentals. Elegant in the way a rollie could never be. Obtaining one of Birgit's continental cigarettes is the object of Gil's visit. He wants to smoke one as he gazes into Granny Iris's dressing table mirror while wearing the green brocade and the pearl earrings. He can practice different expressions. European. Princely. Disdainful.

Birgit smokes, chic and foreign, looking out to sea. There will be no diving today. She wouldn't be standing around smoking if there was diving. She wouldn't be picking and poking at the equipment corralled under canvas. At the stacked crates of finds brought up from the sea, rinsed and photographed, ready to go to the mainland.

Gil scrambles out of the scrub and rounds the camp at a pelt. Slowing his breath, he walks past, raising a hand. *Oh, you're awake, neighbor!*

Birgit sees him. "Want a coffee, Gil?"

Birgit pulls on khaki shorts and knots her man's shirt at the waist. She is barefoot and has long brown toes. She twists her hair up on her head and sticks a pen through it and is catwalk ready. The two men are asleep in the other room yet, so they keep their voices down.

Birgit goes over to the kitchen area: a burner and a small fridge, a sink fed by the rainwater tank. She lights the burner and puts the kettle on. She spoons instant coffee into mugs and mixes powdered milk.

Gil looks around. There's an army bed in the corner with Birgit's sandals under it. The scientists' hut is basic inside, camping chairs and trestle tables. There are metal bracketed shelves with boxes stacked along them, cameras and instruments too. Every corner has things soaking in baths of liquid. On the main wall is a noticeboard with maps and charts pinned on it.

Birgit sets the coffees and a pot of sugar down on a low picnic table and drags over two camping chairs, gesturing Gil to sit and which mug is his. She takes her continental cigarettes out of her pocket and throws them on the table. Gil loves everything about them: the squashy packet, the design on the front, a gilded emblem.

Gil eyes them, raising his mug.

The coffee, though, is disappointing. Pale and milky. Kid's coffee. This probably means Birgit won't give him a cigarette even if she does talk to him like he's an adult. He could ask. Maybe they let kids smoke in her country? In France they let kids drink wine and eat garlic.

"Which country are you from?"

"Germany."

Gil is none the wiser. "Do kids smoke there?"

Birgit gives him a funny look. "No."

Gil studies the map nearest him on the wall: specks of land in a wide, wide sea.

"The Houtman Abrolhos Islands." Birgit sips her coffee. "Abrolhos is a corruption of the Portuguese *abre os olhos*, 'open your eyes.'"

Gil ponders. "The name of these islands is a warning, to stop the ships hitting the reef and sinking."

"Which is what happened to the *Batavia*." Birgit leans forward and shakes a cigarette from the pack, leaving one peeking out. "You know the *Batavia* story?"

"Not really." Only what Silvia's sprouted.

Birgit lights one of her lovely cigarettes and exhales. "Late in 1628 the *Batavia*, a merchant ship, set sail from the Netherlands. Destination: Spice Islands, our modern-day Indonesia. She had just been built and was loaded with more wealth than you can imagine."

"Silver coins."

"Among other things. In charge was the merchant, Francisco Pelsaert, and below him the skipper, Ariaen Jacobsz. The two men loathed each other. So much so that skipper Jacobsz and his supporters were actively planning a mutiny against Pelsaert when the ship wrecked."

"Then everyone was killed?"

"Not quite. The survivors were evacuated to dry land as the ship began to break apart on the reef. Finding no water on any of these bleak islands, Pelsaert and Jacobsz made an impossible decision: they would sail the ship's longboat to their original destination, Batavia."

"And that was a bad idea?"

"It was risky. A journey across open sea in a vessel hardly equipped for it. But if they made it, they could organize a rescue party and return here. They figured the only way they could save their stricken crew and passengers was by abandoning them."

"So they left the people here?"

"The ones that hadn't drowned. Two hundred survivors stranded on this archipelago with limited supplies. Not to mention the seventy men still stuck out on the sinking ship."

"Then everyone was killed?"

Birgit takes another drag. The lit cigarette smells continental, fragrant, not the whiff of stale horse straw a rollie gives. "Then we come to another key figure in the story: Jeronimus Cornelisz, the under-merchant, third in command, a man sly and cruel."

"Jeronimus," Gil repeats dutifully. Leaning into the cigarette smoke.

"Cornelisz very nearly didn't survive himself. Too cowardly to jump into the rescue boat, he remained on the disintegrating ship as the weather conditions worsened. He was the last man to wash up on this island, half-dead and clinging to the bowsprit. It was a miracle."

"A bad miracle, if he was sly and cruel."

"Yes, if miracles can be bad." Birgit tip-taps her cigarette on the ashtray. Gil takes note of the swish of hand and wrist.

"First of all," she continues, "Cornelisz took the weapons and salvaged supplies and put them under guard. He gathered to him men who would do his every bidding: corrupt soldiers and vain young cadets. He ordered boats to be made from the wood that washed up from the wreck. Then he set about banishing the remaining soldiers to another island."

"In case they fought him?"

"Exactly. He believed they would perish there. He didn't know the island had a fresh water supply and food sources that would enable them to survive and organize themselves against him. But that's another story."

"Can we have it sometime?"

Birgit smiles. "Absolutely."

"What did Jeronimus do next?"

"He was in a bind. If the rescue ship returned, he would be arrested for his part in the plan to seize the *Batavia*. Rumors of the mutiny were already spreading—how could they not reach Pelsaert's ears? Mutineers were given the death penalty. But really no one on this island would have expected to be rescued."

"But the others went for help?"

"In a thirty-foot boat, with few supplies, across miles and miles of sea. There was only a slim chance they would make it. The survivors must have felt very alone."

Gil sips to halfway but his coffee doesn't get stronger. He stops, aware that Birgit is watching him.

"Then everyone was killed?"

Birgit puts down her mug with a sigh. "Cornelisz knew that the rations wouldn't last long shared among so many people. He wanted to keep himself and his men alive. If a rescue boat did come, they would seize it, kill the crew, and go pirating."

"Cool."

Birgit throws Gil a look.

"I mean pirates who *don't* murder are cool."

"Well, Cornelisz's gang did murder. They set about reducing the number of survivors."

"To have more food and drink and weapons for themselves."

"At first, Cornelisz pretended the killings were punishments for crimes or misbehaviors. Then people just disappeared. Toward the end—" Birgit stops herself.

Gil thinks. "And kids too?"

She nods. "Cabin boys not much older than you. The children of crew and passengers."

"How were they killed?"

Birgit studies Gil and frowns. "Hard to tell. We haven't found all the remains and we have limited accounts." She screws her continental cigarette out. "I can't imagine what it was like to be abandoned on this island, can you?"

"Yeah. I can."

In the room next door there is the sound of the others waking up. Birgit gathers herself, her cigarettes. Gil has missed his chance to take one. Mick wanders in bare chested and puts the kettle on.

Birgit takes down a box from the shelf and shows it to Gil. On a bed of cotton wool lies a flake of mud.

"This is very exciting, brought up from the reef. We think it's lace concreted in coral."

Gil looks up at the shelves. "Are there any bones?"

"Human? Yes." Birgit makes no move to show him.

"Could they be Little May's?"

"That's just an island story, Gil."

"Is it true?"

"Are you asking a scientist if ghosts exist?"

A milky coffee sort of answer. "Is that *no*?"

Birgit glances over at Mick. He's scratching his armpit and looking at the ceiling. She lowers her voice. "Let's just say this island plays tricks on the mind. The weather, the birds, the history—"

Mick clears his chest extravagantly and lights a rollie to go with his coffee.

Birgit smiles. "I should make a start."

Gil draws the tobacco tin from his pocket and holds it out to her. With a smile she takes it.

"I think it's a bobbin," says Gil. "Ivory."

Birgit looks at him in surprise. "You think?" She inspects it, turning the tin. "You found this on the island?"

"Up at the camp."

Mick, stirring coffee, pipes up. "Joss Hurley's."

Birgit pulls a face at Mick. It says, *Fuck off, I know whose camp it is.* "Is it from the *Batavia*?"

She turns back to Gil. "It might be. Can I hold on to this, see if I can find out more?"

The bobbin rests in its tin on the palm of her hand. Snug there. Gil nods. He's about to ask for a cigarette, a neighborly exchange, only Birgit looks happy and the whole moment is nice.

Instead, he asks, "Will it go into a museum?"

"Possibly. Would you like that?"

"Yeah."

Birgit walks him to the door. She touches his arm. "Come and visit again, Gil."

Gil's elation turns to disappointment up along the path. That wasn't a neighborly exchange; he gave away the bobbin and got nothing in return. Now Birgit will be all over the old man's camp, pissing him off.

Let her.

CHAPTER SEVENTEEN

1629

"Stop cursing!" he says. "Hold fast, little grandmother!"

He is no owl and she is no mouse.

Mayken does hold fast to him, with her hands and feet, like a young monkey. The old sailor has one arm about her back. His arm is slim but strong, like a sound branch. They swing up, up, up, on a rope.

Mayken feels, more than sees, their passage into the sails, for the moon is behind clouds. The ropes this close smell tarry. The sails this close smell of salt. It is a world of creak and snap and billow. When the half hour bell rings, the sound comes from very far below.

He places her carefully on a beam. She feels it solid under her legs.

"You are quite safe," he says.

Mayken nods but her teeth chatter and her legs shake.

"Be brave." He puts his big hands over her small hands. His old rough hands, knuckles gnarled like a tree. "Grip on to the beam here and here, then you will feel better. That's it, trust the ship."

A break in the clouds, a bright moon—Mayken sees she is flying!

She looks down at her bare feet kicked out into—air. She has lost her slippers! Beyond her feet—down through the billowing canvas—is the ship's deck, tiny to her eye. They are unbelievably high. Next to her on the beam perches the old sailor, his India shawl around his head.

"You remember me, little grandmother?"

"I saw you when we boarded."

"You did."

"If you are going to call me Little Grandmother, then I shall call you Holdfast!"

The old sailor laughs, delighted. "My name is Pauwels Barentsz but you may call me Holdfast. Your friend the barber-surgeon is also a friend of mine."

"You know Aris?"

"He asked me to keep an eye out for you."

Mayken frowns. "I can look after myself."

"Of course, but you can never have too many friends."

Mayken considers this. "All right. You keep an eye out for me and I'll keep an eye out for you."

"As you wish, Little Grandmother."

"I thought you were Bullebak when you swooped."

"Meaning big bully?"

"The ancient monster and foe of all humankind that lives in the hold," Mayken explains.

"I see."

"Do you think it could climb masts?"

"No," says Holdfast very seriously. "Its feet would be too slippery."

Mayken nods, relieved. "There are more stars up here."

"There are the same number, only you can see them better. That one there—"

"Don't name them! Let them be wild and not something I have to learn about."

Holdfast laughs.

"I want to be a sailor like you."

"It's a tough life."

"I could wear breeches."

"You could."

"I wouldn't have to dine in the Great Cabin."

"No, you could eat with your messmates and then smoke a pipe."

They sit in companionable silence, looking down on the vast landscape of the sea. The white-peaked moonlit waves and pitch-black troughs.

"I could piss on the soldiers through the hatch."

Holdfast laughs. "It's a tradition."

Mayken has a thought. "You could name the parts of the ship if you like, instead of the stars. The masts and sails and ropes. Then you could teach me all the words sailors shout at one another, especially the curses."

"We'll start with the mainmast. You know enough curses."

"Go on, then."

"The masts are strong, as the ship is strong. The hull is twice as thick as it needs to be and armored against the worm. This mainmast is an ancient tree. Once planted in the forest, it is now planted in the ship. It travels down through the gun deck, orlop, and hold, to rest on her keel. The keel is the ship's backbone."

Mayken doesn't want to think about the hold.

"Close your eyes and press your ear against the mast. You can hear the water under the hull."

Mayken does, and imagines she can hear the hum and rush of the sea under the moving ship.

"Sailors need to learn the language of the ship. She talks to us through rope and sail and the sounds she makes as she moves through the water."

"Like she's alive?"

"She is alive. You're learning fast."

"I know some sailor words," says Mayken. "Larboard and starboard, fore and aft, stern and prow."

"There you are, a fine sailor you are, you know your arse from your elbow."

Mayken smiles. "The world rocks more up here."

"It does."

"Have you any stories?" Mayken asks, suddenly wanting to fall asleep listening to the old sailor's voice, which has a nice rasp to it, like a cat's tongue.

The old sailor obliges. He tells the sleepy child stories of cursed ports and bloodred roses, of the gunner's beautiful daughter, of love knots and promises. His words are snatched up and hauled away by the wind, which picks up as the ship plows on through the night. When Mayken gets cold, Holdfast takes off his India shawl and wraps it around her and says he doesn't mind the wind on his old shaved head.

In the first light of dawn the friends smile at each other. It's a beautiful sight, the sky and the sea awash with brightening color.

"Are you scared in rough weather, Holdfast?"

"Not so much, Little Grandmother. Because I have this."

Holdfast unknots the leather pouch at his waist, takes out a small object, and puts it carefully into Mayken's palm.

"Don't drop it now. That's a long way to fall."

On Mayken's palm, a stone. Perfect, round, with a hole right through the middle. Smooth and cool and nice in her hand. A special stone—magical, even.

"It's a witch stone," says Holdfast. "If you look through the hole, you can see what is yet to come, or what has been already."

Mayken tries it out on the old sailor. "You don't look before or after, you just look old."

Holdfast laughs. Mayken squints down at the sea through the hole. The sea is the same but that's not saying anything, it always was and always will be.

Mayken goes to give the stone back.

Holdfast smiles. "Keep it. If you're going to be a sailor, you'll need a good luck charm."

CHAPTER EIGHTEEN

1989

Gil stands on the moonlit beach and watches the ocean. There is no human voice to be heard, only the call of returning moon birds and the scuttle of ghost crabs and the rush of the wind. The fishermen and their families have gone. In every camp shutters are pulled down, gear stowed away, doors padlocked shut. Gone, too, is the smell of humans: man sweat and rollies, stale beer and tinned-food farts. Gil inhales. He is alone with the mineral air and hard-shelled creatures. Alone with the briny fish and bitter land shrubs and the warm brown birds nesting in their shingly holes. Alone with the lap of the sea on the shingle and the breezes. Alone with a sky full of wild unnamed stars. Gil looks down at his hand, in his open palm the perfect stone with the hole through the middle. Raising it to his eye, he turns in a slow circle: sea, shingle bank, moonlit scrub.

Gil wakes. It's night and he's alone in his room; outside, the murmured voices of his grandfather and Dutch on the veranda. He tries to shake off the taste of the dream, the shiver it's left in his body although the night is warm. In the box in the corner Enkidu scrabbles awake. Gil gets out of bed and goes over to the tortoise.

"Good boy."

It's not a word that Gil catches, or a phrase, that leads him to take notice of the men outside, it's a tone of voice. They are not talking about crays or boats or footy. They are talking about something serious. They are talking about him.

To hear them better, Gil creeps to the lounge room. He crouches to listen. When Dutch speaks, his voice places him just the other side of the open window. Gil is surprised to hear a hardness in his voice.

"Come on, all day, every day, Joss?"

"He doesn't like the boat."

"You blame him for the accident, don't you? He's a Jonah now?"

"The boy has no nerve."

"This is all new to him. Give him a chance. He can get used to the boat."

Joss growls something low.

Silence, then Dutch comes back at him. "He needs company, other kids—"

"Easter there'll be other kids."

"Do you even know what he does all day?"

"Silvia looks in."

"Jesus, that will do him the power of good."

The rasp and flare of a lighter. The smell of tobacco. Gil wants to cough but instead he breathes slowly through his nose until the tickle in his throat goes.

"Maybe there's someone he could talk to. You know, a professional."

"A shrink, you mean? Leave it out, Dutch."

A lull and the sound of seabirds.

"Did he see someone after they found Dawn?"

"How do I know?"

"He's your grandson." There's a pause. "I know you and Dawn didn't see eye to eye."

"She made her bed."

"So now the boy pays the price?"

"What price? I took him in, didn't I?" Joss lowers his voice and continues talking. Gil cranes his head but can't hear.

"But it's not usual kid behavior. And what happened with Dawn—"

"He's all right."

"How do you know that, Joss? Have you ever said more than three words to him?"

There's a creak, one of them has stood up; Gil sees their shadow on the opposite wall, framed by the window.

"Your argument is not with him, Joss. It's with every other fucker you come into contact with but not with Gil."

Gil goes back to his room and lies on his bed. Eventually he hears his grandfather come in off the veranda, the familiar shuffle of feet down the hall. The shuffling stops outside Gil's door. Gil holds his breath until the old man walks on. Gil listens for the creak of bedsprings across the hall. The clearing of lungs. Then, finally, the snores.

CHAPTER NINETEEN

1629

Holdfast tells Mayken to keep her eyes open. What for? Seaweed clumps and a change in cloud formation, different birds flying overhead, slick-backed dolphins racing alongside the ship. These signs mean they are nearing land.

They sit together up in the rigging some nights. When Imke is asleep Mayken patters out on deck and if he's on duty, down swoops the old sailor. They share stories. Holdfast names the parts of the ship but never the stars. Mayken insists that the stars stay wild. At dawn they return to their separate worlds. Mayken aft-the-mast, to sew with the well-to-do passengers. Holdfast to the gun deck, to claim some space between the cannons and sleep. Mayken thinks often about the Below World, of Smoert and Aris. Of John Pinten buying the sleep of a stone, drinking the barber-surgeon's potion to make the dark hours pass.

Imke shows little improvement but there have been no more dreams, no more suspicious bites, no more horrifying nighttime visitors. Perhaps Bullebak has retreated into the hold?

For now, Mayken will live quietly and watch over Imke. This is her main task. Her ship's log entries have waned, after days of *We are somewhere in the sea* and *Imke sleeps and I watch her.* She has not been called upon to accompany Creesje to dine in the Great Cabin again, much to her relief. The two often walk on deck together, for Zwaantie no longer attends her mistress. Gossip is rife of the skipper's growing infatuation for the lady's maid, who denies him nothing, it is said. Pelgrom is busy with carried stories. He trades nuggets of hearsay as if they are sweetmeats. Mayken sees him on his rounds; he does not visit their cabin now. Sometimes Mayken catches him watching her, a fixed smile on his face, dead eyes. She remembers Smoert's warning that the steward is not to be crossed. She wonders what she ever did to Pelgrom to have him abandon her in the hold.

Pelgrom may enjoy stirring the pot but the ship's brew is more noxious by the day. As is the way with souls confined, tempers fray and flare, ill-spoken words fester, coincidences become intrigues. Minds seethe with resentment and revenge like the worms in the water barrels.

As the ship spoils, so does the air between the people.

Cabin neighbors fall out. The crew, it is said, become ever more divided in their loyalty to upper-merchant Pelsaert or skipper Jacobsz. The two men are never seen together. If it were not for their difference in stature—slim and refined versus hairy and stout—you might think it was one man with a costume change. Cornelisz the under-merchant, however, appears to be everyone's friend. He's seen with each of his superiors in turn, thief-thick, whispering in their ears.

The signs of land come, as Holdfast said they would, along with a growing sense of excitement on board, helped by the fine sailing weather. And then the keen-eyed watch at the top of the mast makes the call everyone is waiting for.

Land. After sixty-four days at sea.

Soon Sierra Leone is a shimmering smudge in the distance for everyone to see. The smudge becomes coastline, hills, and a bay. The *Batavia* anchors, for the day is dwindling and landfall must be made in the morning. Few will have permission to go ashore, even though many long to step on solid ground again. All must be content to lie at safe harbor. The rest of the fleet draws in. Mayken can name them: *Dordrecht*, *Assendelft*, *Sardam*, *Kleine David* the little messenger ship, and the warship *Buren*. Where the *Batavia* goes, the other ships must follow. Each vessel has her skipper but Pelsaert commands them all. Now there is much to celebrate: respite from the big sea, peace at anchor, and the convoy together again.

Dawn comes. As the sun rises in the sky, boats approach from the shore. The *Batavia*'s sailors greet the locals, unfurling rope ladders and climbing down to retrieve samples of goods and produce. The passengers marvel at the crafts and carvings, at the wonderful and strange new foods.

The *Batavia*'s yawl is lowered. Pelsaert and a few high-ranking sailors will go ashore. Skipper Jacobsz remains in his cabin. Perhaps he does not agree with this landing, believing, as many of the sailors do, that they should have continued and put in at Table Mountain.

Those on board watch the yawl's progress. The upper-merchant intends to negotiate supplies of fresh water and meat. He will buy livestock and the animals will be slaughtered and butchered on the beach. The salted meat will be pressed into barrels along with the sand flies. The other ships in the fleet dispatch their own boats to conduct similar business and soon the bay is busy with traffic.

At harbor, the soldiers are given extra time on deck. Mayken watches for John Pinten. Once she catches sight of him, dark haired and pale, not as tall as some, but broad. He looks up to where she stands, high on the stern castle. Mayken waves but he doesn't seem to see her.

Music is heard all over the ship now, with the crew at greater leisure. Mayken changes the words of the songs and sings about wild stars dancing in the rigging and the sea at dawn and being a loyal friend to both soldiers and sailors.

Aris the barber-surgeon comes to see Imke. He orders her to be moved onto the open deck sick bay, to take the air, and for the cabin to be scrubbed and purified with burning herbs. The gun decks and orlop decks are cleaned too. The rats are smoked out and chased by teams of roaring cabin boys with brooms. Mayken worries that all this swabbing and sweeping may raise Bullebak from the deep. Then another thought strikes her: what's to stop the creature from abandoning ship and making landfall? Although Mayken wouldn't wish Bullebak on any country.

Imke has survived its bite, but only just. In the harsh light of day, the toll on the old woman is clear: loose-hanging skin, turkey-neck wattles from a too-big gown. She claws at her shawl and feels cold in the warmest breeze. Her eyes haunt. She seems half in another world, so that sometimes she looks right through Mayken. This brush with death has only increased her gift of second sight. She has never been busier.

Only Imke's fortunes are succinct now, plainly told, without embroiderings or deviations. She hasn't the time or the breath for more. Her answers have gained potency; she is even more accurate than a gull flying widdershins around the mast. Imke refuses no one her gift. Messages are brought to her from before- and aft-the-mast, from below deck and the lofty stern castle. Every soul on board seems to seek her predictions, from the provost's wife to the steersman's daughter. Only the older sailors hold back: they have their own means of divination. Even Jeronimus Cornelisz deigns to seek Imke's wisdom. Imke will not tell Mayken his query, but following the under-merchant's visit she shuts up shop as the ship's oracle.

"No more," she says, and shivers.

At night Mayken sleeps outside, cuddled on her nursemaid's cot.

"Will you tell my fortune now, Imke?"

"I'm not in that line of work anymore."

"You've given everyone else theirs!"

Imke hugs her. "Then let me see. I'll divine by the stars and those few clouds."

"You know best."

Imke looks up, then she nods, and listens, as if she's in conversation with the night sky. "You will grow up to be a great lady with jewels and gowns and live in a fine castle in Batavia."

"I won't be a sailor?"

"The heavens have spoken."

"Can they say something else?"

"No. That's your fortune, Mayken."

"I'll change it."

"You can't."

"Why not?"

"That's not how it goes. Your fortune finds you, not the other way around." Imke thinks a moment. "Although some go after their own destiny, that's true."

"Like a pirate after treasure?"

"Indeed."

"Like a merchant after spices?"

"Like a cat after a mouse." Imke goes quiet for a bit. Then in a dreamy voice adds, "What's meant for you won't pass you by."

"So maybe I'm *meant* to be a sailor."

Imke laughs. "Then you'll be a sailor. Although the heavens have put you in a castle wearing a nice gown."

Mayken pulls a face at the heavens. She takes out Holdfast's lucky stone. She carries it everywhere.

"What have you there, child?"

She passes it to Imke, who feels its shape and weight in her palm, then holds it up to the moon. "How did you come by it?"

"Found it." Mayken is glad it's too dark for the canny old nurse-maid to see her face well.

"You know how to use it?"

"You look through it."

"In the old days a man was boiled to death in a barrel of tar for using a prophecy stone. That's what you have here. I expect his customers didn't care for the fortunes he told."

"It shows you what is yet to come or what has been already," Mayken advises.

Imke passes the stone back to her. "Look through. Tell me what you see."

There's excitement in Imke's voice, although she's trying to sound uninterested, as if this is some secret test she wants Mayken to pass.

Mayken complies. "Stars and rigging."

"That's not it. Make your eyes go soft and sleepy. Your mind too. Fortunes have a habit of sidling in from the corners. They won't show themselves if you stare them down."

Mayken tries.

"What do you see now?"

"Bleary stars and rigging."

Imke chuckles.

CHAPTER TWENTY

1989

Gil trains Dutch's binoculars on the sight unfolding: the carrier boat docked alongside the main jetty, unloading mothers, grannies, and children. They arrive with clamor and baggage. They gabble and squabble along the jetty. Gil immediately hates them all, especially the kids. He checks on Enkidu, opening the sports bag to peer in. The tortoise looks fine, pissed off, but fine.

A little kid falls into the water and there's shouting and everyone rushes down the jetty. Kids must drown here all the time, Gil thinks. They probably have to tie them to a stick in the yard, like puppies.

The fishermen aren't here to greet the new arrivals but the seabirds are. There is wild screaming and circling overhead. Birgit is watching the newcomers' arrival too. Cool in sunglasses, sitting outside the scientists' hut, smoking a continental. The two men are inspecting an inflatable dinghy, spreading it out on the ground.

Gil zips up the sports bag. He's traveling light: just Enkidu, some money he found in a coffee tin, Granny Iris's green brocade jacket, and Mrs. Baxter's address in Margaret River.

But now here's Silvia. She approaches two children waiting by the jetty. Roper's kids. She tries to kiss them. The bigger one tolerates it, the smaller one wheels away.

Gil's heart falls. The impossibility of his plan. What was he thinking? That he could just stride down the jetty and throw his leg into the carrier boat and wave goodbye to the island? *Hi, Silvia, yep, just leaving. Oh, didn't Joss say?*

He tightens his grip on the sports bag and waits. Maybe once Silvia with her big mouth has gone, he can slip by?

Silvia is taking her time, talking to some of the mums. She's carrying more than her fair share again, supplies and Roper's kids' stuff too. The bigger boy sulks at her side, the smaller orbits like a gnat.

The skipper's mate is untying the ropes ready to cast off. Gil shoulders his sports bag, willing himself to run—he could still make it, peg down the jetty and jump in as the boat moves off. No time for questions. Boat trip back to the mainland. Make his way to Mrs. Baxter's and not be a stranger.

Mrs. Baxter came to the children's home. She brought Gil a suit and a lend of Mr. Baxter's tie for the funeral. They sat together in the visiting room.

The TV was on cartoons. Mrs. Baxter turned the sound down so she could speak low and serious: about what happened, what was going to happen, how it was for the best and how he mustn't be a stranger.

Gil sipped his soda, then put it carefully down on the coffee table.

The coffee table had sticky rings from other people's drinks. Sometimes they interlinked, sometimes they were separate.

Gil watches the carrier boat motor out of sight, then picks up the sports bag.

He can't bring himself to go back to Joss's camp, so he haunts the Zanetti place. He finds a shady spot under a rusting outboard engine on a metal trolley. He pushes the sports bag in before him and lies down, tasting the grit of windblown shingle. In a while, Roper's kids come outside. They look like Roper: heavyset, turned-out feet, fat faces. The older boy closes a sun umbrella around himself. The younger pulls down his togs and pees, then crouches to watch it sink into the ground. Silvia comes out with a beach bag and fishing nets. She puts her hand on the small boy's back and bends to hear something he says. Gil feels a fizz of jealousy.

She walks with them out onto the coast path and then the kids continue alone, the bigger boy digging the handle of his fishing net into the ground, the smaller lugging the beach bag. When the small one turns to look back, Silvia waves.

Silvia comes out to the lines carrying laundry on her hip. She pegs out the washing and cuts back past Gil's hiding place, swinging the plastic basket.

"You spying on me, Gil?"

"No."

"You want to come in for a while?"

"I'm allowed?"

"Why not? I'm on my own. You want ice cream?"

"Yeah, and some leaves. Where've those kids gone?"

"To play with Mrs. Nord's grandkids."

"They're staying here?"

"Until after Easter. You going to watch from there the whole time?"

Gil scowls and crawls out.

Enkidu wanders about the kitchen floor with a wet flannel over his shell to revive him after the heat of the sports bag. Gil sits at the table and eats ice cream and then a grilled sandwich with meat and cheese and tomatoes.

"Mrs. Nord's very good to take them," says Silvia from the sink. "She used to work at a home for maladjusted boys, so she knows how to handle them. They're little fuckers."

Gil carefully pulls the tomatoes from the sandwich and arranges them neatly at the side of the plate.

"The smaller boy, Mikey, isn't too bad when he shuts up," Silvia continues. "The big one, Paul, will be an arsehole like his father."

Gil says nothing. He is watching Enkidu trying to climb up the side of a bucket of soaking laundry. There are three piles of laundry in the corner of the kitchen. Underpants and singlets, which are white. Bedsheets, which are brown. Then a pile for cargo shorts. Enkidu plows through them, getting tangled in a bra.

Silvia laughs. Glancing at him to join in, her face changes. "Gil?"

Gil puts down his sandwich and wipes his eyes.

They walk out to the grotto because this is where Silvia can think best. She lights a few candles, her mouth pursed in concentration, and sits down next to him.

"Why do you want to leave?"

"I don't belong."

"You think any of us do? A heap of coral in the middle of the sea. Shacks and dead bones and weather. It's not forever. Come the end of the season he'll take you back to Gero."

"I have to go now."

"How? No one will take you off the island without your grand-daddy's permission."

Gil feels his stomach sink, although he already knew.

"Come on. He's not too bad. Does he hit you?"

"No."

"Well, there you go, then."

They look out at the sea.

"It's a big change from when you were with your mum. It was just you and her?"

"Yeah."

"You must miss her?"

Gil can't answer.

"I found something." Silvia rummages about on the lower shelf. "Maybe this should belong to you."

She holds out a photograph. Gil takes it.

Mum. Standing outside an island fisherman's camp. She looks really young, thin, with a boy's cropped hair the same red color as his. Ever since he can remember, Mum dyed her hair—brown, black—it was never red. She stands between two men. They are tanned, shirtless, and each have an arm around her. On her left is Dutch, gaunt and straggly and weathered-looking, even then. Maybe he was born leathery. The other man in the photograph Gil doesn't know. He's dark haired with big sideburns. Dutch looks at Mum, an expression of hungry joy on his face, like he could eat her up. The other man looks at the camera. Mum is squinting at the sky. She has her mouth held funny, like she's in the middle of saying something. Gil turns over the photograph.

EASTER 1979. Dutch, Dawn Hurley, Bobby Knox.

Silvia asks Gil his birth date.

"Then you were there," she says and smiles. "In her tummy, under her denim cutoffs."

The more he walks, the worse he feels. Despite the sea breeze, a stagnant air surrounds him. With it, a constant dripping in his mind, a dammed-up pressure that's sprung a slow leak. The pressure of things he should know and things he half knows and things he doesn't want to know at all.

Everywhere there are people. Milling around by the jetty, gathering outside camps, walking the coast paths. Gil hears the voices of kids playing. On the stony scrap of beach little ones toddle about with arm bands and rubber rings; older kids are out in dinghies. Mums sit with towels at the ready.

The island is too small for all of these.

Gil heads for the quieter path that will take him past the beacon.

At the beacon, he puts down the sports bag. If he had a rollie, he'd smoke it, eyes narrowed into the wind, arms crossed, like Silvia.

He takes out the photograph of Mum. It flutters in the wind. He holds it up high, as high as his arm can reach. Higher. Now he holds it just by the very tip of its corner. He could let go. It might blow into the sea. It might get speared on the scrubby bushes. A sea eagle might swoop and carry it off in its beak. Mum and Dutch and Bobby bloody Knox would find themselves twisted in a nest of string and tinsel.

He knows he could never let go.

A sudden breeze and the photograph is ripped from his hand.

Gil is after it, stumbling, running, as it turns and dances along the ground.

By the waterside, Gil catches up. The photograph settles face-down on the wet shale and he pounces. He pats it dry gently with the bottom of his T-shirt. When he looks up, he sees a flat-bottomed reef boat at the end of a jetty.

They are both old and abandoned-looking; the boat lists, the jetty is crumbling. Gil-the-brave walks down the jetty, jumping the missing planks. He looks down into the boat. It is a mess of mangled feathers and gull shit. Gil pulls the rope and the boat follows. He tethers it closer to the jetty and lowers the sports bag down and then himself. The boat tips and bobs but doesn't sink. The seat is hot on his bare legs and the paint is flaking off. The gull shit is dry at least. He takes Enkidu out of the sports bag for a wander in the bottom of the boat.

A plan grows in his mind. He confides in the tortoise.

The upper-merchant and the skipper of the *Batavia* survived an epic journey. Hundreds of miles across open sea. He and Enkidu could reach Geraldton. They could find oars, steal an outboard. Get maps and a compass. Pack tins, crackers, juice, fuel in a can. Wait for a really calm sea.

They could name the boat.

Little May

Bunyip

He settles on *The Sea Tortoise* in Enkidu's honor. Enkidu, as is his way, looks unimpressed.

CHAPTER TWENTY-ONE

1629

The *Batavia* sails. Some days she's alive to the wave and the wind and cuts through the water, keel sharp and wide belly balanced, canvas taut and lines humming. They could go faster, Holdfast tells Mayken, but the rest of the fleet cannot match the *Batavia*'s speed. This sticks in skipper Jacobsz's craw more than sharing the journey with Pelsaert—he must slow a swift ship when he could be hurtling on to the Spice Islands. But the distant gleam of another craft's stern light in the deep dark night is reassurance to many on board. So the *Batavia* flies, but not too fast, and the souls on board make plans for when they land. On good days, their destination feels closer. On other days, when the wind abandons them and the sea is begrudging and the ship wallows and toils, the hours lie heavy and they feel every weariness of their five months at sea.

If people are to lose their minds it will be now, the sailors say. Now that the deck is blanched with salt spray and the heat of the tropics beats down. The gun deck is rancid and airless and the orlop deck a sweltering hell. The first-class passengers receive their water sieved through muslin. The rest strain it through their teeth.

Four die in not so many days and are committed to the sea. The fifth, a bad omen. A lurch of the ship and the corpse is dropped. The canvas splits. Sailors make signs and look up at the sky. The predikant and the barber-surgeons attend every funeral. Mayken watches from the stern castle but her attention is not on the proceedings. She's watching for patterns in the sea spray, or ripples in a bucket, or unlikely puddles on deck.

She has heard the hushed conversations among the passengers and crew and the suppressed fear in their voices. Those poor souls did not die from the usual afflictions of sea voyages. They say they were carried off by a pestilence unknown and no one has seen anything like it.

Mayken knows the source of this pestilence: Bullebak, on the prowl again.

She walks the sweltering deck, pacing with the movement of the ship. She touches the carved wooden heads, hot in the sun, for good luck. They are losing their features now, their faces worn away by the elements.

Pelgrom cannot be trusted, so she will search the ship alone. Wear her disguise and learn the movements of the crew. Find her own routes to avoid Stonecutter, judge better when to run across the main deck and when not to. She doesn't need anyone's help to catch Bullebak. Only perhaps Smoert can lend a hand.

The corridor outside her cabin is filled with a stagnant odor. By the door an oily footprint lies. A monstrous foot, giant, three toed.

Fearful for Imke, Mayken rushes inside.

Imke lies disheveled in her bunk, twisted in her bedding, in a deep fever. Her foot, hitherto neatly bandaged, is now unwrapped. Her dressings are blood soaked and tangled on the floor. Her foot is hideously swollen, the stump of her big toe raw and glistening. The skin, nearly to her ankle joint, is the color of liver.

Mayken rarely leaves Imke's side, watching for signs that her nursemaid's fever is abating, or for signs that she is slipping under, or for signs of Bullebak. The barber-surgeon calls daily. Aris talks with Imke in a low, grave voice. When he leaves, Imke pretends she's not crying. Mayken knows that they are planning to take off Imke's foot when landfall is made. During this longer stop the sick will be taken ashore to recuperate on solid ground.

Mayken could talk to Aris about Bullebak.

She tries to get everything right in her mind. What has she seen? Rats running away. A strange footprint. An eel curled up at Imke's hip. What has she felt? Fear big enough to crush the breath from her.

Aris does not have the time to listen to such tales, much less believe them. So Mayken, saying nothing, sits on by the old woman's side.

A roar of joy runs through the ship. It can only mean that land has been sighted.

Imke wakes from her doze. "Go and see where we are in the world."

"I don't want to leave you."

"I'll be here when you get back." Imke smiles.

Mayken doesn't like her smile at all. It's the smile from the statue of Mother Mary in Imke's decorated church. It is the smile of someone with higher, otherworldly things to think about. Like Heaven and dying.

Mayken pushes her way onto the crowded deck. She'll take a quick look, then run back to Imke. The whole ship is celebrating. Mayken sees the remarkable sight of the skipper and the upper-merchant out together, albeit at opposite ends of the poop deck. Skipper Jacobsz has his burly legs planted, a wolf's smile on a face ruddy with wine and health. Upper-merchant Pelsaert stands twig-limbed with persistent illness, his red coat sagging off him, his face wan and relieved. Under-merchant Cornelisz slithers between the two, smiling at everyone and no one.

This time the land is no faraway smudge, it is majestic in the clearing sea mist. A great mountain leveled before its peak, like a topped spice cone, beautiful in the morning light. Even hardened sailors weep.

Despite Mayken's pleas, she is refused permission to accompany Imke to shore. It is bad enough that the child has been cooped up in a cabin these past days with a feverish servant. Pelsaert sends Mayken a note saying he has a responsibility to deliver Antony van den Heuvel his daughter alive.

Mayken helps to make Imke as comfortable as possible. The old woman is swaddled in blankets and lashed to a plank that will be lowered into the waiting yawl.

"I had to haul my own arse up into this ship," Imke whispers. "But look, I'm leaving like a queen."

Mayken cannot hold Imke's hand, it is tucked inside her wrappings, so she pats her tightly bound body. She looks into Imke's dear old thin face.

"Please come back."

Imke smiles her otherworldly smile. "Lady Creesje will look out for you. It's all arranged."

"I don't want Lady bloody Creesje!"

Aris touches Mayken lightly on the shoulder.

Mayken bends to kiss Imke. She closes her eyes and two quiet tears fall onto her nursemaid's face. Imke makes tutting noises. No crying now.

"You were peeling apples and the knife slipped," says Mayken. "Then you baked your fingers into a pie."

"Keep guessing."

The convoy is anchored in the harbor. Movement of crew between the ships is forbidden, but a few hours after the upper-merchant departs for the mainland another party sets out. Skipper Jacobsz, Zwaantie, and under-merchant Cornelisz have a boat launched. The skipper commands it to be rowed by four sailors. He demands provisions. Pelgrom produces baskets of food and wine and the deckhands lower them. The boat bobs away. Some distance out, the skipper stands up and the boat shakes and Zwaantie's shriek is carried over the water.

Those on deck watch as the skipper goes visiting.

With her servant otherwise engaged, there is a place in Creesje's cabin for a new companion. Mayken's chest is moved next door. Creesje's cabin is identical but smells a lot better. Efforts have been made to make it homey; there is a rug on the floor and paintings on the wall. The paintings are of country scenes and fruit. This time Mayken must take the bottom bunk; Creesje insists on making it up herself. Mayken watches from the corner, her heart sore. Creesje pats the bunk. "Come, sit with me."

Mayken obeys.

Creesje's voice is kindly, her eyes clear. "Aris will care for Imke. In the meantime, let me care for you."

"I don't need caring for."

"Friends take care of one another."

Mayken considers. "I'll take care of you too, then."

Creesje smiles. "You like to roam, I did too as a child. But be cautious, Mayken. This ship daily becomes more hazardous."

Mayken catches a hint of something in her voice but Creesje's face is serene.

Creesje pats her hand. "Now, shall we tidy you up?"

Creesje undertakes the tidying of Mayken with gentle patience. She is no fierce Zwaantie, vicious with the comb and harsh with the scrubbing. The most pressing problem is Mayken's rampant head lice. If she lived before-the-mast, her head would be shaved and her hair thrown overboard. There are several small girls on the gun deck whose stubbled little heads attest to this. But given her position, Mayken keeps her hair.

Creesje painstakingly douses her in preparations and seeks out her troublesome passengers with a fine-tooth comb. Next, Creesje supervises a thorough wash, having water brought to the cabin. She catches sight of Holdfast's witch stone, which Mayken has taken to wearing around her neck on a ratty leather thong.

"It's for prophecies," she explains.

Creesje speaks kindly. "I have gold chains, if you'd prefer?"

Mayken hesitates.

Creesje kisses her. "You can tuck it under your bodice."

Sometime in the night, Mayken wakes. With Creesje asleep she creeps out into the corridor, opening the door to the deck. She looks up in the hope she'll see Holdfast, then she remembers he's a chosen oarsman for Pelsaert. The sky is dizzy with stars. The flat-topped mountain makes a sharp-edged silhouette against the decorated heavens. On deck, a group of sailors is watching over the gunwale as something approaches. Mayken goes to look and sees a lantern meander toward the ship. She hears the plash of oars and a hollow bumping against the *Batavia*'s flank. Then Zwaantie's dark laugh rings clear in the quiet, followed by skipper Jacobsz's slurs and growls.

Mayken scuttles back to her cabin. She has no wish to be in trouble with the ferocious skipper.

On waking, Mayken lies confused. There is no loud-snoring Imke, just Creesje up and about in her shift, searching Mayken's chest for a change of clothes but finding nothing practical or clean. Creesje will set about sewing new day-clothes for her charge and will send Mayken's linens to be cleaned by a soldier's wife skilled in these things.

Mayken slips out to find some peace and to think about Imke.

No peace is to be had this morning. The ship is a place of upheaval and activity. There is much work to do in preparation for the final leg of the *Batavia*'s journey. Caulkers are busy stuffing up the leaks. Carpenters and sail menders have been set to work; the smell of new-shaved wood and musty canvas fills the air. The decks are sanded with the flat wide stones the sailors call Bibles. On the lower decks cleansing herbs are burnt. The rats that survived the last cull are chased from one end of the ship to the other. The Below World children join in, shrill with glee. With the motion of the ship reduced in the sheltered bay to no more than a pleasant bob, jobs are accomplished with ease. No one dies. The soldiers are allowed another hour a day on deck. With Stonecutter sent to shore on the yawl with the senior sailors, clerks, and cadets, there is a holiday air. Pelgrom has gone too, somehow managing to contrive a place on the yawl. Mayken is struck by the unfairness of it all. A cabin steward is permitted to make landfall, to go about serving and scraping—but she is denied the right to stay with her dear sick Imke!

All the well-to-do passengers remain. The predikant holds daily sermons for them and gives edifying speeches. The passengers are as idle as the crew are industrious. But all are in good spirits. With skipper Jacobsz showing no sign of emerging from his cabin, the under-merchant Jeronimus Cornelisz keeps some kind of order. Cornelisz is mostly to be found out on the poop deck reading, wine at his elbow. He is visited there by the young cadets remaining on board. They flock around him, swaggering with their swords. Ribald laughter is heard. He is the leader of a gaggle of geese in plumed hats.

Everyday rules are eased, distinctions dissolved. People go about their business free from reprimands.

There is no better time for Mayken to revisit the Below World.

With a bundle under her arm, she skulks to the pigpen. It's a quick change into her breeches and cap. She stows her gown with a prayer against the reek of pig shit, grabs her jug, and heads for the gun deck.

There are fewer people below but more commotion. Mayken

makes her way straight to the galley. The door is open. The cook sleeps on a stool, his big red face against a flour sack. A filthy Smoert is scrubbing soot from the firepit. He looks up and smiles.

"What is it we're looking for again?"

Mayken considers. If Smoert is scared he may not help, and an extra pair of hands might prove useful when trying to trap an ancient shape-shifting killer in a pottery jug.

"An eel sort of creature," replies Mayken.

Smoert shivers. "If there's one thing I don't like, it's eels."

"They're better than rats."

"I'll take rats over eels any day."

They climb down onto the orlop deck. Mayken first, Smoert following. The animals stand hock-deep in straw but it's cleaner now. Smoert holds out his hand to a cow and makes soft happy noises. She shuffles over. Smoert pats her cheek and scratches her nose.

"We had cows," he says.

"Your family?"

"No, in the village. My family don't have a pot to piss in."

"Did they send you to sea?"

"No, I sent myself." Smoert smiles a little bitterly. "Seemed like a good idea. I miss the cows and horses, though."

"Will you always be a kitchen boy?"

Smoert considers this. "I've never thought about it. I hope I bloody won't."

"You can come and live with me and Imke in Batavia. My father has stallions. I don't know about cows."

"What would I do?"

"You could be in charge of the animals. Would you like that?"

The cow flicks her ear and gazes at Smoert, as if she's waiting for his answer too. Smoert glances at Mayken shyly and nods.

The soldiers are mostly at ease on the gun deck, gambling with the sailors, but a few stragglers remain. Mayken takes the lantern and bends to the hatch that leads to the hold. It's locked. She looks up at Smoert in dismay. "How do we get down there?"

Smoert shrugs. "Get a key."

Pelgrom had a key, of course. Mayken frowns: who else would have one? "Does the cook have a key?"

"They wouldn't trust that fat bastard with one. The provost might, or the under-merchant?"

Mayken thinks. There's no way they would give her a key. Unless she somehow just took it? She'd likely be hanged for that. She puts down the jug and the bag of bacon rinds that Smoert has contributed to the hunt.

"Let's just wait here for a bit," she says. "Maybe the creature will come to us."

Smoert looks worried. "Like an eel, you say?"

"Don't worry, we have the jug, it'll just flip straight in."

"A small eel, is it?"

"You want to know more about the stallions?"

And Mayken describes the fine stallions and the red and white roses around the doorway of her father's fine house. Just for Smoert, she adds a green field full of pretty cows. She even names the cows. Smoert smiles in the stuffy dim. He begins to smell the clean hay and the fresh air and feel the bright sunshine on his poor scarred face, of this Mayken is sure.

After a while they just sit quietly. There's nothing doing. Smoert picks his scabs and Mayken gets tired of watching out. The creature can't be near because she feels no fear. Only boredom and a slight hunger.

"We must try another way, Smoert."

"All right."

"We'll ask John Pinten's advice."

Smoert rubs his nose. "If you're going down the stinky end, I'll stay here with the jug."

"You're scared of the dark, aren't you?"

Smoert looks embarrassed, his eyes big in his blotched face, bald of eyebrows, tufty of hair.

"Keep on with the jug," says Mayken kindly. "I'll go alone."

She makes her way down the orlop deck. The air is less hellishly fetid now but it is darker because most of the lanterns have been put out.

At the end of the deck, she calls for him. "John Pinten."

Nothing. Perhaps he was taken in the yawl; some of the soldiers accompanied the upper-merchant.

"John Pinten, are you here?"

A glim and a lantern lit.

"To what do I owe the pleasure of your company today?"

John Pinten listens to Mayken's dilemma. The search for Bullebak thwarted by a locked hatch door.

"You have your jug, your bacon rinds ready?"

Mayken nods. "Smoert is lying in wait with them."

"Smoert being?"

"The kitchen boy."

"Of course." The soldier smiles. "I believe it's time to call off your search, Obbe. The creature is not in the hold. It has gone from the ship."

"How do you know?"

"I haven't heard it lately." John Pinten shuffles up on his elbow and reaches for the jug nearby. "I suspect it's taken a trip to shore; who wouldn't, given half a chance?"

Mayken looks at the soldier intently. "Are you telling the truth?"

"Of course." John Pinten smiles, wild-eyed in the half dark.

"If you do hear it—"

"I'll tell it to go and find you and your kitchen boy."

❧

Mayken returns to Smoert.

"It's not in the hold. John Pinten thinks it's gone ashore."

"We could ask around," says Smoert. "Maybe someone's seen it?"

"What if I get you into trouble? I'm not supposed to be here."

Smoert shrugs. "I'm always in trouble. It'll make no difference."

"All right. But if we get caught, I'll take the blame." Mayken pats his arm.

Smoert reddens and looks down at his knees.

The investigation begins.

Smoert opens with each potential witness: "Have you seen or heard anything of an eel sort of creature?"

To this Mayken adds: "It leaves footprints." She measures out the size with her hands. "And gives poisonous bites."

"Stinks like bilge water," Smoert volunteers.

"Changes in size, and . . ."

Smoert nudges her. "Go on."

"Hides in puddles and things."

The soldiers either curse at the children or laugh like it's a game; either way, they get no sensible answers. The sailors are different. They listen carefully, solemnly; sometimes they even ask questions themselves.

One sailor saw a dead eel in a barrel of vinegar. But it might not have been dead, because you know what eels are like.

The gunner's wife saw something unnatural looking in through a porthole.

A carpenter saw an odd figure late one afternoon when he was repairing a yardarm, a hunched shape prowling along the deck below. But it could have been the first mate's shadow.

Soon any number of accidents and annoyances are blamed on Bullebak. Mislaid tools, frayed ropes, broken platters. Bites are revealed. One old sailor exhibits a poisonous toe not unlike Imke's.

But then Smoert is needed in the kitchen and there will be hell to pay if the cook wakes and he's not there. And Mayken must retrace her steps to the Above World and change back into her pig-shit dress.

"Come again tomorrow?" urges Smoert. "We can keep looking."

Bit by bit Mayken and Smoert build up a picture of the strange happenings occurring almost daily on board the ship. People start to flag the two down as they roam the decks with their jug and bag of scraps.

A footprint was seen on the ceiling, would that count?

A sea mist drifted through the cabin with the hint of a burble, could that tally?

Obbe is soon part of the Below World as Mayken is part of the Above.

During the great Bullebak hunt, Obbe learns about the lives lived before-the-mast. And it is Obbe who is responsible for a series of little kindnesses.

Obbe leaves a ribbon for the gunner's wife, who mourns the loss of her front tooth. Obbe finds a pair of clogs for the soldier's wife with swollen feet. Obbe brings pickled plums to the down-at-heart sailor.

Obbe knows the people now and they know Obbe.

Sometimes they say Obbe's name with a wink or an arch look.

"They know who I really am," Mayken whispers to Smoert.

"They won't tell," Smoert whispers back.

Mayken begins to realize that such is the divide between the Above and Below Worlds, her secret may not carry past the mast. As she grows in affection for the people of the ship's belly, the people grow in affection for her. They look out for the small, gray-eyed girl in badly sewn breeches and cabin boy's cap, with her jug and bag of bacon rinds.

The yawl returns with the first results of the upper-merchant's negotiations: food supplies and goods, and barrels of fresh water. Pelsaert himself will follow shortly, those on land returning as the convoy prepares to set sail for Batavia. Creesje is made a gift of a strange downy fruit, which she shares with Mayken. It tastes fragrant and sweet but afterward neither of them can remember the flavor. Creesje is kind and never asks questions as to where Mayken disappears to. As long as Mayken submits to regular hair brushings and face scrubbings she seems happy. If Creesje can smell pig-shit off the gown Mayken is wearing, she doesn't say. The witch stone hangs always around Mayken's neck however she is dressed.

Mayken leans over the gunwale, Creesje beside her. Here, finally, is the boat carrying the sick. Mayken can make out Aris at the prow. As the boat nears, Mayken peers down at the passengers. Some are swaddled and lashed to boards, ready to be raised up on ropes. A few are frail but upright and able to sit on a plank by themselves and be hoisted.

Mayken babbles about the stories she'll tell Imke and the new games they will invent. Creesje, her face sadder than ever, lays a gentle hand on her arm but Mayken cannot stop talking. As the last of the sick are brought on board the *Batavia* Mayken finally falls quiet.

CHAPTER TWENTY-TWO

1989

There are no quiet corners on this island now. The shouts of the children and the roars of the mothers carry even over the arguments of seabirds. Kids in dinghies going about in the water. Kids toddling on the shore and pissing in the sea. Kids roaming the paths, throwing stones at the sea eagles' nests, chasing snakes. Every camp seems to be in chaos, women smoking on beach chairs, scrubbing babies in buckets, all-day visits. The fishermen are relieved to go out. Gil sees that in their faces. They board their boats at dawn when the island is beautifully silent and the rosy light makes the wet shingle shine and touches the sea with fire.

Some mornings, like this morning, Dutch asks Gil to help him carry gear to the boat. Joss will have long gone down, his bed neatly made. Gil wonders why his grandfather doesn't just sleep on the boat, but then maybe he does. Gil has the esky to carry today. It's heavy because inside is the food for the whole day, and fishermen work hard so they eat well. Gil uses both hands. Sometimes he has to put the esky down and have a breather. Dutch usually carries it the last bit of the way.

Even in the early morning Dutch is talkative. He tells lame stories about an odd seal out who eventually fits in, or a mammy sea eagle who dies tragically and leaves her chick but the chick grows up okay after all. Gil should point out that it doesn't work like this in nature; the weak and the young don't stand a chance.

Dutch is looking at him. "Gil?"

"Yeah?"

"I said, have you plans for today?"

Stealing an outboard, finding a compass, fixing up an escape boat.

"Not really."

"A few more kids to play with now?"

"I just like being with Enkidu."

"Do something with your time here, Gil."

"I'm learning the history of the island."

"Good man. There's enough of it." Dutch hesitates. "Only don't *dwell* on the dark things. The *Batavia* story is not really for kids."

"But there were kids in the story, weren't there? Kids on the ship and kids getting killed?"

Dutch opens his mouth and closes it again. Looks out to sea. Starts up again about Mammy Sea Eagle.

Joss is on board *Ramona*, tidying, rearranging. He ignores them. Dutch boards and Gil passes the esky into the boat. Dutch looks up along the jetty and grimaces.

Gil turns to see Roper approaching. His body swelling with argument. A lurid redness to his face in the dawn light. Behind him, Frank and Cherry walk abreast. Frank's baseball cap is pulled down, the lower part of his face looking sour. Cherry is wearing a roguish air of expectation. He keeps his eyes on Roper, as if he's the entertainment.

"You took our deckie, old man," says Roper.

Joss is inspecting the contents of a bucket.

"You hear me?"

"Ah, come on. I'd already left your father's employ, Roper," says Dutch.

Roper turns on him. "Keep the fuck out of it!" Papa Zanetti nudges his son on. "This isn't over, Hurley," says Roper.

Joss mumbles something into the bucket. Roper blows. He's half into Joss's boat, roaring. Papa Zanetti reaches a sinewy arm out, pulls him back, and says something low in his son's ear. Roper goes limp and shakes his head, wiping his nose with his fingers.

"Leave earlier tomorrow," says Frank to Joss.

Joss straightens up and turns to Frank. "I'll leave whatever time I fucking want."

A growl from Roper. Frank marches his son down the jetty. Cherry, smirking, follows behind.

The boats head out. Frank and Cherry are first to cast off in *Sherri Blue*, the biggest, newest vessel moored at the island. Roper follows alone in *Waygood*. *Ramona* sets out after, bouncing through the waves, heading toward the horizon. Joss at the helm, Dutch doing things with ropes. Gil watches them a while, then turns and walks back down the jetty.

Birgit is standing outside the scientists' hut. She smiles at him and mimes drinking from a cup.

"I hear you have a tortoise?"

Gil inspects his coffee. It's less milky than last time. "His name is Enkidu."

"Seriously?" Birgit laughs, working it out. "Then you are Gilgamesh?"

"No. I'm Gil."

"It's quite a story. Bravery, adventure—"

"I like the *Batavia* story better."

"Well, there was adventure in that, setting off in a wooden ship to sail halfway around the world. Bravery too, when the survivors resisted Jeronimus Cornelisz. The soldiers who were dispersed to another island to die, led by Wiebbe Hayes, fought back."

"I thought Jeronimus took all the weapons?"

"They used whatever they could find. Sharpened sticks, rocks."

Gil surveys the boxes on the shelves. There looks to be a jumble of new finds up there.

"I'd like to see where you found the ivory bobbin, Gil. Would you show me?"

Gil hesitates. "It's up at the camp."

"We could take a stroll?" She smiles. "I won't tell your grandfather if you don't."

Gil takes Birgit to the windblown spot between the dunny and Joss Hurley's hut. It's the place where Dutch dries their clothes, only today there's no laundry dancing, just empty lines strummed by the wind. This will be as good a place as any; didn't some bloke on the island discover bones under his washing line?

Birgit crouches down and looks at the ground. She has come alone with a camera, a bundle of sticks, and a notepad. She has a few tools in a canvas bag and a windbreak. Gil helped her carry her gear up.

"The fishermen generally work with us, now that we're here. Your grandfather is one of the exceptions."

"Will you tell him about the bobbin I gave you?"

"Let's just make a few assessments today." Birgit looks at Gil. "We'll take it slowly, don't worry."

Gil nods.

"Where did you find it, Gil?"

"Where that rock is."

"How deep?"

Gil measures the air with his hands, a shallow depth, so she can be done and gone quicker.

Birgit digs, her hat pulled down against the sun, her back bent. Gil watches her from the kitchen window. He wills her to find nothing. Then he feels bad and wills her to find something.

At lunchtime Birgit comes into the kitchen. She pulls trail bars and cigarettes from her rucksack, then goes off to use the dunny. Gil takes his chance and slips three continental cigarettes out of the squashy packet on the table. As an afterthought he puts two back and then there's Birgit returning. The crunch of her footsteps, the outline of her outside the screen door. Gil throws the cigarette into a drawer.

Because Birgit is a guest, they go through to the lounge room. Gil does up plates of crackers topped with tinned meat and dots of tomato sauce. He brings coffee, which he makes powerfully strong for both of them, hoping Birgit will take the hint. Birgit lights a cigarette and the whole room smells of glamorous European tobacco. Gil will have to open the window wide before the others come home.

He goes to fetch an ashtray. When he returns, Birgit is reading the bunyip book. She waves it at Gil. "It slipped out from behind the cabinet."

Gil finds he isn't surprised. "It was my mum's."

Birgit smokes and reads. Gil pushes a plate of crackers nearer and she looks up and smiles but doesn't take one.

"Well, that was disturbing." She puts the book down and takes a sip of coffee. "I'd forgotten about the bunyip myth. You know its origins?"

Gil shakes his head.

"The Moorundi people of the Murray River gave an early account of a terrifying water creature, although instances of the bunyip are found all over the country. Accounts differ, which might have something to do with white explorers asking First Nation people to put into words something so frightening it cannot be described."

Gil frowns. He doesn't follow.

"How do you describe dread, Gil? That's what the bunyip is: an attempt to give fear a shape."

Gil thinks on this.

"Everyone's fear looks different," Birgit continues. "So everyone's creature looks different. But they all eat crayfish, women, and children. That seems to be universal."

"They're just warnings for kids. Not to play near water or talk to strangers."

"Life is precarious. Take precautions against bunyips." She smiles and finishes her coffee. "Come and see what I've been up to."

She's moved a fair bit of coral rubble, creating a shallow trench.

"No bones, I'm afraid. They're not as easy to find as Silvia thinks they are."

Gil is half-disappointed.

"If they're buried below the water table, they could be eroded. Seeping water and abrasive material, like grit, will scour bones to dust." She glances at Gil. "Or maybe it's a bunyip down there crunching everything up."

They both laugh, even though it's lame.

"And generations of nesting birds have churned up the ground. Nothing stays put, not even the dead."

"It's very sad that so many people died here," Gil ventures, feeling as if it's somehow expected.

"It's more than sad, it's shameful."

They look down into the shallow trench.

"The greatest disgrace of humankind is the failure of the strong to protect the weak. We don't need monsters, Gil, we are the monsters."

Gil doesn't reply. He senses Birgit's words are not for him somehow. Maybe she's telling the wind and the sea. Maybe she's telling a listening bunyip.

With Birgit gone, Gil walks out to the Raggedy Tree. The weathered toys and tributes look forlorn. A teddy holds a stuffed heart saying *Marry Me*. A spinning top lies on its side, rusted and fused. A set of crayons have melted to a clump.

He'd thought about what to bring. Not the bunyip book, which would scare even a bloody ghost. Not the jigsaws in the front room with half the pieces missing, they'd be no good to anyone. So he's brought nothing.

"Sorry," he says to no one.

He sits down and watches the ribbons flutter on the branches for the longest time.

CHAPTER TWENTY-THREE

1629

There is no fairness in the world.

That liar Pelgrom lives. The whoring skipper lives. The gunner with the squint who beats his wife lives.

But Imke—good Imke—doesn't.

Mayken's blind with tears. Creesje strokes her wet hair and Aris is summoned to administer a calming cordial. Mayken refuses to drink it. She doesn't want to be calm. She wants to tear the ship apart, rivet by rivet, bolt by bolt, drag the caulking out with her teeth, lever up the boards with her fingernails. She wants to swing off the shrouds screaming and rend the main sail.

Instead, she sleeps.

She is back in her old cabin. Above her, the flame in the gimballed lantern gutters and dies. Darkness! Mayken stumbles out of her bunk. Feeling with her hands she makes her way out of the cabin and along the corridor to the deck.

The deck is empty: no sailors, no passengers, no Stonecutter, no skipper. The sails are slack and the moon above a big white cheese. The sea is mirror flat but reflects nothing. Mayken moves across the moonlit deck, passing the empty pigpen and the two stowed boats.

Here is the hatch to the Below World. She goes to open it but her hands are full. A bag of bacon scraps. A Beardman jug. She hears a noise, the sound of plashing water, and turns. Wet footprints appear, one after another, over the side of the gunwale, plodding down across the deck, three toed, stinking.

She wakes and Creesje is next to her, praying.

"It's back."

The final jobs have been completed, the goods and provisions loaded. Pelsaert gives the order to set sail and the skipper complies. Batavia will be their next landfall.

The deck is full as the *Batavia* leaves Table Bay. The people take one last look at land before they return to their corners before-the-mast or aft-the-mast, to their prescribed places in the Below World or Above.

The *Batavia* sails and the rest of the fleet follows. Soon enough there is no land to be seen, no kind bay or beautiful mountain, just the changing landscape of the open sea.

A thrill runs through the ship as news of the skipper's dressing-down spreads (who would have known Pelsaert had it in him?). The skipper, it seems, disgraced himself, the ship, the Company, his hometown, the mother who gave birth to him, and—most of all—the upper-merchant. Not only did the skipper (with his mistress and the under-merchant in tow) visit the *Batavia*'s sister ships at anchor, he boarded them, outranked the other skippers, attempted to brawl with them, and insulted them richly. As commander of the fleet, the upper-merchant was passed letters of angry complaint.

The cabin steward—Pelgrom being the instrument of this circulating tattle—heard the whole thing. The upper-merchant warned the skipper he would stand trial in Batavia for drunken lewdness. The skipper tried to laugh it off. The upper-merchant's response was steely. The two men parted in spitting hate.

The skipper retained his swagger but it would stick in his craw to submit to Pelsaert. But this is the way with the Company. When a sailing is made for profit, the man who balances the accounts has authority over the man who reads the tides.

The *Batavia* sails and night falls. As this news is digested, tensions grow and factions emerge. The clerks are for the upper-merchant and the sailors are for the skipper. The gunner's wife can't decide, but not liking Zwaantie she opts for Pelsaert. But Pelsaert, it seems, is back in the grips of his old disease, sweating and raving and confined to his cabin. Creesje, who has affection for the man, visits him there and returns to Mayken teary-eyed. She fears greatly for him, she says. He has strength of spirit but his body is weak and he has dangerous enemies. Creesje reddens, as if she's said too much, and Mayken pretends not to notice.

Many are sick again with the renewed motion of the ship as the swell picks up. The weather worsens. The seas are monstrous and a gale shrieks. Creesje has Mayken kneel beside her and they pray together. The cabin rocks, the lantern swings wildly. They cannot help but listen to the scream of the wind and the ship's groans as she labors up every peak to roll and crash in the troughs.

It is too dangerous for the sailors to go out on deck to take in the sails. All hands are called to the pump. The sea scours the deck and washes down the hatches. The gunports are closed and the deck is in darkness. The galley cannot operate in such conditions, so there is no hot food to sustain the sailors. If they can spare a thought it is for the other ships out at sea.

A lull in the storm and the sailors are on deck with the carpenters and the sail menders to see what can be done. It is with dismay that the crew realize that the *Batavia* is alone in the ocean. The skipper, on whose watch the fleet was lost, is unapologetic. Such things happen on rough seas. The stern light went out, making it impossible for the other vessels in the convoy to keep them in their sight. It is a blow felt throughout the ship. The reassurance of other sails in the distance—gone. All feel the hand of fate, some malevolent intervention, of what kind they cannot say.

The *Batavia*'s first baby is born to a before-the-mast girl on a day of squalls and scudding clouds. The girl and her infant are taken up to the Great Cabin to receive good wishes. Mrs. Predikant covers her nose with a handkerchief while the predikant says a few lofty words. In the absence of the upper-merchant, still interred in his cabin, the chief clerk gives the mother a coin. Mayken presents a length of good cloth and the girl smiles and bends down to show her the infant. Mayken touches the tiny fingers with wonder. The baby's head is no bigger than a turnip but she can scream louder than a pig. The new mother's appearance on deck sends the superstitious sailors muttering. One in, one out, says the gunner's wife. If thoughts immediately turn to the upper-merchant, no one mentions it.

The sailors catch an albatross. Its wingspan the height of a man. They bring it down with hooks and poles and it crashes frantic through the rigging and gets tangled in the shrouds. They strangle it on the deck. Mayken weeps to see it killed. The predikant tells her they make tobacco pouches from its feet. Mayken tells the predikant she hates all sailors. He cautions her not to add to the hatred on board and rouses his family in another circuit of prayers.

That night, before they sleep, Creesje and Mayken say a prayer for the majestic bird. Nowadays there are no stories, only prayers. Mayken's life before, in Haarlem with Imke, searching for Bullebak with Smoert, feels like a dream.

Tonight, they will leave the lantern lit and their clothes laid out should they need to dress quickly. Creesje cannot explain why.

In the night the sea is calm; the lantern hangs still. Unknotting the leather cord around her neck, Mayken turns on her side and holds up the witch stone for the first time since the night with Imke. She looks through and sees nothing but the cabin wall.

CHAPTER TWENTY-FOUR

1989

Gil is waiting for the tortoise's reply. Enkidu communicates through shuffles, keeping still, and the retraction of head and limbs. This is important because his facial expressions give nothing away, being uniformly sour. Enkidu's opinion is important; that the tortoise is wise, Gil has no doubt. There is shrewdness in that beaked dinosaur face and those gimlet eyes. Dutch calculated Enkidu's age using the patterns on the tortoise's shell. At nine hundred years old, how could he not be wise?

Enkidu is perfectly still. This means he's deliberating.

On the *For* side, they have tinned meat and crackers, a map, a set of plastic oars, and a boat that hasn't sunk yet. On the *Against* they have sixty kilometers of open sea between Beacon Island and the mainland. But that's never going to change.

"People sail around the world in all sorts of things," Gil observes.

Enkidu slowly lurches forward, nodding.

Gil feels a rush of love for his friend and kisses him on the head. He would pick him up but he's just polished Enkidu's shell with Dutch's surfboard wax. Enkidu looks the business for nine hundred years old. Apart from his toenails.

"We'll give you a manicure before we leave."

Gil writes this on the *To Do* part of his escape plan, under *Steal an outboard*.

A knock, and his bedroom door is pushed open.

"A word," says his grandfather.

They sit out on the veranda, Joss with a beer, Gil with a juice. The sound of Dutch playing guitar in the Love Shack is carried up on the wind. The old man raises his bottle and looks at the sunset through it. Gil does the same with his glass: a juicy orange horizon. Joss holds his beer in his bandaged hand; his fingers can now grip larger things, but not a pen or fork or a cigarette just yet.

"What happened under the washing lines?" he asks.

Gil looks over at the washing lines. Towels and singlets crisp-dried by the sun, waiting for Dutch to take them in. The land beneath has been restored to how Birgit found it. How could Joss even know?

"You were seen. You and the scientist."

Gil glances at his grandfather, confounded. By who? The gulls? No one passed.

Joss is studying his beer. "It's better if you tell the truth, boy."

"I told her I was digging under the washing lines and found stuff from the wreck. Then I gave her the bobbin in a tin from your wardrobe."

Joss takes a sip of his beer. "That's not far off the spot it was found. Was it yours to give?"

"No." Gil thinks a moment. "She's going to take a closer look at it." Joss grunts.

Gil glances at him. "Are you going to beat me?"

"No." His grandfather frowns. "Jesus."

They sit in silence for a while.

Joss drains his bottle and gets up. "You don't take without asking me first, understand?" He holds out his hand for Gil's empty glass. "Want another?"

Gil doesn't. "Okay."

The old man nods stiffly.

Sunset with the sky on fire and the dazzle catching on the ocean and the seabirds revolving with flashes of white just to add to the beauty of it. Dutch joins them on the veranda. The men drink beer and Gil gets a shandy. Dutch puts down his rollie and picks up his guitar.

Dutch has a great voice and can sing any David Bowie or Bruce Springsteen song. Only he changes the lyrics. So that Roper's brain is missing in space or Bill Nord is tearing up the tarmac on the run from Geraldton.

Gil sees, for the first time, his grandfather's face broken in a laugh. Joss is transformed. The best of it is when he turns to Gil and winks. Then Gil is full of sudden joy, with the sunset, the shandy, and Roper's brain orbiting Mars. With Joss laughing and winking with pirate glee and Dutch grinning. Even Enkidu looks a little less pissed off than usual as he bumbles around at their feet.

Dutch sings some of the songs he has written himself. These are about red-haired women letting him down. Joss looks thoughtful at these. Then Dutch sings some depressing Irish songs about dead mothers and wooden crosses. Joss gets watery-eyed at these.

Enkidu likes "Puff, the Magic Dragon." Gil likes the one about a racehorse who never drinks water, only drinks wine, and who has a golden mane and a silver bridle. So Dutch plays both songs twice over.

The sun disappears and the moths begin to reel around the outside light. Joss gets up with a sigh. He walks to the door, stopping only to pat Gil on the shoulder. For a brief moment Gil feels the weight of his hand and it says *You're all right*.

Gil and Dutch stay out on the veranda. Dutch quietly strumming his guitar. Gil thinking. Not about the shipwrecked dead, nor about Mum, nor even about escaping this island in a flat-bottomed boat.

Gil is wondering what makes everyone hate Joss Hurley.

He thinks maybe it's time to ask.

"What's wrong with him?" Dutch wears a half smile and keeps his voice low. "Other than he's a miserable auld bastard?"

"That's why people don't like him?"

"Yes and no." Dutch takes a puff of his rollie and puts down his guitar. "You have to understand something about this life. It's hard graft, dangerous. There's rivalry out here, arguments, disagreements, but the men know that if the shit hits they can depend on one another. For their lives, Gil."

Gil thinks about this. "So they're mates?"

Dutch nods. "Underneath all the bitching they are. But Joss—he's no one's mate."

"No one can depend on him?"

"And he depends on no one. Give and take, the same thing here."

Gil sees it's as simple as that: Joss has no mates. No back-patting or sharing a beer with the other fishermen, no putting the world to rights. But worse than that, people don't even look at him, or talk to him. It would get lonely, even if you weren't the sort that got lonely.

"It's all a question of trust." Dutch lights a rollie. "You know your granda started out as a deckie for the Zanetti family?"

Gil shakes his head.

"Frank's brother, Marco, was his skipper. This was Marco's place." Dutch includes the hut and the shadowy shape of the dunny in a sweep of his rollie. "Then tragedy struck. Marco and Joss were out fishing when a storm hit. Marco went overboard. Joss somehow brought the boat back alone."

"Marco drowned?"

"He did. Then his wife—his widow—gave *Ramona*, this place, and every last craypot to your granda."

"Why?"

"That's what everyone on the island wanted to know. Why would she give everything her late husband had owned to a deckie?" Dutch takes a puff of his rollie. "What makes it worse is that it had been promised to Roper."

"Roper?"

"Marco and his wife had no kids. Roper should have inherited his uncle's livelihood." He pauses. "Fishermen know the risks; these kinds of things are discussed in families."

Gil looks around him. This veranda with its heat-buckled roof, the rattling windows, the weatherworn bench, the generator shed, the bloody dunny, all should belong to Roper Zanetti.

"That's why Roper is so angry."

"Ah, it's one of many reasons, Gil. But the change of plan un-settled everyone." Dutch looks awkward. "Some said Joss had been friendly toward Marco's wife."

Being *friendly* means *doing it*, Gil can tell from Dutch's face.

"Joss returned the next season. Moved into this hut, skippered the boat, started fishing as if everything had always been his. The following season he brought a new wife."

"Granny Iris."

Dutch nods. "The Zanettis were bitter about how things had turned out. They spread rumors. You see, there were no witnesses the day Marco was lost."

"They said he'd been killed?"

"Not outright. But Frank made it clear that your grandfather was not a man to be trusted. As head of the foremost family here, no one would go against Frank. So your granda became everyone's enemy."

Gil considers this. "He couldn't be mates with anyone, even if he wanted to."

Dutch nods. "Exactly."

"That's not fair!" Gil is surprised at how angry he feels at this treatment of the old man.

Dutch continues. "Everyone expected him to sell up but he didn't.

Season after season he returned, even though the Zanettis made life hard for him."

"How?"

"No one would deckie for him, for one thing. He's managed alone all these years. At first because he had to, then I suppose he got used to working solo."

"Now you've come back to deckie for him."

"I'm his last resort. Besides, imagine how much it pisses Roper off." He smiles at Gil. "Maybe you'll deckie for your granda one day?"

"No."

"Then you fancy yourself the skipper?"

"I don't want to be a fisherman."

"Don't be put off. The sea can be mild and boats don't want to sink. Here—" Dutch searches in his shorts pocket then brings something out in his closed fist. "Catch."

Gil does. He opens his hand. On his palm is the stone with the hole right through from Dutch's bedside.

"You know what that is, Gil? A hag stone. I found it here on the island."

Gil turns it over.

"Legend has it if you peer through the hole of a hag stone you will see what is yet to come, or what has been already. I can't remember which."

Gil tries it out on the deckie. "You don't look before or after, you just look old."

Dutch laughs. Gil squints out at the sea through the hole. The sea is the same but that's not saying anything, it always was and always will be.

Gil goes to give it back.

Dutch smiles. "Keep it. If you decide to be a fisherman, you'll need a good luck charm."

CHAPTER TWENTY-FIVE

1629

Creesje knows more than anyone what it is to be heartsore. She says to lose the person you love is to have the light and the flavor and the joy go out of the world. Mayken knows this to be true; she no longer enjoys even cursing and spitting. Creesje believes it helps to say a proper goodbye.

Imke's service is held on an overcast day. The under-merchant presides. Mayken does not listen to his words: she finds him sly, and he didn't know Imke. Instead, she looks around at the people gathering on the main deck. Many have come up from the Below World to pay their respects. They file past Mayken with a nod of recognition, or a smile. No one mentions Obbe but they have much to say about the deceased.

Imke was a wise woman.

A good witch.

An angel.

She was gifted at prophecies.

Mayken starts to cry. "You've all got it wrong, she was just my Imke."

The ship's trumpeters play a refrain, noble and sad. The last note hangs on the air. The *Batavia*'s new baby bawls in the uncustomary silence.

❧

Imke's chest is brought to Creesje's cabin. Creesje will go out for some fresh air. She won't be far away.

Mayken takes a deep breath and opens the lid.

One dress for best.

Five whole cheeses, well-wrapped.

A cross in a velvet case.

A glossy lock of hair, certainly her mother's.

Mayken keeps the dress and the cross and gives away the cheeses. The lock of hair she rubs slowly between her fingers as she walks the deck. She stops, holds it up high, as high as her arm can reach. Higher. It flutters in the wind. She could let go. It might blow into the sea, or get tangled in the shrouds, or snapped up by a swooping seabird.

A sudden breeze and the lock is ripped from her hand.

Mayken watches it dance away down the deck. She makes no move to follow.

CHAPTER TWENTY-SIX

1989

Gil wedges himself in the gap under the rusted outboard engine to keep watch on Frank Zanetti's hut. The screen door has been propped open and the kitchen inside is all in darkness to him. Outside the place is a mess; holes have been dug and planks of wood propped against rubble piles. A pee-stained kid's mattress roasts in the sun.

The smaller boy comes out. Barefoot, he picks over the debris, turns a washtub the right way around and climbs inside, his knees to his ears. He sings a song that increases in volume until the words are shouted. The bigger boy looms in the doorway of the hut, surly and scowling. He holds a hunk of ice cream sandwiched between two wafers. The ice cream melts a channel that runs down his arm and drips from his elbow. He steps out, ignoring his smaller brother. Silvia follows in her usual singlet and shorts, smoking. She makes her way to a lopsided patio chair and sits down without bothering to straighten it. With a few sharp words she turns down the volume on the smaller boy's song, which continues in a stage whisper. She turns her face up to the sun, jaw clenched, frown etched, a decade older than yesterday.

The boys are not at Mrs. Nord's correctional facility today, then.

Gil won't have a chance to ask Silvia what she knows about Marco Zanetti's death, or get a grilled cheese sandwich.

He inspects the engine above him. There's a smell of oil and engine grease. It's a solid piece of machinery resting on a riveted metal frame, badly rusted, pocked in places. He should have tested it first with a kick. He's dug out a burrow in the ground but, even so, if the frame collapses Gil will be a pancake. The shale digs into his legs and belly. This is not the spot for long stakeouts.

He can't leave until they go back inside.

There's no way he'll crawl out and risk being seen by Roper's feral children. Gil has no wish to be near these boys. Ever. They are the image of Roper. Small-eyed, with a tendency to scowl. Long-armed, already paunchy like their father. It's not their appearance that frightens Gil. He can see from the way they hold themselves that these boys have inherited their father's anger. There's a bored kind of menace about them. An easy cruelty. As if they are itching for a cat to torture, or a dog to ill-treat, or a kid weaker than them to torment. The bigger boy goes over to his younger brother and blithely kicks the washtub. Hard, hard, harder. Then he grabs the tub by the side and shakes, his teeth gritted. The younger boy climbs out and picks up the tub and throws it with a roar of fury, not at his brother, but at Silvia. It falls short of her. Silvia stares at the boy blankly, finishes her rollie, stands up, and goes back inside. The boy pulls down his shorts and does an elaborate dance.

As Gil watches, he becomes more baffled. He can't fathom what they are doing. Objects are picked up, thrown, or smashed, apparently at random. The bigger boy pulls faces into a bucket. His brother comes and knocks it over. They both stamp on the spilt contents. They fight with planks of wood. The smaller boy is struck about the head and now he's really screaming. Silvia comes to the door and calls them both inside.

Gil takes his chance, scrambles out and is gone.

Back in the peaceful dinginess of Joss Hurley's kitchen, Gil sips his coffee. It is almost how Mum made it and twice as strong as how Birgit made it. The stolen continental filter-tipped cigarette lies on the table. Gil rolls it backward and forward with a delicate fingertip. The Special Project of the Day is *glamour*.

Only he needs a theme: Day at the Dock, Sangria Nights, Island Life. Then a thought strikes him. Why not hold the island's first-ever fashion show? Gil glances around him. No old fishermen, no craggy deckies, no shipwrecked Dutch ghosts that he can see.

He's definitely alone.

There are three main categories: Day Wear, Night Wear, and Beach Wear. Outfits are laid out on Joss Hurley's lumpety bed. The bonus category is called Fantasia. Gil is working on a historical shipwreck theme. The continental cigarette will feature throughout. Enkidu will be the appreciative audience.

Gil raids Dutch's tape collection and finds Prince and David Bowie. He avoids all Dutch's self-recordings, knowing exactly what he'll get: Red-Haired Women Blues and Irish Death Songs. Gil also spots a bottle of vodka in Dutch's kitchenette. It will be a prop. He'll replace everything after the show apart from the continental cigarette. He'll smoke that until he's sick.

He pushes Granny Iris's dressing table along a bit and angles the center mirror. Now Gil can see himself catwalk along the hallway from the lounge-room door. The mirror doesn't show him entirely; he must lose either his head or his feet. He opts for his head, tilting the mirror down. He climbs up on a chair and tacks his grandfather's bedsheet to the top of the lounge-room door frame as a stage curtain. Enkidu, the guest of honor, is seated on a cushion halfway down the hallway.

༯

Gil knows how to mix a Bloody Mary, he made them for Mum, only there's no tomato juice. Anyway, vodka is better with orange juice, especially the frozen-canister kind. Like an ice pop.

Gil spots an ancient set of heated rollers in Granny Iris's side of the wardrobe. Once the dust smell has burnt off, Gil has a go with them. They don't heat up as hot at he'd like but he manages a mini flick. Spitting in an old pot of eyeliner gets him a decent cat's eye. He lights the continental cigarette, inhales, coughs, heaves, puts out the continental cigarette. It smells much better than it tastes, so he just holds it. He blows a kiss to his mirror-self.

He's in New York, Paris, or Milan. He's a famous fashion model turned singer turned artist. He made it. Without a mother, without a father, without a pearl-blond pixie cut.

Vodka is also good with lemonade. Enkidu makes no comment.

Day dresses, belted, with Granny Iris's slippers shoved inside to make dramatic shoulders. Glitzed with brooches. Textures of silk and lace and dazzling man-made fibers. Layered costume jewelry. Fun with scarves: bandeau, bandanna, sarong.

The best shoes for the catwalk are high ones. Gil can strut in heels. Shit, he can dance in them!

Vodka with evaporated milk is an acquired taste. Enkidu pulls his neck in.

༯

Fantasia. Granny Iris's netted skirt as a giant ruff, a nod to the Dutch ghosts, a pair of patent courts, a cashmere bolero, and a fierce stripe of blush on each cheek. The music for this look will be *spot-on*, Bowie's "Blue Jean." The opening notes find Gilgamesh, Fashion Warrior, poised at the end of the runway. Head high, glaring down his nose, ready to launch. A few steps, perfectly in time, then over on one heel, then the other. Nothing broken!

Vodka is nice with just ice. Enkidu dozes.

Gil readies the final look. Pearl earrings and green brocade. He sets the scene, drawing the curtains in Joss's bedroom and arranging candles on the dressing table and lighting them. He glances in the mirror. The effect is even better than with Silvia. Magical, even. A golden-eyed prince, pale and mysterious in the candlelight! On second thought he runs to his room and grabs Dutch's hag stone. Maybe it will reveal who he really is, or will be? He jumps over heaps of Granny Iris's discarded clothes—he'll tidy them later. Regaining the dressing table stool he holds up the hag stone, thinks princely thoughts, peers through into the mirror—

"What the fuck?"

Joss Hurley stands in the doorway. He's holding a silk blouse picked up off the floor. The garment lies cradled in his arms, limp like a dead pet. The look on his face comes from some deep place where outrage and loathing live.

"You twisted little bastard."

As Gil runs out into the night, he realizes three things. First, he is without Enkidu; second, he is barefoot; third, he still holds the hag stone. Seeking a place to hide, he pushes into a shadowy thornbush, barely feeling the scratches on his torso and limbs. He curls in on himself, numb, like a clam closing. The stone in his fist and his spine set against the world.

Mum didn't believe in boys' and girls' toys, like she didn't believe in boys' and girls' clothes. Kids should have imagination, she said. Who wants to be given a fucking vacuum cleaner aged three and a plastic baby that pisses? Who wants to be told they can only play with tanks? As a toddler Gil's hair grew long and he wore a rainbow of colors. Gil's toys, like his clothes, were thrifted or found. Never vacuum cleaners. Never tanks. A knitted dolphin Mum said looked like a turd. A family of pipe-cleaner swans.

He'd always liked textures, Mum said. Velvet or lace. Soft fur and rough cotton. He'd crawl a mile to feel fabrics between his little fingers. He'd fall asleep wrapped in a net curtain. Mum collected cloth scraps and Gil would play for hours with them. These go together, these don't. These are friends, these are enemies. On date nights, Mum let Gil pick her outfit and she always wore it, however outlandish.

Gil had thought he was alone with Mum in the house that night. He had on Mum's kimono bathrobe and knee-high boots to do ABBA. He reeled in through the kitchen door humming the opening bars to "Fernando," saw Carlo, and ran.

"Is your boy a fruit?" Carlo had later said to Mum, over Friday-night steak and stubbies.

Gil was pretending to be asleep on the couch, where he could keep an eye on Mum through his eyelashes.

"Gil's just wired up different," she'd said.

"Jesus, you're not kidding."

Mum had laughed. Gil's world fell apart.

A skyful of stars can be seen through the tangle of branches, if he looks up. Night birds returning to nest can be heard, if he listens.

But Gil stays numb and closed. Soon enough he'll feel the scratches from the thicket and the cuts from the shingle. At the moment all he feels is the hag stone in his fist. Like an anchor.

It wasn't the fact that Mum had laughed. If it had been her *Yeah, that's my son and he's one of a kind, so go fuck yourself* laugh, that would have been okay. But Mum's laugh sounded embarrassed, even ashamed. Gil couldn't have explained this back then. He only knew that Mum's laugh made him feel bad in every part of himself.

The world can think you're all wrong if there's one person who thinks you're just right.

The night gets cooler. Gil fancies he hears his name being called. The one syllable of his name carried on the breeze. A lost voice, high and mournful. He tells himself it's a bird trying to find her way back to her nest.

Gil wonders if there are any dead Dutch people lying beneath him and, if so, will they get him in the night? Will their skulls rise up through the shingle, budding like pale mushrooms? Will he find himself surrounded by a moat of bones? Will they grab at him with skeletal fingers? The disturbed ground moves beneath him, churned by birds and weather and water tables. Gil sinks.

A touch on his hand.

Light and cold and quick. The merest tap on his tight-closed fist. Gil takes a sharp inhale like he's surfaced in freezing water. He opens his fist and concentrates on feeling the weight of the hag stone in his palm, small and round and real. An anchor in the world above. He can't be dragged under now.

Dawn light comes pink through the scrub. Gil turns his head. He sees his open hand, palm up, stone right there. He closes his fingers around it. Moving slowly with the soreness of cuts and grazes and stiff limbs, he sits up. He is among faded dolls and weathered teddies and melted crayons. Bedraggled ribbons flutter in the breeze. Gil crawls out of the Raggedy Tree.

Silvia finds him first. She comes by wrapped in a blanket against the early freshness. Smoking and walking at the same time, perhaps surprising even herself there.

They sit together on the beach. Silvia has wrapped Gil in the blanket but he still shakes. She says it's likely shock, or blood poisoning from the thorn scratches.

"Dutch came round late last night in a panic. They figured you might have jumped into the sea or something."

Gil glances at her. She's serious.

He draws the blanket closer round him, grits his teeth, wills the shaking to stop.

"What happened?" Silvia's voice is gentle.

"I was doing a fashion show."

"Shit, you were caught wearing Granny's heels?"

Gil says nothing.

"One day it might be funny," Silvia says. "But it will always hurt."

CHAPTER TWENTY-SEVEN

1629

They carry her in, reeking of shit and insensible. Mayken wakes to a cabin full of men and voices. They lay Creesje on the bunk above. Aris arrives with his case. He turns up the flame on the gimballed lamp and shouts for hot water and for everyone to wait outside.

"Do you know me, Lucretia Jansdochter?"

The sound of choked sobbing.

Aris peers down. "Can you help, Mayken?"

Mayken knows that now is not the time to ask questions. Her job is to take the bowl with the foul water to the door and bring the bowl of cleaner water to the table for Aris to use. In between, she stands holding Creesje's hand. Aris tells her she must look away, for her sake and for Creesje's. Mayken fixes her eyes on the wall and listens to Creesje's sobs die and feels her shaking lessen, the hand in hers becoming still.

The cabin still stinks but Creesje is washed and dressed and found to have no serious injuries other than scrapes and bruises to the face and limbs. Aris packs his case. He shows Mayken how to measure the drops to help Creesje sleep. As he leaves, the upper-merchant and the provost arrive. Pelsaert puts his hand on Mayken's head and tells her to go to her bunk.

It is dawn. The open window slats show the sky changing color.

Pelsaert pulls a stool to Creesje's bedside and the provost, Pieter Jansz, stands by the door with his eyes lowered and his big hands folded. Two guards are posted outside.

Pelsaert waits, eyes closed, thin and worn and sad-looking.

Creesje tells the story of her attack. Mayken and the men listen in silence. Sometimes her voice breaks off.

Pelsaert's voice is calm but his face looks troubled. "Would you know your attackers, Creesje?"

"They were masked and silent throughout but one of them spoke, by accident I believe."

The provost leans forward. "You recognized his voice?"

When Creesje speaks again her voice is quiet, grave. "It was a senior member of the crew."

CHAPTER TWENTY-EIGHT

1989

Gil stays in bed until the men have left the camp. Dutch doesn't disturb him, and for this Gil is thankful. He couldn't bear ferrying gear down to the boat under the glare of his grandfather. Or worse, suffer Dutch's pitying glances.

Last night Joss fitted a lock on his bedroom door and took his meal out on the veranda. Dutch sat silent, although Gil could tell he was fishing for words. He felt the deckie's eyes on him as he bolted his food so he could return to his room.

Gil listens. There's the sound of Dutch pulling the door to, and then his feet crunching away through the shingle. And now the sound of the seabirds and of the sea, the backdrop of every single bloody day. Gil closes his eyes and turns over.

A tapping at the door. Gil ignores it. More tapping. A woman's voice calls out. Gil peers into the kitchen.

Birgit is outside the screen door with her canvas bag. Gil opens the door a fraction.

She frowns at his scratches. "What happened to you?"

"I climbed inside the Raggedy Tree."

Birgit nods, as if that's entirely fair enough. "May I come in?"

❧

Gil carries the coffee mugs to the kitchen table. Enkidu has joined them. Birgit is stroking the tortoise's shell as he sits among the sauce bottles.

She takes a sip of coffee and lights a continental.

"I've come to say goodbye. We're catching the carrier boat today."

"Will you be back?"

"Not this season."

Enkidu launches himself at a sauce bottle open-mouthed. Birgit laughs. Gil stirs his drink.

"I'll be competing in the swimming race before I leave. Bill Nord's orders. You'll come and cheer me on, Gil?"

"Okay."

"I also wanted to thank you for putting in a word with your grandfather."

Gil looks up. Birgit is smiling.

"He came to speak to me and said he wanted to encourage your interest in the history of the islands. He's agreed to let us survey this camp for excavation."

"He said that?"

"Can you believe it? He thinks your finds might be from a different spot originally. He'd hauled shingle to that area under the washing lines."

The old man had even given Gil a cover story.

Birgit opens her bag and pulls out a book.

"Your grandfather thought you might like some reading material."

Gil takes the book. It's on the *Batavia* shipwreck. He flicks through. It has a good number of photographs and maps.

"Come and visit when the season's over? I'll give you a behind-the-scenes tour at the museum."

Gil nods.

"Bring Enkidu."

Gil smiles.

Gil goes down to the main jetty, where people are collecting to mark the start of the Easter festivities. He holds back from the larger groups, staying at the edges, avoiding eye contact. Boats are arriving from other islands. Trestle tables have been set up just down from the scientists' hut. Beach chairs and sun umbrellas are dotted around. There's a long grill and an awning with a couple of older men moving crates about.

Gil spots Silvia. She's with the mums and grans unpacking Tupperware boxes and handing out drinks to the kids that roar past in sun hats and long tees. Roper's boys are among them. Roper himself arrives in a small boat, in a storm of noise with a cassette player on full volume. There are three men on board with him, wild-looking with straggling hair and no shoes. Gil doesn't recognize them from the island. They carry up the kegs of beer they have brought with them. Roper high-fives a few of the kids, then grabs and kisses a mum, who pushes him away.

Gil finds himself standing next to Bill Nord.

"He's an awful prick, isn't he?" says Bill.

There are five contestants in the swimming race, Birgit and Silvia among them. Bill Nord tells Gil that it's an Easter tradition to swim out to the wreck site of the *Batavia* and back again. It's called the Wybrecht Dash and he invented it five years ago. Wybrecht was the name of the servant girl who swam out to the wreck to try and bring back water for the shipwrecked survivors. Hence the competition is open only to the ladies.

Bill Nord's eyes are teary. "The bravery of that young woman, Gil."

"Is it dangerous?"

"Not so much if you're sober."

Bill is called upon to start the race. He fetches a stepladder, climbs to the top, and blows a referee's whistle. When the people simmer down, he tells them just what he told Gil about the race and the servant girl. Only his eyes don't get teary this time. Then Bill climbs back down the stepladder and everyone marches behind him to the starting point, which is a golf flag stuck in the shingle by the side of the water. The crowd gathers round, laughing, talking. The five contestants stand apart, shaking out their legs, stretching their arms.

Birgit is next to Silvia. When Birgit nods to her, Silvia looks away.

The contestants all wear swimming shoes and different colored caps. Birgit stands out among the women. Gil knows she'll be fast. Her shoulders and arms are muscled, her body sleek and long. She's looking out to sea, toward the buoys that mark the route. The others are fiddling with their goggles, looking nervous.

Bill climbs back up the stepladder. The islanders shush one another.

"Our contestants are swimming for a romantic weekend break at the Royal in Geraldton."

Hoots and cheers and a wolf whistle.

"Only there's a catch."

The crowd boos.

"The winner has to take Roper Zanetti as their date."

"He's the bloody booby prize," someone shouts.

The crowd laughs. Cherry nudges Roper and he laughs with effort.

"Out between the buoys and back again." Bill turns to the women. "Have any of you taken alcohol today?"

No, none of them have.

"All right. If you get into trouble, raise your arm and you'll be picked up." Bill waves to the rescue boat already out in the sea, three men on board. They wave back; they're ready.

"On your marks. Get set—"

Bill fires the starting pistol and everyone jumps and then laughs, because didn't they see him there with it in his hand.

The swimmers run into the water.

✂

Birgit is way out in front.

"Jesus, she's fast," someone says.

All eyes are on Birgit. The others can't touch her, the gap just keeps widening.

Gil watches with the rest of them, one of the crowd now. A woman smiles at him. An old man nudges him and points out to sea, saying something about breakers that Gil can't hear above the cheering.

Shouts go up from the onlookers. One of the swimmers is in trouble. The conditions have changed, a sudden sharp wind, a swell.

A name is repeated, carried by the crowd. Silvia.

The rescue boat bounces across the waves. There are only four brightly colored caps bobbing out there now.

Gil closes his eyes.

Let her be all right. Let her be all right. Let her be all right.

Repeat three times. Three times three makes nine. Then begin again.

Let her be all right. Let her be all right. Let her be all right.

It worked with Mum one time.

The ambulance crew spoke in loud voices, breaking out plastic tubes and packaged face masks. Dawn. Dawn. Are you with us? She's a user. You're her kid? You got anyone you can call? Mrs. Baxter's number was by the phone. She came across, red-faced in a housecoat. Yes, yes, she would take him. No, no, he couldn't go to the hospital with Mum. Mum had to go on her own. Only she wouldn't be on her own, she would have paramedics with her and doctors waiting at the hospital.

Mrs. Baxter put the television on in the lounge for Gil. He sat down with the smell of the meal she'd been cooking: onions and stew meat. The meal was abandoned now because Mrs. Baxter was on the phone, telling people about Mum. Each time she told the story differently: the number of ambulance crew, where and how the poor girl was found, her own role in the drama. Then Mrs. Baxter would lower her voice to say it didn't look good and it was the child she felt for. Mr. Baxter came in with a bag of oranges and told Mrs. Baxter to get off the bloody line else the bloody hospital wouldn't be able to get through. Mr. Baxter gave Gil an orange. Mrs. Baxter wondered if she ought to phone her daughter in Cheltenham, England, but then there was the time difference.

Gil stared at the orange in his hand.

Let her be all right. Let her be all right. Let her be all right.

Bill Nord is standing in the water, looking out toward the rescue boat. The crowd watches, silent, breath held. Birgit, unaware, keeps swimming; she has an easy win now. Two other swimmers have stopped and are treading water. The third is way behind. The rescue boat rocks as the men pull Silvia on board. The crowd goes mad cheering. Gil won't cheer until Silvia's on dry land.

Let her be all right. Let her be all right. Let her be all right.

They'd walked the length of the ward, himself and Mrs. Baxter. They'd walked past Mum in the bed, even though she had her name written on a whiteboard on the wall above her.

Dawn Hurley.

She looked small and pale and young, propped up against the pillows with a hospital gown on. A tremble like a low current ran through her. She wanted a cigarette. She wanted a cold drink for her throat. She had chapped lips and marks on the sides of her mouth where tubes had gone into her. There was a needle fixed in the back of her hand, which was attached to a drip. She had a plastic bracelet with her name written on it. Mrs. Baxter had bought her a new pair of slippers from Target. Mum smirked at them behind the old girl's back. Gil hated her for it.

When they were leaving, Mum grabbed Gil by the arm and pulled him down to her. Her breath was stale. She spoke into his ear. She said it was an accident. She said she'd never leave him. He knew that, didn't he? That he was her whole world?

Mrs. Baxter washed Gil's clothes and ironed them. Mrs. Baxter ironed everything because ironing kept her sane. Tablecloths, knickers, curtains, tea towels, Mr. Baxter's underpants and handkerchiefs. Gil's fiercely laundered clothes saved the day. That, and Mum wearing a skirt and brushing her hair up in a bun so that she looked like an organized secretary. Yes, they could stay together, said social services, a care plan is in place. Mum had a folder with all her appointments written up. On the way out, she binned the folder. They left town that night. There was no time to say goodbye to Mrs. Baxter.

Silvia is landed. The crowd cheers, Gil among them. She shakes hands like a celebrity. Accepts back pats like a hero. Someone hands her a beer, a towel. Gil pushes forward, driven by an urge to touch her, to make sure it's true that she has survived. Silvia's skin is mottled and cold to the touch but she is definitely alive. Feeling his hand on her arm, she turns and gives Gil a quick rough hug. He lets himself sob into her damp neck and then she's gone.

The islanders march the swimmers down to the main jetty, spirits high. Isn't it great that none of the contestants drowned? With the carrier boat an approaching speck in the sea, Birgit, still in her bathers, disappears into her hut. The other scientists have been hauling down the equipment ready for the leaving. They wait with their gear, smoking, on the jetty.

The carrier boat draws in. Easter supplies for the islanders are unloaded and the scientists, their boxed finds and kit are loaded.

Birgit makes her way down the jetty, accompanied by Bill Nord, who hands her into the boat as if she's a queen. She's changed into khaki shorts and a man's shirt and carries her wide-brimmed hat. Her hair is almost dry in the late-morning sun. She's looking around, searching the crowd for someone. Gil ducks behind a trestle table in case it's him.

The carrier boat pulls away. Bill Nord stands on the jetty with one hand raised, all serious and noble, like some olden-days figure. He still has his referee whistle around his neck.

Gil sees Birgit turn away from the island and set her face to the open sea.

He sits on a crate, near a group of people but not with them. A tucked-away place where he can watch everything unfold: the mums clucking about, the blokes holding stubbies and lighting the grills with mad quantities of smoke.

Roper and his wild men take seats nearby. The talk is whether Birgit will summon him for a weekend of passion at the hotel in Gero. Roper's ears are lit red, his smile forced; he's offended but can't show it. Silvia drifts among the crowds, still with a towel around her shoulders, telling the story of her near-fatal cramp over and over again. Gil is given a burger and eats it, one eye on Roper's children, who have run over to their father. The big one, Paul, stands scowling near his dad's chair; the small one, Mikey, wheels about the gathered men. Stare at anyone long enough and they will look back. Gil ought to know that.

Gil glances over his shoulder. Mikey flitting on and off the path. Paul with a dogged plod trying to catch up.

"Wait the fuck, will you?"

Gil quickens his pace but tries not to run. Running will set off some kind of instinct in this sort of boy. Paul draws level with Gil on the path, red-faced but keeping pace. Gil sees the sweat patches on the boy's too-tight tee.

"You live with Old Man Hurley."

Gil keeps walking.

"Is he a faggot, like you?"

Gil keeps walking.

"Your mum did herself in, didn't she?"

Gil keeps walking.

"An' you didn't tell anyone for weeks, sick fuck."

Mikey spins closer to his brother, letting out a howl.

"Shut the fuck up, Mikey."

Mikey spins away, grinning. Gil quickens his pace.

"Wait, will you?" Paul scrambles to keep up. "What did she look like when she went rotten?"

Gil walks faster.

"You wear your granny's dresses, don't you?"

Mikey laughs wildly.

"Faggot." Paul spits.

Mikey takes up the word, spins with it. "Faggot, faggot, faggot."

Gil runs now. A bitter sickness rising. His heart crashing. He glances back. Mikey still spins. Paul has stopped on the path. He hawks up a spit from the depths of his soul.

"Keep away from us," he yells. "Or our dad will take you out to sea and drown you."

CHAPTER TWENTY-NINE

1629

The story is on everyone's lips. Lady Lucretia, stepping onto the moonless deck to take the sea air before retiring, was set upon by eight, six, twenty men.

The aft-the-mast account: maltreated by unknown assailants and left insensible by the mizzenmast.

The before-the-mast account: jumped, gagged, and dangled by her ankles over the side of the ship, pinned down, gown lifted, smeared with shit, head knocked against the deck, left for dead.

The motive for the attack baffles everyone. Nothing was taken and her body was not used. A dark and scandalous undercurrent ripples through the ship. Creesje was set upon for being Pelsaert's whore—there's no denying the two are close—an assault designed to anger the upper-merchant. Punishments are predicted; hanging for the instigator, keelhauling for his gang. Special tortures will be dreamt up by the provost, who walks the ship in a glower.

Three days pass and Pelsaert makes no inquiries, no arrests, calls for no tortures, no hangings. Creesje emerges on deck wan and determined, hand in hand with Antony van den Heuvel's feral daughter. The other passengers keep their distance. A guard is placed at Creesje's cabin door, day and night.

Creesje will not let Mayken out of her sight. She says that dark forces are at work on this ship and that the upper-merchant must tread carefully. Pelsaert has enemies and their hostility toward him is growing. This is taking a terrible toll on his already poor health and he remains in his cabin. Respect for him among some of the men has dwindled in favor of the skipper. If those men are disciplined, they might do the unthinkable.

Mayken puzzles. "What is the unthinkable?"

Creesje's voice is barely a whisper. "Mutiny."

Mayken must not repeat this, nor must she utter the name of the attacker whose voice Creesje recognized. *Jan Evertsz. Bosun.* Creesje has discreetly inquired of his reputation, to be told he's a hard-brawling bastard of a man who commands the loyalty of the sailors. He is close to the skipper.

Bloody flux.

Creesje asks God to forgive the upper-merchant, who cannot act for fear of greater disorder. Mayken asks God to bestow scurvy and catastrophic accidents on the men who hurt Creesje. She considers death by Bullebak but it feels as if enough evil stalks the decks now. Creesje no longer dines in the Great Cabin; the skipper reigns there now; their meals are brought to their door. She won't step out after dark and sits apart from the other passengers on deck. She prays often and counts the days until she sees her own dear husband again. She cries out in her dreams and wants to keep Mayken always nearby.

Mayken's jobs are: singing to Creesje, telling Creesje stories about kittens and babies saved from floods by miraculous floating cradles, and holding Creesje's hand until she falls asleep.

When Creesje sleeps, Mayken can leave the cabin. By night she walks on the deck, hoping that Holdfast will swoop down from the shrouds but he never does during these watchful, uneasy times. By day she makes her patrols. The guards know her and let her pass. The sailors know her and nod their heads. Under Creesje's care she has become more regal, less itchy, able to assume a demeanor of un-questionable purpose. Mayken always takes her Beardman jug, even with the worsening quality of the scraps.

Her route varies but generally begins at the officers' crapping stations. Two triangular cupboards, one each side of the stern castle for the easement of the higher orders. Mayken peers down through the seat to the sea far below. She half expects Bullebak to stick its head up through the hole. Eyes burning, tongue lashing. The horror of it.

But Bullebak is not to be found.

Yet daily there are signs. Bullebak leaves its mark everywhere. Bitten ropes and gnawed clogs. Unlikely puddles and the persistent smell of rotting fish. Tendrils of black mold on walls and ceiling beams.

The ship dankly sours.

Old superstitions are rife now. The sailors lead the way. Words must be chanted over knots. Messmates must be served in a particular order. A change of wind direction must be greeted. Portents are looked for and translated. The cut of the wake noted. The shape of clouds debated. Imke is sorely missed.

A lamp taken down into the hold will now burn green. Monstrous births plague the onboard animals. Their issue is hastily thrown overboard to prevent alarm. Eyeless lambs. Mouthless piglets. A litter of rabbits joined together, a mass of heads and limbs. The gardener harvests only fork-tailed carrots from his boxed plot outside the hen coop.

"It's the way of long journeys," says Creesje. "They alter what people think and see."

It's Bullebak, says Mayken to herself.

She catches sight of Holdfast early one morning. He has lost his India shawl and his poor old head is sunburnt raw and hot to the touch. She puts her small cold palms on it and Holdfast laughs. He sees the stone around her neck and smiles.

"Any prophecies?"

None.

They climb up to the stern and watch the wake fall away behind the ship. Imke is miles and miles away now, buried in a land Mayken will likely never see again or visit. She cannot bear to think of Imke's loneliness. One who so loved the bustle of Haarlem market, the crowds clamoring to her for their fortune, the gossip and chatter of everyday people always around her. Now Imke is all alone in strange soil.

Holdfast names the birds that fly by. Mayken watches them with envy. To drift away on kind winds. Drink raindrops and eat clouds. Away from the rotten water and moldering food dredged up from the fermenting belly of the ship. It's hardly surprising that spite and intrigue grow in this stale confinement. That people start to hate and choose sides, whisper in corners, plot abominations, discuss the unthinkable.

"Why the worried face, Little Grandmother?"

"I was thinking, you can't trust anyone these days."

"You can trust the ship."

"What if she sinks?"

"A well-made ship no more wants to sink than an honest dog wants to bite."

Mayken looks back at the well-made ship. Decks newly scrubbed with seawater and quiet yet. The painted fittings faded now. The sails weather-stained.

"What about the barnacles and the leaks?"

Holdfast smiles. "Have we not had brutal seas? Have we not had storm after storm?"

"Yes."

"Yet she held together?"

"I suppose."

Holdfast's dark eyes shine. "This ship is our mother, Mayken. She rocks us, we are safe in her arms."

Mayken starts to cry. She doesn't know why.

Holdfast wipes Mayken's face roughly with his hand. "If you stop that, I'll tell you a story."

"What story?"

"The story of the wood nymph and the cradle."

"Is it frightening?"

"Not very. Will you still hear it?"

Mayken sniffs. "Go ahead."

There was once a strong young woodcutter who lived alone in a hut in the forest and enjoyed his work. He respected the trees he felled and helped them in many ways.

"What ways?"

"If they had sick branches, he'd cut them off. He'd collect the baby birds that fell out of the trees."

"To eat?"

"No, he saved them. He fed them on stew until they grew fat and strong."

"Then he ate them?"

"Then he released them to sing in the treetops."

"So he was a hungry woodcutter?"

Holdfast laughs. "Can I get on with the story?"

The woodcutter loved his life and his cozy hut. He loved the kettle on the hob and the little black range that he lit with wood chippings. And the pot above it, full of good rich stew. And the shelf he had built, with his pipe upon it. His bed was made warm with feather-filled bolsters and the hides of the animals he trapped. Although poor, the woodcutter lived like a king! Most of all he loved his work. For the trees would greet him with a swaying of their branches and the birds would greet him with their bright songs. But for all that, he was lonely.

"He had the trees."

"Trees don't talk back."

"And the birds."

"He was lonely for another person."

"Why didn't you say?"
"Listen, now."

One day the woodcutter came upon a maiden. She was beautiful and strange, with dark green hair and smooth limbs, the green white you'd find in saplings stripped of bark. She started and made to run. He calmed her and invited her back to his hut for a bowl of stew and a smoke of his pipe.

Soon they were married and were very content living together in the hut in the forest. The strange wife of the woodcutter made her husband promise her one thing—he must let her walk alone among the trees at every full moon. The woodcutter agreed gladly. Soon a baby came along, with dark green hair like her mother's and the green white limbs of a sapling—she was the delight of her parents.

The woodcutter began to worry about all the things his daughter might need to make her happy: a house made of bricks, costly gowns, gold plates and crystal goblets, a pony with a ribboned mane.

His wife calmed him. Weren't they content here in the forest? Didn't they have everything they needed? But the woodcutter didn't listen.

He began to fell more and more trees to sell to the greedy timber mill owner. Soon the birds stopped singing and the trees stopped swaying their leaves when he approached. Now the birds turned their beaks away and the trees glared down at him and pointed their stick fingers.

The woodcutter's wife begged him to take only what they needed and no more.

But the woodcutter didn't listen. He became mean-hearted, rotten of spirit. Then came the night of a full moon.

"Look after our dear daughter," his wife said. "I'm taking my moonlit walk."

The woodcutter sat in the hut, looking out of the window at the full moon. The baby was asleep. His wife was gone. Restless, he took up his axe and went out into the woods to cut more trees, for the moon was very bright that night, almost like daylight. He walked through the woods, sparse now, because he had taken so many trees. But he didn't notice the damage he had caused.

He came to a tree he'd never seen before. The tree glowed green in the moonlight with long-leaved hanging branches, flowing like a willow would. The tree somehow reminded him of a lovely maiden with dark green hair.

He hesitated, for the tree was so beautiful! But thinking of the good price he could get for such choice wood, he began to chop. As he struck the first blow he heard a distant scream. Then another scream at the next blow, then another. But he kept on until the tree was felled and the forest was silent.

The woodcutter trimmed off the branches. Seeing the sapling green white of the tree's limbs, he lost the will for the work. Tomorrow he would bring the mule to drag the tree up to the timber mill but now he must return to the hut else his wife, returning from her walk, would know he had broken his promise to her.

Reaching the cottage, he heard his daughter screaming. The baby cried all night, she cried at dawn and then cried all morning. The woodcutter paced the floor with her. He was worried for his infant and worried for his wife, who had not returned from her moonlit walk. He carried the child into the woods to look. Perhaps his wife had met with some misfortune and was lying injured?

The baby stopped crying when they reached the beautiful fallen tree. The woodcutter put the child on the ground and she crawled toward the tree, laid her face against its trunk, and closed her eyes.

"That tree was her mother, the wood nymph."

"Little Grandmother, would you ever let me finish?"

In the days that followed, the baby could not be separated from the felled tree. The woodcutter did not have the heart to cart the trunk to the timber mill. He took his carpentry tools and shaped and chiseled the tree into a cradle. When he placed the child inside, she fell fast asleep.

That night the woodcutter, who had taken a drop to soothe his sadness, saw that the cradle was moving by itself. It was rocking the child. Listening, he heard a distant voice. It was the voice of his wife singing a melody. The melody she would always sing to the child.

In that moment he realized—

"He'd killed his own wife."

"Yes."

"So, you're saying this ship is made of dead wood nymphs?"

"I'm saying that this ship is a forest, that she once had her feet in the soil, just like we did."

"But you don't have your feet in the soil."

"I grew up on land, I want to return to land again. In the meantime, I choose life at sea."

Mayken thinks for a moment. "I choose life at sea too. I will become a sailor and sail everywhere with you."

Holdfast laughs. "I am old and this is my last journey. I plan to settle in Batavia. That will be my land."

"I don't want to settle there. I don't want to live with my father. He whips his horses and tortures his roses."

"He's a fine rich man."

"Being rich doesn't make him fine."

"No." Holdfast looks up at the sky. "Close your eyes and listen to the song of the ship."

Mayken closes her eyes and listens, to the billow of canvas and the rasp of rope and the plash of water on the hull. The ship creaks, heeling as her massive sails fill with wind. And beyond this, the ship's own song in the accent of the forest she is made from— a whole forest of trees! In the ship's song is the memory of branches and leaves tasting the wind. The heartbeat of the slow-growing oak, the rushing pine.

Mayken opens her eyes.

"Did you hear it?"

Mayken nods.

"She will keep us safe, though there'll be storms and shipworms outside and in. To *Batavia* we must cling."

CHAPTER THIRTY

1989

Gil chooses quiet times to go about, at night or before dawn. During daylight hours he keeps to Joss Hurley's camp. Gil is not scared of the dark or even of ghosts in the dark. Or at least Gil is scared of the dark and of the dead less than he's scared of the living, now that the whole island knows him as the weirdo who dresses in his granny's clothes.

He can guess how Roper's kids found out, and he hates Silvia for it.

Wherever Gil walks he sees the debris of busy days. The barbecues and beach picnics. Sometimes, when he's holed up at the camp, he fancies he hears raucous voices and laughter and detects the smell of charred meat carried on the wind.

Mostly he lies on his bed reading the book Birgit gave him about the *Batavia*.

What is left of the mighty ship and all those people? Jawbones and pottery shards, silver bedposts and water-logged wood. You can touch the things they touched or hold a piece of the actual person in your hand. You can read a letter from a preacher who was there or the diary of the upper-merchant.

None of this information came easy. The cannons on the seabed waited hundreds of years to be found and winched up. The stuff in the sea turned into coral and had to be chipped out. Stuff on land was messed up by the burrowing seabirds. The scientists had to piece it all together, bit by bit.

Gil imagines the' survivors. Everyday people who probably moaned about the weather and having to eat bony fish. Then they battered one another to death as the water ran out. In Birgit's book there's a picture of a skull with a piece knocked out. It belonged to a man who was killed while running away. If you listened to that skull, held it up to your ear like a seashell, you might hear the clashing of swords and gurgling, then three hundred and sixty years of nothing. Why wouldn't the dead Dutch be pissed off when the fishermen arrived, and the scientists, stirring up their old bones, trying to tell their story?

Somewhere between very late and very early Gil lowers the sports bag out of his bedroom window. He steps up on his bedside crate and climbs out. This way is quieter than creaking down the corridor and through the kitchen. Once outside, there's nothing he can do about the sound of his footsteps on the shingle.

It's a bright night, so he does a circuit of the island with the sports bag unzipped so Enkidu can see the stars. Gil knows the pathways so well now that he rarely stumbles, even in the dark. The trick is to use all your senses; cats and other nocturnal creatures know this. Their eyes are wide, yes, but also their ears are pricked and their whiskers are twitching and their paws are light stepping. This night world looks different from the daytime world and feels different too. Breezes are read by the skin. The smell of the land is released.

Gil heads down to the old jetty and with care climbs down into the flat-bottomed boat. With Enkidu settled, he spools out the rope and the boat floats away, right to the end of the tether. Little May is probably watching from the shore; she wouldn't want to risk another sailing. Sometimes Gil thinks about untying the rope and letting the boat just drift. Out past the shipwreck site. Out past the teeth of the reef. They would brave biblical storms, putting their trust in *The Sea Tortoise*. There would be calamities: lost oars, forgotten tin openers, sharks. But sure enough, they'd wash up on some distant shore with fresh leaves and coconuts and no people.

Gil looks up at the indifferent auld stars. The indifferent auld stars twinkle back coldly.

Visits to the scientists' hut are the most perilous. The main jetty is the busiest part of the island. Expeditions must take place before dawn, when the fishermen head down to their boats. The scientists' hut was left unlocked.

The place smells musty. The moonlight through the shutters patterns the floor. Gil keeps his torch aimed low and steady. Moving light attracts attention; if he can see moonlight inside, someone outside might see his torch flicker.

The scientists' hut has an abandoned look. The remaining equipment has been packed into boxes and stacked in corners. The shelves are empty, the boxed finds gone. The dishes on the sink drainer have a layer of dust over them. The tap is dry, the water from the tank has been cut off. Some of the notices on the pinboard have been taken down and there are tack holes and darker patches of cork where they used to be. In the room where the men slept, the steel-framed bunk beds are empty of mattresses.

Gil unzips the sports bag and lets Enkidu out to roam. He checks his list by torchlight.

First aid box
Flares
Map

The first aid box is screwed to the wall next to the door. Inside there are mostly bandages. Gil can find nothing else on his list but he'll take the cap he found in the bunk room. The cap has a badge on the front that says *Monaco*. He opens up the camp bed in the corner, the one Birgit used. It has a faint smell of continental cigarettes.

He lies down, listening to the scuttle of claws and the knocking of Enkidu's shell as his friend skims along the walls.

Gil wakes late morning, by the clock on the shelf. It's too late to go back up to Joss Hurley's camp unseen. There are voices outside, a kid's high whine, the low rumble of an old man, the sharp bark of a mum. Gil will have to stay put and wait it out.

Enkidu is asleep under a square of tarpaulin. Gil sits cross-legged next to his friend. He licks a finger and draws a portrait of Enkidu on the floor in the dust. Then one of himself. Enkidu is much bigger than him. In real life the tortoise would be the size of a small car. Gil would start again, only now he has a gritty taste from the dust and his mouth is dry.

Gil stares through the hole in Dutch's hag stone for ages. He sees only the ceiling. Nothing magical happens. Nothing happens, except that after a while Enkidu wakes up. He gives his friend half a can of evaporated milk he found in the cupboard. Enkidu looks at him with an expression that says *I'm not a bloody cat.*

The light is mellowing when Gil opens the door to the scientists' hut a crack. There's no one around. The fishermen will be at home with their families, boats moored, crays sorted, gear packed away. Even *Ramona* will have returned by now. Dutch will be up at the hut preparing the meal. Joss will be dozing on the veranda. Gil stows the sports bag behind the camp bed. He'll travel light and hope to slip back to the camp unnoticed.

Enkidu rides in Gil's arms. Steady and level because Enkidu doesn't like to be tipped. The breeze after a day inside the hut feels good to Gil. The island is in a soft mood. He hopes for sight of a sea eagle, a seal, some interesting seabirds.

The sun is behind them so that by the time Gil spots Roper's kids they are making a beeline for him, kicking up the coast path.

They are in their swimmers, hair still wet. Paul wears footy boots with no socks. Mikey is barefoot but doesn't seem to mind.

Paul looks narrowly at Gil. "What's that?"

"Nothing."

Mikey hops over. "Le' me see!"

"Show him. It's a *tortoise*, Mikey."

Gil holds the tortoise lower so the smaller boy can see. Mikey sticks out a prodding finger.

"Not like that," Gil says. "You have to be careful."

"I want to hold it!"

"Let him hold it."

Gil sees with dismay how this will pan out. Paul's expression has changed from boredom to malicious interest. Gil has made a mistake in showing that he cares about the creature.

"Give it here," says Paul.

Mikey, his face pulled into a grimace, is coming at the tortoise again with a finger. He pokes the tortoise hard. The tortoise struggles in Gil's hands. The boy spins away, shouting.

"GROSS. GROSS. GROSS!"

"Shut up!" says the big brother. "Fuck's sake."

Gil thinks about running but he might not get away and Enkidu would hate being jostled.

"Give it."

Gil hands Enkidu over. Enkidu looks back at him. A look of panic on his poor old face, his thin neck darting.

Paul flips the tortoise over, nonchalantly.

Careful. Gil wants to scream. *Careful.*

Paul holds the tortoise up to his face. "Hello, little fucker. Funny little fucker."

Gil can't bear it. "You've seen him. Give him back, now."

Roper's boy smiles. "Ask nicely, faggot."

"Give him back, please."

"Beg me."

"I beg you."

Roper's boy smiles. He goes to hand the tortoise back. Still smiling, he dropkicks the tortoise. Hard and fast. A dull thud as the tortoise makes contact with his footy boot. Enkidu draws an arc in the air. A sickening clack as he lands on stone, tummy upward. Paul laughs and Mikey spins.

Gil, suddenly able to move again, picks up his friend and runs.

Joss looks up from his newspaper. Gil's nearly taken the screen door off its hinges. He's sobbing with the tortoise in his arms—*Enkidu*—surely dead already. Legs drawn in, the nubbin of his head showing, his shell cracked open. Along the jagged edges blood wells.

Joss gets up and gently takes the tortoise from the boy.

Surgery happens on the kitchen table. Joss places the tortoise on a clean towel and carefully wipes ooze away with damp cotton wool. Then he takes up strips of medical gauze and glue. Gil crouches and talks to the tortoise, although his friend's head is still tucked inside. Dutch is on hand with hot water, like in the films. He's brewing tea; they'll have it with a rake of sugar in. This is the Irish remedy for shock and disaster.

"Enkidu, can you hear me?" whispers Gil. "You'll be all right."

Joss lays the gauze in thin strips across the cracks. He paints each strip, then rubs the glue in with a delicate touch. When he is finished, he removes the residue with a rag. He picks up the tortoise very tenderly and puts him in the box Dutch has prepared, lined with a folded towel.

"We'll have that tea, Dutch," he says.

"Righto."

Gil and his grandfather sit at the table with the box between them.

"You'll need to put him somewhere quiet and dark."

"Thanks."

The old man glances at Dutch, then back at Gil. "You could call me Grandpa, if you wanted."

Gil nods. Dutch, at the sink, smiles into the tea caddy.

"What about you?" asks Joss. "Gilgamesh the Warrior Prince?"

Gil grimaces and is ashamed to find tears coming again.

Joss gets up. He puts his hand on the boy's shoulder and Gil cries.

Gil lies on his bed. He is watching Enkidu sleep in a nest of pillows. Outside on the veranda Dutch starts a low song on his guitar.

Certain his friend is resting comfortably, Gil slips out. Dutch taps the bench next to him. Gil sits down.

"Where's he gone?"

"For a walk. How's Enkidu?"

Gil shrugs.

"We've done all we can do," says Dutch. "Brave Enkidu's fate is in the hands of the gods now."

Gil looks out at the sea. "I should have defended him."

"From a boy twice your size?" Dutch asks. "And mean like a fuckin' rat?"

"Even so," says Gil.

"Noble Gilgamesh. If there's any fairness in the world, your friend will live."

Later still, Joss stands in the doorway. There's a sway to him, and when he comes farther into Gil's room, a booze smell.

He puts something down at the foot of the bed. Gil watches through narrowed eyes, keeping perfectly still. It reminds him of the times Mum played Santa. Late-night rustlings and stubbed-toe curses that left behind filled footy socks or half-stuffed pillowcases.

Joss retreats, patting the door frame, looking back, closing the door gently.

Gil stretches out his toes. Something lies on the bedsheet. He sits up to investigate and finds green brocade, folded neatly, rich and festive in his torchlight.

CHAPTER THIRTY-ONE

1629

She has been blind—every part of this ship is alive! Just like the carvings in the Church of Saint Bavo, the jewel of Haarlem. Back then she didn't believe that a wooden toad on the choir stall could wink, or a stone gargoyle could grin. Imke told her to open her eyes and take notice.

Mayken looks anew with wonder. The ship lives!

The sailors have always known and now Mayken does too, she feels it in the taut ropes and keening timbers. At night, Mayken waits for Creesje's drops to work, then she steals out.

She roams wider, no longer dreading Stonecutter, no longer fearing punishment. Everyone is off whispering in corners, not taking notice of some wandering child. After seven months at sea the people are ghosts haunting the same worn pathways. Their eyes have turned inward to watch their thoughts brood. Their mouths spit out the bitter cud of these broodings. Dark tales and intrigues and gathering clouds. Even Creesje has sunk into a gloom.

Now Mayken unobserved sits for hours on the forecastle deck, waiting for the figurehead to wake. If she watches closely enough, she might see the red-maned Lion of Holland yawn and stretch and creak off along the bowsprit. To snap at the leaping waves and dip his wooden paw into the ocean. To catch the sea spume like blown dandelion seeds. Mayken glances away and when she looks back the lion's position has changed. His rump is higher in the air! His tail curls differently! The painted wooden heads on the quarterdeck turn to watch her—she's sure of it. Their faces are quite worn away but when she pats them, their startled expressions turn into smiles.

Every part of this ship is dear to Mayken. The air through her cabin window slats is the *Batavia* breathing. The gunports are the *Batavia*'s eyes. The keel her mighty backbone. Nightly Mayken thanks the ship for keeping her and Creesje safe. They don't need the guard snoring outside the door! The *Batavia* won't let them be harmed.

Mayken returns to lie on her bunk as the lantern burns low. Creesje slumbers soundly. A shadow flickers in the corner of the cabin. Mayken's eye is caught. The shadow worms out from the listening hole Pelgrom made. The same hole she would press her ear to, on the other side of the wall, in the old days when Imke was alive and Creesje would bicker with Zwaantie.

The shadow slides down the wall. It takes the shape of an eel-like creature. Spreading out from floor to ceiling, stretching its notched spine, turning this way and that. A head with bulbous eyes, whiskered like a catfish, gills beating, turns to her. There's a sudden stink of stale water. The pop and burble of draining sludge.

Mayken lies on her bunk rigid with fear. She no longer needs to search for Bullebak. Bullebak has come to her.

The shadow crouches and pools by her bedside.

She takes a deep breath. "You are a creature of water, go back to the water."

The shadow deepens.

Slowly, slowly, Mayken sits up and takes up the jug and the stopper from under her bunk.

"You could be a great sea monster," she continues. "Not some worm feasting on the toes of old nursemaids. You could ride the storms. But you'd rather be a stowaway, hiding in the hold, creeping around the decks."

The shadow shrinks a little. Then it begins to spiral around the room. Slowly at first, then building speed. There's the sound of fast-draining water.

"I won't pretend we are friends, because you killed my Imke with your poisonous bite."

The shadow stops turning and collects in a patch on the ceiling. The sound changes into a steady, thoughtful drip.

"I've no bacon rinds but if you climb into this jug, I promise to set you free."

The shadow diminishes and races back to the corner of the room.

"Are you not weary? Are you not cramped? You who have stretched out along the canals of Amsterdam? You who can grow to the size of a hill? You're not wanted here, by this ship or by these people, who have troubles enough. Here you are just a worm in a bobbing apple."

As if in answer, the shadow lengthens across the ceiling.

"Jump inside." Mayken holds up the jug. "Do it!"

There's a noise, a low whistle like a note blown over the jug's mouth. Mayken quickly stoppers it. She listens to the jug's potbelly and hears a distant rushing sound, the sea in a shell held to the ear.

Mayken turns the jug in her hands and almost drops it with surprise.

The clay face has changed; it has lost its expression of pop-eyed horror and found a smirk.

Mayken steals out to the main deck and leans over the gunwale. She holds the jug over the boiling waves. They greedily lick up the side of the ship. She lets go.

The watchman sends for the barber-surgeon, recognizing a fever when he sees one. Aris carries Mayken back to her cabin, waking Creesje. Now it is her turn to hold Mayken's hand. Mayken turns to her, flushed, hair wet, glassy-eyed, her breath bitter.

"It's gone," she whispers. "Can't you tell?"

CHAPTER THIRTY-TWO

1989

Gil is reading aloud to the tortoise that sits on the kitchen table. Dutch started it last night. He said Enkidu would enjoy listening to *The Epic of Gilgamesh* because it's ancient like him and who doesn't like to hear their name read aloud? It would take Enkidu's mind off his injuries. Dutch had read the first few pages in an easy, warm voice and then handed Gil the book.

Gil picks over the words and gets stuck often but Enkidu has a comfortable nest among the sauce bottles and seems content to listen.

The attack has changed Gil's friend. Now Enkidu moves in a halting swim and there's a dip to his right side. Sometimes his back legs give out, so he must drag his hindquarters. Enkidu's mouth is crooked now and his eyes dim.

The crunch of shingle. Gil looks up from the book. Silvia is standing outside the screen door.

Enkidu ignores the leaves Silvia brings. He knows a snake in the grass when he sees one. Silvia, polite, smiling, will have a glass of water if it's not too much trouble.

She sits, picks up the book on the table, flicks through it too quickly to read, puts it down again.

Gil takes the seat farthest from her.

"Your granddaddy came to see Frank, to complain about the boys."

Gil keeps his face plain.

"They swore blind they didn't touch your tortoise."

"They're lying."

Silvia frowns at the tortoise. "Is he all right?"

Enkidu gives Gil a lopsided glance. Gil says nothing.

"I'm sorry we haven't been able to hang out. Roper has taken against you. He doesn't want you near his boys, you understand?"

Gil concentrates on unclenching his fists under the table. Silvia, unconcerned, takes out her tobacco tin, fishes out a rollie, and lights it.

"They teased me about Granny Iris's clothes."

"I had to tell Frank about us dressing up that night." She smokes, picks at a fingernail. "He wanted to know why I came home with makeup on. Old blokes get jealous."

Gil gets up from the table.

"Frank just thought it was funny!" She laughs, and it's hollow.

Gil picks up Enkidu with the greatest care. He closes the kitchen door quietly behind them.

In a while, Gil regains the room. There's no evidence of Silvia apart from an empty glass on the table. He straightens her chair and goes to close the pantry door, catching sight of the sherry bottle. It has leapfrogged over whole regiments of tinned ham. He takes up the bottle, sniffs Silvia's glass on the table, then refills it. He carries the drink back to his room.

He toasts the sleeping Enkidu in much the same way Mum would toast a beautiful sunset and settles down again with his book.

CHAPTER THIRTY-THREE

1629

The witch stone is heavy in her hand, an anchor. The rock of the ship in the before-dawn quiet. Her fever is not yet broken, so she senses the pulse of her blood and the beating of her heart and the growing of her hair. Her teeth feel soft and her mind unrooted. Mayken lifts the stone and peers through the hole.

On the other side—an eye—widening.

The eye pivots. Golden-brown, unblinking. A child's eye, perhaps. It fixes on her, *sees* her.

She blinks, looks again, but all she sees is the gimballed lantern swinging above.

CHAPTER THIRTY-FOUR

1989

The hag stone is heavy in his hand, an anchor. The spin of the room in the darkening dusk. The glass on his bedside crate is empty of sherry, so he senses the slump of his blood and the beating of his heart and the hurting of his hair. His teeth feel soft and his mind unrooted. Gil lifts the stone and peers through the hole.

On the other side—an eye—widening.

The eye pivots. Gray, unblinking. A child's eye, perhaps. It fixes on him, *sees* him.

He blinks, looks again, but all he sees is the strip light above.

CHAPTER THIRTY-FIVE

1629

Mayken is thrown sideways. She slides along the floor and lands halfway up the wall. Creesje follows, banging her head on the table that's also in flight. There is a tremendous rending, the scream of splintering wood, the sound of heavy objects falling. The ship stops, juddering down her entire length, pitching sharply to the left.

The gimballed lantern still burns but at a bizarre angle.

Creesje's head is not bleeding, although she has a fierce knock to the temple. She ignores it. Taking the warmest shawls from her chest, she swaddles Mayken in one and winds the other about herself. Next Creesje casts around for their small valuables. Mayken feels for her witch stone at her neck.

Together they get the door open and fall into the corridor. The noise is terrifying. A deep *boom*, *boom*, *boom* and a grinding, somewhere low, the keel maybe. Opening the door to the upper deck presents a strange new landscape. Mayken clings with one hand to the door and to Creesje with the other.

It is dark yet, before dawn, and raining heavily. The ship slopes steeply and is lashed by waves, spray covering the main deck. The skipper barks orders at the sailors frantically stripping the sails. As Mayken watches, one man is washed screaming into the sea. A slight figure staggers across the deck in a night robe, barefoot, coatless, and hatless. It takes her a moment to recognize the upper-merchant.

She hears the bitter words Pelsaert roars into the face of the skipper: *You have put a noose around our necks.*

The well-to-do passengers collect in the Great Cabin with the clerks and cadets. Soldiers guard the door, should order break down. The predikant leads the prayers. Judick and Mrs. Predikant sit pale-faced with the rest of the children. Their servant, Wybrecht, with her strong high cheekbones, sits capless, like so many of them roused in the night. Mayken sees that her hair is reddish brown, the color of leaves turned. She smiles at Mayken and all the angles go out of her face. Roelant lurches about the room, ignored by his family deep in prayer. He falls asleep wrapped in the tablecloth. The wind keens and the shouts of men are heard even above the constant scrape and boom of the ship against rock. Pelgrom is back and forth with reports and such food and drink as he can get from the stores, for the ship is in chaos. A line of sailors and soldiers and their wives has been established to pass buckets hand to hand to try and bail out the rising water on the lower decks.

Dawn comes, gray and rain lashed, and the gravity of the situation is revealed. The forepart of the ship is impaled upon sharp rocks. They sail out a kedge anchor to try to winch her backward. With the wild weather, they are in danger of losing the boat they launch. The sailors proceed with patience and skill, watching the swell, timing the rise and fall. One false move and the boat will dash to splinters against the side of the ship, drowning the men in it. All hands are called to the capstan to wind, but the ship does not budge. Torrential leaks are sprung in the hull, caulkers and carpenters work relentlessly. Mayken thinks of her friends in the Below World and her heart turns sideways. She speaks to God in her mind. *If you save these people*, she says, *I'll mind my father and not run away to sea.*

❧

The passengers sit quietly; some of them cry. Creesje puts her arm around Mayken, who feels her friend tremble despite her brave smile.

The steward returns, drenched and near hoarse. "They've jettisoned the cannons, did you hear?"

The passengers look up at Pelgrom, numb, disbelieving.

"They rolled them through the open gunports right into the sea. The gunners wept to do it. The skipper has ordered everything to be thrown off that can be. They are trying to float her off the rocks."

Pelgrom battles with the door and is gone again. Mayken moves to follow but Creesje grabs her arm.

"This time you must stay, Mayken."

The passengers wait. The clerks gather account books together and put them into a trunk. The cadets ready the silver chests, find carrying straps, bindings.

Creesje, understanding what this means, knots the pouches she took from the cabin into her skirts. These are the jewels her husband gave her.

Mayken looks out. The stern window is blind, rain lashed, but she watches as the day outside turns lighter gray.

The upper-merchant, clothed now but wet through, enters the Great Cabin, wiping rain from his eyes. Pelsaert talks in a low, urgent voice to the cadets and the clerks, sees their preparations, and seems gratified. With a nod to the passengers, he leaves.

One of the cadets addresses the room. "To save the ship, they are cutting down the mainmast."

"But what does that mean?" asks Judick.

The cadet turns to her. "The mast's weight on the keel is punching through to the rock below. We need to prepare ourselves for the worst."

"God help us," says the predikant and reaches for his wife's hand, and she lets him take it.

CHAPTER THIRTY-SIX

1989

Good things happen to good people and bad things happen to bad people; that is the law of karma. Good deeds get rewarded and bad acts get punished. Help someone out, you'll win the lottery. Steal from a shop, a bird will shit on your head. Sometimes you'll get bad karma for something you don't do, like not helping an old lady who falls down in the road. In a few days, a month, or a year, a hole will appear in your pocket and your wallet will fall through it. That's karma.

Lying brings bad karma. Even a small lie can make something really bad happen and the karma will grow to match it.

If a man comes to your house, said Mum, and cooks you steak every Friday and fixes your boiler, he wants to be your only one. Then Mum laughed. She looked really happy. She had shining eyes and clear skin and was dressing nicely. It's been just you and me for long enough, she said. You need a dad, Gil. He's not your dad, okay, but think of all the boy stuff you could do? Fishing, camping, footy. You like him, don't you?

❧

Carlo emerged from the bathroom. Too-small towel around his too-wide waist. Mum had gone to the store for some coffee, pancake mix, and rashers, with a rattle of car keys and a bright shout from the door.

Gil was on his way to his room.

"Wait a minute, mate."

Carlo in the hallway, steaming from the shower, broad smile, thick pelt of wet hair from shoulders to shins that ended at the ankles, started again on the feet and toes. Yeti.

"You're okay with me hanging out with your mum, yeah?"

Gil shrugged.

"I like her, Gil."

Gil picked at a paint chip on the door frame. "Mum has loads of blokes."

He glanced up, saw Carlo's smile falter and his hand clench the towel around his middle.

"You mean before me?"

The paint chip gave way; under the green paint there was more green paint. "When you're out of town."

Carlo was gone before his footprints were dry on the landing. The pancakes stayed unmade. The rashers left out on the kitchen counter. It didn't go back to how it was before. There were no show tunes, no dressing up, no Mum and Gil against the world. Mum began staying out after her shift and sleeping all day. When she heard Carlo had left town, she didn't get up for a week. Gil thought about telling Mum what he had said to Carlo. But he didn't. He couldn't. He waited for the karma.

Sometimes bad karma hurts someone else, because that way it will hurt you more.

The flies were knocking themselves out against the window: that was the first thing Gil noticed as he walked up the path. The front door was locked, so he had to find his keys in his schoolbag. Mum was in the lounge room, stretched out on the couch. There was a heavy sour smell, sick and something worse than sick. Mum's cheek was resting on a cushion, her topmost eye open a sliver. Her mouth looked thin and smeared and her hand was twisted funny underneath her. She wasn't asleep and she wasn't awake. Gil knew what she was.

He backed out into the hallway and closed the door a bit. Now he could only see Mum's foot, pushed into the arm of the couch. Her toenails painted dark plum. Her foot was narrow, pale green in the light through the closed curtains. A foot as rigid and planted as a tree root. Maybe Mum was growing into the worn foam of the couch? Tiny tendrils uncurling from her hairline. Her knees sprouting green leaves, her ankles and hips too. Gil opened the door a little wider. No, Mum wasn't growing. Silly thought. She hadn't moved.

Gil watches Enkidu for signs of movement.

Gil was used to taking care of himself when Mum was at work. He knew when to finish his homework, or brush his teeth, or put his clothes out for school. He did everything the same. He even sat on the veranda sometimes but he couldn't quite manage the show tunes. Mum had a name for every sky color, like a paint chart. Gil named the skies for her now.

Sunset Peach
Sangria Red
Holy Blue

Gil watches Enkidu for signs of movement.

Gil picked up groceries on the way home from school. He fixed the same snack every day: a grilled cheese sandwich. The only time he sat with Mum was when he had his snack. He had always eaten his snack in the lounge room. Only it was getting hard to eat anywhere in the house now because of the smell. He thought about covering Mum over but he was used to her now. She wasn't so scary. She just looked like a sunken version of herself, with the thin smear of her mouth and her planted feet. Sometimes he was sure she moved; a flick of the eyelid, a twitch of a smile. But she never did.

Gil watches Enkidu for signs of movement.

Mum's boss at the servo came to the house. He knocked and knocked. When he started walking round the side, Gil opened the door. Was his mum in? Where was she? She'd missed shift after shift. No sight nor sound from her for over a week, ten days. He'd stopped. Frowned. What was with all the fucking flies?

Gil watches Enkidu for signs of movement.

Mum's boss had a nice home with wall-to-wall cream carpet and a smoked-glass coffee table in his lounge room. Gil could see that from where he stood on the doormat. Where he was to stand and wait while Mum's boss spoke to his wife.

Mum's boss was called Tony, his wife was called Lynette. Gil couldn't see them but he could hear them. They spoke in furious whispers.

Tony came back, red-faced. He told Gil to go with Lynette into the kitchen-diner while he made some phone calls. Lynette put newspaper on a breakfast bar stool and told Gil to sit up there. The stools were high and it was difficult to get up without the newspaper slipping off. Lynette pretended not to see this.

She asked him why they didn't have a phone up at their house. Gil didn't know. Then she gave him melon balls with an unpleasant juice served in a wineglass. While they waited for the police to arrive, Tony told Gil about the pinball machines he refurbished in his workshop.

Gil watches Enkidu for signs of movement.

The police officer led Gil past the cordon, which was police tape that went all around the front of the house. They had to go straight upstairs to his room, DO NOT PASS GO. Gil wasn't allowed in the room Mum had been in, although they had taken her away now. There were people in suits and masks walking about the ground floor. But the house was no longer a crime scene, which was why Gil was allowed in. The police officer told him to pack a few bits for the night. She stood by the door watching so that Gil got flustered and couldn't think what to take. In the time that followed he wished he'd taken very different things but he wasn't to know he would never go back. Sometimes he wondered what had happened to all their stuff; Mum's clothes and jewelry, their books and records. Even daft things like their inflatable flamingo. He wondered if Tony and Lynette took that. Maybe it's sitting on newspaper up at their breakfast bar.

Gil watches Enkidu for signs of movement.

CHAPTER THIRTY-SEVEN

1629

The blow of axes on the mainmast is felt in the Great Cabin as well as heard. Then the sound of the great mast falling—the terrible groan of it—with a crash that shakes the ship. Roelant wakes and wails in fright. And now the screams of the sailors are heard even above the keening wind and the people in the Great Cabin know that something has gone very wrong.

The upper-merchant comes in, soaked to the bone, his eyes dead with fatigue.

"You have to understand," he says. "We thought we'd stand a chance of keeping her hull in one piece."

"You've done what you could," volunteers the predikant.

Pelsaert looks harrowed. "We cannot save the *Batavia*. I come to order you to abandon ship."

Mayken is spray blind. She's hung over the gunwale. A sailor holds her under each arm. A rope is knotted tightly around her chest. Other sailors hold off the surge of people onto the deck. They rush up from the Below World, herd into the driving sea mist, are drenched by the slant of rain. They push and stumble and fight over the fallen. Sometimes they are swept away by the waves washing over the deck. All of them are frantic to get off the ship into the boat alongside.

The sailors move differently, steadily, with purpose, without panic. Using hand gestures when they are close enough to see one another. The trumpeters relay commands, audible still above the lashing wind and the breakers. The sailors must clear the sails and rigging that came down with the mast to allow the people space to evacuate from the flooded decks below. But the canvas lies sodden and vast and just traversing the sloping deck is a feat. The fallen mainmast lies crossways and has destroyed the balustrades.

The sailor holding her shouts in Mayken's ear. "I have to drop you. Do you understand?"

He drops her.

Mayken falls through the air and the sea rises up.

The rope around her chest snaps her up again. It bites hard under her arms. Hands scrabble to catch her legs before she is dashed against the side of the ship. The boat pitches and leaps insanely and she tumbles into the crush of drenched bodies. With each evacuee it is the same. The sailors on both sides must wait and watch until the boat is lifted on the swell almost to the gunwale of the ship, then the people jump, or are dropped before the sea gives out under the boat and it plummets again, leaving Mayken's stomach in her mouth every time.

The sailors row miles around the breakers. At a distance, and with the change in tide, the survivors see well the bony knuckle of the reef and the broken ship lodged upon it. They come to a channel of calmer water. Up ahead lie flat plaques of gray, which are a scattering of low islands. Farther in the distance there is higher land. The sailor in charge says that the skipper has directed the survivors to be set on a stretch of scrub and shingle that will not flood at high tide. They must wait here until as many people as possible are taken off the stricken ship. Then the sailors will return to ferry them to one of the larger islands.

Mayken is shoeless and has lost Creesje's good shawl. The coral rubble underfoot cuts her, so she stays where the sailors put her down, at the water's edge. This is where Creesje finds her. The rain has stopped but the sky is gray and the wind continues to blow bitter. The survivors huddle together on wet ground. Mayken tucks her cut feet into her skirts. Creesje wraps her shawl around them both.

Creesje starts to pray. A low murmur on the exhale. Mayken listens, her body calming with every breath Creesje takes.

When Creesje has finished she raises Mayken's chin. "Look at me, Mayken."

Mayken struggles to see the face before her.

Creesje, wet haired, pale lipped, the clearest eyes. "We are alive."

During the course of the day more people are landed. A water barrel is brought to shore and strong men run into the sea to claim it. The water is drunk quickly and not shared.

Mayken and Creesje watch with dismay.

"So this is the way it will be," Creesje says.

With weather conditions worsening, the sailors cannot safely reach the wreck: they will not risk their boats being dashed to pieces against the side of the ship. Instead, they begin the slow process of ferrying the survivors from the strip of rubble to a nearby small island. Mayken, with Creesje's arms around her, cannot stop shivering as they approach. The formless scab of an island has already been named Batavia's Graveyard.

Each boat full of new arrivals swells the population so that soon Batavia's Graveyard is thronging. It is without shelter and no natural supplies of water or food have been discovered. Groups quickly form, with the soldiers organizing themselves on one side of the island and the sailors on the other. Smoert is landed with a group of cabin boys and searches out Mayken and sits down next to her.

"I caught the creature," she says.

"You did?" Smoert's slow smile. "The big eel?"

"It was just a shadow in the end."

Smoert rummages in his tunic. He holds out a piece of ship's biscuit to her. She hesitates.

"Go on, you're in need of it. Hide it, though, there's people that would steal the food from your mouth on this island."

Mayken puts the biscuit away in her skirts.

"They've told me I'm to set about mending nets now, for the fishing," says Smoert. "Least I'm out of the bloody galley."

Mayken kisses Smoert's cheek. "For the biscuit."

Smoert reddens and looks down at his knees.

The passengers and the landed sick are gathered together. Mayken is thankful that Imke did not live to see this. To her profound relief Aris and John Pinten arrive in the same boat. John Pinten is carried up onto the shingle. He has a bad break to his ankle, sustained when he fell in the rush to come up from the orlop deck. Aris binds Mayken's cut feet but without shoes she cannot walk far. And those with shoes struggle anyway, for all are land sick. As night falls the swaying lessens for Mayken. At some point she sleeps fitfully with her head on Creesje's lap.

Mayken has shoes made from salvaged barrels by a crewman who is not Holdfast but knows Holdfast and hasn't seen him. The crewman has a wife who is lying curled up, whispering into the shingle. Mayken tries out her shoes although there is nowhere to walk to. There are no landmarks on this island, not a tree, or a cave, or any kind of structure. Surely no person has ever made landfall here?

Mayken, light-headed, sits. She has been without food and water for many hours. She unties the witch stone from her neck and holds it. She concentrates on feeling the weight of the stone in her palm, small and round and real. An anchor in this new gray world. She can't be blown away now.

Holdfast finds her. With his arms about her he cries and says *Little Grandmother*, over and over again.

The two people who died in the night are carried to the highest ground by the soldiers, who make a pit with their bare hands. Stones are piled over them. Everyone gathers and the predikant says a prayer and the wind seems to die down to listen.

In the distance the *Batavia* is breaking up. Wave by wave, swell by swell. Caught between the gathering clouds and the rising waves. Seventy souls are stranded in her tilted stern castle. There is no way to save them; the sea won't let them be saved. The hold is flooded and the water is thigh height on the gun deck. The stores of wine will be breached by the abandoned. The men will turn lawless, feral in their fear. They will rifle the Great Cabin. They will scream and fight. They will spend their final hours insensible with drink. Some will try to swim the distance, leaping from the battered ship into the sea to be dashed on the reef and dragged under.

A watch is stationed on the mean strip of beach and at other points around the island for salvage. As the ship crumbles, whatever is inside her will spill out. Crates and cargo. Barrels and bodies.

The people scour the island for food. They cry for water. Some of the survivors have had the sense to bring useful things, like warm clothes or cooking pots, but then there is little to put in the pots. There are strange marine snails. There are small birds to trap. Some of the sailors have line and hooks for fishing.

❧

Mayken rests in the shelter of the sick bay, one of the first makeshift tents to go up on the island. Aris lowers himself stiffly to sit beside her. He has lost his bloodied apron but kept his weary look.

"How are the feet?"

"I have these shoes now."

"You do indeed." He looks at the family groups gathered nearby. "If we can salvage more canvas, everyone will have relief from the weather."

Mayken looks, too, at the people; they are blank-faced and exhausted. The small child among them picks through the coral rubble, wearing a deep frown.

"Although this weather may aid us. If it were summer . . ."

Aris lets his reflection trail away, and Mayken is glad of it. She doesn't want to think of this island beaten by heat and of an even greater thirst.

"I'm going to join the sailors. I'm a good fisherman," says Aris. "I'll catch you something."

They sit quietly for a while.

"John is very sick."

"Can you mend him?"

"No, Mayken. Neither can he sleep through this; we have little medicine."

"Will he die?"

Aris's face is calm and sad. "We are none of us in a good place but John especially not. He's in a great deal of pain."

"What can I do?"

"Sit with him."

Mayken kneels down next to John Pinten. He is among the sick who lie on scraps of canvas. Some bear injuries sustained during their escape from the ship. Others lie with fever or sickness. Canvas billows above. John Pinten is watching it; he seems far away in his mind. Mayken puts her hand on his arm and he turns to her, his eyes dull with pain, his beard matted.

He forces a smile. "Did you ever catch your creature?"

"Yes," says Mayken. "I caught it in your jug and threw it in the sea."

"Well, now, isn't that one good thing?" He touches the witch stone around Mayken's neck. "Curious."

"It shows you what is and what will be and what was."

"All that? Then you're a magic woman, just like your nursemaid."

Mayken lifts the stone to her eye, peers at her friend, and puts on a sonorous voice. "I see you in fine clothes and a big hat walking around Batavia."

"Limping, surely." John Pinten gestures at his ankle. "But I like the big hat and the fine clothes. That's good fortune indeed."

They fall into silence. Mayken makes to go.

"Wait. You must be paid for your prophecy." His hand scrabbles under the scrap of canvas. He brings out an object. "I traded my wine rations for this but I haven't the breath. Take it."

It's a bone whistle, beautifully made. Mayken turns it over in her hands, smiling in delight. John Pinten shows her how to play it, how to patter tunes into the mouthpiece with her tongue, how to make the sound raspy or shrill, soft like a blown note across a bottle, or strident like a call. How to answer the whistle's voice with her own.

Mayken loves the sounds she can make, like some strange sad island bird. She starts with some simple sailor songs, then begins to invent her own. Until, exhausted and dry-mouthed, she must stop. She looks around. The sick listen; some are crying. Creesje listens, a covered jug in her hand.

John Pinten turns to his fellow patients and announces, "Our whistling Mayken."

❧

The soldiers have been all around the island and there is no fresh water to be found.

Fights break out over the remaining water, with few barrels and many people. The strongest make their claim. Some speak of harvesting rainwater, only there's no saying when the next squally winter storm might be; the gray sky gives nothing away.

The seaweed is salty and Holdfast warns Mayken not to eat it, or drink from the sea, however thirsty she might be. Her tongue feels like it doesn't belong to her. It swells and cleaves to the roof of her mouth, making talking difficult. Her lips crack and bleed. Holdfast finds her a cup of water and stands over her while she drinks it, his brow low. He will knock the head off anyone who tries to take it from her. Mayken uses her two hands and is careful not to spill it. She tries to give him some but he makes her drink it to the last.

CHAPTER THIRTY-EIGHT

1989

Just before dawn, on Easter Sunday, Enkidu rises from the dead.

Gil wakes to a rustling sound coming from Enkidu's box. He lifts the tortoise out and sets him on the floor. Enkidu stumbles haphazardly the length of Gil's room. The glue has dried on his shell, the cracks blackened under it. He refuses water but takes a lettuce leaf, snatches it, his dinosaur face grim.

Gil wipes his tears on the bedsheet.

Joss and Dutch are drinking coffee at the kitchen table. Dutch gets up and brings a mug for Gil.

Gil sets the tortoise on the table. "He ate a leaf."

Dutch holds up his mug. "A toast to brave Enkidu. Back from the land of the dead."

Gil holds up his mug and so does Joss. The tortoise craps on the table.

"Bastard! Get him off," laughs Joss.

Dutch hoots. Gil smiles. Enkidu topples a sauce bottle.

Joss finishes his drink and gets up. In passing, he taps the tortoise gently on the shell. Then he shoulders his bag and is gone out the door.

Gil turns to Dutch. "Aren't you going with him?"

"Day off. Deckies get motherless on Easter Sunday, it's tradition. Your granda will take *Ramona* for a spin, find a quiet spot, get away from the ructions."

Gil can well understand that.

Dutch turns to the tortoise. "This fella is nearly as good as new."

"He's ruined."

"You think so?" Dutch looks thoughtful. "In Japan, if they smash a bowl or a vase they repair it with gold. That way the cracks make it more beautiful."

Gil studies Enkidu. His cracks look anything but beautiful.

"I'm not sure that he'd like that. Would you, Enkidu?"

Enkidu lifts his head.

Dutch goes all over the island for a tiny pot of enamel paint. Only it's not gold, it's copper but it will work just as well. They put the tortoise down with rolled-up towels around him to stop him rampaging. Dutch prizes off the lid of the pot and Gil stirs the paint carefully with a matchstick. Dutch takes a fine brush and dips it in the paint. He starts on the biggest fault line, a jagged crack right across the shell. When he's finished, he hands Gil the brush.

"Maybe come down to the party later?"

Gil dips the brush. "Maybe."

With Enkidu's crazy-paving shell outlined in shiny copper, the damage is much clearer. Gil would rather Enkidu had been unbroken but he can see why Dutch suggested it. To celebrate Enkidu's scars is to celebrate his survival; he is a warrior, after all.

"I promise to fight for you," says Gil. "For as long as I live."

The tortoise bows his old thin head. Gil puts him gently back in his box. Enkidu swims on tired legs to the corner. Gil cleans off the paintbrush. He looks at the flyer Dutch left on the table.

BEACON ISLAND EASTER 1989
COMPETITIONS, PRIZES AND RACES
GOODY BAGS, BARBIE, MUSIC AND MORE!!

Gil doesn't want to be with other people but he could watch them for a while. Just while Enkidu is sleeping.

The party is by the main jetty. The trestle tables are out again. They have bright tablecloths pegged to them and are set with baskets of buns and bottles of sauces. The awning flutters, tied down against the sea breeze. Beer kegs and bags of briquettes are stacked in piles. Mums and grans are fussing with cool bags and boxes. People from other islands are coming in, fishermen and their families. Boats crowd along the jetty; the sea is dotted with them. There are many more people than on Birgit's race day. Gil sees that they form groups. The deckies keep apart, a straggly crew in weatherworn clothes, drinking steadily. The fishermen make another group, with their puffed-out bellies. Dutch isn't with either group. He's nowhere to be seen. Bill Nord is abroad, everywhere, patting the chefs' backs, pouring beer for the deckies, finding chairs for folks not much older than him. Gil takes a juice from a bucket of ice and sits down behind a windbreak. From here he can keep an eye out for Dutch.

A little girl in a summer dress hands Gil a burger. It's on a paper plate with relish and a napkin too. When he remembers to say thank you, she's already hopped off again. A mum smiles at him from behind a trestle table. Gil quickly looks away.

Dancing breaks out. A gran waltzes with a deckie, and the little girl who gave him the burger hops about with an old bloke. Her feet are on his feet. He pretends to wince with every step and she giggles until she hiccups. The islanders are together, laughing and singing along. Smaller kids run about roaring. The barbecue smokes up. Stubbies are handed out from eskies full of ice. More ice is brought down from freezers. Babies are corralled in a nest of cushions under the shade of beach parasols. And here comes Papa Zanetti and Silvia, Cherry the deckie, Roper and his boys, to the party.

Gil should return to the camp.

He can't help but watch them. The Zanetti family. The fishermen turn and greet Frank, shaking hands, nodding respectfully. Silvia joins the mums, chatting and eye rolling, eating, collecting plates.

Roper and his boys have a mock fight, then stand with Cherry and the deckies. Paul is given a beer and Mikey reels about, circling the group. He's a plane, he's a bird, he's a lunatic.

Gil is careful to keep down behind the windbreak.

The deckies are just drunk enough to be entertained by Roper's kids. Paul and Mikey are telling them a story. Paul becoming talkative with the attention, Mikey becoming more erratic. Roper looks on, his hand on Paul's shoulder. Paul mimes a dropkick, the sailing of an object through the air, someone crying boo-hoo!

Mikey copies the mime, performs it again and again, taking up his brother's words. Louder and louder.

"I beg you! I BEG you! I BEG YOU!"

The deckies look amused; a couple just drink. Cherry turns away and spits on the ground. Roper glances around. His eyes meet Gil's. He opens his mouth and laughs heartily.

Enkidu is old, nine hundred years or more. He has seen many sights. He holds many wisdoms. He will never be the same. The dip to his side, his back legs giving out, his beautiful shell broken and traced in copper. The work of a moment.

The adults get drunker. The kids run out of steam. The party lights strung along the awning are switched on. Sunset approaches: the one true spectacle the island will see today, like every day. Gil watches from his quiet spot.

Mikey is sitting under a trestle table, scratching in a picture book with a Biro. He startles when he sees Gil.

Gil hears his own voice, sweet and wheedling, Bunyip-sly. "Do you want to see the tortoise?"

Mikey's eyes widen.

"You never got to hold him, did you?"

Mikey hesitates, perhaps sensing a trick.

Gil holds out the lollies he's taken from goody bags. "We can share these on the way."

Mikey gets to his feet.

CHAPTER THIRTY-NINE

1629

Five children all in a row, two below-deck girls and three cabin boys. The soldiers tuck shingle all around them so they won't be cold, for the wind is biting for the unsheltered. But it's too late, they're already frozen, Mayken saw their faces: lips blue and eyelids veined in blue too. The soldiers lay the stones gently, apologetically. Sand flies swarm.

The thirst gets terrible. Some drink the sea and some drink their own water. Mouths thicken and lips crack and eyes sink. The end isn't so bad, they say, once the thirst stops you can just lie down and sleep. The predikant prays for rain and the sky darkens. Others join in and nothing happens. Holdfast finds a half cup of something brackish. Mayken can barely swallow. He takes her everywhere with him as he searches for food. He makes her eat sea snails, grinding them into a paste with flat stones. He scrapes up the mess with his fingers and pushes it into her mouth.

Aris comes with his catch. Creesje cooks it and shares it among the sick. Mayken gets a portion. She takes it down to Holdfast on the beach where he is watching out for salvage.

"You eat, Little Grandmother."

"Not unless you share it with me."

Holdfast shakes his head.

"Go on, it's mostly bone, anyway."

Holdfast laughs.

The fish is awful but they pick it apart.

The longboat is seen heading east. On board are the upper-merchant, the skipper, and a crew of good sailors. They are looking for water, the people say, they are searching all the nearby islands. The yawl waits farther out at sea. It has been busy salvaging from the wreck site but the weather is still against them. Several chests of silver have been landed on the strip of coral rubble the survivors first stepped upon, but no more souls have been saved from the ship. Mayken and Holdfast keep watch for the longboat's return.

"They will bring us water." He says it like a prayer.

Mayken looks at her friend. He has found a scrap of canvas to wind about his old head. He wears it as well as his lost India shawl. It makes him look more himself. Only he's not himself. His hands, once steady, shake now. His mouth, like hers, is cracked and stiff. He turns to her and smiles with his eyes. They have lost their shine.

The longboat approaches Batavia's Graveyard. The people who can walk gather at the water's edge rejoicing. The upper-merchant and the skipper bringing news and supplies! Word goes around that they have found a better place. A higher island with fresh water, more vegetation—shelter, even.

But hope turns to confusion in the watching crowd as the craft nears. They can see that something is wrong. Pelsaert is shouting but they cannot hear what he says, the wind takes up his voice and carries it away. He's trying to climb overboard and wade to shore but the others are holding him back. Now the longboat is changing direction—not toward their island—it's sailing away!

The survivors rush out into the sea, shouting to the upper-merchant, to the skipper, to the men on board the longboat. They plead for water. They plead for food. But the longboat holds its course, moving farther and farther from the island. Pelsaert with his face in his hands, the sailors still holding him.

The longboat puts in briefly at the stretch of coral rubble that was the people's first landing place. A sailor disembarks and wades to the shore. He stands there waving. The keen-eyed spot something in his hand. He is leaving it behind. Wading out again, he is helped back into the longboat. The craft turns, more decisively now, and makes progress out to sea. The yawl follows.

The stretch of coral rubble is named Traitors' Island by those left behind.

The sailors believe that the skipper intends to steer toward the South Land to find supplies, although that dry coast is inhospitable and likely uninhabited.

The survivors curse their abandoners. They have taken both boats and left no water and no food. Seventy men remain on the broken *Batavia* but the islanders have no means to help them. Those poor souls must see to their own rescue now. A few, clinging to pieces of timber, ride the tide and reach the island. They recount their experiences on the sinking ship. The hold is flooded and much of the cargo ruined. There are barrels of drinking water and food that may yet be salvaged. But how, without any kind of craft to sail there? Order has broken down on the ship. The chests that remain on board have been opened and their silver hoard scattered.

The predikant's servant, Wybrecht Claasen, takes off her clogs and her skirts and her cap and leaves on her tunic. She walks to the water's edge with her face full of purpose.

Mrs. Predikant calls out to her. The predikant starts up with a shawl to wrap around the girl.

"Let her go," says Judick. "She was brought up by eel fishermen. She is a strong swimmer."

Wybrecht wades into the water, ankle—knees—thigh-deep.

Everyone watches her. They see that Judick is right, the girl is made for the sea: her shoulders and arms muscled, her body sleek and long.

Over the horizon, beyond the stricken ship, the sun is breaking through a bank of cloud. It skims the sea with mackerel streaks of light.

The predikant takes it as a sign. He starts praying and others join in.

Wybrecht pays no mind. She baptizes herself in the shallows of the sea. Cupping the water over her legs, stomach, shoulders, her head. When the water is to her waist, she folds the long curve of her back into the sea and pushes away.

She stops at Traitors' Island, where the sailor from the longboat put ashore. They see her walk up and down the length of it. She lifts a small barrel and looks back. Hesitating, as if making a decision. Then she's back in the water, striking out for the ship.

The others watch until she's out of sight. The last thing they see of her, she's dipping under a breaker. The predikant prays. The soldiers pace. The sailors mutter old charms.

Midafternoon Wybrecht is sighted and a call goes up. She swims toward them awkwardly, dragging something behind her. She struggles up the beach, red of face, limbs cold-bitten, holding a small barrel of water. A fight breaks out.

"So this is the way it will be," says Holdfast.

The men on the ship have gone insane, Wybrecht says. They bristle with weapons; knives in their hats, swords at their waists. They prowl the half-sunk ship and have made the stern castle their lair. The Great Cabin is like a dockside tavern, wine brought up and beer. They get drunk. The remaining chests have been opened and the men throw silver coins at one another and overboard. All the while the ship breaks away all around them. The noise is maddening. The constant scraping and booming and splintering and sea spray. None that remain can swim or make a raft and sail it to safety. They

did not harm her, the wild men. A few even cried when she climbed
back into the sea.

The predikant reads aloud the note Wybrecht found under the empty
barrel on the lick of rubble. Written by the upper-merchant, signed
by the skipper, it tells of their plan to sail along the dry coast, and if
that does not prove fruitful, make a course to Batavia and there raise
a rescue party for the survivors. The people take this news bitterly.
Without water and food, how could there be survivors? They have
been deserted. Pelsaert and Jacobsz are whores' sons.

A cold squall. The sky opens and Mayken lies with her mouth open
and her eyes closed. The people catch the water in every vessel they
can. They crowd under the few tents erected, seeking shelter. Holdfast, with no way to keep Mayken dry, embraces her to keep her
warm. Her teeth chatter but she's alive.

CHAPTER FORTY

1989

The boy runs ahead and then back again, in a way Gil finds irritating. Once they are clear of neighboring huts, Gil relaxes. They've got away. No one will be on this stretch of path, it only leads to Joss Hurley's. Behind them the faint sound of music. Before them the sky flares orange over a sea of molten iron.

Mikey is asking Gil something. His face is unbelievably dirty. Smears of tomato sauce, something blue above his eyebrow. He's lost his two front teeth so that he lisps.

"Finish your lolly first," replies Gil, disgusted.

"I want to hold the tortoise."

"Didn't I say you could?"

There's no sign of the old man on the veranda, no lights on inside the hut.

"Be quiet," Gil says. "Or you'll scare the tortoise and he'll run away."

But the boy is already struck silent, unsure in these new surroundings. Gil opens the door and Mikey follows him inside.

The familiar kitchen smell: cigarettes and fried breakfasts and mice. At this time the dying sun illuminates everything. All the day's light, collected by the sea and the sky, pours in. A honeyed soup of light. Even Mikey must feel how magical it is.

He follows Gil to his room, hesitating to come any farther.

Gil, carefully, carefully, gets Enkidu out from his box. The copper fault lines on the tortoise's shell catch the light and shine.

Mikey looks amazed. He reaches out a finger to trace the bright pattern on the tortoise's broken back.

"You can't touch him because he hates you and your brother."

Mikey opens his mouth to whine.

"We can play another game, though."

CHAPTER FORTY-ONE

1629

After ten days on the island everyone has shelter because when the predikant prayed long and hard the *Batavia*'s spars washed ashore with sails and rope attached.

Now there is a council to tell everyone what they should be doing, apart from the soldiers because they are doing everything already, like building shelters, killing seals, and fishing. The council is made up of the island's senior men, including Pelsaert's highest-ranking clerk, the provost and the predikant.

Mayken walks this strange new canvas village, doing her rounds as she did on board the *Batavia*. Sometimes she takes her bone whistle and the people call out for a tune. But the whistle makes every song sad and sweet and a touch unearthly.

The sick tent is at the edge of the settlement. This is where John Pinten lies and where Creesje tends to the injured and feverish. There is also the main tent where the council meet and where supplies, such as they are, are held. The shared tents for family groups are set round and about. Creesje and Mayken have a screened corner in one.

The sailors and carpenters have shelter across the way. This is where Holdfast and Smoert live. The predikant's family have their own abode and their servant Wybrecht stays with them. The soldiers have the best camp, well-ordered and at a distance from the other survivors.

Aris sets up camp wherever he wishes, moving to where the fishing is good. He is the island's best fisherman by far. These past few days he has pitched his shelter at the farthest point from the settlement. Mayken sets out for it. The weather is cold and overcast but she has borrowed Creesje's shawl and her barrel shoes fare well on the shingle. She says a prayer to encourage raindrops and the small nesting birds the sailors catch at night. Everyone prays for this, or else for more salvage to be found. The more hopeful pray for a rescue ship, even if this constitutes a miracle.

Mayken walks the length of the island slowly, this way she gets less thirsty. She can do nothing about the hunger, which makes her stomach a tight grumbling fist.

Seeing the barber-surgeon's canvas ahead, she approaches quietly. She has learned not to shout out to Aris when he's fishing. Besides, she likes to watch him, his slow and patient dance of lines and hooks, then the flash of a catch, landed, gasping. He makes the dispatch quickly, stone in hand. There's no cruelty in the man, he seems rather part of the water, the fish he seeks. He says that one day he will grow gills and swim away. He keeps every fifth fish for himself, the rest he gives to the council to distribute.

He glances round at her. "How are the sick?"

"No one has died."

He nods. "I've a piece of fish for you, in there, under the canvas."

"I'll take it for Holdfast."

"Take it for yourself." He frowns into the water. "Else you'll disappear, you're as slippery-looking as an elver."

"What's an elver?"

"A young eel."

Mayken shudders. "I'd rather not be an eel."

"What would you be?"

Mayken looks up at the sky. "A gull. When you grow gills and swim away, I'll fly after you."

Aris laughs.

Mayken, head down, follows Holdfast's bare feet along the beach. She does not know how he can stand walking on this sharp shingle. But then his feet are leathery and callused from all the years climbing ropes. Everyone strong enough must scour the island for anything they can find. But here, now, there is only Mayken and Holdfast. She matches her steps to the old sailor's trudge. They are a good salvage team. With Mayken's sharp eyes and Holdfast's wiry strength they have hauled out big kegs and nail-studded planks, coils of rope and a wooden sewing box. It claimed no owner so was given to Creesje to mend the clothes of the sick.

Farther along the beach, Holdfast's feet stop. He raises his hand.

"Stay there, Little Grandmother." He wades out into the water.

Something is knocking in the shallows.

Human remains have been washed up. Because of the breakers, they are not complete. When they have faces, they are blue. When they have torsos, they are bloated and stinking. Holdfast says that such sights can never be unseen. Mayken knows he is right because she often thinks of the five dead children lying under softly heaped stones.

The body in the water is intact, lying faceup, eyes closed. The limbs twitch.

Holdfast exclaims with wonder. "He's alive."

The men peel him from the bowsprit. His hands are claws. He has petrified to the wood. The very bowsprit the Lion of Holland used to prowl upon! But now there is no carved lion, only a half-drowned man whose face is recognized.

A shout goes out—Jeronimus Cornelisz has survived!

They carry the under-merchant up the beach. Mayken straggles behind. She spots something in the sea foam washed up nearby. She wades out into the water and picks it up. It is a piece of broken pottery. Part of a face, with a beard and a pop-eyed smirk. She drops it onto the stones, wiping her hands on her skirts. Bullebak's broken jug sneers up at her.

The under-merchant quickly regains his voice and tells his story. He was the last to leave the ship and only because she crumbled into the sea. He had lived alone on the wreck after all the others had jumped in or been washed away. As the stern castle finally collapsed, he looked about himself for a piece of timber big enough for a raft. Seeing only the bowsprit, he lashed himself to it. The wood floated, him along with it, for days and days in the water, riding the eddies and waves to arrive at the island.

The people agree that it's a miracle.

Mayken thinks of the pottery shard and its pop-eyed smirk.

Under canvas, Mayken dreams. The night is clear and cold, the stars shine and the moon is bright. The people of Batavia's Graveyard slumber, cold and exhausted, on hard ground. The tents flap in the breeze, otherwise all is quiet. Something else is moving this night. A shadow crawls out from the sick tent, to pool and collect outside. In the light of the moon the shadow deepens and grows. It forms a shape: tall, hunched. The shadow stretches its notched spine, turning this way and that. The outline of a head, bulbous-eyed, whiskered like a catfish, the gills beating. The wind stirs up deepwater badness; a stale stench fills the air. Then the sound of low burbling. Words form, they drip. A voice, honeyed, intimate, seeks an ear to lean into. The shadow wishes just to whisper—

Under canvas, Mayken wakes. Creesje sleeps beside her. Mayken fancies she sees a shadow steal by, hears it hiss. She closes her eyes tight and presses her hands over her ears.

CHAPTER FORTY-TWO

1989

"It's part of the game."

Mikey shakes his head, his face pinched with tears.

"Have another lolly."

The boy takes a lolly solemnly. He sits on his haunches behind the generator and eats it.

"I've put it over my head, now it's your turn." Gil holds out the bait sack. "Just put the bloody sack on!"

Mikey retreats farther, pushing backward with his grubby feet.

Gil doesn't blame him for refusing. He had planned to shut Mikey in the broken-down freezer and pile stones on top. The boy refused to get in, given that it smells like Hell. When Gil tried to lift him, Mikey went limp in resistance. Mikey may be small but he's sturdy. He's also so snotty and filthy it horrifies Gil to touch him.

Gil tries being furious. "You'll ruin everything! You won't see Bunyip!"

"I don't want to see Bunyip!"

"If you put the sack on your head, I'll give you ten dollars."

Mikey says nothing.

"Twenty dollars."

"I don't want to." Mikey draws up his legs and starts to cry.

Gil feels exhausted. He looks at the small boy sobbing in the harsh light of the one working strip. Dirty blond hair, face pressed into his knees. He's lost his sandals and has a bloody graze on his ankle.

Gil sits down near Mikey. Eventually the boy stops sobbing and looks up, his face flushed and miserable.

"I'll take you home," Gil says.

The night is overcast and the wind calm. The sea is a flat blackness against a charcoal sky. Gil takes the track down to the Zanetti camp. Mikey drags alongside, sandals found, slap-slapping against his feet.

As they near the Zanetti camp, Gil says, "That game we played is a secret. Okay?"

Mikey's small voice. "Okay."

The porch light is on at Papa Zanetti's but the place looks empty. "Go inside."

Mikey won't. He starts crying again. Asking for something.

Gil makes out a word. "You want me to take you back to the party?"

Mikey stops crying.

The party has mellowed. They've lit a campfire and gathered around it drinking. Groups of people, the men together and the women separate, the kids going between. The fire crackles. Gil wishes it would catch and spread and burn this island to nothing. Then nature would start again. He learned this about the bushfires. That there were good fires and bad. Some fires cleansed. Some fires cleared the dead wood and burst open seeds. Without people, nature would be queen. The plants and animals and birds would reign. The islands would be how they had been for millions of years. Empty of the sound of boat engines and generators. Uncluttered by kero stoves and jetties. Let it all burn to dust. Let the islanders, him too, melt and twist and howl and then lie silent. Let the island breathe again.

❧

Dutch sits with the people, tuning his guitar. He starts to play. Everyone falls quiet from talking and laughing.

Dutch's voice is some beautiful broken thing.

The listeners are lulled. Grannies pull kids nearer. Fishermen glance at their wives. Old men close their eyes. Gil could cry. He doesn't know why.

Mikey stands beside him.

"Go on," hisses Gil. "Off you go."

Mikey hangs back, then spots his father sitting by the fire and runs to him, exploding into wailing.

Mikey clings to Roper. Roper looks at Gil.

"What the fuck did you do to him?"

The music stops. Mikey sobs. Everyone is watching.

"He was lost."

"Lost—on an island this fucking size? Are you fucking serious?" Roper loosens his son's grip and sways toward Gil.

Silvia steps forward to comfort Mikey and he cries louder. She picks him up. The boy looks at Gil over her shoulder. He's finally playing a game he knows the rules of.

Roper livid by firelight. "Stay away from my boys, you weird little fuck."

Dutch puts down his guitar and stands up. "That's enough, Roper. He's only a kid."

Everyone watches. All the eyes around the fire. No one moves, only the flames. No sound, only the snap of the flames and Mikey's crying.

Dutch holds up his hands, like he's stopping a horse. "Roper, leave it."

Roper kicks over a chair and heads for Gil.

❧

Gil knows well the dark paths through the scrub. He hurtles along, not running from Roper anymore; no one is chasing him. He runs from their faces, firelit eyes watching him and the sting of that word and other words. *Weird, weird, weird.*

The cloud cover clears and the stars put on a big cold twinkling show. The brightest moon shows all the details: the stones on the path, the dark-windowed huts, the coils of rope, the abandoned gear. At the beach Gil lies facedown, hardly feeling the shock of cold shingle. Knowing there's no part of him that's right or good. As his breathing calms he becomes aware of a stirring. Far, far below in the silty water table there's a shifting. A tongue flickers, a knotted spine uncoils, limbs shift the shale. Bunyip swims up through bone dust and seabird shit and dead coral. Bunyip comes to claim him.

CHAPTER FORTY-THREE

1629

Jeronimus Cornelisz stands at the entrance of the new large tent pitched at the northwestern corner of the island, just above the mean little beach. He wears found finery: a red coat from a salvaged chest that once belonged to Pelsaert. Cornelisz changes his costume three times a day, appearing in stockings and hats and capelets. If a feather can be stuck somewhere, it's stuck. If something can be beribboned, it's beribboned. His superior's clothes are made for a slighter man and are worn too tight, adding to the grotesquery of the strutting.

No one questions his appropriation of Pelsaert's possessions. After the upper-merchant and the skipper, Cornelisz is next in command according to Company law. He already has his devotees—"his boys"—a rabble of rowdy high-family cadets, a clutch of burly German mercenaries, and steward Pelgrom on the periphery. And Stonecutter, who has lost none of his shipboard menace. Cornelisz's retinue follows him everywhere about the island. There's something of the parade about this, absurd and obscene before so much suffering.

The days continue cool and overcast. Any further squalls are met with hectic water-gathering in canvas funneled for that purpose.

With the ship scoured and broken on the reef, her full cargo has been released into the sea. Barrels and casks bob in the currents that pass by the island. They are hooked out of the water by the constant watch set up all around the coastline.

Cornelisz organizes the supplies in a central place, this being his tent. But greater order has been established with the rationing of water, ship's biscuit, and the allocation of wine to the sick. Cornelisz has directed the digging of latrines. The soldiers, apart from the few German mercenaries that dog his step, recognize Cornelisz's authority but do not like it. When he orders them to bring their weapons to the main tent where they can be kept safely, the soldiers are disgruntled. Cornelisz talks of pirate attacks. This hardly seems plausible, but then he's an educated man. He sets the carpenters to building boats from the wreckage, the sailors to fishing or watching for salvage. The women and the children must search the island for edible berries and plants or walk the tidelines looking for sea snails and sea urchins. Birds are hounded from their nests at night and strangled. Seals are slaughtered wherever they haul up. Eggs collected. When a beach-made boat is ready, trips are made out to the carcass of the ship, but nothing can be brought back.

Cornelisz has insisted that Creesje and Mayken take a tent of their own near his, as befitting highborn passengers. He sets them a guard, which Creesje has tried to refuse. It is enough that he has set them apart from the other survivors, with a bed and rugs salvaged from the ship. This is attention Creesje does not want. Her nightmares return, as in the days following her attack on board the *Batavia*.

When Mayken isn't visiting Aris or John Pinten, or gathering sea snails, or helping Holdfast with the salvage, she watches Cornelisz's tent. If he comes out, she's careful to look away. If their eyes meet, he will make a bow and there is something mocking in his gesture.

Tonight, as the light fades, he sits outside his tent with his gaggle of goose boys. They've a good fire and wine. Pelgrom hovers with skillet and jug. The oily stink of roasting seal meat fills the air, which, along with the taunting laughter coming from the group, makes Mayken feel queasy.

She huddles at the entrance of their tent. Creesje will be back soon from tending the sick, then they will see what they have to eat. More often than not they just crawl together into their straw-stuffed canvas bed, the under-merchant's gift. Creesje says she would prefer to sleep on wet shingle.

Outside the under-merchant's tent the talk has become ribald. Mayken knows this from the way they are flashing the hilts of their swords around. Pelgrom tries to join in but the group take no notice of him. As Mayken watches, Cornelisz leans forward to speak into the ear of the cadet next to him. The firelight crackles and jumps, and a familiar shadow is cast large on the wall of the Great Tent.

Early morning and Mayken finds Smoert down on the beach, mending a net. The kitchen boy is one of the few people to look better since the wreck. The many burns on his face from the fat splatters have had a chance to heal. Smoert's scorched eyebrows have grown back, along with his hair, which is russet in the early sun.

Smoert glances warily at Mayken.

"Don't worry, there won't be any kisses."

Smoert, reddening, looks down at his net.

"I've come to tell you that it's back."

The investigation begins.

Smoert opens with each potential witness: "Have you seen or heard anything of that eel sort of creature?"

To this Mayken adds: "The one that leaves footprints." She measures out the size with her hands, to remind them. "And gives poisonous bites."

"Stinks like seal stew," Smoert volunteers.

"Changes in size, and . . ."

Smoert nudges her. "Go on."

"Might hide in tents and things."

One soldier saw a dead eel in his boot. But it might not have been dead, because you know what eels are like.

The caulker's wife saw something unnatural in her cooking pot, among the sea snails and seal gristle. She could swear it had beating gills.

A strange figure was seen by a carpenter late one afternoon. He was shaping a stem post and caught sight of a hunched shape prowling along the shingle, but it could have been the provost's shadow.

Soon any number of accidents and annoyances are blamed on Bullebak. Fires that won't light. Fish that won't bite. Bedding that won't dry.

Mayken and Smoert search the sick bay for probable bites. They find a cabin boy with a poisonous-looking finger, although he's unsure whether he was bitten or not. A frail John Pinten beckons them over.

"You're on the hunt again?" he whispers. "For your Bullebak?"

"It's not *my* Bullebak." Mayken frowns. "And we've no jug."

"Or bacon rinds," admits Smoert.

John Pinten reaches under his canvas bed and produces a cracked jug. "Find something to stopper it and try seal meat."

But now Smoert must return to his nets and Mayken must look for salvage.

"Meet again tomorrow?" says Smoert. "We can keep looking."

Bit by bit Mayken and Smoert build up a picture of the strange happenings occurring almost daily on the island. People start to flag the two down as they pass by with their jug and nub of seal meat.

A footprint was seen on the canvas wall, would that count?

A sea mist drifted through the camp with the hint of a burble, could that tally?

During the second great Bullebak hunt, Mayken learns about the lives lived by the survivors. It is Mayken who is responsible for a series of little kindnesses.

She gives her last ribbon to the gunner's daughter, who cries for her lost friends.

She finds a cap and apron for a soldier's wife who still wears her night shift.

She brings a perfect speckled gull's egg to a down-at-heart sailor.

When she has nothing to give, she gets out her bone whistle and plays a tune.

The under-merchant has wine, fine furniture, and jewels in his Great Tent; his followers dine on extra rations. Mayken knows this to be wrong. There should be no divide between the survivors of Below and Above Worlds, all should have their equal share. As she grows in affection for the people of the island, the people grow in affection for her. They look out for the small, gray-eyed girl wrapped in a borrowed shawl.

They begin to notice an air of Imke about her. It's as if the old nursemaid has imparted her wisdom to the child. The people start to seek out Mayken's advice and she proves gifted with the reading of portents, clouds, waves, seaweed, and the like, although she prefers just to look through her prophecy stone.

What Mayken sometimes lacks in accuracy she makes up for in spirit. Many come away infected with renewed hope and even charitable feelings.

CHAPTER FORTY-FOUR

1989

That Mikey would tell was only natural. That Mikey would invent new twists to the story, Gil didn't expect. All the ingredients were there: bait sack, freezer, bribery. Added to this: threats with a nail gun and the binding of Mikey's hands and feet with rope.

Gil knows the severity of the situation. From the look on his grandfather's face and from the fact that Bill Nord is sitting at the kitchen table wearing his Community Watch badge and writing everything down.

Dutch tops up their coffees and takes a seat.

Bill looks up from his notepad. "So you're saying there was no nail gun, Gil?"

"Ah, come on!" says Dutch. "You know the Zanettis as well as I do, Bill. They've fed that kid what to say. They're making the whole thing sound worse."

Bill holds up his hand while with the other he continues to write, slowly, meticulously. After reading back his lines to himself, he closes the notebook.

He addresses Gil, a stern note in his voice. "Keep to your grandpa's camp for your own safety. Spirits are running high on this island right now."

Gil finds himself crying. "I didn't mean anything."

The three men sit silently. Even Dutch looks away.

Roper is coming for him. He will kill him, hack him up like bait, and throw him overboard in deep water. Today Joss is out on the veranda. Dutch is with him, strumming his guitar. But tomorrow they'll both be out at sea and Gil will be left alone.

Cray bait. Who'll care? Even if people suspect Roper, they won't risk losing Papa Frank's favor by speaking out. And Joss and Dutch will probably be relieved to be shot of him. Gil will just be that weirdo kid who disappeared. Some story will be told about him: he drowned, went raving into the waves. He ought to have been tied to a bedpost like a toddler or a sleepwalker.

Enkidu sleeps soundly in his box. Gil strokes his copper-crazed shell and wonders if his friend is dreaming. He clears away uneaten leaves.

Dutch returns late. Low voices on the veranda. Gil slips out of bed and into the lounge room. He crouches by the window and listens.

Dutch's voice, grave. "They want him off the island."

"They can fuck off."

"That little kid is really shaken up. Roper's gunning."

"What's new?"

"They're saying you brought Gil out here knowing he's wired up wrong. You need to send him away."

"Yeah, where?"

"To another relative."

"He has no other relatives."

Silence out on the veranda.

Then Joss again. "End of season, I'll take him back with me to Gero."

"In the meantime?"

"He can stick to the camp, like Bill said."

"Great, Joss. Days carting a dying tortoise around dressed in his granny's clothes and Roper on the warpath."

"Roper won't touch him, it's me he's after."

A lull, then:

"Maybe he should see someone?"

"Dutch, I'll put you through that wall." Then the old man, quietly: "They'd take him away."

"What happened with Dawn. Was that right, was that healthy?"

The old man doesn't answer.

"Gil needs routine, contact with other kids—"

"He just tried to shut one in a fucking chest freezer. I'd say he's a loner."

"Joss, come on, think about what would really help him now."

"Not seeing those fucking Zanettis again."

Gil holds out his hand and touches the wall. His grandfather is on the other side. He's there in the creak of a chair, the pop of a lighter. In a while, one of the men stands. His shadow passes by the window but Gil is already in bed.

CHAPTER FORTY-FIVE

1629

The under-merchant's most trusted men take the beach-made rafts and sail out from Batavia's Graveyard. They are going to explore the nearest islands. The survivors have little hope they'll find anything but they keep this to themselves. For hadn't Pelsaert and Jacobsz (curse their souls) taken the longboat all about? There was nothing to be had in this wide sea but dry scrub and coral rubble.

The survivors watch the progress of the boats. They head northwest and then up farther toward the higher land. The beach-made vessels don't go fast and there isn't a decent sailor among them. The decent sailors have all been left behind, much to their bafflement. Late in the day the men return surly and go into the Great Tent, where they stay for the longest time. There is no wine drinking and reveling this night.

A dark ripple spreads through the island: a carried story whispered. It is about the unthinkable, a word people cannot say out loud.

Smoert says the word in Mayken's ear. They are sitting on the beach, mending nets. His breath is warm and tickles, too close to hear.

"Say it again, Smoert."

"Mutiny."

This is not a charmed word but it is a word which wrongly spoken can make luck turn. This word can only bring a bad ending.

The seaman had been grumbling for days but no one listened. He was a hothead on board. On the island, with the cold and hunger and thirst, his fury grew. Something stewed in him until he could bear it no longer.

He opened his mouth and out fell the tale of a conspiracy.

If the wreck hadn't happened, a mutiny would have.

The night of the storm, the skipper ensured they became separated from the convoy so none of the other ships could come to the *Batavia*'s aid. He gave orders for the stern light to be put out.

Skipper Jacobsz was involved in a mutiny?

He was.

The orlop-deck hatch was to be nailed down with the soldiers inside. Pelsaert would be run through with a sword. The sailors would be given a choice: follow or die. The passengers thrown overboard. The silver and valuable goods were to be divided among the mutineers. Had she not collided with the reef, the *Batavia* would have sailed into very dark waters.

None of the survivors will go anywhere near the angry seaman. They will not share food with him or even look at him. Suddenly fearful, he swears blind he cannot name the mutineers, for all were recruited in strict secrecy.

❧

The angry seaman is missing, on an island no bigger than Haarlem market.

The angry seaman is found dead in the bushes. His throat has been slashed with a ferocity that has almost taken his head off. Everyone is quiet that day. Everyone suspects someone. Most everyone suspects Stonecutter.

If they can walk, they must come to the beach by order of Jeronimus Cornelisz. It is a day of gentle weather, of sun and kind winds. A sea scattered with diamonds.

The under-merchant arrives flanked by his men. The soldiers come in from their corner of the island. They stand apart and look on grimly. Aris leaves off fishing. Creesje and Mayken stand holding hands. The members of the council are among the crowd, as baffled as everyone else.

The under-merchant starts to talk. His voice, raised above tide and seabird, is smooth and cheerful. He says that this place, now called Batavia's Graveyard, won't sustain everyone. He intends to set up camps on the surrounding islands. High Island, where the scouts found water. Seals' Island, where the animals, wise to the slaughter here, now haul out. Traitors' Island, which offers the best fishing. Regular supplies will be rowed out until each group is established. Cornelisz calls this the Great Dispersal.

"So this is how it will be," says Creesje.

When their names are called, they must quickly gather their possessions and walk down to the beach. They will be transported by beach-made boats to their appointed settlement. The under-merchant reminds the crowd that his selection cannot be appealed. Mayken sees Stonecutter grasp the hilt of his sword, his eyes sweeping the crowd. The under-merchant has armed his gaggle of geese. Now they are no longer ludicrous.

The group is named for Seals' Island, a place more barren than where they stand now. Married men and their wives, a few older soldiers and sailors, cabin boys, including Smoert.

Fifteen to Traitors' Island, a desolate strip of rubble. The provost will go to keep order. His wife sobs at having to leave. Cornelisz smiles into her hand as he kisses it. Holdfast's name is called.

Mayken follows Holdfast into the sailors' tent. He has little to collect and has gathered his things in moments. In the time they have left, they sit quietly together.

"Hold fast, Little Grandmother."

"I want to go with you."

Holdfast nods. "Look to your friends here, Creesje and Aris, the soldier John Pinten."

Finding she can't help herself, Mayken begins to cry.

Holdfast wipes Mayken's face roughly with his hand. "If you stop that, I'll tell you a plan."

Mayken takes a breath.

"Good. There's this star—"

"Don't tell me the name!"

"I know, the stars stay wild. It's very bright. If you look up and I look up—"

"We'll be together in our looking?"

Holdfast nods. His old eyes are teary.

"All right. I'll look for this star. Do I have to say some charms or something?"

Holdfast laughs. "You're every bit a sailor."

⁓

Crowds gather on the beach, survivors with their possessions, on-lookers; many are crying. The first boats go out, full of people for Seals' Island.

The members of the council are trying to talk to the under-merchant. Cornelisz holds up his hand and walks back to his tent. The council members look at one another in disbelief.

Mayken waits with Holdfast. She sees Smoert. She will say a quick goodbye. Holdfast nods, take your time, the boats have yet to return.

Mayken runs to Smoert. She just stops short of flinging her arms around the kitchen boy. Perhaps Smoert knows it, because he gives his slow smile—

Mayken feels the shock of hands.

Stonecutter lifts her and carries her up the beach. She tries to get free, twisting and turning, but his grip is iron. She fights against him, screaming, shouting, trying to get her teeth on him. His hold tightens, crushing the breath from her.

Now Creesje's voice, raised, imperious, ordering Stonecutter to put Mayken down. He complies, dropping her. Mayken is to stay off the beach. If Creesje can't control her, the child will be dealt with.

Mayken lies on the shingle bank, watching the boats tack back and forth to the other islands. Taking Smoert. Taking Holdfast.

The under-merchant's men return with a great find from Seals' Island. Cornelisz comes out of his tent to inspect it. Pelsaert's secret box of delights, saved from the wreckage by the longboat and left on the hitherto deserted island for safety. The under-merchant is transported. He calls for wine.

Creesje is summoned by the under-merchant. She has orders to join him in his tent for a private viewing of the contents of Pelsaert's secret box.

Creesje sends her apologies. A guard arrives to escort her. Creesje promises Mayken she will return. Mayken promises she will sit quietly and wait.

To Mayken's relief, Creesje is back within hours. She creeps into their bed in the dark.

"The inside of his tent is just like the Great Cabin," Creesje whispers. "He has Pelsaert's bureau. How, I don't know."

"What was inside the box?"

"An ugly agate carving of a horse and cart." Her voice is bitter. "I hate him."

Mayken feels Creesje's tears on her neck but neither of them says anything.

Creesje cries out in her sleep. Mayken speaks to her softly and she settles. Unable to sleep, Mayken gets up and puts on Creesje's shawl. She walks as quietly as she can in her barrel shoes.

She watches out for faint moving lights on the islands across the water. These are the shell lamps the survivors make, lit by seal oil, that flicker with a smoky glow. But the islands are in darkness.

Mayken looks up at the sky. There's no bright star that she can see.

CHAPTER FORTY-SIX

1989

The children are leaving the island, running along the jetty and hopping onto the carrier boat like so many little rats. Gil is not among them. He is lying on his belly in the scrub with Dutch's binoculars trained on the proceedings. Faithful Enkidu sleeps beside him in the sports bag.

Goodbye! Fuck off, now!

Silvia walks down the jetty. She holds Mikey's hand and bends down to him. Maybe she's telling him to walk properly. Mikey is hopping and dragging on her arm in a way that's annoying for adults. Big brother Paul follows, scowling, his feet out-turned, plod, plod. Gil takes aim with an imaginary gun. Bang. Paul's fat head explodes.

There's no sign of Roper or any of the fishermen. They said their goodbyes last night. Easter is over and they went out to sea hours ago.

Silvia hands Mikey onto the carrier boat. The bigger boy climbs past her without a backward look. Silvia's shouting something to the skipper's mate, and he gives a thumbs-up.

The carrier boat pulls away, the passengers waving to the handful of islanders left behind on the jetty. Up in the scrub the last child on Beacon Island waves back.

Fuck off, now! Goodbye!

Walking back to Joss Hurley's camp along the coast path, Gil sees a fishing boat anchored a little way out. It's Roper's.

CHAPTER FORTY-SEVEN

1629

The soldiers, Dutch and French, are to be sent to High Island, the most habitable of all the islands, even Batavia's Graveyard. There is drinkable water, small, hopping animals, and good fishing. The soldiers have their instructions: When they locate water they are to light three fires to alert the under-merchant.

Creesje's voice, an uneasy whisper: "If Cornelisz's men have already found water there, then why are they sending the soldiers to look for it?"

Mayken walks the pathways made by the feet of the survivors. She must hunt sea snails and salvage now. Not Bullebak.

She wishes for Imke's wisdom, her mystic gifts, so that when she looks at the under-merchant through the witch stone, he'll appear how he really is. No longer speaking Dutch but rather a watery language of burbles and drips. His face running with water, gills beating at his neck, skin crazing into scales.

Then Mayken will see just what has crawled behind this man's eyes.

But he's always just a middling man in ill-fitting finery.

❧

A day of glorious weather and calm sea. The boat goes back to the wreck and strikes lucky. Salvage waits to be found on a reef ledge. Garments, gold braid, fine cloth. They are hauled back and spread on the shingle banks around the main tent to dry. Jeronimus Cornelisz's cheap market stall.

The carpenters want to build a boat capable of sailing to Batavia to bring back a rescue party. Cornelisz refuses. Their efforts are best employed mending nets and strangling birds.

Creesje is distracted. She walks the floor and frowns into the cooking pot. She sweeps the rug and moves around their few possessions. She sits down on the bed next to Mayken.

Mayken glances at her. "Whisper it."

"He's sent no supplies to the other islands. Everyone thinks it, no one says it."

They look out at the guard posted at the mouth of their tent. He seems to be sleeping, his back to the tent prop, but you can't always tell.

"No signal has been sent by the soldiers. I fear for them, Mayken."

The guard glances over his shoulder, then closes his eyes again.

A young soldier with a sturdy aspect and a gunner old enough to know better are found insensible after stealing into the stores and tapping a barrel of wine.

Cornelisz rules: the death penalty for both men.

The council disagree: the soldier was the perpetrator, the gunner coaxed into drinking with him.

The gunner is spared but the soldier is gagged, bound hand and foot, and rowed out into deep water. The survivors watch silently from shore as the accused is pushed off the side of the boat. It is over in moments, a struggle and a splash. Cornelisz's men look down into the water, then row back again.

Cornelisz disbands the council and forms a new one, more to his liking.

This is the way it will be.

Mayken makes her island rounds. The survivors are quiet today, keeping under canvas, pensive, as if waiting for an approaching storm. Mayken takes out her bone whistle, playing as she walks. No one calls out their request. No one even looks out. The sky is overcast. She feels chill, despite the borrowed shawl knotted around her.

Two of Cornelisz's men approach. They tell her to stow her noise. She pretends not to hear. One comes forward to snatch her whistle but she's too quick, hiding it in the folds of her shawl.

"Keep your whistle, then, Lady Mayken," he says, "but play another note and we'll take you out to sea and drown you."

It is said laughingly but with such a cold eye Mayken does not doubt it.

CHAPTER FORTY-EIGHT

1989

Joss Hurley's camp appears to be just as Gil left it. Even so, he takes a paring knife from the sink drainer and goes through the hut. There's no sign of trespass. He runs back, locks the back door, and closes all the windows. Thankfully Joss's hut has plenty of locks, probably on account of everyone hating him. Gil checks the kitchen clock: three hours until *Ramona* returns to the jetty, three and a half before his grandfather and Dutch arrive back at the hut.

Gil thinks of racing down to Bill Nord's. The old man opening the door and the baffled look on his face. What would Gil even say? That Roper's boat is anchored off the island instead of out fishing? Bill would send him away, or worse, he'd have to sit there with him. The clock ticking. One long silence.

Gil carries Enkidu into his room. He puts pillows on the floor beside the bed, where there's a view of the window. He climbs into this nest with the tortoise.

A noise outside. Gil's up on his knees, holding his breath, listening past his own heartbeat crashing in his ears. It's the wind, sending something scrabbling past, an empty bait bag. He lies back down with Enkidu, tracing the patterns on his shell. Telling himself to tighten the screws.

༈

Gil wakes with a strong sense that a shadow has just passed by the window. He sits up, his face stiff where he dribbled. The room is sweltering with the window closed and the day's heat beating in.

He turns to the tortoise. "The hut is locked. We're safe."

Enkidu looks doubtful.

Gil knows that Roper could put his fist through the window. He could kick out the door frame without trying.

Gil drinks squash, three mugs. Enkidu ignores a saucer of water.

Gil thinks about pissing in the sink. There's no way he's going outside to the dunny.

Gil looks out of the kitchen window, opens it, and gets up on a chair to peer out, in case Roper's crouching on the veranda, waiting to pounce. There's no one outside.

He puts Enkidu on the kitchen table. "You keep watch."

Gil scoots out the door, full scuttle, like a dunny crab, like the little creatures out there waiting with their pincers waving in the air, full of excitement, beady eyes twitching. He can't keep the hut in his sights because the dunny door keeps blowing shut in the wind. But he's quick enough.

Seconds and he's back in the kitchen, sun-blind from the dazzle. As his eyes adjust to the dim, it becomes clear: sitting at the kitchen table is a man shape.

CHAPTER FORTY-NINE

1629

From her tent, Mayken watches the island's new council gather about their commander. There are celebrations with wine. Pelgrom runs with the jug, laughing, grinning. The under-merchant has promoted the bold, the cruel, and the ruthless. Rewarding loyalty, not former rank. A lowly clerk on board the *Batavia* is now a figure of glowering authority, despite his wispy beard. A strutting young gunner stares down men twice his age. A rough locksmith from Groningen has won himself a place at the commander's right side. There are seasoned soldiers among their number. Unlike the cadets and the clerks, they don't mock-slap one another and no one mock-slaps them because they would knock their fucking heads off. As for the rest, the highborn cadet officers stride about as if the sky and the sea and the shingle are theirs.

The youngest member is a cabin boy promoted to the mascot that stooped, long-faced Pelgrom likely wants to be. The boy has blue eyes and a handsome look to him. Mayken knows of him by reputation from Haarlem. His family don't live in a nice part of town. His mother takes in babies and washing.

The survivors understand the threat latent in these men; they are not fooled by the lolling and the joking. The good fellowship gives way to blank coldness when these men address someone not of their group. The most terrifying of all the under-merchant's men is Stonecutter. He has fashioned a tunic from sailcloth and wears it open, his bare chest like the pelt of an animal. His beard grows out and is threaded with gray. He looks like some terrifying god of old. Sometimes he growls. Mayken is afraid of him; she can still feel his grip on her, his easy violence.

The island has transformed these men. They have grown bigger as everyone else shrinks and cowers. Those that held a position shipboard—who tried to establish order before the coming of the under-merchant—are diminished. They no longer have the ear of the island's self-appointed commander. And threaten Cornelisz's authority and you may find yourself at the bottom of the sea or in a shallow shingle grave.

Creesje beckons to Mayken. She is holding up a comb. Mayken begins to complain but something in Creesje's expression stops her. She yields and sits down before her.

"Be careful what you say and who to. Be only where you are allowed to be," Creesje whispers. "Don't talk to them or even look at them. Don't draw attention to yourself. Don't give them reason to take you away, Mayken. Do you understand?"

The guard at the entrance of their tent inclines his head.

Mayken nods, but only very slightly.

Mayken has hidden her bone whistle under the bed. Sometimes she takes it out and mimes a song, resisting the urge to fill her lungs and make the biggest, angriest sound. To stomp all around the camp playing as loudly as she can. To shout out her own requests. Let them drown her! More than once Creesje has quietly, gently, taken the whistle from her hands.

❧

This shell is Mayken, small and gray. Here is Holdfast, a beautiful dappled turban of a shell. John Pinten is a spiky anemone cast. Aris, a smooth conch. Smoert is a starry limpet. Creesje, a piece of bright glass. Imke is the witch stone, smooth and perfect with a seeing hole right through. Mayken will never let it go.

They all live happily together in a coral slate house with walls and courtyards. There are feather trees, and seaweed grows around the door. There are no stallions but there are pieces of wood which look to be winged. They fly and gallop and are decorated with char-coaled eyes and stripes. Calico creatures. They are gentle and tame and named for the stall holders at Haarlem market.

Two carpenters stand accused of stealing a beach-made boat. They intended to sail to another island. The under-merchant's appointed court gathers. It seems that justice will now be served by bold cadets, leering gunners, and rotten soldiers.

The accused wait outside the Great Tent. The predikant stands with them, reading from the open Bible in his hand. Mayken pre-tends to move her shells about. After a little time, the council and their leader emerge. The predikant comes forward to ask what the verdict is. Mayken doesn't hear the answer, but one of the carpenters starts to cry.

Mayken looks to her shells as the procession passes. She takes sly glances and sees that the procession is made of the convicted men, Jeronimus Cornelisz, and his council. The predikant lags be-hind, wearing an expression of dismay. The prisoners walk between two soldiers, their hands bound. Too late Mayken realizes that the under-merchant is watching her. He breaks away from the proces-sion and walks over, holding out his hand.

He talks to her in his honeyed voice all the way to the beach. About her noble father, about Creesje's kindness and beauty, about his hopes for their rescue. He holds her hand tightly. His grip is too hard. Mayken fights against biting him and pulling away.

They stand on the bank and watch as the carpenters are half carried, half dragged down onto the beach. They are instructed to kneel. They do so with difficulty, bound as they are. Cornelisz's men help them, putting steadying hands on their shoulders.

Two young cadets, with a sword each, approach along the beach, in easy conversation. As they near the kneeling men, the cadets give a jubilant shout and run the final distance. They fall upon the accused, teeth-gritted, hacking.

Mayken stands very still. Her face is stiff from tears. Cornelisz crushes her hand in his. Cloud shadows cross the shingle.

Cornelisz sends men to help the soldiers find water. The reinforcements are rowed out by members of his council. The boat returns, bringing one of them back. He wears a smile that isn't real. When Cornelisz's men slap him on the back he flinches.

It becomes a regular occurrence: a group of recruits are rowed out by Cornelisz's men to follow in the wake of the soldiers. Sometimes one of their number returns.

Mayken knows exactly what's going on.

Once upon a time Bullebak lived in the Great Tent. It guarded stolen chests of glittering treasure. It stretched out on the rug. It nuzzled around the under-merchant's neck like a shadowy stole. Swelled by grief and fed on fear, Bullebak grew too big for the island. One night they towed the monstrous shadow away, slumped behind a boat, low and bloated in the water. They gave it an island of its own. They tended it, like worker bees do their queen, bringing it men to eat from the inside, as a beetle eats a soft log. These men still walk upright but there's nothing behind their eyes.

A soldier and his wife are invited to dine with the under-merchant. They eat seal meat and drink good wine. They enjoy the light of wax candles, and the soldier's wife strokes a rug and agrees it's the best thing she's ever seen. They return to their tent to find their little daughter gone. All that's left is a hair ribbon and a tangle of hair. Overnight a new mound appears in the shingle bank, so small as to be almost imperceptible.

Creesje whispers, "Don't go off on your own, Mayken."

"Will they kill me too?"

Creesje's voice is too bright. "No. You are with me."

Creesje Jansdochter is to be taken into the Great Tent under council guard for her own protection.

A soldier waits as she gathers her belongings. The soldier is listening. Creesje makes subtle faces at Mayken, who cannot interpret them.

Creesje gives Mayken her shawl and her sewing box and is led away. The guard returns directly. Mayken is to vacate the tent and seek other shelter. He takes the sewing box but leaves her the shawl.

Mayken makes her camp in a hollow thornbush. She carries seaweed up from the tideline and, ignoring the hopping flies, arranges it for a bed. She furnishes the camp with shells and ties strips of canvas to the branches to flutter prettily in the wind. When it gets dark, Mayken looks out at Seals' Island. She watches for the tiny shell-lamp flames, which mean the people are still alive. But the island is in darkness again tonight.

Mayken studies the sky. There are many stars to choose from and she can't tell which is the brightest. She chooses one and gazes and gazes. Across the water Holdfast may be gazing too. She misses the old sailor until her heart hurts.

When it gets too cold to sit out, she crawls inside her shelter and covers herself with Creesje's shawl. The flies bite her senseless and every footstep on shingle fills her with sudden dread. Toward dawn, she falls asleep. She wakes late to find a piece of cooked fish and a bowl of water have been left for her.

CHAPTER FIFTY

1989

"All because of this"—Roper gestures—"tortoise."

Gil stands very still.

Roper sits at the table like a reasonable interviewer. He looks at Gil over the sauce bottles, nudges aside a dirty ashtray with his elbow, recoils, looks at his arm, and wipes it with a tea towel.

"Don't you people ever clean this place?"

Gil stands very still.

"Help me out. I'm just trying to understand what's going on in that fucking head of yours."

"I didn't mean anything."

"You didn't mean anything."

Gil dives toward the back door but Roper is quicker than he could imagine. In one move his chair is over and he has Gil by his shirt. Gil hears himself screaming. Right up in Roper's face: redfacemeat-sweatfucker. Roper slaps him.

A rushing pain to the side of Gil's head. For a second, Roper looks as shocked as Gil is. Panic sweats off the man. Gil starts to scream again. Then Roper really goes to town.

Roper uses his palm, not a fist. He doesn't mean to kill him.

❧

Of course he means to kill him. Then gut him, dice him, and scrape him into the water. Pieces of Gil sinking fathoms deep, out beyond the fishing ground.

Gil twists from his shirt, drops to the floor, and then he's up and running.

CHAPTER FIFTY-ONE

1629

A plume of smoke from High Island. Mayken hears shouts of joy all around.

The soldiers have found water!

Nothing happens.

No boats are sent.

Cornelisz's council gathers in the main tent. When they come out, their faces are like thunder. The islanders stop smiling and go about their chores. No one speaks.

Mayken, searching for sea snails, rounds the island to see the under-merchant's men run down to their boats. They are armed with swords and knives. Mayken follows the direction of their sailing, running along the coast path.

Making its way past Seals' Island is a flotilla of roughly built rafts. Dipping and slow, overloaded, the rafts move through the water propelled by frantic paddling. They are heading toward the far smoke signal at High Island. Cornelisz's men are setting a course for them.

They clash in the deepwater passage.

The rafts are dragged back to Batavia's Graveyard. Cornelisz's men stand waist-height in water holding them there.

On the rafts survivors cling. Mayken sees them and knows them: the provost, his wife and their little girl, a cooper, carpenters, caulkers, an old sailor—*Holdfast*.

Holdfast crouching on the edge of a raft, thinner than ever, drenched by the sea. Mayken starts to race toward him.

Cornelisz stands on the bank, watching. One of his men wades out of the water and walks up to talk to his commander. Cornelisz speaks. The cadet listens and nods. Then he half runs, half falls back down the shingle bank.

"Kill," he shouts. "Kill."

Holdfast staggers, fights the waves, runs out of the sea.

Mayken watches, frozen on the path, riveted in horror. Cornelisz's men are on him with their pike and swords. She cannot look away.

Holdfast won't die. There is nothing of him but he still won't die. Not with the hacking of his neck or the stabbing of his sides. He keeps trying to rise up. He's stamped down. A pike is driven through his throat to the shingle below.

The pike is stuck; it cannot be withdrawn.

His murderers take turns to kick it.

Holdfast lies, arms open, palms turned upward. In supplication to the sky and the wheeling seabirds. Pinned in the shingle. He's left like that. By degrees, Mayken nears him and lies down beside her friend. She rests her hand, palm upward, in his. The old sailor's expression is not to be feared; his sightless eyes are fixed on the heavens; his mouth, in death, shows neither grimace nor smile.

CHAPTER FIFTY-TWO

1989

Bill Nord has him take slow breaths. Bill's voice is calm but his hands shake. Gil can feel them shaking as the old man holds him by the shoulders.

"That's it, son, slow breath, in, out. Then I can understand what you're trying to say."

No, Bill doesn't think Roper will kill the tortoise. The tortoise will be where Gil left him. Roper has likely legged it. Yes, Bill will go up to the camp himself to see about the tortoise but first he needs to take care of Gil's injuries.

"You've a sprain on that wrist, not a break, which is one good thing."

Gil nods. His teeth are chattering, although he doesn't feel cold.

Bill makes a proper sling with a triangle bandage and safety pins. He's seen active service. Blood and guts, he says. He works carefully. First, he lays out supplies from the first aid kit on the kitchen table. Then he sets about cleaning the cuts, the welts. Applying ointment to the already darkening bruises.

Bill finds some of his grandkid's clothes, shorts and a T-shirt. He shows Gil where he can change.

"Take your time, son. I'm going to radio this in."

Gil nods, hardly understanding. There's something funny going on with his eye, a narrowing of his vision, his eyelid sticky. To say nothing of the ringing in his ears.

Bill gives him a smile. "Just hang in there. Okay?"

Gil's legs won't stop shaking, so he sits down on the bed, holding the clean clothes on his lap. There's a mirror. Gil gathers himself to go and look in it. His right eye is busted closed. There's an apple-sized bruise to his temple, and his lip is swelling too. There are welts on his face and body, marks where the ring Roper was wearing cut in. Otherwise, Gil's feet and limbs are casualties of the coral rubble and the scrub.

He gets dressed stiffly, trying not to make noises like an old bloke. The T-shirt falls lower than the shorts but the bandages look really neat. He puts his sling back on the way Bill showed him, straightening the folds carefully.

The Nords' kitchen is like theirs, only cleaner. The layout of the place seems much the same. Gil finds this reassuring. Bill has two sons out at sea. They each have a mug with their name on it. All the mugs live on a mug tree when they are not being used. They don't live on the table, or under the bed, or in the sink. Bill is clear about that. Bill has angina but back in the day he pulled pots with the best of them.

Gil is to sit up at the table for his drink. It comes in a cold glass and is fizzy and has ice in it. Next to Gil's drink are two biscuits on a saucer. Gil wants to cry. Instead, he eats his biscuits and sips his lemonade. His lip makes it difficult to chew politely, his mouth stings, and he tastes nothing. Bill recounts the entire history of the Nord family. Gil looks out of the window at an outboard that's been taken apart and at the dunny.

Bill is talking about the scientists. Gil makes an effort to listen.

"Maybe it's a wing bone, but if it's a human shoulder blade it could be the mass burial they're looking for."

"What burial?"

"A whole family wiped out, wife, all the kiddies. Only the father, a preacher, was spared and the older daughter. Some kind of cruelty right there. That man had to go on living. I couldn't."

Gil looks at his empty glass. "Do you see ghosts?"

Bill smiles. "Not that I'll admit to."

"Silvia talks about a dead Dutch girl."

"Little May?" Bill finishes his drink and closes his eyes a moment. "The dead can't hurt you, Gil. It's the living you need to watch out for."

Gil has another lemonade. Bill has a whisky for his angina. He makes them both a sandwich. It's tinned ham.

"He shouldn't have done what he did." Bill's eyes are rheumy. "No matter what."

Gil finishes his sandwich and wipes his fingers underneath the table.

"Just so you know that, son."

Mum had a rule if something bad happened: no talking about the bad thing, no thinking about the bad thing, no remembering the bad thing. Mum only wanted to hear about this good meal, or that funny prank, or this nice servo restroom. Never of this fight, or accidentally running over that dog, or the time they were caught leaving without paying.

Gil has always liked the idea that if you stop talking or thinking or remembering something bad, it vanishes from your mind altogether.

He should try it on Roper.

Bill doesn't have the same rule. He sets out a notebook and a tape recorder.

"Now, Gil, suppose we get a few facts down while we're waiting on the cavalry?"

Joss and Dutch arrive off the boat. Bill's big sons are not far behind.

When Joss sees his grandson, he's straight back out through the door. Bill's big sons head him off. Bill orders the old man to take a seat. This is not the time to play silly bastards.

Men fill the kitchen, talking. The room becomes airless. Gil's ears ring and his head swims and all he wants is his tortoise.

He's to lie on the couch with a wet flannel on his forehead. He hears the men debate in the kitchen. The words sometimes distinct, sometimes not. Gil doesn't fish for them, he doesn't try to understand what they are saying. He just drifts.

When his grandfather comes in to check on him, Gil pretends to be asleep on the couch.

Joss leans down and touches his head, gently, very gently.

Through his eyelashes Gil watches him leave the room. The old man briefly leans against the door frame, like he has to prop up the whole hut.

CHAPTER FIFTY-THREE

1629

It's a fine day, so John Pinten has been brought to the mouth of the sick tent and propped there. His pallor is not helped by the strong light but he's over the worst, Aris says; he'll most likely starve to death now. The under-merchant has allocated the sick half rations, and what they get is already poor: water barely drinkable, food hardly edible.

Mayken kneels next to the English soldier.

He leans nearer and whispers. "We'll steal a boat and go where the others have gone. High Island."

Mayken frowns. How can she tell him that there is no one there? They've all been fed to Bullebak.

"They'll invade, you know," he continues. "They have good soldiers among them who will have worked out what's going on here."

He closes his eyes and moves his leg, trying not to show pain.

Mayken attempts to distract him. "When we escape, can we bring Creesje too?"

"Of course."

"And Aris?"

"Most welcome."

"What if the rescue ship never comes?"

John Pinten smiles. "Then we'll build our own marble house, with red and white roses. Will that do?"

"The longboat sank, didn't it? In that big storm."

"And you visit to lighten my mood?"

Mayken unknots the pouch at her waist. Inside are two perfect bird's eggs. Small and bluish white. She puts them in the soldier's hands.

"Found outside your camp?"

Mayken nodded.

John Pinten tries to give them back. "The good soul that put them there meant these for you."

"Then they're mine to share."

Mayken makes to go.

"Wait, Mayken. Stay. Until I fall asleep."

The light and shade cast down by the moving canvas passes over John Pinten's sleeping face. Mayken lies close to him. The wind picks up to dry her salt tears.

Mayken must not stay out alone anymore by order of the under-merchant. Now that Judick is married to a favorite cadet of the commander, there is space in the predikant family's tent for Mayken.

She is to sleep behind a canvas partition with Agnete, who is younger than her and spiteful. Agnete claims all the blanket and spits in the stew. Mayken is careful to keep her precious possessions from the girl; the witch stone and the bone whistle and Creesje's fine shawl are always with her.

The family have changed very much. The predikant looks shrunken in his skin; Mrs. Predikant is always red-eyed and never speaks; even Roelant has forgotten how to smile. Every night the child wakes screaming and everyone in the tent holds their breath in panic. Mrs. Predikant puts her hand over his mouth and he swallows his sobs with little frantic choking noises. It doesn't do to draw attention on this island. Every day the boy asks for Judick over and over. The predikant children are not allowed to walk around the island on their own, they must always be with their mother or father, even the grown boy. The grown boy keeps mostly inside, for the bold young cadets mock him and Mrs. Predikant is scared that their games with him will prove fatal. Nightly the father leads his family in whispered prayers. The under-merchant has banned open services. At the last public sermon Cornelisz's cadets descended upon the congregation flapping bloody seal flippers and jeering. Now the minister must spend his days guarding the boats, running to help launch them when he sees the men coming. Whenever Cornelisz sets eyes on the predikant, he communicates his astonishment that he's still alive.

When the family pray, they send their servant, Wybrecht, out to keep watch. Mayken offers to go with her but she's told to stay and join in. Agnete pinches her until she moves her lips too. Mayken only pretends. Used to the turbulent passion of Imke's worship, the predikant's prayers go down like dry ship's biscuit.

Day by day the family becomes quieter and more hollow-eyed. Shadows of themselves. Mayken wonders if she's becoming a shadow too.

She thinks about Bullebak. She left her jug up at her camp. But would the creature be lured inside even if it was on the island?

Wybrecht takes it upon herself to keep the family from starving to death. She goes about the island finding things to put in the pot. She begs scraps from the fishermen. She swims out with a spear. If any of Cornelisz's rougher men call out to her, she tells them to go fuck themselves. Mayken follows her everywhere. She adores her. At night she creeps from her place next to Agnete to where Wybrecht lies. The servant girl bundles her up in her shawl. Mayken finds comfort wrapped in the warm smell of woodsmoke and dirty hair.

Wybrecht slips Mayken a paring knife. They are sitting together, tending the fire that's heating something terrible in the pot for the family's main meal. A foamy soup of seal meat and shrub leaves and some kind of inky creatures found at the tideline.

"Take it," Wybrecht says of the knife. "For when they come for you."

Mayken is shocked.

"As the stores run out, they will kill more people, us before them."

A cadet passes by. Wybrecht gestures to Mayken to hide the knife.

They watch the pot as it rests in ashes. The wood they burn is the *Batavia*. These are the charred and glowing remains of the great ship. What isn't given to the carpenters for beach-made boats and structures is shared for fuel. Wybrecht blows on the fire, nudging the flame with her breath. She is careful not to waste their allotment.

"Are you scared, Wybrecht?"

"Yes."

"I'm not sure about dying."

Wybrecht smiles. "So be like the eel, don't die. Just when they think you're dead—off you go, slithering from their plate."

"If there's one thing I don't like, it's eels."

"No one does, because they are a mystery. Even to me, and I fished for them." She puts her arm around Mayken and makes her hand go slithery. "Neck-deep in an eel pit with my little hook. Grabbing those slimy bastards under the gills."

Mayken laughs.

Then it strikes Mayken: if anyone could catch Bullebak, it would be Wybrecht the Brave.

When Mrs. Predikant is sleeping, they take Roelant about the island to find food. He is allowed to hold the basket when they walk and he does so with both hands and a serious expression. He is a different boy from the one Mayken knew on board the ship. He moves slowly and sleeps all the time. His arms and legs look thin and his head looks big. Sometimes when they walk, he sits down and refuses to move. When he cries for food, they give him a small stone to suck. If he falls on the sharp coral, they grab him up and kiss his face quickly, quickly, his eyes widening at their sudden love. Wybrecht points out the place where his hair is falling out. She says he grinds his teeth when he sleeps; they're as worn as an old mule's.

"We must be thankful that he's too young to remember this," says the servant. "This will be just a dream to him when we are rescued."

"Will we be rescued?"

Wybrecht considers this. "We've prayed enough for it."

They sit down at the land's edge as the sun sets, the small boy between them. They look out to sea.

"Forty-four days we have been here," says Wybrecht. She shows Mayken the row of black stitches in her underskirt. "This is how I remember."

Roelant takes the stone from his mouth and throws it at the water.

CHAPTER FIFTY-FOUR

1989

A soft tap and Joss is standing in the doorway. "What are you doing?"

"Looking through my stone."

The old man hesitates. "Righto. You want a drink?"

"Okay."

The old man lingers. "We'll get him, Gil."

"Okay."

At lunchtime, Dutch brings in a tray and sets it on Gil's bed.

"How's it going?"

"Okay."

"Don't see much of Enkidu these days."

"He's asleep." Gil glances at Dutch. "Hibernation."

"It's not winter."

"He doesn't know that."

"You still have that auld hag stone?"

"Yeah."

Dutch sits silent for a while. When he gets up, his knees crack. "Come out on the veranda, for a bit of fresh air?"

"Maybe."

Gil ignores the tray. He lies back on the bed and looks through the stone. Still just a strip light.

CHAPTER FIFTY-FIVE

1629

This morning the sick tent is empty, aside from Aris spearing bloody bedding with a stick, moving it toward the fire at the entrance. Mayken runs to him. He holds a finger up before his lips and shakes his head. His eyes run with tears from the woodsmoke.

Mayken walks around the whole island looking for John Pinten. Here is a mound and there is a mound, only she can't remember which are new and which are old. And would they bury the murdered or just roll them into the sea? They do that, too, these days. She walks the coast path looking down into the water, in case he's somewhere in the shallows. One of the jewels knotted in her skirt bought Holdfast's burial. A shallow grave under shingle dug by one of the net menders.

There is no sign of the English soldier. Not a button, nor strand of hair.

She cannot bear to go back to the predikant's tent. To sit in the anxious gloom listening to the nervous whispering of prayers. To startle at every sound. She stays outside with the wheeling seabirds and the wind and the waves.

When she gets to her old camp in the bushes, with the raggedy strips fluttering, she finds Jan Pelgrom there.

༄

He's sitting under the branches, hunched and awkward with his long legs folded up. He is thinner than ever, although as a servant to the commander he does better than most. On signing an oath of loyalty Cornelisz's followers, Pelgrom included, have been given rich materials to make clothes, red wool, gold braid, and silver lace. He has sewn a collar for himself and a short cape. In his costume he looks like a hawker's dog. He beckons her inside.

It's dank in the camp, with the seaweed Mayken piled up for her bed. In front of the shelter there are the ashy ghosts of her small fires. They sit with their legs and shoulders almost touching. Pelgrom holds one of her shells in his hand; Mayken fights the urge to snatch it from him. But the shell is only a minor character in her game of Haarlem Market: a barrow boy or a fat pigeon.

"You know there will be no stallions and roses and marble houses for you, Mayken dear?"

Mayken sets about moving her important shells away from him.

"There will be no rescue," he says. "We'll never leave here."

She takes up the starry Smoert shell.

"By our honorable commander's reckoning, supplies will only last another fortnight, given the present number of people on the island."

She takes up Holdfast, the beautiful dappled turban of a shell.

"Do you understand what he's trying to do?"

She takes up John Pinten, the spiky anemone cast.

"The commander will scour this island of traitors, those who would rob the stores, steal the food from our mouths. Imagine! When there isn't enough to go around? What sort of person would steal from the hungry? From the weak?"

Pelgrom picks up another shell, turns it over in his hand. It's a shell that serves as an unpopular Haarlem butcher.

His face changes, drops. His voice is suddenly weary. "I want to confess. Will you hear it?"

Mayken makes no answer.

"Do you know what happened on Seals' Island?"

Mayken has heard rumors and the little lights have long been out.

"They went over and killed all the men," he continues. "They left the women. The cabin boys ran away and hid."

Mayken looks at the shells in her lap. She names them in her mind, Holdfast, John Pinten, Smoert—

"I went back to help them clean up. We cut the women and pulled them into the water. We stabbed the boys and bashed their heads in."

She wills him to stop speaking.

"I killed your friend, Mayken. I killed the kitchen boy."

It was almost dawn. Surprise attack, Pelgrom tells her. As he delivered the blows, he had screamed and screamed, as if it hurt him more. Smoert had an injured foot, so he was easy to catch. Pelgrom had thought of seals as he dragged the boy into the sea, the way they play in the water, the joyful bulk of them and their kind dog faces.

Pelgrom sobs. He forces his knuckles into his closed eyes and takes a deep breath. Then he turns to her, a watery smile. He points to the entrance of the tent. "I left those things for you."

Pelgrom was the good soul. Mayken looks away.

"Stay here. Hide. I'll bring supplies." His voice is urgent. "Promise me: don't go back to the predikant's camp."

Pelgrom's knee knocks the coral slabs that make up part of Haarlem. He levels a church and a corner house.

CHAPTER FIFTY-SIX

1989

Let all the dead Dutch people rise up and gather. Let them moan and weep and call out to him. Surround his bed in their tall Dutch hats and wide Dutch bonnets, their white lace collars and ghost faces.

Gil isn't scared.

Let Bunyip come too, slick from whatever foul hole it has crept from. Dripping stagnant water at the end of his bed, breathing bubbles. Let it lick its chops and flex its claws. Lash its tail and do its worst.

Gil isn't scared.

His nightmares are real. Not some olden-days ghost shit. Not some made-up kid-scaring monster shit.

Roper with gritted teeth, meat-sweat stink, dead fucking eyes.

Gil knows it: Roper Zanetti is coming for him.

Gil screams and the hall light's on and here's Joss. The cauldron of his naked belly resting on the band of his underpants. A slept-in face and his last wisps of hair on end.

Gil sobs against the old man's chest. He smells engine oil and tobacco and sea air.

"You're all right, lad," says Joss. "You're all right."

❧

Bill Nord comes up to sit with Gil while the others go out looking. Gil looks through his stone and Bill nods off in the chair. In the afternoon they go for a walk.

"What's in the sports bag there, Gil?"

"Tortoise."

"Righto."

A sunset like you would not believe. The colors cocktail-magical. A tropical dream. Gil is persuaded outside.

"Here he is," says Dutch.

Joss and Bill Nord sit side by side on the veranda. They turn and nod, as if the whole world has been waiting on Gil.

Silvia comes up to the camp after sunset. She brings leaves for En-kidu and gets teary when she sees Gil, although his eye doesn't look so bad today.

She calls Roper a fucker.

Gil is to sit in the kitchen with Silvia and the men. There are things he should hear, now that he no longer wants to listen.

The cops won't get involved. Bill Nord looks pained when he says it. Silvia curses. Dutch balls the tea towel and throws it in the sink. Joss stares out of the window at nothing, it's dark.

Waygood is still moored off the island, where Gil saw it the day of the attack. This is no news to anyone. Silvia confirms that Roper has taken a dinghy and supplies. He's on the run.

Joss turns to Bill. "Your boys searched Seals' Island and West Wallabi?"

"Not a peep."

Joss turns to Silvia. "What did your old man say?"

"He doesn't know where he is."

Dutch lets out air like a hiss. "You believe that?"

"I have to."

Gil puts his palms down on the table, lifts one finger after another, feels the usual sticky resistance.

CHAPTER FIFTY-SEVEN

1629

The men in the council tent re-enact their kills, with wine and laughter. Or else they go with the women they have set up in tents. Their husbands, if they have them, are dead or dispersed or they give their consent.

None of the women give their consent.

Agnete, the predikant's spiteful daughter, has a fascination for the women. When Mrs. Predikant is asleep, she sneaks out to look at them as they sit at the entrance of their tents in between visitors. Agnete, wearing her pious face, informs them that she prays for their souls. Mayken says their souls would probably prefer it if she just left them alone. Wybrecht has secretly entered into an agreement with the women; they give her their fuel rations and she cooks their food. At quiet times she sits with them. These women paid their respects to Imke. The gunner's wife still wears the ribbon Mayken gave her. They wave when Mayken passes, and smile at her.

When Mrs. Predikant finds out, Agnete is forbidden to visit the women again.

"For what reason, Mama?"

Mrs. Predikant won't say.

"It's in case their sin rubs off," decides Agnete.

Wybrecht, cutting something unholy into the pot, glances at the girl. "It's in case the men set their eyes on you next."

The under-merchant emerges from the Great Tent twice a day. In the morning, he takes a stroll with his favorites, the bold cadets. In the evening, he walks with Creesje.

Creesje keeps her eyes lowered. She's shook-looking. A young clerk was killed just for talking to her. He was chased to the beach and hacked down. The under-merchant looks ridiculous in Pelsaert's finery and his own gold-trimmed creations, but that doesn't make him any less dangerous. Wybrecht says that someone will cut his throat yet. His followers are made to sign new oaths of loyalty daily.

The *Batavia*'s firstborn is not thriving. The wizened scrap of a thing cries day and night. The girl does her best but the baby will not settle. Mother and baby are escorted to the tent of the under-merchant.

Wybrecht is back late from her foraging. She weeps into the foamy soup. Mayken has never seen her cry before. She touches her cautiously.

A dark story is passed among the survivors.

Cornelisz dosed the baby with a medicine he prepared himself, for wasn't he an apothecary? The young mother expressed due gratitude and was sent away but her infant weakened. When the baby lingered, a man was sent to dispatch it.

The *Batavia*'s baby is buried in a dip of coral shingle.

❧

Halfway to the south end of the island, behind a bank of scrub, they are digging a pit. Mayken stops to watch and the sailors stop, too, and wipe their faces and glance over at her.

"Why are you digging?" she asks, for none of them are the under-merchant's men and so are likely to answer her.

"He directed it."

"Are you searching for water?"

The sailors look away and fall back to their work.

Pelgrom is shouting in the shallows, wild-eyed, thin and shabby.

"Come now, devils with all the sacraments, where are you?"

When he notices Mayken he stops a moment, his face puzzled, before lurching onward.

"Who wants to be stabbed to death?" She hears him roar. "I can do that very beautifully."

CHAPTER FIFTY-EIGHT

1989

Joss knocks early on Gil's door.

"With everything that's happened, it's best if I send you back to Gero."

"On my own?"

"I can't leave until the end of the season, Gil."

Gil thinks on this. "Where would I live?"

"There's this place for kids. People you can talk to. About how things are. How they've been."

"What place?"

Joss takes off his cap and rubs his head.

Gil reaches for his hag stone. "A kids' home?"

Joss nods.

"No."

"Gil—"

"No."

"Of all the kids to try and shut in a bloody freezer, you pick Roper's?"

"They started it. They hurt Enkidu."

Joss puts his cap back on. "They did."

"I'm not scared of Roper. I want to stay here. I'm fine."

"You wet the bed. You scream in your sleep. How's that fine?"

Gil has no answer.

"When your mother died, what you did, was that fine too, Gil?"

Gil stares at his grandfather. There's spittle at the corners of the old man's mouth. Joss frowns, gets up, and walks out.

CHAPTER FIFTY-NINE

1629

Let all the dead rise up and gather. Let them moan and weep and call out to her. Surround her in their tall hats and wide bonnets, their white lace collars and familiar faces.

Mayken isn't scared.

Let Bullebak come, too, slick from whatever foul hole it has crept from. Dripping stagnant water, breathing bubbles. Let it lick its chops and flex its claws. Lash its tail and do its worst.

Mayken isn't scared.

Her nightmares are real, not some child-scaring tale.

Shingle mounds, empty tents, costumed killers.

Mayken knows it: Cornelisz's men are coming for her.

CHAPTER SIXTY

1989

He didn't touch Mum, he only looked at her. Mostly her feet, pushed out to the end of the couch, toenails painted dark plum. Her feet became narrower as the days passed, they became hard and gnarled like a tree root. Pale green bluish. But maybe that was the light through the curtains.

He listened out, in case Mum started moving again and called for him. Or tried to get up on her twisted feet, to walk across the floor and turn the door handle.

Did you know your mother was dead, Gil?

Why didn't you get help, Gil?

Was there no one you could tell, Gil?

The kindly police officer tried to understand. She smiled at Gil to show she was on his side, as if to say, who was she to judge?

It was the flies that gave it away. Knocking themselves out against the window. Mum's boss pulled his shirtsleeve down and covered his mouth, pushed Gil aside, and went down the hallway. He came back out retching, staggering like a drunk. He stared at Gil, just stared.

❧

Gil could go and live in the kids' home. Have regular bedtimes and maybe make friends. Even without Mum, Gil reckons he doesn't have to be average. With Mum, he didn't mind being weird. She put the weirdness in him, or else she brought it out. He just has to remember he's one-of-a-kind-so-go-fuck-yourself.

Sleepless, Gil goes walking. He's scared, but should he meet Roper he'll run; he's quick, he knows the paths. He pats Enkidu goodbye and climbs out of the window.

He heads to the Raggedy Tree and sits down beside it with a clear view to the path. The sky is lightening. There's a bright streak on the horizon but the sea stays dark with bad intentions. Now he can see the detail in the ghostly shape of the gifts left for Little May. The rusted spinning top, the weatherworn dolls, the faded bears. He wonders what she makes of them. He watches the ribbons on the branches flutter. The rising sun skims the sea with mackerel streaks of light. Gil, suddenly chill, stands and stamps life into his feet. He takes from his pocket the hag stone and puts it carefully under the bush and says goodbye to no one.

The wind carries the smell of burning. Now strong. Now faint. Gil stops, traces back, changes direction to find the source of it.

Out in the water, moored a little way out, Roper's boat burns. The flames rage from prow to stern. Embers float upward to turn and drop into the sea. A plume of black smoke rises. A signal that will be seen for miles.

CHAPTER SIXTY-ONE

1629

It's a soft, windless night and there's a worn-out peace in the predikant family's tent. Wybrecht is making soup from a seal carcass. She has her shawl tied over her mouth, for she hates the smell of this creature's meat and the oily fishy texture of it.

The predikant and Judick have been ordered to dine with the commander tonight. The family wonder what Judick and the predikant will be dining on in the main tent. They would rather suck stones and eat air than be at the table of the under-merchant.

Mrs. Predikant and the older children read the Bible.

The soup simmers. Wybrecht skims off the scum. Mayken and Roelant play a game nearby. It's called the Game of Remembering.

"Remember trees, Roelant?"

"Remember buttermilk, Roelant?"

The boy shakes his head or nods to respond. In all cases he is deadly serious.

He remembers canals but not mules.

He remembers apples but not cheese.

Mayken smiles and gives him a shell, which means he has won.

Between readings the family whisper together. There is great news to be discussed. Today the bosun's mate escaped in a small craft he had made from wreck wood and hidden from sight at the end of the island. He left at dawn and was too far out to be caught by the time the watch saw him.

It can be done.

The predikant's grown boy speaks of it with shining eyes.

A cadet at the tent flap. One of the under-merchant's favorites.

"Come for a walk, Wybrecht Claasen."

Wybrecht stands up from the pot she is tending. She looks at Mayken. "It's dark," she calls out.

"Doesn't matter. Hurry up."

Mayken moves to follow but Wybrecht shakes her head, her face stern. Mayken sits down again.

Wybrecht goes to the tent opening. "Do you mean me harm?"

Outside the smell of tobacco, laughter. "Come on!"

Mrs. Predikant looks up, face ashen. "Wybrecht—"

Wybrecht wipes her hands and is gone.

Muffled voices, steps on shingle, men fill the tent.

CHAPTER SIXTY-TWO

1989

Gil smells his grandfather before he sees him, the reek of smoke and the stink of gasoline. When he rounds the veranda he finds Joss looking out to sea. He glances up at Gil.

Gil sits down beside the old man, although the smell is overpowering.

The dinghy is dragged up on the foreshore, just past the dunny. Fuel cans roped together in the back.

Joss gets out his tobacco tin, thinks better of it, puts it away. The dressing on his injured hand is filthy.

A twitch to the corners of his mouth. "To catch a demon you have to flush him out."

Gil's eyes meet his grandfather's. The old man's smile widens.

"Stay close to the camp until this business is finished, you hear?"

"Okay."

Gil gets up and goes inside. He finds what he needs on the dresser.

Joss, eyes closed, is leaning back on the chair, the early sun on his face. He opens his eyes when Gil sits back down beside him.

"Bill Nord taught me."

"Is that right?"

The old man doesn't protest as Gil unwraps his hand, wipes it gently with cotton wool, and opens new packages of lint and bandages. When Gil is finished the dressing is bulkier, and perhaps a little tight over the thumb, but it's clean.

The old man turns over his hand, tries his fingers. "Thank you, Gil."

"You're welcome, Grandpa."

Dutch isn't talking to Joss. The deckie goes about the kitchen with a tuneless whistle on his lips. Slamming doors and throwing pans. Joss flinches every time.

"He's worse than a bloody woman," he whispers to Gil.

Dutch brings their breakfasts to the table and clatters the plates down with a dark glare in Joss's direction.

"Looks good, Dutch."

Dutch points with a fork. "Don't. Just fecking don't." He sits down and starts spearing eggs, his eyes on Joss.

Joss reaches for the salt cellar and delicately dusts his breakfast.

Ramona is sailed out of harm's way, in case of retaliation.

Dutch makes coffee when Joss returns. Strong for everyone, Gil's is no different.

"Will they go to the police, for the arson?"

"It's not their style, Dutch."

Late afternoon and the visitors gather outside the porch, kicking the shale, looking narrowly at the hut. Joss finishes his coffee and pours another, making them wait. In a while he puts on his cap, gets up slowly and goes to the door.

Dutch and Gil watch from the kitchen window.

Dutch nudges Gil. "The face on Papa Zanetti. Like Judgment Day."

Joss steps out to meet them.

"It's *High Noon*," mutters Dutch. "Look at Grandpa drawing himself up to his full height. Good man yourself, Joss!"

"I thought you weren't friends anymore?"

Dutch keeps his eyes on the action. "He's a rotten auld bastard, granted. Wait now, until I go out and give him some backup. You stay here."

Frank Zanetti is flanked by two men. One of them is Cherry, who smokes and squints up at the sky like a gunslinger. The other is a middle-aged bald bloke Gil hasn't seen before. He looks like Roper's stunt double; red-faced and with a paunch on him. Dutch steps out behind Joss and pats his shoulder. The old man turns and nods to him.

The exchange between Joss and Frank is conducted in a volley of low growls. Then Frank raises his hand and makes an emphatic gesture. Joss rears, stepping forward. Dutch moves to hold him back.

A grunt from Joss, and Frank raises his fists. Cherry throws away his cigarette and Roper's stunt double pulls his shorts up over his gut. They grab Frank and pull him back.

Gil thinks it's like a dance: step away, lunge forward, haul back.

Frank, half an inch from Joss's face, hisses something. All at once Joss's expression changes. A smile breaks out, then he throws his head back and laughs.

Frank's expression is baffled. Joss responds with his own gesture: a gentle pat on Frank's cheek.

Now it takes three men to drag Frank away.

Gil is not even allowed to go to the dunny alone. Dutch has to watch from the veranda.

It's late when Bill Nord calls round.

Joss unlocks the door and ushers him into the kitchen. The men glance over at Gil, who quickly puts his head down and pretends to be reading.

Bill hands over the package. "You didn't get this from me."

Joss nods.

Bill hisses. "And for fuck's sake, don't use it unless you have to."

Gil, thirsty in the night, comes across his grandfather doing a crossword. On the kitchen table, by his good hand, lies a gun. Joss looks up and covers the gun with the newspaper.

"You need to go outside, lad?"

Gil shakes his head. He feels strange, a little queasy, as if the world has somehow flipped over. Everything seems less real: his grandfather, sitting at the table in his singlet and underpants, the sauce bottles, the dishes stacked to dry. All could be a painted backdrop. The only thing that feels real is that black metal shape. Even though it's hidden, Gil feels its pull. It's the heaviest, most solid thing right now.

By dawn, it's just Dutch making coffee. A wired aspect to him. Grandpa and the gun have gone.

CHAPTER SIXTY-THREE

1629

"You are accused of the theft of Company property."

Mrs. Predikant rises slowly and her grown son moves in front of her slowly. They are marked by the under-merchant's men, who move slowly too. Agnete stays seated, holding the family Bible on her knees.

Mayken reaches for Roelant's hand. The faces of the under-merchant's men are blank, unreadable, but Mayken is not looking at their faces. She's watching Roelant. He is staring at the canvas wall. She follows his gaze and sees a shadow flit. The boy points after it. And now the sudden stink of stale water. And now the pop and burble of draining sludge.

And now the pit of fear growing in Mayken's belly.

The lamp sputters, the fire flickers, the shadow grows. A hunched shape from floor to ceiling, it stretches its notched spine, turning this way and that. The outline of a head with bulbous eyes, whiskered like a catfish, gills beating.

Roelant's eyes widen. He is watching the shadow, which spreads and bleeds across the ground, across the walls, across the ceiling.

A glance passes between the men and then it begins. The cooking pot is kicked over and the lantern is thrown and there is darkness and screaming and pleading and cursing and grunting with the hot and furious labor of slaughter and the sound of adze and sword and dagger through flesh and bone and heart and guts and throat and face.

Mayken has Roelant's hand. She sees the entrance of the tent, a square of night, and pulls the boy toward this lighter dark. The figure of a man steps into the entrance.

They run past, ducking around legs, out, out, into the night. Somewhere in the rush Roelant's hand slips from her grip. She stops and looks back. The man shape straightens over the little slumped shadow and turns toward her.

CHAPTER SIXTY-FOUR

1989

They're out on the veranda. Dutch, frowning, reads the *Batavia* book Birgit gave Gil.

"Tell me the good bits."

"There are no good bits," murmurs Dutch. "As you know, Gil, there are mostly very bad bits. What with all the death."

"Some people didn't die."

"Granted."

"The book should give their story."

"They got shipwrecked, didn't die, then they went home again?"

"Yeah. Wasn't there a kid who survived?"

Dutch lights his rollie. "Not that I know of."

"People aren't just their bloody deaths, you know."

Dutch looks up at him in surprise. "Gil, mate—"

"No. I don't want to bloody talk about it."

Gil gets up, walks down to the dunny, and slams the door closed behind him, two, three times.

Then he just sits.

Even here the wind and the seabirds and the sound of the sea won't leave him alone. He picks furiously at a scab on his knee. It's not ready but he pulls it off anyway and watches the blood bead. Don't bleed on this island, Silvia said. Well, he already has.

❧

Dutch is still reading when Gil makes his way back up.

"You okay?"

"Yeah."

"This about your mum?"

"No."

They sit in silence.

Dutch, gently: "Is Enkidu still hibernating?"

"Yes."

Dutch turns off the kero stove. The cutlery is set and the sauce bot-tles. Gil has buttered the bread, cut it into triangles, and arranged them nicely.

They sit down at the table to wait for the old man.

Dutch gets up, finds a torch, and tests it. "I'll go and have a nosy for him, else his meal will spoil. Lock the door now and don't put a foot outside."

Gil locks the door behind Dutch. He looks into the pot; it's the stew they've had three nights in a row. There's no spoiling about it.

Gil sits at the table. He concentrates hard on the *Batavia* book. He starts with the pictures. An olden-days drawing of Dutch people wearing tall hats and fighting. The island is flattened out into an oval shape and there are a few giant tents. Little waves are drawn here and there, to show there's sea all around. Next there are pho-tographs of divers floating above bits of wood at the bottom of the sea. Next there is a picture of a woman scientist looking through a microscope. Next there is a cracked jug. The jug has a face on it and a broken handle. The face has pop-out eyes and a beard. In the last picture the bits of wood are arranged to look like a ship. Gil turns back to the book's introduction to read about underwater photography and cataloging wood. Something difficult that needs his concentration. He wants to think only about scientists who spend their days patiently digging about in shingle or scraping coral off a bit of ancient lace. People who know what words like *predikant* and *adze* mean. People who patiently explain these things to other people, taking the feeling out of the old violent stories and putting them in the world of facts.

Gil pushes the book away. He folds his arms and lays his head on them, never-minding the sticky tack of the table. He thinks about the ivory bobbin lying comfortable and safe in a museum. In a glass cabinet with a label and everything. He thinks about bored schoolkids filing past it. He thinks about nothing.

CHAPTER SIXTY-FIVE

1629

Mayken walks with the certain knowledge that the killings are not over tonight. The men follow at an amble, one with a sword unsheathed, one with an adze held easy across his shoulder. Where can she go?

She circles the camp, then heads to the center. She draws out her bone whistle and stands a moment. There is silence but for the flapping of the tents and the lapping of waves and the low murmur of the approaching men.

She takes a full breath, knowing this will not be her usual sad strange tune. Mayken stands in the middle of the camp and plays a shrill and urgent alarm. To the last of the *Batavia*'s sailors, frozen under canvas, listening with dread for a heavy footfall. To her friend Aris, alone in his makeshift shelter, hands stiffened with sea brine. To Creesje, lying awake not an inch from her captor. To the women who no longer dream, kept apart for the mutineers.

A note of outrage that demands attention, demands witness. It echoes all around Batavia's Graveyard and beyond, out into the listening night, the black sea.

CHAPTER SIXTY-SIX

1989

Gil startles. At the kitchen table he wakes to silence, but with the certainty he was roused by a sound. He listens hard. Beyond the camp, night's familiar orchestra plays. A note rises out of it once again. Shrill and urgent. Birdcall or weather's clamor, most likely.

Gil cannot think of closing his eyes. He gets up from the table and unlocks the door. He doesn't stop to take a torch; there's a moon behind the cloud cover, enough light to make out the paths and anyone on them. He runs down to the main jetty but all is quiet, just the sound of the ropes twisting on the moored fishing boats.

Where else would trouble head to?

Every light in the place is on.

Gil approaches with stealth, scrabbling under the abandoned outboard.

Dutch is standing on the doorstep, illuminated by the porch light. Frank and Silvia stand in the doorway. Silvia is smoking; Frank has his arms crossed. Voices are raised. Frank closes the door abruptly.

As Dutch walks away, Cherry steps around the hut. The two men talk low, then Dutch slaps Cherry on the back. They walk quickly toward the coast path.

Gil takes another way back. It will take him past the wreck of Roper's burnt boat but that can't be helped. With any luck, he'll be in the door and at the table reading about maritime museums by the time Dutch walks in.

A sheen on the sea in the moonlight and the burnt-out hull. The cabin has collapsed in on itself and the boat sits buckled in the water.

The moon goes behind clouds. On the path up ahead is a dark, slumped shape. Gil slows his step and approaches with caution. The shape shifts with a sticky breathing sound, a low bubbling. Gil freezes. Thinks of the bunyip. Waits for its attack.

The shape doesn't move, Gil moves nearer, kneels down to it. He smells tobacco and sea air.

Groaning low, his grandfather gropes around on the ground. Gil sees the dropped torch, picks it up, tries the switch, shakes it and the torch flickers on with a weak beam that brightens. He shines it on Joss. His heart turns over.

The old man's nose is broken, that much Gil can see. His face is wet with blood. He reaches out and puts the strap of a bag in Gil's hand, making gestures. Inside the bag there's an orange flare gun, a length of rope, and a bottle of whisky. Joss nudges the flare gun. Gil passes it to him but there's no strength left in the old man to take it.

Gil shines the torchlight on the flare gun. The old man touches the safety catch and points up to the sky.

The catch is stiff but Gil manages it. He stands, points the gun directly upward, and pulls the trigger. A red star bursts high above, burning brightly even as it descends.

CHAPTER SIXTY-SEVEN

1629

Mayken keeps playing. Her pursuers run toward her with their weapons raised.

She looks away, up at the sky. The stars are clearer now. They burn cold. She can't name them and wouldn't want to. Her whistle sounds clear and loud with the last of her breath.

She keeps her eyes on the star that bursts high above, burning brightly even as it descends.

CHAPTER SIXTY-EIGHT

1989

Gil shouts and shouts and could cry with relief when the men begin to shout back. Then they are here, rushing toward him out of the night: Dutch, Bill Nord, and his big sons. Lanterns are set around, a first aid box, and a stretcher. Now that Joss has been found, the men work quickly, talking to one another in low, calm voices. The old man groans until whatever Bill Nord injects him with starts working.

Gil races alongside the stretcher to the jetty. The men carry his grandfather as smoothly as they can but they are going at a pace. Joss's head is held in a neck brace and there's a blanket tucked around him. His eyes are on the sky. It's nearly dawn.

Along the jetty a boat is ready. The navigation lights are on, the engine growling. The men carefully lift the stretcher on. Bill Nord boards with it.

Gil runs ahead but Dutch grabs him.

Frank Zanetti prepares to cast off.

"Why is he taking him?"

"His best bet is with *Sherri Blue*, she's the fastest boat we have."

Gil sobs. "But *Frank*."

"Bill is with him. He'll take care of your granda."

❧

Silvia comes up at lunchtime with a radio update. *Sherri Blue* did good time, but it was still a long haul. Another hour and they would have lost him.

She smiles at Gil and rubs his arm. "He's going to be okay."

Dutch speaks low. "And Roper?"

"They picked him up on West Wallabi. Frank told them where to look."

Bill Nord will have a whisky for his angina. Dutch will have a whisky for his nerves. Gil will have a juice and join them.

Bill takes off his cap and rubs his eyes. It's been a long night and a day. "Five fishers have come forward saying they caught Roper in the act of attempting to murder Joss Hurley on the coast path on Beacon Island."

Dutch nudges Gil. "Your granda is popular after all."

Bill takes a slug of his drink and visibly relaxes. "The police will take that with a pinch, Dutch."

Dutch tops up Bill's glass. "But they'll make this stick?"

"They have the wrench Roper used in the attack and the clothes he was wearing, found by Cherry." He glances at Gil. "It will stick, all right."

"Dutch?"

"You okay, Gil?"

"I don't think Enkidu is hibernating anymore."

CHAPTER SIXTY-NINE

1989

The child sails in the fishing boat out from Beacon Island. There is much to see: the birds and the waves and the changing colors of sea and sky. A breeze gets up and *Ramona* bounces over the water. Gil holds on tight.

Dutch is the skipper, Cherry's the deckie, but they are not here to pull pots.

They know a good spot, clear of the wreck and the ghosts of the wreck. Where the water is as calm as it's likely to be and the seabed sparkles and the whole world is a fierce, beautiful blue.

Dutch cuts the engine. *Ramona* dips and bucks.

Cherry takes off his cap, lowers his eyes, and bows his head.

Gil looks up at the sky, at the far-off point of a white bird turning. They would be a speck to that bird.

Enkidu lies nestled in a basket. He could be asleep. There are stones lining the bottom of the basket because that's how you do a burial at sea. Gil touches his friend's shell, patched with copper lines, splendid and broken. When he is ready, Dutch helps him buckle the lid on. Together they hold the basket over the side.

"You ready, son?"

Gil nods and together they let go.

Dutch reads a passage from *The Epic of Gilgamesh*, something about friendship and honor, loss and bravery in the face of death. Gil throws leaves on the water.

It's a champion's send-off.

It's what Enkidu would have wanted.

EPILOGUE

*We learned from their own confessions, and the testimony of
all the living persons, that they have drowned, murdered and
brought to death with all manner of cruelties, more than 120
persons, men, women and children as well . . .*

—Francisco Pelsaert's journal, September 1629

Of the stranded survivors, numbering more than two hundred,
fewer than eighty remained alive when the rescue party returned
three months after the *Batavia* wrecked.

Francisco Pelsaert would record the trial that took place over the
ensuing weeks as the rescue party on board the returning ship, the
Sardam, scrupulously salvaged the Company's remaining goods.
The skipper of that ship lost his life in pursuit of a vinegar barrel.
Of the thirty or so children on board the *Batavia*, only one babe
in arms survived, making the remarkable journey with its unnamed
mother on the longboat with Pelsaert and Jacobsz to Batavia.

Jeronimus Cornelisz and his key followers were executed by
hanging on Seals' Island, the only island in the group whose ground

would support a scaffold. The youngest mutineers were sentenced to flogging. Stonecutter Pietersz was taken to Batavia to be broken upon the wheel, a horrifying method of execution. Jan Pelgrom and a fellow mutineer were marooned on the mainland. It is questionable how long they survived on the inhospitable coast.

Lucretia Jansdochter arrived in Batavia to find that her husband had died. She remarried and may have lived to her late seventies. Skipper Jacobsz was arrested and languished in Castle Batavia, where he most likely died. Zwaantie, too, was taken into custody but whether she was released or died in prison is not recorded.

Wiebbe Hayes, the young soldier who resisted Cornelisz's attack and mounted a counteroffensive, was rewarded with promotion.

The predikant, Gijsbert Bastiaensz, left a survivor's account in a letter. His one surviving family member, Judick, would marry and lose two husbands to sickness. The Dutch East India Company recognized her misfortune, compensating her for this double widowhood and the suffering she sustained following the wreck of the *Batavia*.

Pauwels Barentsz, sailor of Harderwijk, was murdered on Batavia's Graveyard, July 9, 1629.

Smoert was one of many cabin boys on board the *Batavia*. He was murdered by Jan Pelgrom on Seals' Island, July 18, 1629.

Jan Pinten, English soldier, died on Batavia's Graveyard. The original sources give two different dates for his murder: July 10 and 19, 1629.

Aris Jansz, under-barber, escaped to the safety of High Island on July 21, 1629, the night Maria Schepens, the predikant's wife, and six of their children were murdered on Batavia's Graveyard.

Francisco Pelsaert's fortunes failed with the *Batavia*. He finally succumbed to the fever that plagued him on board less than a year after he executed Jeronimus Cornelisz on Seals' Island. He died in Batavia in September 1630.

Cray fishers began using Batavia's Graveyard as their base during the 1950s. During this time speculation grew as to the location of the missing wreck of the *Batavia*, spearheaded by the writer Henrietta Drake-Brockman. She was instrumental in reviving the *Batavia* mystery and bringing it to a wider audience with *Voyage to Disaster* (1963). The book featured Pelsaert's journals, a key account of the *Batavia* story, which included his documentation of the rescue of the survivors and the trials of the mutineers. Drake-Brockman also correctly predicted the location of the wreck site.

In 1960, the fisher "Pop" Marten uncovered human remains and other finds on Batavia's Graveyard. Another fisher, Dave Johnson, in the course of setting his craypots, discovered the wreck site and later revealed his find to journalist Hugh Edwards and Geraldton-based Max Cramer, who were searching for the final resting place of the ship. On June 4, 1963, exactly 334 years since she had wrecked on the reef, Cramer and his colleagues dived on the site and confirmed it was indeed the *Batavia*.

Beacon Island, Batavia's Graveyard, is now a designated archaeological site uninhabited by fishers. Their structures have been dismantled and the island exists in its natural state.

ACKNOWLEDGMENTS

The Night Ship was a true collaboration between teams in the U.K., U.S., and Australia, so it feels right to thank everyone collectively. To my wonderful agent Sue Armstrong, a huge thank you for your faith and commitment as I sailed off into uncharted waters with this story. Much gratitude to my editors extraordinaire Francis Bickmore and Megan Reid at Canongate, and to Leila Cruickshank for your proofreading magic. To the C&W and Canongate families—for your ongoing support, thank you. To Luke Speed and Anna Weguelin at Curtis Brown, big thanks as always. Across the pond, I would like to thank my amazing agent Amelia Atlas and editors Loan Le and Lindsay Sagnette at Atria for your dedication and vision. A heartfelt thank you to Mark LaFlaur and Janet Cameron for your ongoing support and encouragement; it means the world to me. To Daniella Wexler, a truly inspiring editor, whose early notes shaped Mayken and Gil's connection across time, much love and gratitude to you for championing my work all these years. Thanks also go to Nikki Christer and Rachel Scully at Penguin Random House Australia for your brilliant insights.

The highlight of writing this book was learning about the *Batavia* and her final resting place in the Abrolhos Islands, off the coast of Western Australia. (Please see the Author's Note on the very last page.) I had the pleasure to meet some remarkable people who generously shared their knowledge, thoughts, and experience and gave me the confidence to tackle this story. Needless to say, any discrepancies are the result of my own omissions and oversights. A debt of gratitude to my friend, the multitalented Howard Gray, whose knowledge of the flora, fauna, and history of the Abrolhos Islands, and the *Batavia*'s place there, is unmatched. I will remember our trip out to the islands with much joy, along with the time spent in Geraldton with you and Sapia. As an author and researcher writing nonfiction and fiction, Howard brought the *Batavia* story vividly to life for me, not least in *Lucretia's Batavia Diary*. I was thrilled to have Howard cast his eye over many iterations of this book. His enthusiasm and support never waned, and his guidance helped me shape and unravel both Mayken's and Gil's worlds. My warmest thanks go to Henk Looijesteijn, especially for bringing Mayken's Haarlem past to life. Not only did Henk bring his keen historian's mind to this project but he also inspired the folkloric elements. The Bullebak is entirely down to you, Henk. Huge gratitude to Mike Dash, who has written a wonderful nonfiction account of the *Batavia* story in *Batavia's Graveyard*. Mike gave me much early encouragement and commented on the evolving drafts, and this was greatly appreciated. My appreciation to the staff and helpers at the Western Australian Museums in Geraldton and Fremantle, in particular Zhen Ang and Catherine Belcher. Thanks also to Corioli Souter, Curator, Maritime Archaeology, who took me behind the scenes at the museum. To Professor Philip Mead and family, thank you for your warm welcome and for expanding on the *Batavia* story and hosting a wonderful evening of literature and history, food and talk. My gratitude to Patrick Baker, marine photographer, and Brenda for also generously welcoming me into their home. The time spent at the Shipwreck Museum in Fremantle with Patrick, who dived and documented the *Batavia* as she was brought up from the seabed, was magical. To the volunteers and staff aboard the

Duyfken, especially Mirjam, thank you for sharing your knowledge. Your accounts of sailing your wonderful vessel were riveting and invaluable. To the volunteers and staff at Batavialand in Lelystad, your patience and enthusiasm and the chance to walk and wander through Willem Vos's remarkable replica helped me to picture life on board the *Batavia*. Thanks also to Geraldton Air Charter for making the trip out to the Abrolhos Islands unforgettable.

Last, but not least, to Gavin Clarke: thank you for telling me the *Batavia* story. Without you, this book wouldn't exist. Much gratitude also to Sally Wood and Barrie Selwyn for your kind contributions to the manuscript. To my mother, sisters, and daughter, Eva, thank you for putting up with me at my most reclusive. To my friends: ditto. To Howard Sykes, thank you for the love and the tea in equal measure.

ABOUT THE AUTHOR

Jess Kidd is the award-winning author of *The Night Ship*, *Himself*, *Mr. Flood's Last Resort*, and *Things in Jars*. Learn more at JessKidd.com.

A NOTE FROM THE AUTHOR

Batavia Images Online

I knew nothing about the *Batavia* story when I set out to write this book. Initially, I read both fiction and nonfiction accounts, which only intrigued me more. I wanted to see the relics of the sunken ship and the bones of her myself. My research took me all over the world, from the *Batavia*'s final resting place in the Abrolhos Islands, off the coast of Western Australia, to Batavialand in Lelystad, in the Netherlands, which features Willem Vos's remarkable replica of the *Batavia*. The found and retrieved objects in the museums in Geraldton and Fremantle in Western Australia were remarkable, but so too were the stories of the people I met on my travels. The shipwreck and the events that unfolded on that bleak island had echoed down the centuries to be heard all over the world by fishers and historians, sailors and boat-builders, treasure hunters and archaeologists.

Some of the images I took to inspire and inform me as I worked on the book are collected on my website, jesskidd.com. These were taken for my own research purposes—and there is a wealth of more detailed information online—but you might find these images interesting with regard to building a picture of Mayken and Gil's lives.

J. K.

jesskidd.com

THE NIGHT SHIP

JESS KIDD

This reading group guide for The Night Ship *includes an introduction, discussion questions, ideas for enhancing your book club, and a Q&A with author Jess Kidd. The suggested questions are intended to help your reading group find new and interesting angles and topics for your discussion. We hope that these ideas will enrich your conversation and increase your enjoyment of the book.*

INTRODUCTION

Based on a real-life event, The Night Ship *is an epic historical novel from the award-winning author of* Things in Jars *that illuminates the lives of two characters: a girl shipwrecked on an island off Western Australia and, three hundred years later, a boy finding a home with his grandfather on the very same island.*

TOPICS & QUESTIONS
FOR DISCUSSION

1. Through all five senses Jess Kidd evokes both being aboard the *Batavia* and life among the seasonal fishing community on Beacon Island. What descriptions made these settings come alive for you? Were there any parts of Kidd's sea voyage that felt familiar, or some that felt new?

2. How does Kidd mirror Mayken and Gil's separate journeys in chapters 1 and 2? As the story progresses, do you find Gil's outsider identity important to the novel? How does his 'otherness' reflect Mayken's experience?

3. How would you characterize the tone of the story, or what seems to be the author's attitude toward the subject and time period? How does the language contribute to the tone? What else contributes to it?

4. Discuss the differences and similarities between Mayken and Gil. Despite their being more than three hundred years apart, what are some of their shared experiences?

5. As tensions rise during the *Batavia*'s voyage and after the shipwreck, what role does the Bullebak play in the novel? How is this reflected in the use of the Bunyip in Gil's time?

6. Storytelling is woven into *The Night Ship* in various ways, including through folklore and family histories. What do you think the author is trying to achieve with these layers of storytelling?

7. Each child has parental figures who step in at different times in their journeys (for examples, Imke, Holdfast, Dutch, and Silvia). How would you describe these stand-in parents? In what ways were these adults important for Mayken and Gil?

8. Loss is central to both Mayken and Gil's experience; for starters, each child has lost their mother. Discuss some of their major (and minor) losses throughout the novel and how these may have shaped them as characters.

9. Each character brings something different to the story. Did you relate to any of the characters in particular? If so, please explain who, and why.

10. As we reach the conclusion of the novel, the chapters become shorter. Why do you think the author chose to do this? Do these quicker chapters add to the urgency of the conclusion?

11. Given that this book is based on real-life events that took place during the voyage of the *Batavia* (as we are reminded in the epilogue), what do you think we should take away from Mayken's story?

12. Jess Kidd's novels cross genres, blending light and darkness, whimsy and mystery, the real and the supernatural. If you had to sum up this book in one line, how would you describe it?

ENHANCE YOUR BOOK CLUB

1. The Bullebak is a creature of Dutch folklore. Research a bit more about its history, or take a look at other folktales from the Netherlands. Is there a common thread throughout the folktales?

2. *The Night Ship* is based on actual events surrounding the *Batavia*'s shipwreck near the Abrolhos Islands off the west coast of Australia. To see more about Kidd's research, including photos from the Abrolhos Islands today, check out http://jesskidd.com/night-ship-gallery/

3. If your reading group has not yet read Jess Kidd's other novels, *Things in Jars*, *Himself*, or *Mr. Flood's Last Resort*, choose one of them and discuss it at your next gathering. What similarities do they share with *The Night Ship*? What differences? What themes do you think interest Jess Kidd as a writer?

A CONVERSATION WITH JESS KIDD

Q: What interested you about the *Batavia*? Why did you decide to set a novel around this famous shipwreck?

A: I was searching for a story, and a friend came to me and said, "You have to write about the *Batavia*." I had never heard of the ship, but as soon as I started researching, I was hooked. I was both daunted and reassured to find that there hadn't been a great deal of fiction written about the *Batavia*. I had previously written historical novels, but this would be the first time I would take real people and their lives for the basis of a story.

Q: What research was involved in your writing process?

A: A great deal of research went into the writing of this book, not least because I was telling the story of people who really

lived and died on this ship or the island. It felt like a very big responsibility to not just get the facts right but also to build a vivid picture of what life would have been like on board and how the survivors would experience life on the bleak little island they found themselves on. My obsession with gathering information led me to Amsterdam, Haarlem, and Lelystad in the Netherlands to trace the start of the *Batavia*'s journey and to find out more about the way the ship was constructed and the people who sailed on her. I spent time on replica ships, which was invaluable as it gave me a real sense of life on board. I visited museums in Western Australia to see the *Batavia* artifacts retrieved from sea and land, along with the remains of the great ship herself, which was a very poignant experience for me.

Q: What was the most surprising thing you learned from your research?

A: I flew by light aircraft over the scarred site of the wreck to the Abrolhos Islands. It was there that I really got a sense of the isolation and terror that must have struck the survivors, even without the terrible events that followed the shipwreck. At this point, the research became very personal to me, and I wanted to tell this story in the best way I could. Other sur-

prising highlights included meeting Patrick Baker, a marine photographer who catalogued the wreck after it was discovered and brought up from the seabed in the 1960s. I also met some people who sail historical ships, and they gave me wonderful insights into life on board a ship.

Q: The novel moves back and forth in time between Mayken and Gil. Why did you choose to tell these stories through the eyes of children?

A: Initially I intended to focus just on Mayken, but I realized that the *Batavia*'s story didn't end with the death of her survivors. Archaeologists were still uncovering her secrets on land and sea. I became fascinated by the cray fishers who made Beacon Island their seasonal base and the families who would join them there at certain times of the year. I hoped that the dual narratives could show how much the *Batavia* story continues to have resonance today, how the past can inform the present. One of the major difficulties for me was how to frame a violent real-life story. Taking a child's eye view allowed me to weave in an element of curiosity and playfulness. I wanted to show that in both time periods, the use of the imagination can be an act of survival for these children who find themselves in the gritty reality of an adult world.

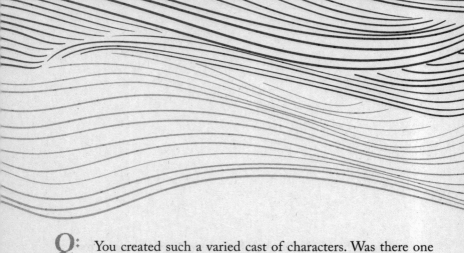

Q: You created such a varied cast of characters. Was there one character who was your favorite to write about? If so, why?

A: So hard to choose! The characters in Mayken's time are a mix of fictional characters and actual people who sailed on the *Batavia*. For example, Mayken's best friend, Holdfast, is based on a real-life sailor noted in contemporary sources. Holdfast is a storytelling character (who finds an echo in Gil's time with the character named Dutch), and I particularly love writing stories within stories!

Q: This novel is a fantastic blend of genres, with many mythological and literary allusions. Were there any books of mythology or novels that particularly influenced *The Night Ship*?

A: *The Epic of Gilgamesh* inspired Gil's name and also the name of his best friend on the island. This felt apt, as it's a nod to big themes of mortality, bravery, and friendship. I also bring in both Dutch and Indigenous Australian folklore in the forms of the bullebak and the bunyip, both water monsters. This is just one imaginative link between the times and the children. I was fascinated to find the existence of similar entities in such different cultures. Two epic sea tales also influenced

the writing of this book, *The Old Man and the Sea* by Ernest Hemingway and *The Rime of the Ancient Mariner* by Samuel Taylor Coleridge. From these I think I got a sense of the strangeness and relentlessness of the sea, and how small and frail we are to pit ourselves against it.

Q: As a writer, what do you hope readers take away from this story?

A: I hope that readers will feel that I've brought the story alive and created an immersive world for them. This is what I love to get from a book when I read. I'm also hoping that they will go on to discover the *Batavia*'s incredible story for themselves, as there are so many fascinating resources out there.

Q: Do you have a next project in mind? And, if so, can you tell us a little about it?

A: I'm embarking on two projects! A novel from the world of myth and a cozy (but twisted) crime tale. Two very different worlds, but I'm loving meeting my new casts of characters.